EASTER

A Novel

by H. B. Coates

DORRANCE
PUBLISHING CO
EST. 1920
PITTSBURGH, PENNSYLVANIA 15238

Dorrance Publishing Co
585 Alpha Drive
Suite 103
Pittsburgh, PA 15238
Visit our website at *www.dorrancebookstore.com*

ISBN: 978-1-6442-6081-4
eISBN: 978-1-6442-6060-9

SUICIDE IS AN EVENT OF HUMAN NATURE, WHICH, WHATEVER MAY BE SAID AND DONE WITH RESPECT TO IT, DEMANDS THE SYMPATHY OF EVERY HUMAN BEING, AND IN EVERY EPOCH MUST BE DISCUSSED ANEW.

(J. W. Goethe)

CHAPTER 1

Rev. Henry "Bud" Caine
12 April 1998

Early on the first day of the week, a hint of sunrise still hiding behind the ridge of Newberry Caldera, I prepared my grieving heart to bury my dead.

Mary Magdalene, Joanna, Mary the mother of James, and Salome, I cannot imagine your distress that Sabbath long ago, having to wait until Sunday morning to observe your burial custom of anointing the crucified body of Jesus. But at least you awoke that morning with a clear and simple task before you.

I wish my task were so clear and simple. I awoke this morning to the unsettling discovery that I'm burying my dead a second time – as if once were not enough. A second time because I could not come to terms with the first time. Unable to sort out all of our emotions when a death occurs, we sometimes end up facing that death at the next funeral we attend.

I've lived with this delayed reaction before when my dad's half-brother died two months after I had left for college twelve hundred miles from home. Our last living connection with my dad's family, Uncle Willie was our favorite Sunday afternoon guest when my brother George and I were growing up. After his requested chop suey dinner, we respectfully stood on either side of our Kimball upright piano to try and stump him with the latest pop chart hits. Single all his life, living on disability from the Western Electric Co. since injuring his back during the Great Depression, an "up-town kind of street bum" (his description), he had little exposure to contemporary music on radio

1

or television. "Just whistle me the tune, boys, and let's see if I can't pick it up." Black keys – "there's less of them to confound me" – soon reproduced our suggested melody. "Moon River," Henry Mancini, 1961. Always brought gifts for us, usually free brochures and small calendars collected during the week at the post office or local bank. Sunday evening then, too soon to say goodbye, we rode with our dad to take Uncle Willie home to his senior living facility in the Mojave Desert town of Acton, what he called the Old Fogies Farm.

I remember the Friday I flew home for Uncle Willie's service at Our Savior's Lutheran Church. I returned to school Monday morning unaware of the strain on my heart to accept my uncle's death. My short-circuited emotions had left me too numb to even think about his death, let alone his funeral. Three years later, when our family attended the funeral service for my dad's boyhood chum, Wayne Berg, I had to excuse myself, so stricken with grief over the death of my Uncle Willie.

For the first time in fifteen years, I don't need to practice my sermon one more time this morning, so I'm focused on the complicated task before me. Easter had been dying one death at a time for me, but I refused to face those deaths by switching OFF my broken heart and switching ON my clergy brain so I could fulfill my ordination vows and pass on the faith I had inherited. In denial all this time of the increasingly diminished role my mother's Easter has played in my adult life, my broken heart could wait no longer. In the wake of my current clergy brain shut down, my broken heart decided to show up at the door – had been waiting until *here* and *now* to catch up with me.

Here: My favorite getaway in Central Oregon.

Now: Easter Sunday.

The Resort at Sunriver, where Denise and I have celebrated most of our April 11 anniversaries, reminds me of the Grand Canyon because I'm encouraged to think about our natural place in the universe, about what is important and what is not. From the dry, pine-scented air to the uninterrupted solitude to the countless days of high desert sunshine to the unmatched nighttime showcase of star systems, it's easy to forget what doesn't matter.

A doe and her fawn surprised us yesterday on our bicycle ride back from the Nature Center, the two deer prancing alongside us for the entertainment of it. As we followed the path leading to Circle Four, Ft. Rock Park, and the North Pool, we came across a small red STOP sign that read, "Please Walk

Your Bike: Baby Toad Migration in Progress." The doe and her fawn also slowed down. Where else?

This extreme attention given to Nature's superior place in the order of things is part of Sunriver's sacred allure. Called the Ecologium when it first opened, the eight-acre Nature Center and Observatory led the way for similar projects across the country, establishing the resort as a private sanctuary where people and wildlife share a single living experience. Every morning is a Sunday morning at Sunriver. Its beauty and its recreation are an embellishment of life, not a condition.

The South Meadows golf course at the resort is where I played a roguish round of golf with my three best men who stood beside me that day in church, the three men with whom I have shared a separate and private vow to always stand by one another in life. The four of us played only nine holes that spring morning before I stood before the altar to marry my bride. Thankfully, only nine holes. We fully expected our embarrassing scorecard, but scores were not the point.

After we had picked up our gimme putts on the ninth green, we raised our clasped hands together in a promise to one another. Regardless of what may come, we would have each other's back through it all. We stoked our Hav-A-Tampa cigars and strutted off the ninth green like a just-married couple parading out of a church.

In the parking lot, the four of us – groom, best man, and two groomsmen – shook each other's hand as if we were exchanging rings to remind us of our promise. Andy began singing Ben King's "Stand By Me," and George, Karl, and I provided a little vocal background. We would not be afraid of those nights that lie ahead, no matter how dark the land. We knew the future would take us in different directions, but we would stand by each other forever. That Saturday morning in 1970 – our stand-by-me pledge, our declaration of sentiments – opened the doorway to adulthood when the past is closed behind, and the future becomes real for the first time.

The future did take us in different directions, sometimes as each of us had planned, sometimes against our will.

One of us would become a toolmaker.

One of us would become a lumber broker.

Another would attend seminary and become a preacher.

And one of us would become a teacher.

Within five years, though, our ninth-green promise to stand by each other had begun to unravel, barely perceptible at first because we saw each other often enough. And that would be part of our shortcoming; we saw each other as if that were enough. Life was asking more questions than our Sunday school faith could answer. Every year produced one excuse after another, each sufficiently compelling to spoil any plans for an anniversary reunion. We slowly drifted apart, like two married people who drift apart, two married people who see each other all the time.

I kept trying to schedule a yearly reunion for this second weekend in April, thinking such a gathering would be one way to renew our ninth green promise. Not easy to maintain my enthusiasm, though, after so many years. It's not that we didn't see each other over the years; it's that our seeing each other hardly plumbed the depths of what we each faced after making that promise. The whole point of our original pledge was to help each other deal with life's ups and downs, to prevent what seems to happen to other people. At least Denise never had to share me with a groom's party anniversary reunion here at Sunriver.

Of course, this is where my broken heart would catch up with me. What other here and now should I have expected? This *here* is where we had made our promise, and this *now* – conveniently falling this year on the first weekend after the paschal full moon – marks the anniversary of the weekend we made it. And this is the weekend I'm renouncing whatever part I have played in the proclamation of that supreme promise made long ago in Jerusalem, a promise that has sustained my three best men and me about as well as our feeble ninth-green promise made on my wedding day.

Which brings me to why my task is so complicated.

The next funeral I attend is my own.

Preaching on Christmas Day this past December, a Christ Mass that included the baptism of little Sarah Schreiber – who seemed to appreciate my abbreviated liturgy that morning – I continued asking my questions about why our childhood faith (my mother's Easter) often falls short when we grow up and confront adult challenges. "What impact will these 'glad tidings' have on your everyday life this coming new year?" I began my sermon.

Parishioners at Trinity Lutheran Church that morning weren't too interested in answering my question. Sons and daughters home for the holidays, gifts carefully selected and wrapped waiting under the tree, dinner already roasting in the oven. My pensive theological inquiry was no match for singing "Away in a Manger." I was trying hard to camouflage my waning faith. I had my own answer to that question, and my response was nothing less than an unfolding death of who I am.

Asking the question about why our childhood faith doesn't always translate into a meaningful adult faith can be traced far back before my first days at the Graduate Theological Union in Berkeley eighteen years ago. I had begun searching for an answer to this question the day I figured out I could ask it; by the first of the year, I was living an answer. Alfred Steiner read my letter of resignation at our congregation's annual meeting the end of January. I officiated for the last time on February 22, The Transfiguration of Our Lord Sunday. I descended from that mountaintop, I tried to explain how I had met God and Moses and Elijah, and then I said goodbye to the congregation. And goodbye to the person I had prepared a lifetime to become.

Voluntary death can be an impatient partner when it is forced to accommodate our grandiose schemes to play God. After forty days alone in the wilderness with my introspection, I thought it best to finalize plans and arrangements. Enough with mulling over the consequences of what I'm about to do to myself; I can't go on forever analyzing such a decision. This past Good Friday, I declared with genuine relief, "It is finished." Only this: like another who said that long ago, I'm not feeling so confident now about what that declaration means.

Since that Sunday in February, Denise has helped me recall the path I have followed to this point in my life, what it means to walk away this year from my childhood faith and my calling to share that faith with others. It was Denise who first connected my questioning heart with my broken heart. My broken heart catching up with me in this here and now made perfect sense, but perfect sense seldom assuages a broken heart.

The story of Holy Week has only two possible endings: sundown on Good Friday, or sunrise on Easter morning. I have come to a Good Friday sundown of my own making. When you have grown up surrounded by the voices, the places, the events, the teachings of my mother's Easter, finally facing its death and burial calls into question the foundation of your being. No wonder I have tried to avoid this day of reckoning for so long.

Whatever you first Easter women told the world, your report would become for my family the greatest story ever told. If I merely have been playing a part on life's stage, then my inherited Christian faith has been the director of my performance. When I was baptized on July 4, 1948, at Hill Ave. Grace Lutheran Church in Pasadena, I was sealed by the Holy Spirit and marked with the cross of Christ forever. After my godparents, my mother's Aunt Gertie and Uncle Wally, promised to fulfill their obligations to raise me in the Christian faith, Pastor Olson declared that I had been liberated from bondage to sin and death. God had given of His only begotten Son to open the way for me to the joy and freedom of everlasting life; I was reborn a child of God and an inheritor of eternal life. That's how much God loved the world and me! I was only a week old then so Aunt Gertie would remind me of those words every Fourth of July. "On the birthday of our nation today, Buddy is celebrating his birthday when he became a child of God."

When we were young, my brother and I thought we had been born in Galilee, not Glendale. All of our friends were church friends; my best friend Andy was the pastor's kid. Seems like every clock we turned to told us it was time for church.

When we attended Sunday school, we sat at the feet of Jesus, asking him questions. Like that popular painting by Harry Anderson. "What happened to your hand?" I'm that little guy holding the model airplane. Or, if you're my brother, he's that little guy. Had to be one of us because that WW II fighter the kid is holding looked exactly like our gray P-51 Mustang model. We sat below this painting every Sunday morning, reminded that we could talk with Jesus any time. This painting can lay claim to the first portrait of Jesus depicted with modern-day children – caused a stir in the 1950s.

When we knelt at the communion rail to receive an unleavened wafer and small glass of wine, we were sitting down with Jesus at his Last Supper that night he was betrayed. After he took bread and gave thanks, we heard him say, "Take and eat; this is my body, given for you. Do this for the remembrance of me." And after he took the cup and gave thanks, we heard him say, "This cup is the new covenant in my blood, shed for you and for all people for the forgiveness of sin. Do this for the remembrance of me." Didn't understand what was happening, but we did hear him say those words.

When we gathered for our Luther League youth group Sunday evening, we sat amongst those followers on that hill – or on the plain, wherever it was that Jesus comforted the crowd. "Blessed are you when men revile you and persecute you and utter all kinds of evil against you falsely on my account.

Rejoice and be glad, for your reward is great in heaven, for so men perse-cuted the prophets who were before you." So when other kids teased us about all of our church stuff, we should be happy, because someday when we die and go to heaven, we'll be rewarded.

When we attended catechism class on Monday afternoon, Jesus taught us to be His disciples. "Behold, I send you out as sheep in the midst of wolves; so be wise as serpents and innocent as doves." "Be wise as serpents," we liked. We didn't always have to be so meek and mild-mannered as we had been taught the night before. We could be sneaky like a slithering snake.

Our Boy Scout Troop 316, sponsored by our church, met in the base-ment Sunday school hall on Tuesday nights. This is where we learned "to do justice, and to love kindness, and to walk humbly with our God." Pastor Messner used to talk about our Lutheran Church's PRO DEO ET PATRIA religious Scout award in the same sentence he spoke about the Eagle Scout badge. You weren't keeping the Twelfth Scout Law – A Scout is Reverent – if you hadn't earned this religious award. Always laws and commandments with Pastor Messner.

Our church youth choir practiced on Wednesday evenings. "Sing to the LORD a new song, his praise from the end of the earth! Let the sea roar and all that fills it, the coastlands and their inhabitants. Let the desert and its cities lift up their voice, the villages that Kedar inhabits; let the inhabitants of Sela sing for joy, let them shout from the top of the mountains. Let them give glory to the LORD, and declare his praise in the coastlands." "Except for you, Buddy," Mrs. Messner usually pleaded. "I know you're trying, but your strong voice is off key and flat. Perhaps you could simply mouth the words for now. We'll work on your tone deafness later."

So I asked my mother, "Why do I need to show up for choir if I'm just mouthing the words?"

"Because showing up for choir is what we do on Wednesday."

My brother and I attended Weekday Religious Education classes right after lunch every Tuesday and Thursday. We gathered in a sixty-foot long, single-wide classroom trailer my grandfather delivered along the sidewalk in front of Coolidge Elementary School. We created our own elaborate map of the Holy Land; apparently, those professionally prepared maps included in the last few pages of our Bible weren't good enough. We would tell the old, old story over and over again each week, placing our map on an easel to help us pinpoint the life and times of Jesus. We knew His neighborhood better than our own.

We never missed a Sunday morning, except for our Scout overnight weekend campouts; but even then, Pastor Messner usually showed up Sunday afternoon with a shorter version of his morning sermon.

Every summer, we spent a week at Camp YOLIJWA (Youth Living Jesus' Way) east of Yucaipa and Redlands in the foothills below Mt. San Gorgonio. Celebrated my June 27 birthday there in 1959. A Saturday, I recall, but still a day full of church stuff. Happy Birthday, Buddy!

During the spring of my high school junior year, we focused on career dreams and the necessary preparation those dreams would require. Assignment: Interview someone who is doing what you would like to do someday. I interviewed Peter Gutknecht, the young intern at our church. After college, I planned to attend seminary and become a Lutheran pastor.

Scripture accompanied me everywhere. Two and a half years had passed since JFK's assassination; his eloquent rhetoric had been a favorite resource for our debate team. For the individual tournament event of oratorical interpretation, I had delivered his undelivered speech scheduled for Dallas. Recognizing America's limitations in achieving "peace on earth, good will toward men" – especially our country's military power to combat communism and support Vietnam – Kennedy was prepared to conclude his speech by invoking the help of Providence. "Except the Lord keep the city, the watchman waketh but in vain." I concluded my San Gabriel High School graduation speech using those same words of the psalmist.

Along with our Christmas Lionel trains and Hopalong Cassidy cap guns, my brother and I also unwrapped the baby Jesus. The baby Jesus was our main gift every year, and our mother expected us to think about nothing else at that moment – although I remember unwrapping the baby Jesus while my brother fired off his two cap guns.

On Easter Sunday, we were surprised and filled with awe (year after year) to hear that announcement. "Why do you look for the living among the dead? He is not here, but has risen." We heard Pastor Messner declare, "Almighty God, through His only Son, has overcome death and opened for us the gate of everlasting life." We knew Jesus loved us because the Bible told us so; that meant we were destined for heaven someday when we died, and all would be well. Our hope was built on nothing less than Christ the

Solid Rock; that's where we took our stand because all other ground was sinking sand. If my kid brother wasn't singing "Fishers of Men" every day, he at least was whistling the tune.

Like Israel, though, I had grown up. I was questioning God's Goodness and what was not so good about our here and now world. God seemed less attentive, seemed more remote than how I remembered Him from childhood. I didn't always feel the spirit of joy in His presence. I couldn't count on His help in times of trouble. I knew I wasn't the only one who was tested in life, but God didn't always provide the way out so I could endure it. I didn't know for certain that all things work together for good to them that love God. Goodness and mercy did not always follow me all of my days. And what is the definition of *good* here? Is that for God alone to define? God's lamp to my feet, His light to my path, had grown dim and unreliable. My relationship with God had come up wanting; I was out of sorts with my Creator, out of sorts for all kinds of reasons. I heard people talking about God and His mysterious ways and His promise of salvation, but I didn't always feel like praying. How I sympathized with Job and Elie Wiesel!

Growing up, I had fallen asleep every night under Sallman's painting, "Jesus Savior, Pilot Me."

Jesus, Savior, pilot me
Over life's tempestuous sea;
Unknown waves before me roll,
Hiding rock and treach'rous shoal;
Chart and compass come from thee
Jesus, Savior, pilot me.

But I no longer felt the hand of Jesus on my shoulder. I no longer felt Jesus behind me, pointing the way to safety.

So, like Israel, I was waiting for a Savior. Looking for salvation, I had gathered along that road leading into Jerusalem with all the other bystanders on Palm Sunday. Looking for salvation from living life without a safe hold against life's tempestuous sea. Looking for salvation from whatever subtracts from an abundant life. My mother's Easter conceded unbearable pain and fear and desolation and depression in this here and now by promising life existed beyond. My mother's life-after-death Easter is the ultimate solution to the problem of theodicy. How do we justify an omnibenevolent and omnipotent God in the face of suffering and evil in the world? Answer: Our here and now is not the final word; if it is, then it cannot be that God is perfectly good and all-powerful. I was hoping, though, for a here-and-now-friendly version of salvation. I too, Cleopas, had thought He was the one, the one to save us.

When hope was a young man, my prayers seemed to matter. But as hope grew up, older now, kicked around a little, hoping against all hope seems a stretch. Along with whom I had spent a lifetime becoming, hoping against all hope was running out of hope. As each passing year separated me from my childhood, I found myself further separated from the voices of my mother's Easter. Contending voices grew louder as I grew up, some more powerful than others, even in their silence.

Like a child whose hand God is no longer holding. If you have been taught all your life that your worst fear is a child-like fear of God letting go of you, how do you go on when you have chosen to let go of God's hand?

Which complicates my task even further.

For the first time in my life, dear Easter women, after fifty years on the planet, I'm waking up on Easter morning without an Easter faith. Am I also waking up on Easter morning without God? My own little Nietzschean crisis, waking up to a world now devoid of the Christian faith I had inherited.

My mother's Easter has devalued the here and now by claiming those two premises about God's goodness and God's power require a hereafter life. So trusting in my mother's life-after-death Easter has deprived my here and now world of ultimate meaning. But without my mother's Easter, I'm not sure about any meaning at all. Rejecting my mother's Easter deprives everything of meaning because my Christian faith is how I have interpreted the world, how I have tried to understand my existence, how I have tried to make sense of my reality. If my world no longer includes my mother's Easter, does it also no longer include God?

Again, without the promise of life after death, a good and all-powerful God makes no sense. How do I escape from this nihilism? Am I Nietzsche's madman running around Sunriver this morning with my lantern searching for God?

Faulkner's Quentin Compson knew what I'm facing here. For his father, all of life was absurd, including any outrage over his daughter Caddy's loss of virginity. But if Quentin had accepted his father's cynical dismissal of any indignation, he would have abandoned his value system that provoked such anger in the first place over his sister's pregnancy. Quentin couldn't live, though, without his value system. So if he stood firmly by his value system, his disgust over his sister's terrible sin drove him to such torment and conflict of emotions, he could hardly cope with the shame and family embarrassment. His values had been shattered by her transgression. His escape from this nihilism? Suicide by drowning himself in the Charles River.

I have built my whole life around the Good News of a Savior. As they say at the casino table, "I was all in." When I was young, I never heard alternative voices questioning my mother's Easter. When you are convinced that what you have been taught is right teaching, hope does not exist outside of that created, ordered world. So what happens when your mother's Easter dies? Life can't go on as usual, because without this, I'm back to Nietzsche's nihilism.

Dear Easter women, please wait. You're in such a hurry. I don't know, but do we share the same space and time? I know I share with you this morning your fleeting version of hope. You had been waiting for a messiah to save you from Roman persecution and oppression, and now it is the third day since your Jesus of Nazareth, mighty in deed and word, was crucified. My mother was waiting for that same messiah to save her from death, the wages of sin. I have been waiting for a salvation that transforms the meaning of Christ's life, death, and resurrection into a celebration of our life in the here and now. Waiting for salvation from nihilism.

I too am nervous and afraid. I met you once a long time ago. Like you, I awoke this morning with a broken heart and a faraway hope disappearing over the horizon. Maybe I'll discover more than you discovered that first Easter morning – when nothing changed in spite of everything changing.

CHAPTER 2

George Caine

Might as well have been handcuffed, the way our mother held our hands when we were young. We could have crossed a raging river together. My older brother Bud once tried to squirm loose from her protective grip, but it was no use. She would not let go. Even when we stood perfectly still and paid attention to something right in front of us, she would not let go. Didn't seem to matter where or when.

The three of us stood one Saturday afternoon at the Griffith Park Zoo in front of those old beat-up cages where those old beat-up lions lived. Bud and I weren't moving until those two old beat-up lions woke up and looked at us. Our mother wasn't moving either. She would not let go.

We spent another Saturday at the L.A. County Natural History Museum in Exposition Park, standing lifeless like sculptures in front of that diorama with sculptures of a mastodon and a saber-tooth tiger. "Which one would win in a fight between the two?" I asked. "Which one would end up killing the other?"

No answer, just a comment, and an awkward point with her finger while still holding our hands. "Well, that would have been a sight to see now, wouldn't it boys?"

Bud and I could stand all day by that gigantic garden railroad display out at the L.A. County Fair Grounds in Pomona. Like the prototype, we watched trains with seventy or eighty freight cars meander their way around this model train layout the size of a football field. Our mother could have left

13

us there all night and found us in the exact spot the next day with our faces against the fence. She didn't, of course. She just stood there with us and held our hands.

We were sure this Sunday morning in 1955 would be different. How could she possibly hold our hands and still participate in the Easter sunrise service at Our Savior's Lutheran Church? We walked with her up the narrow steps to a level paved area behind the church, a tennis court belonging to the retirement center around the corner. One hundred and twenty dark brown wooden folding chairs arranged in a semi-circle faced a row of stately California Fan Palms. This provided the makeshift altar with an authentic Holy Land backdrop. The whole point of this outdoor worship service depended on a faithful recreation of the original setting where Jesus had been buried outside the walls of Jerusalem.

This Sunday, though, of all Sundays, my brother and I expected to be fun. Everyone dressed up in their newly bought best, contagious smiles all around after a gloomy forty days of Lent, and a baked ham and scalloped potatoes dinner with a lazy afternoon to play with cousins. Most other kids were running all over the place dashing between rows of chairs and clusters of grown-ups. Even our best friend, Pastor Messner's son Andy, got away with climbing the twelve-foot-high chain-link fence that surrounded the tennis court.

Andy enjoyed certain privileges denied to the rest of us, but he also lived with certain expectations not required of the rest of us. The Wrath of Almighty God loomed like a dark shadow behind his father's standard parental warnings. Ignoring what would be forbidden in Andy's kid world might result in plagues of frogs and gnats and flies and locusts. Ignoring the same in our world would result in a short lecture from our big-hearted dad. But our friend could count on almost total freedom at most church-related functions. His father would be preoccupied with the unending demands of parishioners, and his mother would be equally preoccupied with those demands to which his father did not attend. Easter Sunday for Andy Messner? About as much fun as any kid could imagine.

Not us, though. We sat on either side of our mother with her "Be still now" grasp, making it clear we would not be running all over the place. How could she do this and still hold her hymnal? Didn't matter, she had it all memorized. How could she fold her hands for prayer? Didn't matter, she would hold our hands tighter when she prayed. So there we sat, watching the other kids revel in the predawn anticipation of Easter morning. There we sat with our mother and waited for the report from those women hurrying to the tomb of Jesus of Nazareth.

Bud must have felt our mother nudge forward before I did because he leaned back enough to catch my attention before she gently raised us from our chairs. We kept exchanging quizzical looks behind her back until the three of us carved our way through the dense fan-like sprays of the arborvitae hedge on the other side of that sunrise service altar.

"Bud and George," my mother began with a soft whisper that belied her tightened grip on our little hands, "I want you to meet these friends of mine. Mary Magdalene, Joanna, Mary the mother of James, and Salome, the mother of the sons of Zebedee."

Bud and I hesitated to look away from each other because we both knew our Sunday school friends were no longer nearby. I don't know what magic our mother performed that Easter morning behind Our Savior's, but I knew we weren't in Alhambra anymore. No one observed this queen of all liturgical festivals like our mother; she is the queen of all Easter observers. Walter Cronkite's *You Are There!* crew didn't need to help her reenact the events of Holy Week. She lived all year long for this morning, a chance to rediscover the empty tomb of Jesus and hear once again the promise that she too would be raised someday from the dead. Don't know how, but Bud and I were there at the empty tomb. All things were like they were then, except the three of us were there.

"We had to wait until after the Sabbath," Mary Magdalene explained to us like a schoolteacher explaining a history lesson. "We were nervous all night about how we could complete what our custom expected of us, to prepare his body for burial. We could hardly wait for the sunrise on this first day of the week. We have set out from Bethany to anoint the body of Jesus of Nazareth because the approaching Sabbath prevented us from our task after his crucifixion on Friday afternoon." My mother leaned down and kissed me on top of my head, but that didn't help my shaking. "Take a deep breath, boys," she murmured with a smile.

Bud and I could forget about having any fun this morning. He and I had never attended a funeral, I was only five years old, so I didn't understand what we were doing. I copied my brother and instinctively latched onto our mother's hand with my other hand so she did not let go. Those women walking ahead of us now mumbled something about who would roll away the stone that had been placed in front of the tomb. Then, all of a sudden, I saw the outline of an angel in a flash of bright light. Bud saw a young man sitting on the right side of the tomb entrance dressed in a white robe. My mother claimed it was two men standing by us in dazzling apparel. Whoever we saw declared in a clear and comforting voice, "Why do you look for the living among the dead? He is not here, but has risen." All of us, the women, my mother, Bud and I, didn't know what to make of this announcement. Afraid, trembling, excited, bewildered. My mother's friends hurried around the north wall of Jerusalem. We turned and walked through that hedge to the now empty tennis court behind the church.

Those women eventually reported to the original eleven disciples and to all the rest. After twenty centuries of all the rest, whoever that may be, theologizing about this report from Mary Magdalene, Joanna, and the other women with them, this is what the Church had taught my mother about Easter.

Someone had to pay the price for my sweet mother's sin, confusing for me because I could not imagine any such thing. What sin, I had to ask, and why did she have to pay for it? Why did God set things up like that? When she was my age, her German mother Florence Koehler had taught her to pray what her mother Maria Schinkel had taught her to pray: "*Lieber Gott, mache mich heilig, damit ich in den Himmel gehen kann.*" ("Dear God, make me holy so I can go to heaven.") The day before yesterday, at her Good Friday Service, my mother had sung,

There is a green hill far away, Without a city wall,
Where the dear Lord was crucified, Who died to save us all.
He died that we might be forgiven, He died to make us good;
That we might go at last to heaven, Saved by his precious Blood.
There was no other good enough, To pay the price of sin,
He only could unlock the gate Of heaven, and let us in.

Honest to God, I was convinced our mother, Margaret Anita Caine, was as good as they come. If heaven was where she wanted to go, who was I to question her wish? Although I did wonder why God locked His gate to heaven. And why didn't God make people pay for their sins as they go? Why wait to pay for their sins at the last when they die? Why not get it over with by paying for their sins each morning? Seemed to me a person would be much more apt to sin all life-long knowing the payment for such a life would-n't be required until they finally died.

The Irish poet Mrs. Cecil Frances Alexander didn't have any answers for me, but she had written that hymn to help her children understand what had happened to Jesus on Good Friday, why he had suffered under Pontius Pilate, was crucified, died, and was buried. "That we might go at last to heaven!" was the reason why God had given of His Son to die for us. To save us from the wages of sin, to save us from death.

When she was twelve years old, my mother had memorized Luther's meaning to the Third Article of The Apostles' Creed. I would memorize the same truth in Pastor's Messner's catechism class when I turned twelve. "And on the last day God will raise me and all the dead and will grant eternal life to me and to all who believe in Christ. This is most certainly true."

Thanks to the resurrection of Jesus, my mother could look forward to her own resurrection from the dead some day. Someday, that is, after she had died. Someday when it is her Easter time, she would be saved from death, the wages of sin. Our mother's parents had taught her, and she, in turn, had taught us, the empty tomb of Jesus is a gift we receive when we die. "In my Father's house," Jesus had said, "are many mansions: if it were not so, I would have told you. I go to prepare a place for you." I was sure my mother's death someday would be one of Pastor Messner's Easter sermon stories. No one was waiting with such faith and confidence like her, waiting to go at last to heaven. My mother could hardly imagine the good and wonderful things God had prepared for her when it was her Easter time.

In the meantime, though, many Americans were curious about the good and wonderful things God had prepared for us here on earth. Like any two brothers growing up, Bud and I sure were, but we would soon adjust our earthly expectations to conform more closely to our Lutheran Reformation heritage. Thanks to hand-me-down teachings deeply rooted in my mother's family tree, most of our family accepted the futility of our earth-bound existence.

Except for our Grandpa Caine.

My dad's father enjoyed his earth-bound existence whenever he could. After my grandmother, his wife Amelia, played the church organ on Sunday morning at Christ Lutheran Church on Parkside Ave. in Chicago, she rushed home to concoct my grandpa's latest brew request on their homemade still in the basement. Prohibition would not be repealed until the end of 1933, but until then, life was still good on a Sunday afternoon for my grandpa. "Amelia darlin', come sit down here and tell me all about your morning at church."

My mother's parents attended that same Lutheran church. I should say, *belonged* to that church, not *attended*. "Belonging to the Lord and to His House" is what they said. Their five-dollar offering each Sunday, before the Great Depression, was a brand new bill acquired at First City Bank on Friday afternoon. On more than one occasion, their belonging to Christ Lutheran was contrasted with William Caine's not belonging.

I'll never forget the day when Bud proudly announced his latest genealogical discovery about our family. He did this after his first son was born. "Grandma Florence, guess what? According to the 1910 Census, you're a year older than it says in our family Bible (a document demanding more respect than any from the Dead Sea Scrolls). Your parents might have fibbed a little when you were a teenager so you could earn some money in the workforce. And Grandpa, as near as I can figure out the dates on these church records I've collected from Topfseifersdorf, you were born six months after your mom and dad were married in 1893. Get a load of that, would ya'? Suppose we should change the dates in our family Bible?" I couldn't believe my brother's moxie sometimes, how he could stir things up. "What the hell were you thinkin', Bud? Change those dates in our family Bible?"

I usually walked in the shadow of my brother's confidence. Like weeds in a garden, maybe all my fears growing up smothered out any confidence trying to plant a foothold in me. I know I was the better athlete. I was the catcher for our Little League team, the Greens, and I was expected to hit the ball over the fence every time I came up to bat. I often did. Bud had played right field, the last position in Little League any coach is too worried about. And when he was up to bat, Bud had a tendency to duck away from a curveball he didn't trust would break over the plate. He didn't like batting as much as I did.

My parents have spent their energy and love on Bud and grappling with the messed-up marriages of our two sisters. I'm like a best-supporting actor in most of the photographs with my brother. I'm there in the photo when Bud earned his Eagle Scout badge. I quit Scouting after I earned the rank of Star. We're standing together when he graduated from the University of

Washington. I quit college halfway through my sophomore year. I'm there at his left side, the best man in his wedding. I never needed a best man. I'm standing there with him in front of the church where he was ordained. I don't have any photos of him and me standing in front of our dad's machine shop.

While most of the world is frowning with sadness and strife, Bud is out searching for the sunny side of the street. "Mr. Silver Lining," our dad always said of Bud, although my brother has trouble finding much silver lining about me.

When we were growing up, he avoided any mention of his six scars, four on the back of his head, and one on either side. From a bicycle accident when he was six years old. He tried to cover them up as best he could. Always sat in the back of the classroom so kids wouldn't tease him about how those scars looked. Second grade was the worst. He ended up punching more than one kid who bothered to comment, "What a stupid hair-cut. Did your dad do that to you?" I can't be sure, but that accident might have messed up the shape of his skull because he was forever towel-drying his hair 'til he could create the style he wanted. He still towel dries it like crazy. He spends way too much time on his hair, but you wouldn't believe that at first glance. His disheveled look says the opposite of someone who's always blow-drying or towel-drying his hair like he does.

Our orthodontist Dr. Gawley had declared Bud's mouth of teeth an exceptional case study, so you would think my brother would have been inclined to show off his rearranged teeth. But because he was such a case study, he ended up with those braces well into his senior year of high school and had chosen early on to smile with his mouth closed. Still does that today in photographs, although his expressive, forest green eyes and rise of his cheeks draw attention away from his closed mouth.

He grew a neatly trimmed beard after moving north with his family to Bend, Oregon. At six feet four inches, an inch taller than me, my brother inherited our mother's natural ability to fend off unwanted weight. Even if Bud weren't older than me, he still would look older. The guy's always thinking about what we have been taught about God. Can't be sure if he has found many reasonable answers to his questions, especially answers provided by our parents and grandparents.

I don't know how they managed to keep it all straight, but our mother's parents could talk about their faith and their church and the Lord's work smack dab in the middle of a serious Friday evening pinochle game. They had nurtured their Christian faith through the years by listening carefully to hundreds of Lutheran sermons and reading daily from their King James Version of the Bible. Year after year, Bud and I spent many a Friday night at their home on Hellman Ave. listening to them visit while we watched the boob tube. After our liver sausage sandwiches on rye, German potato salad, chocolate milk, and tooth tingling chocolate sundaes, we settled into *The Adventures of Rin Tin Tin* with Lt. Rip Masters and Rusty and then watched Rowdy Yates in *Rawhide* while the ghost of Luther explained himself in the kitchen between trick-taking rounds.

Here's what we overheard from our Grandpa Koehler, explaining things to our dad.

"It's all about your priorities, Hank. You have to ask yourself, 'What reason is there to try and reform a society that is doomed to collapse sooner than later?' We're like guests in a foreign land. We don't need to chase after temporary comforts or concerns. We only need to think about His kingdom to come where we have our permanent home. Sometimes, Hank, I even find myself sighing and hoping for the Day of Judgment. Luther taught us, 'If you believe it, the resurrection of the body and the life everlasting, you must truly wish it with all your heart and love the Last Day. For as long as we live in this vale of sorrows we will have little peace and rest. Today we are plagued with one, tomorrow with another misfortune. Furthermore, the world is our bitter enemy and persecutes us cruelly. Such misery we cannot shed as long as this life lasts. In our sad condition, our only consolation is the expectancy of another life. Here below all is incomprehensible.' Luther's right, here, Hank. Once you've lived as long as Florence and me, you'll know he's right."

"I know he's right, Dad" we heard our mother exclaim. "Luther hoped and prayed the Lord would put an end to everything and not regard the astronomers who claimed a new golden age would begin in the year 1540. Luther suggested we pray for our day of death to approach without delay. We should look forward to it! None of us are home yet. Goin' home someday, but not home yet. Like the apostle Paul said in his second letter to the Corinthians, 'We are of good courage, and we would rather be away from the body and at home with the Lord.'"

Did my Grandpa Koehler, my mother, Luther, and the apostle Paul just say, "The sooner we get this burdensome life over with, the better?"

Then we heard our dad finally respond. He had been staring at the embroidered plaque above our grandparents' pantry:

> "Love not the world, neither the things that are in the world. If any man love the world, the love of the Father is not in him. For all that is in the world, the lust of the flesh, and the lust of the eyes, and the pride of life, is not of the Father, but is of the world. And the world passeth away, and the lust thereof: but he that doeth the will of God abideth forever." (1 John 2:15-17)

"Wouldn't have taken much of a visit with Martin Luther to figure out why he yearned so much for the hereafter. Look at when he lived. The whole church was corrupt from within, including the pope who claimed authority in place of Christ. And the advancing military might of the Turkish Empire, the tyrant armed with the sword, threatened the land. He had his reasons, I guess, for thinking the way he did."

That sounded awfully close to something our dad might have heard from his father. Before our Grandpa Koehler could collect his thoughts and continue his amateur theologizing, our grandmother, like a supporting partner in a tent ministry team, had begun to softly sing one of her favorite hymns to punctuate our grandfather's Luther lecture.

> *Be still, my soul: the hour is hastening on*
> *When we shall be forever with the Lord.*
> *When disappointment, grief and fear are gone,*
> *Sorrow forgot, love's purest joys restored.*
> *Be still, my soul: when change and tears are past*
> *All safe and blessed we shall meet at last.*

At least our dad was ready to dig in a little and give life before death a chance. Before we all shall meet at last, that is. We sure liked to listen to him whenever he visited with our Uncle Willie on Sunday afternoons. "Ya' see, Will, planted in our front yard around Margaret's immaculate dichondra lawn and neat little border of bougainvillea is peace, opportunity, and prosperity. In the backyard, though, and not so visible to everyone, is the testing of H-Bombs and those Russian Communists. Ozzie and Harriet and Ward and June can be found out front. But McCarthy and Khrushchev are hiding out back. It's important, Will, we keep up our front yard in spite of that backyard. You can't let that backyard ruin your life. Thanks to Ike adding that phrase to our Pledge of Allegiance, we now at least officially live 'under God.' How we have made it up until now without living 'under God' I don't even want to think about. I'm feeling a lot better, Will, with God on our side."

My dad handed his pack of Benson & Hedges to Uncle Willie. The U.S. surgeon general had not yet declared cigarette smoking a major cause of sickness and death, a warning that only matters if you think life before death is worth such a caution. My dad shook the ice cubes around in his Tanqueray gin martini, and calmly announced, "Ya' know, Will, I might install one of those nuclear fallout shelters in our backyard." He said this so casually, as if shifting from his installation of our new water heater to the installation of a fallout shelter was no big deal.

Ours was a dangerous world. That goofy grin on The Beav's face didn't fool me! I listened carefully to those Friday evening conversations in my grandparent's kitchen and to my dad's Sunday afternoon visits with my Uncle Willie. Unbeknown to most Americans, the U.S. had exploded a hydrogen bomb on Eniwetok atoll in the Pacific two years after I was born. But at a weight of over ten tons, it couldn't be delivered anywhere as a weapon. In March of 1954, though, our scientists exploded a second hydrogen bomb that was small enough to use as a weapon and destructive enough to vaporize Los Angeles. The Soviets weren't far behind us. Many of those scientists responsible for the original atomic bomb we had dropped on Japan were opposed to any further development. They argued that little would be accomplished except the speeding up of the arms race. They were right.

I never felt reassured by Bert the Turtle and his *Duck and Cover* film we watched in the third grade with Mrs. Draper. Trying to figure out how to "beat the bomb," Americans worried more about the tremendous heat and blast damage than we did about the dangers of radiation and fallout. We had heard a rumor that some schools were even distributing metal dog tags like those worn by World War II soldiers. We didn't think much about how the bodies of dead students could be identified after an attack. We just thought that was kind of cool, to have dog tags like soldiers. Ducking under a desk and covering your head might have helped the children of Hiroshima and Nagasaki if they had been located far enough away from ground zero. But Bert the Turtle and that built-in shelter on his back wouldn't have had much of a chance with the explosion of an H-bomb. The first one tested produced the equivalent of ten and a half million tons of TNT, over 450 times more powerful than the atomic bomb we had dropped on Hiroshima.

The Red Scare wasn't called that for nothing! On a clear October night in 1957, Bud and I stood at our dad's side, necks craning backward to visualize the entire breadth of the star-filled universe above. Our dad spotted it first, and we stood silently as though we were staring at God in heaven. Our dad explained that we were staring at the Soviet's 184-pound *Sputnik* satellite running past us in the space race, claiming first place that year as the world leader in space technology and missile development. Could it be those Russian schools were superior in math and science to American schools?

Ike and the Department of Defense had no time to lose. Within a year, NASA and Project Mercury were underway. Intermediate-range missiles were placed in Turkey and Italy along with ICBMs deployed underground across the U.S., all aimed at the Soviet Union. Nuclear-powered submarines with nuclear-armed Polaris missiles were built to increase our range. And the National Defense Education Act was passed in 1958 to improve our training of future rocket engineers who would use their New Math to develop Project Apollo for a manned landing on the moon. Before those goddamned, godless Reds could get there!

Overheard one Friday evening. "So how cold is this Cold War we're in now, Hank?" my Grandpa Koehler asked. "Doesn't seem so cold to me these days. I've read that nuclear weapons poised by both superpowers have brought the world closer to the brink of Armageddon than at any time in history. And I hear our Secretary of State Dulles likes to force the Soviets into tense situations to test their resolve."

That didn't sound like the kind of *war* my brother and I played with Dennis Pruitt and Craig Glasgow in the empty lot behind our house on De Sales Street. You could count to one hundred to return to life whenever you were shot (and no fair counting by tens!). This kind of represented your recovery from a bullet wound. Would there be any counting to a hundred after nuclear annihilation, my generation's version of war?

"I can tell you this," our dad replied. "Our CIA is hard at work, replacing pro-Soviet leaders with pro-Western leaders. To protect America, Ike is building a new forty-two thousand mile interstate highway system for moving troops and tanks around the country if the Reds invade Long Island or Long Beach. That's not exactly cold, I would say."

Overheard one Sunday afternoon. "Hank, maybe I'm the only one, but I'm baffled about why we're so interested in Southeast Asia these days. I don't see this turning out so well in the long run, do you?"

"You've got to appreciate, Will, it's our American duty to protect the free world from communism. Since 1955, we've poured more than a billion dollars into South Vietnam, most of it in military aid. After the French were defeated at Dien Bien Phu, we took over the job of stopping the Reds in Southeast Asia. Honestly, Will, this ultimately serves our own interests, because we would end up the last domino standing once we let dominoes fall to communism around the world. That would be unthinkable for the American Empire we have become. Thanks to *Washington Post* columnist Joseph Alsop, we know how this domino thing works. Communism would take over the world country by country. 'You have a row of dominoes set up. You knock over the first one, and it's only a matter of time before the last one follows.' And we, Will, would be that last domino to fall."

Thanks to his machine shop contracts for building military aircraft parts, my grandfather and my Uncle Willie relied on my dad to help them understand why everybody seemed so nervous about the Cold War. I couldn't figure out how this was any different from Luther's day and those advancing Turks. Was our Grandpa Koehler right after all? My brother and I were learning a lot by listening to those Friday evening and Sunday afternoon conversations. And each year, things seemed to get worse.

Our Cold War-Space Race was complicated by all kinds of mistakes and ill-advised decisions. Had that Air Force U-2 spy plane pilot betrayed his country? Most Americans figured he could have destroyed his plane and taken his own life as instructed. Not my dad.

My dad was thinking about this incident in a different way. We desperately needed to know what the other side was up to, but we sometimes asked more of our technology than it could provide. And maybe we asked more of our pilots than we should. "What were we becoming," my dad asked, "when our instructions to a spy plane pilot taking high altitude photos included the use of a suicide pill (a tiny saxitoxin-impregnated needle hidden inside a fake silver dollar) if shot down behind enemy lines?"

After Ike had denied the existence of any such spy program, Khrushchev produced Gary Powers and his shot down spy plane. This revelation was embarrassing enough, but then Khrushchev took advantage of this debacle by walking out at the nuclear test ban treaty summit in Paris.

Some Americans hoped this superpower lunacy might face more reasonable minds with the election of Camelot in 1960. Not hardly. Ignoring Ike's warning about the growing military-industrial complex's influence on our government, President Kennedy embarked on the most extensive military build up in our nation's peacetime history. By 1961, our arsenal of nuclear weapons had increased by 150 percent, including the deployment of 1,000 Minuteman missiles, surpassing the Soviet ICBM build up at that time.

And then this harrowing confrontation in the Caribbean during the fall of 1962 cranked up the intensity one more notch, as if we weren't already scared enough. "We're protecting Cuba against any Western invasion," Khrushchev explained while twenty-five Soviet ships steamed toward the island. Khrushchev's navy was loaded with offensive military equipment and weapons capable of reaching most U.S. cities with a blow twenty to thirty times the force of the explosion at Hiroshima. To prevent further supplies arriving from the Soviet Union, JFK announced our military's quarantine of Cuba (use of the more accurate phrase "search-or-sink blockade" would have been considered an act of war). Fortunately, this was a line in the sand the Soviets chose not to cross.

But the standoff escalated when a Soviet SAM missile shot down an American U-2 plane. Who knows what would have happened if we had invaded the island? The Bay of Pigs invasion the year before had not gone well for JFK, but those stakes were minor league in comparison. Imagine three World Wars, all in one century. And this last one would have been a wrap-up! But six days after JFK's television announcement of the quarantine, the two Ks agreed to remove missiles from Cuba and Turkey and install a telephone hotline between their two capitals to provide more effective communication in such a global crisis. Neither of the two leaders, though, bothered to share news of their accelerated efforts to build more weapons. Within five years, the Soviets had surpassed us in the build-up of ICBMs.

Mutual Assured Destruction hung over our lives like a mushroom-shaped cloud. These fears I now felt played right into the hands of my Grandpa Koehler's theologizing. MAD sounds an awful lot like something

Martin Luther might have described four hundred and fifty years earlier, longing for God's day of judgment as he did.

The year after our flirting encounter with World War III, on a Friday in late November, an assassin named Lee Harvey Oswald snuffed out any hope or inspiration JFK had left to give us. Two days later, we watched on national television the murder of this assassin by a Dallas nightclub owner named Jack Ruby. One hundred years had passed since the assassination of Abraham Lincoln, and this was as far as we had come. Maybe the Day of the Lord was imminent. Thank goodness we had our sights on God above, and not on this transitory vale of tears below. The threat of those advancing Turks in Luther's day had nothing on our Cold War arms race with the Soviets. Thank God for my mother's faith!

And what the hell were psychologists thinking? Did they have any clue about how such a threat of nuclear annihilation affects a young child? If you feel trapped, as I did growing up, in a 1950s horror movie that only ends with your vaporizing death under a classroom table, but followed by your Easter reward in heaven, maybe your mother holding your hand like she did all the time is about all you've got.

After our cousins had left for home that Easter Sunday in 1955, our mother sat down between Bud and me to read the rest of the story she had begun for us on Good Friday, the same story she read for us every year over Easter weekend. Lew Wallace's best-selling classic, *Ben-Hur*.

The Civil War general-turned-author had reexamined his Christian faith after a lively debate with a Colonel Ingersoll. So ashamed of his indifference and ignorance, Wallace at once committed himself to a thorough study of the subject. The tale of the Wise Men utterly fascinated him. But he expanded his original short story draft, "The First Christmas," to cover the entire story of Jesus of Nazareth through the eyes of a Jewish aristocrat named Judah Ben-Hur.

Won't ever forget that spectacular chariot race at Antioch when Ben-Hur outraced his childhood friend and now Roman adversary Messala. And every schoolboy agrees Messala got what he had coming to him! But our favorite part of the story tells how the Nazarene's procession on Palm Sunday before he was crucified briefly paused so he could heal some lepers along the road to Jerusalem. Ben-Hur had been watching all of this but did not know at first that the two women healed by Jesus were his mother

Miriam and his sister Tirzah. He had searched for them in vain day after day in the caves of the lepers beyond the city gates. How wonderful that Jesus could heal people who suffered so from this wretched disease. But why some, and not others? Why only Miriam and Tirzah, and not all the lepers in that miserable cave?

A full day that Easter Sunday in 1955 for my brother Bud and me. For our mother, for those women Mary Magdalene, Joanna, Mary the mother of James, and Salome, and for Judah Ben-Hur, his mother Miriam, and sister Tirzah. Walter Cronkite would add, "What sort of day was it? A day like all days, filled with those events that alter and illuminate our times, and you were there."

We were there, all right. And we were there the next month when *LIFE* magazine published those eerie photos of a million dollar replica of a town used for one of our routine atomic bomb tests. Even included the use of department store mannequins to demonstrate the effects on people. Did I say, *routine*? During the first half of the year, the U.S. had already detonated more than a dozen nuclear test explosions in Nevada alone. Viewing the mushroom clouds rising above Yucca Flat had become a tourist draw for Las Vegas sixty miles away. This atomic bomb explosion in May of 1955 was our forty-fourth nuclear test. I bet Luther wouldn't have bothered to plant his apple tree if he had lived with us in the 1950s!

Maybe two minutes before midnight, the closest ever setting, wasn't close enough for the infamous Doomsday Clock. Those scientists who had worked on the Manhattan project in 1947 had hoped otherwise when they created the thing. Seen as an indicator of the likelihood of a disastrous nuclear conflict, this closest to midnight setting remained until 1960. Did Luther operate with his own version of a Doomsday Clock? How about my Grandpa Koehler?

As I have thought about these days, I count P. F. Sloan as my own personal Old Testament prophet, praying for me what I meant to pray. We couldn't be the only ones feeling this way. All you had to do was look around you and you were bound to be scared. Who in their right mind didn't believe we were living on the *eve of destruction*?

I believed we were living on the *eve of destruction*. Growing up, I didn't have much context for my fears when I listened to my dad and Grandpa Koehler and Uncle Willie. When I later learned about all of this and was able to patch together those childhood fears with the threatening reality around me, I felt more frightened than ever.

Whatever's happening around us when we're coming of age has a lot to do with how we handle the rest of our lives. Seems like some people draw the lucky straw, grow up on a bright morning in history, the dawn of a new day full of promise and hope. Seems like others might have to work through some early morning clouds until the blue skies break up that overcast, but their day in history still ends up promising. Of all the goddamned timing, though, I had to come of age on the *eve of destruction*.

And I've been afraid of life ever since.

CHAPTER 3

Henry
9 April 1998
Maundy Thursday

For as long as I can remember, I have spent Thursday evening of Holy Week at church, either receiving Communion – hearing those words of Jesus as He shared the bread and wine, His Body and Blood – or presiding and distributing that bread and wine. So leaving home this morning for our three and a half hour drive from Portland to Sunriver was a first that Denise could not help but acknowledge.

"How are you feeling about missing the Lord's Last Supper tonight?"

"You know how troubled I am these days about leaving parish ministry, about what's ahead for us. And I know this isn't easy for you."

"Well, we both know your questions have been brewing for a long time, so it's not as if you're betraying Jesus because you're not showing up at His supper tonight."

I paused before responding. I hadn't thought about betraying Jesus. "Ya' got that right – brewing for a long time, I mean."

Denise accepted my silence then while Highway 22 took us from the Willamette Valley floor out of Stayton, up past Detroit Lake and the junction with Highway 20, and then up again over Santiam Pass before we descended into Sisters.

I couldn't help but smile, recalling a Maundy Thursday long ago when life seemed so much lighter. For my kid brother, anything that didn't make sense about our mother's faith only exacerbated his fears. Acute anxiety lurked around his every corner. "What's with 'Monday Thursday'?" he asked our mom.

She deferred to Pastor Messner. "Ask Pastor next week before your catechism class."

"Not a chance. He likes to embarrass us when we ask stupid questions."

"Well, it's not a stupid question. It's Maundy Thursday, George, M-a-u-n-d-y, and you're not the first person to wonder about that name. Some Christians call it Holy Thursday. On this night during Holy Week, we reenact the Lord's Last Supper when Jesus shared the Jewish Passover meal with his disciples before he was betrayed and arrested in the Garden of Gethsemane. To show his disciples how much He loved them, Jesus humbly knelt before each of the twelve and washed their feet as an example of what it means to serve others."

"I hope Pastor Messner's not gonna try and wash my feet tonight. No one's touchin' my feet."

"We usually just celebrate Holy Communion tonight. But Jesus gave his disciples that commandment to love one another, and so we get the word *Maundy* from the Latin word for commandment: *MANDATUM*." Our mother was so quick and handy with her Bible, always ready to cite chapter and verse whenever she was teaching us anything. She was finding the passage, in the Gospel According to John, the thirteenth chapter, even as she spoke about that Latin word for commandment. "So if I, your Lord and Teacher, have washed your feet, you also ought to wash one another's feet."

"Yeah, well, that's fine, but like I said, no one's touchin' my feet tonight."

Once a kid brother, always a kid brother. While George was growing up, he retained most of his childhood features – an adult version of his fourth-grade school photo from Coolidge Elementary. Like his thick blonde hair still combed in that Elvis wave my mother had created when he was five-years-old; like his wrinkle-free expansive forehead that remained so smooth even when he squinted his bluish-gray eyes in bright sunlight; like his turned-up nose a comic-strip illustrator had drawn on his face to emphasize his youthfulness; like his disproportionately small mouth surrounded by remnants of baby-chubbiness for jowls that framed his perfectly-rounded chin; and like that initial connection he seemed to make with most people he met (winning the affection of others came easy for George) – a connection a child makes and evokes from us an offer to ask, "How can I help you?" It was all those things, but the giveaway was my kid brother's five thousand freckles! To irritate him, I would call him Alfalfa, and he would instinctively wave his hand across the top of his head to check for any cowlicks. Come to think of it, he might have had six thousand freckles.

George was one of those lucky guys – born with large bones and an athletic physique that seemed to require little effort to maintain it. Couldn't tell if he had forgotten to shave, his whiskers were so light-colored. During his drug-induced heyday, my brother weighed maybe close to 165 lbs.; at six foot three, his clothes hung on him like he was recovering from major surgery, only he wasn't. George did let his hair grow long during those days but kept it clean. Even when he had gained weight, he still looked younger than his age, in spite of his bulging front torso where excessive twenty-four-ounce bottles of Budweiser had settled comfortably for the long haul.

George and I couldn't stop giggling that Maundy Thursday service in 1963. He kept whispering in my ear something about how smelly the whole place would get if Pastor Messner washed everybody's feet that night. As my brother looked around behind us, he predicted who would be the smelliest. Our mother was furious, and she didn't even know what we were giggling about. She didn't have to.

I recalled another Maundy Thursday long ago when I asked my mother to explain the difference between her book about Ben-Hur and the film version about Ben-Hur. As it turned out, my question planted the seed that grew over my lifetime into this Easter weekend about to unfold at Sunriver. I was a seventh-grade catechism student returning home after our Luther League field trip back in 1961 – the Saturday before Palm Sunday – a matinee showing of the Academy Award-winning movie *Ben-Hur* starring Charlton Heston. I couldn't shake off this notable disparity. The screenplay writers (the one Oscar the film didn't get) did not show Ben-Hur's mother and sister healed on the Palm Sunday before that first Easter, like the story my mother had read for George and me when we were younger; they are healed on Good Friday when the sky darkens, and the clouds burst open with a torrential downpour over the three criminals hanged on Calvary. Watching that dramatic moment – Esther, Miriam, and Tirzah huddled in a cave, suddenly cured of leprosy – was the first time I ever thought about Easter as something more than a price paid for some one's sin so they could go at last to heaven. Ben-Hur's mother and sister would now live new life in the here and now, not waiting for some future Easter time and the hereafter, but healed for life in the here and now. There's no question that whatever was dead isn't dead anymore when flashes of lightning reveal their astonished faces, this miracle set to the impassioned musical score by Miklós Rózsa. Living with leprosy was a life good as dead.

At twelve years old, I didn't fully understand sin and salvation, but I was not new to what death and resurrection was all about. On Labor Day in 1954, the sixth of September, the day before I began first grade at Fremont Elementary School, my older sister Cathy was taking me for a bicycle ride to the Thirty-One Flavors ice cream parlor by our old house on Campbell Avenue. At the top of the hill where we lived on S. Meridian Ave., she declined my offer to race to the bottom, so I set out like a flash anyway to show her it would have been in vain. As I crossed the intersection of Ross Ave. and Ramona Terrace, I turned around with a shout to my sister, "Come on, Cath, what are ya' waitin' for?" In that brief moment of reckless eternity, a '49 Ford pickup truck from Childer's Nursery swerved to the left hoping to avoid my careening bicycle and me. I, however, did not avoid it.

The accident proved fatal, for at least three minutes before the ambulance arrived at Valley General. When I was pronounced clinically dead, my mother made a promise to God – much like Hannah's promise to God, that if she were blessed with a son, she would dedicate him to the Lord for the rest of his life – that if my life were spared, my mother would turn me over someday to serve the Lord. A brain concussion, three hours of surgery, two and a half months recovering in the hospital, a shot every day, alternating left or right side of my buttocks, and I was returned to life with my mother's vow to fulfill. I was preordained to be ordained. I'm surprised she didn't rename me *Samuel*.

I learned I wasn't the only one with this kind of death and resurrection experience, coming back from the dead to live life in the here and now. Later that Easter Sunday in 1955 after George and I had first met those women behind the sunrise-service altar at Our Savior's, Cary Middlecoff defeated the best in the game of golf, Ben Hogan, by a seven-stroke margin to win the Masters Tournament in Augusta, Georgia. Middlecoff had opened with a round of seventy-two on Maundy Thursday but followed with a second-round sixty-five on Good Friday. Sam Snead had defeated Ben Hogan by one stroke in an eighteen-hole playoff the year before, so this was Hogan's second year in a row as the runner-up, after winning the Masters in both 1951 and 1953. Hogan's remarkable record of nine majors, including three in 1953, doesn't mention the incredible number of times he stared at a finishing leaderboard with his name one slot below the leader. By 1955, Hogan sat atop the pantheon of American sports icons – although his achievements were not often cited by Lutheran pastors in their Easter sermons.

What made the past five years of golf so memorable was Hogan's miraculous comeback from the dead after he had thrown himself across his wife as a Greyhound bus trying to pass a truck slammed head-on into their Cadillac. Before this near-fatal accident on southwest Texas Highway 80 in 1949, on what would have been his father's sixty-seventh birthday, Hogan had established the sport's standard for dogged determination, an indefatigable work ethic, and absolute self-reliance. No one refused to give up like him, no one in golf practiced more than him, and no one overcame self-doubt like Hogan did. There is golf before Hogan, and there is golf after Hogan; the little paperboy from Dublin, Texas, can be credited with overthrowing the feudal world of country club golf.

For many years, though, fellow touring pros, sports writers, and fans had to reconcile the Hogan demeanor – brusque, intimidating, intensely private, ambitious, and obsessive – with the public acclaim he so deserved for his near perfect game. The 1951 movie about Hogan's life, *Follow The Sun*, starring Glenn Ford and Anne Baxter, ideally focused on his indomitable spirit in the face of overwhelming odds; but it was hardly the story of Ben Hogan's life. The movie did not know, could not know, the most likely source of the Hogan mystique, the closely guarded secret kept by Hogan his entire life – his father's suicide.

On a wintry Monday evening the day before Valentine's Day in 1922, at his family's house in Fort Worth, Ben's father Chester, a thirty-seven-year-old blacksmith, decided his quarreling with Ben's mother Clara was pointless. Confused and hopeless, Chester walked into the next room, pointed a .38 caliber revolver at his heart and pulled the trigger, unaware his nine-year-old adoring son Ben had followed him into the room. How many times Ben Hogan asked himself why the man he loved so much would do such a thing, no one can ever know. Ben's mother was not holding his hand that day; he was all alone, and he would remain all alone with this unimaginable horror for the rest of his life.

Feeling desperately alone is how his father's path to self-destruction had begun after his horse-based business slowly declined with the advent of the automobile. Debts mounted, his fear of failure intensified, his self-image in the eyes of his wife Clara diminished, and his steadfast churchgoing habit gradually gave way to a demoralizing drinking habit. How is it that Chester's Easter faith did not sustain him? Looking for salvation, looking for life – he obviously didn't find it in that empty tomb of Jesus.

In those days, the path itself was called melancholia, and it usually led down an emotional hole out of which few were able to climb. This malady of the spirit was as much the subject of quackery as it was of legitimate medicine, although no one knows for sure how Chester was treated at Arlington Heights Sanatorium. However his bipolar depression was treated, Chester's spirits lifted enough for him to think he was cured and ready to move his family back to Dublin. That's what the argument had been about with Clara.

How this unspeakable family tragedy eventually shaped the ambitions of Ben Hogan the golfer is not easy to establish, but his unwavering survivor instinct in the face of repeated failure to achieve his goal of becoming a respected golf professional may have been Hogan's way of living his father's failed life as well as his own. Can we live our life with double the effort to make up for another's life? Did Ben Hogan ever contemplate suicide, ever contemplate following in his father's footsteps as a way out? If we run fast enough away from our pain, does that mean we also run fast enough away from suicide? Is that one way to find our here and now salvation – in the rigors of discipline and hard work?

Chairman of that 1955 Masters Golf Tournament – had chaired the tournament for forty-five years – was the Wall Street investment banker Clifford Roberts, who finally found his true love in the grandeur of the magnificent Augusta National Golf Club he co-founded with amateur golf sensation Bobby Jones. Hogan, Roberts, and Jones shared a curious alchemy: one part Roberts the enigma plus one part Jones the Hollywood star equaled the one and only Ben Hogan. Tellingly, Roberts and Jones drifted apart when Roberts discouraged the ailing Jones, suffering from Lou Gehrig's disease, from attending the Masters. So worried about his partner's image and health is something Hogan would have been concerned about. And like Hogan, Roberts rose above his circumstances to achieve his lofty goals, sometimes too high-minded for those around him – like arguing with his partner that their new tournament at Augusta should be called The Masters.

But unlike Hogan, Roberts did follow in his father's footsteps, and his mother's, when he finally determined eighty-four years of life was enough. When Clifford was nineteen, his forty-four-year-old, unhappy mother Rebecca had used a shotgun to end her back pain and headaches and depression; eight years later, the year before Hogan's father Chester killed himself, Clifford's father Charles had decided to end his battles with ill health by stepping in front of a train.

Early in the morning of September 29, 1977, tired of dealing with cancer and the debilitating limitations of a recent stroke, wearing a trench coat and trousers over his pajamas and galoshes with no shoes, "Mr. Cliff" headed out the door for a middle-of-the-night stroll down to the par-three course east of the clubhouse. What was once a parking lot in 1955 was now a little fishing pond he had built at President Eisenhower's suggestion, for whom he had served as chief financial adviser and campaign finance chairman.

Shortly before 3:00 AM, he found the perfect spot near the water's edge, lifted a Smith & Wesson .38 to his head, and with the calculating efficiency that drove every endeavor in his life, he ended it – "controlling everything down to the last shot," one reporter quipped.

All suicides begin with a different story, but it would seem all suicides end up the same way.

From Sisters into Bend, and then south on Hwy 97 to Sunriver, less than an hour, and we were driving around the circle to park in front of the lodge.

"Mr. Caine, welcome to Sunriver Resort, and Happy Anniversary to you both! Saturday, the eleventh, right? How many years, may I ask?"

"It'll be our twenty-eighth. Thanks for noticing, and Happy Maundy Thursday to you."

Chapter 4

Karl Benson

To sing the closing hymn that Easter morning at Ebenezer Lutheran Church in Bend, Oregon, we rose from our pew in the exact spot where we had stood the summer before for my mother's funeral service. We had stood in this same spot with her when we were baptized two years before her death. We became children of God just in time, I guess, before He took her away from us. And six months from now, I would be standing in this same spot to watch my dad marry the woman who was supposed to replace my mom.

For the moment though, the sixth of April 1958, I was trying to imagine what good and wonderful things God was providing for my mom in heaven. My seven-year-old sister Denise held our little sister Kristin's white-gloved hand on one side and my hand on the other while our dad and Grandma Genevieve flanked the three of us. My dad held my hand and my grandma held Kristin's hand because our mother had gone at last to heaven this past August after suffering for two years with skin cancer. My dad leaned down and kissed me on top of my head, but that didn't stop my trembling. The three of us weren't trying to squirm loose, we weren't interested in having any fun, and we weren't looking forward to any Easter dinner or playing with any cousins. We just wanted to know why God had taken our mother away, why our mother wasn't holding our hands today, why we had no answer for that question on the plaque now hanging in the hallway outside our bedrooms, the poem by Dorothy Aldis. Since our mother drew the shade each morning to wake us up, and tucked us in each night with a kiss, who was supposed to start our night and day if our mother ever went away?

I've been trying to figure that out since the day she died. In a panic, my dad had listened carefully to well-intentioned relatives and church friends who thought they knew best who should start the day for Gordon Benson's three children. Did these people think this was a job opening to fill, like organizing some kind of talent search for a replacement mom? My dad's sister, Aunt Adeline, volunteering before the funeral to offer her home for my two sisters, was the first in line.

"It will be impossible for you to provide what those two little girls need now, Gordon. This way, you'll only be responsible for raising Karl." Hard to know how to feel about all of this. People were telling my dad that some arrangement was necessary for life to go on for us. Were we sick and dying too?

Our family was broken up enough over my mother's death, so my dad rejected any proposals that would break us up any more. An angel by the name of Mrs. Suma appeared before us, recommended for her nurturing way with children and, it would turn out, an almost supernatural understanding of what we truly needed to help us carry on with our lives. Don't know how she knew, but she did. Why we couldn't have stuck with Mrs. Suma, I will never know.

My dad regretted taking the advice of Al and Mary Jean Sawyer who had provided their large and comfortable farmhouse for the wake following my mother's service. They had thought it wise to keep Denise and Kristin away from the funeral, thought it would be too difficult for them to attend. So my sisters had stayed with the Sawyer's teenage daughter Charlene. They're relatives of a sort. My Grandma Genevieve had married Al's dad, Charlie Sawyer (her third husband), two years before. But the Sawyer's advice to separate our family for my mother's service felt like a bad omen. My dad and I wasted no time leaving the church and returning to hug my sisters. I remember them watching from the deck overlooking the red brick patio, watching people they did not know arrive from the church, many still crying and then turning away to cry even more after they had made eye contact with Denise and Kristin.

My mother was heavily sedated with morphine when she was taken away that Monday afternoon. I remember waving goodbye to the rear door of the ambulance. Family and friends had gathered at our house, but all I remember is feeling utterly alone. I knew then she was gone forever. She died two days later, the twenty-first of August, 1957, and the good and loving God to whom we had prayed for her recovery has been hiding behind a permanent cloud of gloom ever since. I was eight years old.

That Wednesday night, all I could think about was my mother touching and sniffing my hair. Last year, before my mother had begun to weaken midway through each day, we had spent a week in July riding our speedboat around Paulina Lake and camping along the eastern shoreline. My dad's cousin, we called him Uncle Bill, and his wife, we called her Aunt Lorna, had joined us with their kids and travel trailer. My dad and I both were due for a haircut but didn't have time the week before, so my mom offered to step in and take care of us. Sitting next to each other wasn't the best idea because my Uncle Bill had challenged us to hold perfectly still while he made faces to make us laugh. My mom got so frustrated with my dad that she used his ears to stop the comb whenever she rearranged his wet hair. "Ouch, aren't you supposed to stop combing before you hit my ear?" She never got frustrated with me. She simply held my head steady with her gentle hands whenever I snickered. I could already feel this memory fading, as though that ambulance pulling away had taken this memory away too. Memories can fade away quickly if you let them.

I would learn as I grew up that my mother's death, as well as her life before death, was shrouded in layers of secrecy, layers I had to investigate and uncover over many years. Which is so unlike how she chose to live her life, how she decided to express herself each day. Always honest with herself and with those around her. All of the family deceit that has followed her death is a betrayal of her memory. I couldn't reclaim my stolen childhood, but I could try to restore my mother's honor.

I asked questions whenever I had the opportunity to visit my Grandma Genevieve. My dad wasn't talking to me about my mom's death. I wanted to know why medicine and doctors and prayer and God had failed to save my mom. I didn't realize at the time how much I didn't know. I knew I had to blame someone. This was not my mom's fault. Do I blame my dad, my Grandma Genevieve, my Grandpa Sam, Mary Baker Eddy and her Christian Science? Do I blame God? That's kind of scary, but I would go there if I had to.

As the years passed following her death, I realized my quest would require a much broader scope of inquiry than merely asking questions of my grandmother. Who was my Grandpa Sam? Who was Mary Baker Eddy and what was Christian Science? What were the circumstances surrounding my mother's death, and why was it so difficult to find some answers? I owed her this pursuit of the truth.

My grandmother had wasted little time in finding another man after her divorce from my real Grandfather Frank Ralston, a Montana cowboy who had left her just before the Great Depression. My mom was only four-years-old then. Could have been traumatic, but her new stepfather created a loving relationship and enduring bond with her that lasted until his death in 1953. Before the War, my mom's real dad had appeared at Bend High School one day, out of nowhere, hoping to pick up the lost pieces. He wasn't in the best of health and probably wished to explain himself before it was too late. I think she was uncomfortable seeing him, so content now with her life. I don't think she harbored any ill feelings toward Frank Ralston. I think she respected Sam Sheldon too much to try turning back the clock to what could have been. As always, my mom was honest.

The five-foot-ten, kind and loving Sam Sheldon introduced his two favorite ladies to Christian Science, a religious movement he had devoted his life to with an unwavering passion that surpassed even his devotion to God. First as a Lay Christian Science practitioner, then as a Church officer, Sam was as trusted a disciple of Mrs. Eddy's teachings as she ever could have imagined.

"My dearest ones," he explained one day with extraordinary courtesy and genuine concern, "you must trust that God is good, that it is never His will for anyone to suffer, be sick, or die. God only wills for us our good health and life. Why not believe that the same Galilean Prophet who healed the sick two thousand years ago can touch and heal our lives and the world today? We have neglected that cornerstone of His ministry, to heal sickness and disease, to make the blind see, to make the crippled walk. I want to share with you this profound feeling of being loved and being well."

So one of the many layers of secrecy surrounding my mother's death was the extent to which she had embraced that well-meaning counsel offered by Grandpa Sam. I learned that Sam Sheldon was a practical man, a well-groomed gentleman who had led his church's religious discussions in the evening and directed daily operations at the local hospital he co-founded in 1946. A brilliant businessman, he had managed the magnificent Claremont Hotel in the Oakland-Berkeley hills above the San Francisco Bay. I'm sure his evening group of fellow members and his daytime colleagues at the hospital were interested in how he reconciled his two lives, his personal commitment to Eddy's principal work *Science and Health with Key to the Scriptures* and his personal commitment to the mission and goals of the hospital.

Did he consider the medical care provided by his hospital on a par with his church's teaching about healing the sick? My grandmother explained to me that he was quick to answer. When it came to health care decisions, Christian Science people were free to make their own choices about what to think and do. Grandpa Sam respected medical professionals who professed their belief that prayer and health are related.

Mrs. Eddy, however, had drawn a clearer distinction between the two. For their motives and philanthropy, the best of physicians deserve our great respect. But if they only understood the science of mind healing, they would abandon their false theories and would flock to our superior cause. Faithful followers of Christian Science have no need to visit doctors or use medicine. Once you ask for medical help, you have admitted you are sick. This is exactly how the false belief in illness can threaten a Christian Scientist's confidence in the power of mind alone.

Turns out, your first call to make when you're dealing with the illusory belief you're ill or in pain isn't to Grandpa Sam's daytime colleagues. Your first call is to a Christian Science practitioner who will help you realize the errors of your thinking so you can focus on driving those mistaken thoughts from your mind. According to Mrs. Eddy, my mom needn't have worried about an abnormality on her skin. It wasn't an abnormality. It was an illusion. What is termed a *disease* does not exist.

Grandpa Sam's church promoted the power of prayer to heal physical and mental illnesses and disorders. Every week, the Christian Science Sentinel, and every month, the Christian Science Journal, reported accounts of healing through prayer. He would have been asked, I'm sure, why The Journal did not generally report on cases where prayer had failed. I sure would have asked him why such prayer was unable to save my mom.

For followers of Christian Science, though, God was not held accountable when prayer failed to heal the sick. Your prayer had asked for right thinking, not for God's Holy Hand to touch your sick and dying mom. Her sickness and her death were illusions, and her lack, your lack, of right thinking prevented both of you from accepting this. My grandmother gave me a

1956 issue of the Christian Science Sentinel my mom had read and marked. Here's what I read in the article "How Prayer Can Help You":

> "'The prayer of faith shall save the sick,' says the Scripture. What is this healing prayer? A mere request that God will heal the sick has no power to gain more of the divine presence than is always at hand. The beneficial effect of such prayer for the sick is on the human mind, making it act more powerfully on the body through a blind faith in God."

I know what Mrs. Eddy thought about the problem of evil. She simply denied its existence. Not exactly a logical argument, but a clever way out. Evil is an illusion. My mom's cancer was an illusion. Since God is good and God is everywhere, Mrs. Eddy figured good must be everywhere, and therefore evil could not be anywhere. Like I said, not exactly a logical argument.

I wish I knew how much of this teaching Grandpa Sam had shared with my mom and my grandmother. I've tried to imagine my mom listening to some of the proof offered by Mrs. Eddy's writings, evidence that sickness and disease are unreal. My grandma did remember Grandpa Sam telling her and my mom this story about how Mrs. Eddy had deceived a patient suffering from edema. Mrs. Eddy, fully aware this patient was improving, but fearing a prolonged use of the prescribed remedies, decided to give this unknowing patient unmedicated pellets and watch the result. Amazingly, the patient was cured! (Chapter VI, Page 156, Lines 5-27) My grandmother told me that Grandpa Sam sure knew his *Science and Health* like a preacher knows his Bible. He liked to add that Eddy's cover page included this quote from Shakespeare: "There is nothing either good or bad, but thinking makes it so."

I wish I could have visited with my Grandpa Sam about all of this. I would have asked him how Mrs. Eddy's story could be considered scientific proof that disease is an illusion. So was she cured, Grandpa Sam, as in no longer suffering from edema, or did Mrs. Eddy assist this woman in accepting the reality her edema was never real in the first place? She didn't need some medical treatment for her edema; she needed help in overcoming the illusion that she was suffering from edema, right, Grandpa Sam? As a practitioner, Grandpa Sam, why couldn't you have helped my mom overcome the illusion that she was suffering from cancer? "Believing makes it so," right, Grandpa Sam?

"For the assurance and encouragement of the reader," the last one hundred pages of Eddy's *Science and Health* include case studies of those "who have been reformed and healed through the perusal or study of her book." It is essential to Christian Science that its claims be supported by testimonies of the healing power of thought. Searching for some connection I could make with my mom, my grandmother, and Grandpa Sam, I read all eighty-four of those letters, submitted from De Funiak Springs, Florida, to North Yakima, Washington, from parts in between, and from Canada, Panama, and the United Kingdom. I honestly can't imagine my mother finding much assurance or encouragement here as she contemplated her choices to seek help during those early stages of her melanoma.

These letters were supposed to provide the necessary credibility for a religious mind-cure movement my Grandpa Sam had lovingly shared with my grandmother and my mom. Reacting to a religion of fear and anxiety sweeping across our country, such beliefs like his had originated in the latter half of nineteenth-century America. It didn't help that medicine at this time had little to offer those suffering from anxiety.

Medical care still looked much like the nightmarish practices of medieval practitioners. Antibiotics were not developed until the 1930s and 1940s. Before that time, doctors knew little more than how to help a patient's own body do its healing work. Diet, rest, and ingestion of needed body fluids. Drugs used by doctors in the 1800s were mostly ineffective.

Mrs. Eddy had borrowed some of her ideas from an uneducated clockmaker named Phineas P. Quimby who had once traveled around the country in a covered wagon selling snake oil. He eventually gave that up and concluded that neither his nor anyone else's medicine was genuinely effective. Our healing begins, Mrs. Eddy claimed, with the power of suggestion, a patient's motivation, some faith in the process and the healer, some rituals and drama. Sounds to me like the placebo effect.

I do not know which tradition had more influence on my dad and mom during her illness. If Grandma Genevieve were visiting, it would be Grandpa Sam's Christian Science teachings. If Grandpa and Grandma Benson were visiting, it would be my dad's Lutheran teachings inherited from Sweden.

Both traditions stressed God's promised goodness and love, and that seemed to make the days leading up to my mom's death even worse, not better.

I cannot know the extent to which Grandpa Sam's beliefs alone were trusted for my mom's well being. How much bearing did Christian Science have on her decision to forestall any treatment for that serious skin lesion on her leg, a concern dating back to my sister Denise's birth in 1950? My grandmother's Dr. Langer had turned his practice over to his son, my mom's close friend from high school. That's who had delivered all three of us. In friendship, had the younger Dr. Langer assented to my mom's confidence in the teachings of Christian Science to heal her? Had she waited too long before she acquiesced and accepted his diagnosis and treatment? Whether or not her premature death from cancer can be blamed on irrational beliefs, I will never know for certain. But if Mrs. Eddy's folly influenced my mother in any way to avoid the medical care she needed, I'll point to God as the source of such folly. My mother's wisdom and honesty tells me that her deep respect for Sam Sheldon and the teachings of Christian Science were placed on one side of a scale with the current medical advice of Dr. Langer on the other side, and she bravely fell victim to cancer that no mind healing or medical treatment was going to prevent. That may be what I am left with after all of my inquiry.

Except for this one thing. The more committed a family stands by the presumption that God is good and loving and has a plan for our lives, the more perplexing and unfair, then, is the human suffering that befalls a family. Like Christian Science, my dad's Lutheran background asks us to expect God's goodness. But I have to ask in return, "How does a good and loving God with His plan for our lives square with my mom's death at thirty-one, leaving behind three children?" How am I supposed to make sense of this God "who only wills for us our good health and life," but who takes our mother away from us when we are children? Who was supposed to start our night and day?

At least Mrs. Eddy had an answer. My mother had let the truth slip away, the truth that could make her free. She had not overcome the delusion. Ridiculous logic, but still an answer.

My dad's Lutheran teachings reminded me that God can turn this unbearable moment to good if I but trust in Him. Some things that happen to us may not make much sense at the time, but they are all part of God's greater plan. We may not always be able to see clearly His purpose in our suffering.

That's ridiculous. What kind of a God comes up with a plan like that? All those church people were so concerned about our proper grieving and lack of any counseling or therapy. I just wanted them to help me understand how God's Plan for my mother's death made any sense for my sisters and me. Please help me understand that. Those church people did remain diligent, though, in their quest to find a permanent replacement mom for the three of us. Was that part of God's plan?

I'll never forget this well-meaning remark a friend of my Aunt Adeline made: "Here's what you can say to those people who will try to confuse you about God. They will say, 'See, Jesus took your mom away.' But you don't have to blame God. You can say, 'Yes, death did take my mom away, but Jesus took my mom away from death.'" Yeah, well, my mom is still gone!

As I grew older, my Aunt Adeline tried to explain exactly how God's plan made sense for what had happened to our family, why my mother had died. I remember her holding on her lap a copy of C. S. Lewis's *The Problem of Pain*, her hand tapping that confident source of wisdom as she explained this to me. What I needed to understand, she told me, had more to do with my dad than with my sisters and me. My dad's pride and self-sufficiency had prevented him from turning all of his thoughts toward God, surrendering himself to his creator. For my dad, I was told, God was like a parachute, there for emergencies but hopefully never needed. God could even feel like an interruption in his life sometimes. What my dad didn't realize is that his happy life wasn't happy at all; it was a false happiness because in the end, whatever life he had put together for himself and us wouldn't mean a thing if we had not known God the right way. Our happiness lies in God. My dad was living under the illusion of self-sufficiency. But to my dad, life seemed agreeable enough. Why surrender it to God? So God was left, as cruel as this may seem, with making my dad's life less agreeable by taking away the plausible source of false happiness. The creature's illusion of self-sufficiency must, for the creature's sake, be shattered. This illusion of self-sufficiency may be at its strongest in some sincere, kindly, decent, capable, hardworking, and temperate people, and on such people therefore, misfortune must fall.

Ridiculous again! I could hardly sort out the differences between such folly and the folly of Mrs. Eddy's Christian Science. My sisters and I sure weren't the only ones with questions about why God needed to shatter our dad's self-sufficiency. But when you're eight years old the day your mother dies, every future connection you make with a pastor, with a church, with the Bible, with an Easter Sunday, with relatives who want to help comfort you and explain why this happened, every such connection must be reconciled with the twenty-first of August, 1957. Every such connection for the rest of your life.

Ever supportive of my struggle to find some answers, my Aunt Lorna always had time for my questions about those layers of secrecy. What I appreciated most about Aunt Lorna was that she listened to me share my confusion about all of this and then refrained from trying to provide any answers.

Because there are no answers.

Because there is no answer to my question. Since God took my mother away, who would start my night and day?

One year after my mom's death, my dad met Eva Kimble at a weekly Bible Study some friends had arranged for that expressed purpose. Just widowed three months before, she was struggling financially to support her two daughters. Melissa was fifteen, and Diane, adopted at birth, was my age. Eva had chosen to ignore any professional help to work through the painful illness and death of her husband Milt. That was the topic of their first conversation. My dad had made the same choice. Their faith was sufficient, they told each other, and they married three months later. A marriage of convenience, ignorance, and denial, multiplied by two!

Here's what I remember about that first month after their wedding. I went from being the oldest brother of two sisters to being the only boy and middle kid among four sisters. Sharing a bed with my dad on nights too dark and lonely was no longer an option. Honest to God, I don't know how I would have lived through the night sometimes if I hadn't been able to put my hand on my dad's chest and feel his breathing. I know that's how my two sisters made it through so many nights. They had each other and held each other tight.

Eva had lost a son during childbirth when she was thirty-one, so in a dysfunctional but genuine urge, she sought to bond with me. I had lost my mom when she was thirty-one, but the last thing I wanted was to bond with a stepmom and two stepsisters. And to complicate things even further for our two grieving families, Diane longed for a replacement dad to fill the void now left by the death of her loving father Milt. My close relationship with my dad interfered with that, so Diane and I ended up picking a fight with each other at least twice a week. Of course, I'm the one who got in trouble for those fights. Our playroom where my punching bag and drums were set up was converted into a bedroom for Diane, so my stuff was stuffed into a corner in our carport. That didn't help.

Eva didn't appreciate Mrs. Suma staying on after the wedding and interfering with her relationship-building efforts with my sisters and me. I loved Mrs. Suma and her oldest son who brought her every day and treated me like a kid brother. "The day you arranged Mrs. Suma's last day for us, Eva, felt a lot like the day I learned my mom was not getting better." Every day I lived with my stepmom was a confirmation my mom was gone and never coming back.

I could hardly wait for Saturdays when I would escape to the sawmill with my dad. During the week, my dad timed his log or lumber deliveries so he would pass by my school and pick me up for the rest of the day. One way to keep me out of the fray. But he gradually shifted his loyalty and devotion to Eva and seemed to grow tired of my moaning and complaining. "Karl, look, Eva's your mother now, you'll have to flip a switch. We need to move on as best we can!" The more my dad spoke this way, the more I felt abandoned by him. Not by my mom, but by him. He was still living, and his marriage to Eva announced his priorities loud and clear. Half-orphaned can be worse than losing both of your parents. It didn't take long to figure out that my dad had abandoned me for a woman. Not a replacement for our mom, but a wife for himself.

If circumstances had been reversed, if my dad had died instead of my mom, and she had now remarried to provide a substitute family to help us carry on, I cannot imagine her ever suggesting to me that I needed to "flip a switch" and move on. She would have shared memories with us about our life with our dad, and she would have explained how this new man in our lives was there to help our family, not to replace the father we had lost. She would have been honest about what had happened to our family, and about how difficult it would be to deal with all of the changes.

I tried Cub Scouts for a few months. That didn't take. Our den mother, Mrs. Osborne, reminded me too much of my mom. You would think that might have helped a little. It didn't. I couldn't stand baseball, too boring, so Little League was out. My dad didn't like baseball either. I had more fun crushing pennies on the railroad track than playing baseball.

Thankfully, lots of boys in our neighborhood to play with and forget about things. Except for Jimmy Laughlin who snuck into my bedroom when we were gone one weekend and stole my fourteen dollars I had hidden in a model airplane.

Eva had a difficult time figuring out how to make it all work. She never did, and most of her efforts backfired and added to the strain on our family. She tried to prevent as much contact with our grandmother as possible, concluding that this would only make things more difficult for the three of us. It would only make things more difficult for Eva was the real problem. Our grandma was the only way we could reconnect with our mom. Like orphans searching for their lost home and family, we invented excuses to visit our grandma, claiming we needed more time in the morning to reach school.

All of our family albums with treasured photos of us with our mom were purposely stowed away in a closet. Whenever our dad and Eva were gone, we would hide in the closet to look at them while one of us sobbed to keep nosy stepsisters at bay. Which wasn't necessary, we soon discovered, because they were both holed up in another closet trying to recapture what they could of their life once lived.

Each passing year after 1957, I could feel my anger toward God growing, what would become a lifelong battle I chose to fight alone. I did teach my two little sisters to join with me in prayer. All three of us ended our nighttime prayers with "And God, why did you let our mother get sick and die? Why did you take our mother away?" Our dad never questioned us about it. I don't think Mrs. Eddy had that in mind when she spoke about the power of prayer.

What's puzzling to me now is that my battle with God back then assumed God was still in charge of the universe. I didn't agree with how He was running it.

Battling with God by spouting off my frustrations and disapproval of how He was running things was hardly satisfying. So the school ground became my main battlefield. I was bigger than most kids my age and often teased about my raw emotions. A lot of kids didn't know about what had happened to our mom. I found myself outside the principal's office door more than I was in my classroom. Fight after fight, I confronted and bullied those insensitive kids, all the time directing at them the real anger I could not physically direct toward God.

Feeling every morning that I was the victim of incredible unfairness and an uncaring God had a way of taking a toll on my classroom attention. Hard to care too much about multiplication tables, spelling quizzes, stories to read, or science lessons to explore. Didn't seem to matter, didn't seem real. The only thing that mattered was my mother's death. That was real.

Will never know how much professional counseling might have made a difference. I only know it would have had to compete with the same circumstances my nonprofessional help faced each day. The family and friends who helped me return to 1957 to mourn my mother's death, who listened to my questions, who encouraged me to cry when I needed to cry, who offered to tell me more about my mom, were increasingly shut out of our lives. My Grandma Genevieve, Aunt Lorna, and Mrs. Suma. My dad and Eva were leaving 1957 behind as quickly as they could. Leaving my sisters and me behind too, because our grieving was controlled to maintain a respectable family reputation. Little did they know, but my dad and Eva, by their deep denial of so much pain in our family, were losing ground even as they claimed our family was moving forward.

Whenever my two sisters and I have shared 1957 and the years following, we quickly agree. Our own burdens of sorrow we now deal with each day were born of grief we were denied and our dysfunction as a family because of that denial. My dad chose to deal with his pain apart from my two sisters and me. That was not too helpful. Denial creates its own version of pain, in addition to the pain caused by whatever is denied.

My dad wasn't singing this Easter morning, even though he loved to sing. My mother had fallen in love with him the day he soloed at her First Church of Christ, Scientist. She had been dating my dad's brother Hubert who had foolishly asked his brother to fill in for him that evening. What this auburn haired Hollywood starlet with gorgeous dark brown eyes saw in my Uncle Spud my dad could never imagine. Besides, my dad was a crooner, my Uncle Spud all operatic. Today, though, my dad stood quietly holding my hand, probably trying to figure out, like I was, what good and wonderful things God had provided for Robin in heaven.

Lo, Jesus meets thee, Risen from the tomb!
Lovingly he greets thee, Scatters fear and gloom;

Let his Church with gladness Hymns of triumph sing,
For the Lord now liveth; Death hath lost its sting!
Thine is the glory, Risen, conqu'ring Son;
Endless is the vict'ry Thou o'er death hast won!

CHAPTER 5

Henry
9 April 1998
Maundy Thursday

Denise and I have celebrated our anniversary every year by recalling details of our wedding day. It's our own little version of *The Newlywed Game*, testing each other's memory, sometimes alternately embellishing a favorite recollection until our reminiscences spiral out of control into total laughter and delight. But we hardly felt like playing our quiz game this Maundy Thursday evening while we waited for our dinner at the Trout House. We shared our breadbasket, we toasted our years together with a glass of Beringer White Zinfandel, and we stared at the sunset calm of the Deschutes River. Like dude-ranch saddle horses returning to their stable, our bikes had led us along the path from our lodge guest-room out past the first four fairways to the south, around to the west of the resort air-strip, and then north past the stables to the restaurant by the river-landing. Our yearly ritual.

Denise turned away from our corner window overlooking the river. "You blame both, don't you, for what happened?"

I knew what she meant. My three best men and I had not done well by our promise on that ninth green twenty-eight years ago, and God had not done well by His promise in Jerusalem two thousand years ago.

"You're going through with it, aren't you?"

I stared at the endless flow of the river and let the spot where I was staring remind me of how past, present, and future so often flow together both

51

in nature and in life. My spot had turned into a future even as it was becoming a new past. Even after someone's death, we can still feel their life around us. Will I still feel my mother's Easter around me?

When the four of us had walked off that ninth green the day of my wedding, we believed our vow of faithfulness to each other was no less binding than the vows of marriage I would exchange that afternoon. As Denise walked down the aisle that day, it was already clear to her that the person she had fallen in love with also shared his soul with those three men standing by him to his left. The four of us shared a bond few people understood. We were a part of each other. I was not giving up my life with those three guys that afternoon; when I said my vows to Denise, I was adding a new partner in my life. More than one Scripture source offers the simple equation to describe this moment: "For this reason a man shall leave his father and mother and be joined to his wife, and the two shall become one." Denise and I thought it was a bit more complicated than that; the two of us were becoming four. Now I was Denise's spouse, but I was still who I was the day before. And now Denise was my spouse, but she did not give up who she was the day before. Same spot in the river – how past, present, and future so often flow together.

My mother-in-law had failed to appreciate the double ceremony of our wedding day.

"Was it necessary for you boys to play golf this morning?" Eva greeted us after our twenty-minute drive from Sunriver Resort back to Bend. "A stunt like that has no place on your wedding day. Why didn't you play golf yesterday before your big bachelor party – like a last hurrah for the boys?"

A last hurrah for the boys? Our foursome exchanged quick glances. As Andy began to offer an explanation, Karl seized the reality of the moment by simply apologizing. Karl was the expert when it came to Eva; for most of his life, he had been forced to cope with her peculiar insensitivities.

Don't know this for sure, but I imagine Eva harbored some resentment toward Karl and his Hollywood good looks – a constant reminder of his real mom and not a damned thing she could ever do about it. Never more than three weeks out of Roy's barber chair, so couldn't always tell when Karl had had his last haircut. His whiskers were darker than his reddish blonde hair, so usually noticed any days he missed shaving. His forehead crevices, not unlike a complex Chinese character, he could have lived without. But that distinguished dimple accenting his prominent chin and his strong jawline didn't make it any easier for poor Eva.

If Karl's comforting hazel eyes could speak, they would say, "Everything's gonna be all right." Like a medic injecting a Syrette of morphine. Deep within, though, his heart knew better; nothing had been all right since that day in 1957 when his mother had died. So you had to savor his pleasant smile because you never knew how quickly it would succumb to the growing sadness he endured.

His disproportionately long torso brought added attention to his broad chest and strong shoulders. Standing shirtless in a photo from Vietnam, he could have passed for G. I. Joe's brother. His drink of choice, a refreshing blend of grapefruit juice and vodka, the Greyhound never left him with any next-morning regrets. Sure liked to wear a winter vest over his hickory shirt, wore a hat better than Greg Norman, and always greeted you with a gentle slug to your upper arm – his way of shaking hands. He liked to make a face whenever he was thinking about something serious, eyes half-closed, and lips pursed but curled back inward. Karl had a lot of his past flowing together with his present most of the time.

When the South Course first premiered a few weeks before I was married in 1970, only the front nine holes were open for play.

Although the Cascade Range to the west blocks most of the moist Pacific Ocean air from reaching this region, the temperature of the ground and grass often falls below freezing overnight. Trampling down this fragile terrain can cause costly damage to the course. The tiny strands of crushed grass do not usually recover. Although such concerns seemed oddly overstated – the geological formation of this terrain was anything but fragile – we had to wait for the frost-covered fairways and greens to thaw before we could play golf that morning.

In the beginning, before the invention of writing and recorded history, much of this region was destroyed by cataclysmic volcanic activity. Toward the lava plains of the southeast, Paulina Peak marks the highest point around the caldera formed after the intense eruptions and collapse of the massive Newberry Volcano over 80,000 years ago. During the 1960s, NASA considered the bleak and inhospitable lava fields covering the outer slopes similar enough to the lava and nearby pumice-dusted surfaces explorers might find on the moon, so this area became a training ground for lunar astronauts.

More recent fissure eruptions along the fault line extending northwest from this volcano formed a five hundred foot cinder cone now called Lava Butte. About seven thousand years ago, indigenous inhabitants who hunted and fished this area were forced to temporarily relocate after the westward lava flows from a subsequent eruption of Lava Butte reshaped the Deschutes River and its surrounding pine forest into a shallow lake and marshland. Any footprints left under that burning magma would have been cast in lava for discovery by archeologists who would be grateful someone had traipsed all over this meadow. Benham Falls marks the drainage point where this seventeen-mile long lake eventually receded to create the Great Meadow that is now Sunriver Resort.

Over sixty-five hundred years ago, not far to the south, Mt. Mazama had erupted and eventually formed the caldera known today as Crater Lake. Using the Bible's timeline, that would be about five hundred years before the earth was without form and void, before the Spirit of God was moving over the darkness that was upon the face of the deep.

None of the early Native American inhabitants of this region – the Northern Paiute, the Tenino, or the Klamath – would have bothered to wait for the grass to thaw before they collected their obsidian tools and arrowheads. The early French fur trappers who named the Deschutes River ("river of the falls") would not have waited to set their traps. The trader and explorer Nathaniel Wyeth would not have waited in 1834 before he pitched camp in this meadow. Such celebrated explorers as John C. Fremont and Kit Carson surely would not have waited until mid-morning before setting up their camp in this area. The Lost Wagon Train led by Steven Meek in 1845 did not wait each morning before searching for the way West. In 1855, U.S. Army Lt. Henry Abbot did not wait for the thaw before he surveyed this area for the railroad proposal connecting Sacramento to the Columbia River territory. Cattlemen ready to move their herds for summer grazing in mountain meadows didn't worry about trampling the frost-covered grass. And Chief Paulina of the Snake River Walapi tribe – whose name is immortalized by that peak above the Newberry Caldera – did not wait until noon each day before he defended his homeland against white settlers from the East. None of these people had to be concerned about early morning frost on the grass, but we did.

We had to wait.

The World War II soldiers of Camp Abbott – the U.S. Army's Third Engineer Replacement Training Center that occupied this meadow – welcomed the frost-covered conditions in 1943. Anything that could simulate winter conditions in Europe was helpful for the Army's ninety thousand combat engineers who would be trained here. These camp trainees weren't dodging golf balls in those days; they were dodging bullets on the obstacle course laid out around the present location of the tenth tee. They weren't swinging at golf balls on the driving range; they were firing rifles and launching grenades. Bridges were built over the Deschutes River to prepare for bridge building over the Rhine River.

The landmark Great Hall, Sunriver Resort's community centerpiece, originally served as the Officers' Club for Camp Abbot. Thanks to local materials available for construction, and built as a training project, this classic mountain lodge was completed in six months at a cost of $4,796. The camp's northern barracks were located on ground that is now between the twelfth and fourteenth holes. So dazzled by the mountain scenery of Central Oregon, one of the young soldiers wrote in his diary, "This is absolutely the prettiest country I have ever seen in my life."

After the Government sold the 5,484 acres that had been Camp Abbot, the Great Hall was neglected and began to deteriorate in the late 1940s, even used at one time to house cattle. In the early 1960s, after Oregon industrialist John Gray had purchased the land and before any of the Sunriver development had occurred, this site was used as a movie location for a film titled *The Way West*, starring Kirk Douglas, Robert Mitchum, Richard Widmark, and Sally Field. In this movie the Great Hall was depicted as Fort Bridger. Instead of accepting a cash payment for the use of the facility, Gray asked the filmmaker to install a new roof on the Great Hall. This renovation eventually resulted in the marvelous building standing today: a fitting memorial to the men and women who trained here and later fought in World War II.

After my brother George had proudly announced the occasion for our round, the attendant behind the counter waived the five-dollar-weekend green fee.

"I still can't believe Caine is playing golf today."

"What, you think he's still drunk from last night?"

"I heard that, Andy. Silence from the gallery, please. I need silence here; I need to concentrate on this drive." Standing over a golf ball the morning after my bachelor party and expecting to concentrate didn't make too much sense. I could hardly pay attention to our natural surroundings; I had a difficult enough time standing up! My brother had wisely checked with the pro-shop the day before, so we knew the frost would delay our starting time – giving me more time to recover from the night before but adding nervous strain to both already-over-stressed families.

But I didn't want this stress to affect my golf game. I had enough to ponder that morning. Like the question, "When does drunkenness switch to a hangover?" Was I switching from one to the other this precise moment as I tried to balance myself with the fifty-three-inch shaft of a MacGregor one wood placed firmly on the ground next to my teed-up ball? I raised the clubhead off the ground – a third and fourth time – dizzily concluding the hangover must at least be on its way.

"For God's sake, Caine, swing the club, or we're gonna be late for your wedding this afternoon."

Ah, yes, my wedding today at 4:00 PM.

I raised the clubhead a fifth time – counting now like I had counted the drinks last night that we raised in celebration of my big day. I had my count of gin martinis under control until Matt what's-his-name showed up to challenge the intoxication limits and manhood of this groom. That no-good bastard, a short-term boyfriend of my wife's stepsister, Diane, hadn't even been invited.

"Everclear," he declared, "one hundred and ninety proof, or you're not ready to make the leap!" His recommendation is a brand of pure grain alcohol illegal in many states.

I shoved my little Tanqueray friends away from the edge of the table, seven empty cheerleading glasses having already worked their intoxicating pep-rally in my system. I felt like an Old West gunslinger accused of card cheating. So bold was I, jerking back the shot glass and swallowing without hesitation. Another? Of course, why not? All cheered. What a man! And wasn't this the whole point of a bachelor party? Given the advanced stage of our party consciousness, passing such a test seemed to indicate my readiness for marriage.

I may have been ready for marriage, but I sure wasn't ready for the night ahead. Denise and her sister were called to provide safe transportation home. I vaguely remember someone saying, "Cover your eyes, Caine, you're not supposed to see your bride on your wedding day." Not to worry. I didn't have a clue at this moment that it was my wedding day! I locked myself in the downstairs bathroom of my future father-in-law's home, dozing off-and-on while slouching awkwardly on the covered toilet seat – in case the Tan-queray and Everclear decided to rebel.

"Bud," my father-in-law checked on me about 3:30 AM. "Are you OK in there?"

"Yeah, I'm fine, just making sure, that's all."

I raised the clubhead of my driver again, a seventh time, and slowly turned my shoulders into the backswing. Such contortion protested my sleeping position from the night before. "Hit the damn ball," I mumbled to myself – along with a few other concerns. "Oh crap, I hope Gordon didn't tell my dad about how I slept in the bathroom last night. Why didn't I stick with my martinis? Why did I stay in that bathroom 'til morning? What will people think of me when they hear about this? I can hardly wait to see Denise this afternoon."

Easy money that day would have bet on a slice. Sure enough, my Slazenger #2 faded off to the right, flew within inches of a ponderosa pine, bounced onto the cart path, and rolled into the thick clumps of Idaho fescue that border the south Great Meadow.

"Jesus, this is gonna be a long day," Karl murmured. "Maybe we should-n't be playing golf after all."

"On the contrary," Andy answered. "Golfing with the boys is just as important as his wedding. Bud's not giving up any relationships; he's adding a relationship. He loves Denise more than anything else in the world. But he believes you can have both, not one at the exclusion of the other. You don't have to give up who you've been; with marriage, you add to the person you are. This morning means as much to him as this afternoon will. Something like that is what he told me last night after his third martini."

It was only 1:30 PM, plenty of time yet before my wedding. But plenty yet to do, and the mere thought that we could walk off the course and into the church for the ceremony did not meet with Eva's approval.

Eva was sharing her thoughts now with various relatives who had gath-ered at the house to prepare for the family reception later that evening. She reminded everyone that Denise and Bud had been working in Southern Cal-ifornia up until two weeks ago, that she had been left alone to take care of so many things for our big day. She was staring at me as she spoke.

"I am my brother's keeper," I murmured loud enough for the other three to hear.

"What was that?" she asked.

By 4:00 PM, we were all in our places at Ebenezer Lutheran Church in Bend, an old Swedish congregation affiliated with the original Augustana Synod. With the side windows of the sanctuary opened this April Saturday afternoon in 1970, the temperature inside was a pleasant seventy-three degrees.

The resort at Sunriver may be sacred, but this sacred place traced its history back to the beginning, so the Bible begins, when God created the heavens and the earth. In the seventeenth-century CE, an Irish Archbishop by the name of James Ussher had enough time on his hands to figure out, with no help from a modern calculator, the precise date of this beginning – a Saturday evening like our wedding day, but in October, the twenty-second, 4004 BCE.

Paying close attention to the opening chapters of Genesis reveals two different accounts of creation, suggesting that writing about the beginning is a lot more challenging than first meets the eye. And we can read in the Bible other accounts of creation, including a considerably different account in Psalm 104.

Genesis chapter one is the priestly version of creation – a revision of King David's temple history – that tried to explain how the state priesthood of the late sixth century BCE viewed its world and how that world had come into being. The earlier account of creation recorded in chapters two and three was written to validate the establishment of King David's royal house shortly after 1000 BCE, uniting both Israel and Judah with Jerusalem its capital. Centuries before, God had saved King David's people, once a band of disenfranchised, oppressed laborers, when He delivered them from Egypt; centuries later, God would need to save them again, this time from Roman rule, and they looked for the coming of a messiah who would save them in the here and now, not in the hereafter.

But most of God's chosen people did not accept a descendant of the House of David, one Jesus of Nazareth, as that long-expected Messiah. Some who did recognize him as God's Son, however, interpreted those creation accounts as serving a broader purpose – trying to explain who we are as human beings, and why it is a savior must save us from our fallen humanity, our sinfulness, and the curse of death. This expectation defined individual salvation, and over the course of two millennia, theologians and church officials worked out enough details to claim Jesus' life, death, and resurrection from the dead had fulfilled that expectation. These theologians added to Jesus' name the Greek equivalent of the Hebrew word *Messiah: Christos.* His followers became known as Christians.

A lucky crowd, though, that first Easter Sunday. Most didn't understand what had happened. But what had happened raised more questions than Easter could answer. "Why were so many things still the same the day after?" would be one of those questions. So theologians debated. Church leaders assembled to agree about what believers should believe (established dogma and doctrine); they split apart if they disagreed (Eastern Orthodox Church, Martin Luther and the Reformation, and a parade of other reformers splitting apart to this day); they excluded and persecuted those who didn't care one way or the other (Spanish Inquisition, treatment of Native Americans by European explorers); and to this day, they differ enough about such questions that many still don't know what happened. That original message about Jesus is lost on many who can't understand what all the fuss is about. But make no mistake: Western Civilization and Christianity are practically synonymous. For fifteen hundred years after Jesus, Europe was the Roman Catholic Church – one language (Latin) and one Holy Roman Emperor. CHRISTENDOM.

White paraments, the liturgical color of Easter Sunday two weeks ago, and the color for the season of Easter, adorned the pulpit, the lectern, and the freestanding altar. The altar guild ladies instructed us about the rules for using their worship space. "Do not move, for any reason, the six-foot-high paschal candle behind the baptismal font to the right of the lectern. You can only place floral arrangements on either side in front of the steps leading up to the communion rail. No rice or birdseed after the ceremony, please, because it is too difficult to clean up the brick surface of the entryway."

A large cross was suspended from the ceiling above the chancel, hung at a slight but noticeable angle to represent how it might have looked as Jesus of Nazareth carried it along the VIA DOLOROSA the day he was crucified. Unfortunately, this sight was hard to imagine because this cross, instead of a rugged, wooden cross, was made of polished brass.

Andy and I had asked about it the night before at our rehearsal. We were told the story about the widow who bequeathed this gift and idea of a crooked cross, about how some disgruntled members tried at first to gradually reduce the angle each week but were then questioned the next Sunday by that widow and her family. Don't mess with church memorial funds and bequests!

This church had a way of helping you think about things other than God's Holiness. Richly-engraved memorial plaques were posted below each of the stained-glass side windows, drawing your attention to the names of members who felt deserving of such an honor: Mr. & Mrs. Hjalmar Svensson, Mr. & Mrs. Gerhard Hegnell, Mr. & Mrs. Hans Larsson, Mr. & Mrs. Nils Lindkvist.

What did ol' Gustaf do for a living? What kind of neighbor was he? Did Gustaf say grace before every meal? How generous was he when it came to those in need? Were he and the Mrs. happily married? No doubt ol' Gustaf was one of the original boys who had built the new sanctuary after World War I with mostly donated lumber from the various local mills operated by members of the church – proud craftsmanship in the tradition of Old World cathedral builders. After hearing stories about how your Pa had re-measured lumber cuts a fourth and fifth time on the remodeling project, the hanging of that goddamned crooked cross could have been a real bone to pick in later years. But who knows, maybe Gustaf's daughter was the crooked cross lady.

When the organ chords of "Lohengrin" signaled my gorgeous bride to walk down the aisle to meet me, I felt my brother's arm reach around to pat me on my back. I turned enough to notice Karl's arm patting George on the back and Andy patting Karl on the back. When I returned my attention to Denise and her dad, my vision included the front pew to my right – the drained-face expression of Eva staring at the Caine foursome. Wedding photographers sometimes miss the most memorable pictures.

On the eleventh of April 1970, I made a commitment that would shape every day of the rest of my life. I promised faithfulness twice that day. But to how many people can you make such a promise? My promise to Denise would end up extending to our three children; we uttered those stand-by-me words the moment each was born. We would stand by them in the darkest of nights. As life has turned out, plenty of long nights and dark land to go around. And not always easy to keep that promise.

CHAPTER 6

Andy Messner

When I was in the seventh grade, listening to my father preach on Sunday morning was a welcome respite from the teasing I endured at school. Twice humiliated, because kids making fun of me were also making fun of him. I was beginning to understand and appreciate what he stood for, even though this automatically branded me a dull and wimpy Christian – too wimpy to stand up and confront the school bully, too wimpy to cuss or swear when someone on our flag football team screwed up the play, and too wimpy to get excited about the cool stuff everyone else was doing after school. It only took one kid to churn up this hackneyed nonsense about pusillanimous PKs, but one kid was one-too-many.

Respect for my father was evolving in step with my growing faith in God over the past year. When I was eleven years old, I had my hands full being a kid; adding PK to the equation sometimes overloaded that task. I remember how I tried to ditch my father and his pastor job – a formidable challenge because that meant I was trying to ditch God and His job.

We had to introduce ourselves the first week of my sixth-grade year using a list of required questions to answer. Oh great, "What does your father do for a living?" I decided in a split second of child apostasy to go with *submarine commander*, U.S. Navy. Hardly wimpy. For the next three weeks, I lived this fantasy by embellishing my father's career with tall tales of heroic actions all over the Pacific in World War II. I spent hours each afternoon in the school library researching the necessary details. Strangely enough, or maybe not strange at all given the general lack of logic and deductive reasoning skills of typical sixth graders, none of my friends whose families belonged to Our Savior's Lutheran bothered to question my outlandish claim. Fortunately, my best friend Bud Caine attended Coolidge Elementary across town; I know he would have stepped in to call my bluff.

By back-to-school night the end of September, though, I knew my jig was up; it didn't take Mrs. Cathcart long to figure it out when she met my parents and asked my father to visit our class to tell of his high seas adventures. That evening, my father explained to me how he felt about his part in the work of Christ. "Be careful next time," he said, "because we end up belittling ourselves when we try to cover up what we might be embarrassed about. We could give people the wrong impression about how much, or how little, we trust in God and how much we count on God's love each day. I'm a servant of our Lord, Andy, and I don't ever want to betray him like Peter did that Thursday night. And you know that story, son."

Of course, I did, but my father recited it anyway.

"We don't ever want to betray our Lord like Peter did!"

"But Father, at least Peter stood up for Jesus and tried to help him when he was arrested. I would have done the same thing to that servant named Malchus; only I would have cut off more than his right ear. And then I would have fought off those Roman soldiers and religious leaders."

"But Andy, you know Jesus did not approve of such violence. He even said He could have asked God to send down twelve legions of angels to protect Him, but that was not what was supposed to happen. And Jesus healed that servant's ear, right then and there."

"Twelve legions of angels? I would have called in the U.S. Navy!" My father smiled. Maybe the seventh graders remembered my submarine stories from last year, and now I was paying for my deceitfulness. If only I owned a sword, I would have shown them how wimpy I wasn't. I'm discomfited now about that whole sad charade last year, ashamed I was ever embarrassed about what my father did for a living.

Sitting in the front pew with my mother and two sisters, I couldn't help turning around enough to glance the faces of over three hundred people, all listening to what my father had to say this Easter Sunday in 1961. Only half, if that, would be returning the next Sunday; maybe what he said was so compelling and convincing that the other half didn't need to return every Sunday after Easter to hear it again. Maybe, maybe not. All I know is that Our Savior's was filled this morning with people listening to my father preach. He was the most important person in the church today. I was beginning to worship my father the Lutheran pastor.

My friend Bud was sitting two rows behind my family with his brother, two sisters, and mom and dad. His brother was sneaking a bite of a hollow chocolate egg while his sisters munched on their jellybeans. My two little sisters couldn't help but take notice; our family didn't participate in any neighborhood Easter Egg Hunt or worry about baskets full of little chocolate bunnies and chicks. Holy Week at the Messner residence was HOLY WEEK.

Bud and I listened carefully because we were required to take sermon notes for catechism class. We had a worksheet my father had prepared to help us identify the three main points of his sermon each week. Always three main points. And then we had to write a single sentence about what we would tell someone if they asked us what the sermon was about. What central message would we take away from this morning's sermon? My father's first point was his promise that when our Easter time has come, we will have a difficult time trying to describe the wonder of it all.

"Who among us here today," my father began his sermon, "has not experienced that awkward moment when your ability to speak fails to express what you are so certain about in your brain? You simply find yourself at a loss for words. Can you remember such a moment that truly took your breath away, that left you dumbfounded? Asked to describe it, you discover you have no words to utter; your brain can visualize it, but that image might as well be some unknown foreign language by the time you are ready to speak. 'Indescribable,' we barely murmur. 'Words fail us,' we excuse ourselves. 'Speechless,' we proclaim in a word. I can tell you this: for me, it happened every time one of our children was born.

Well, you haven't seen anything yet! I will make you three promises this Easter morning. My first promise is this: when it's your Easter time someday, you'll be fortunate if you can even think some clear thoughts, let alone try to express them. Talk about a disconnect between brain and speaking. Oh, our brain hears the Gospel accounts of that morning long ago and then creates images and visuals to help us comprehend the moment. And playing over and over again in our heads are those bold words proclaimed by the apostle Paul: 'O death, where is thy victory? O death, where is thy sting?' Triumphant words, indeed, and that is the essential promise of Easter. By his death, Jesus has destroyed the power of death, and by his resurrection has opened the kingdom of heaven to all believers. Because he lives, we shall live also.

And by the way, we will not be alone in our speechlessness when it's our Easter time. Mark's gospel tells us that trembling and astonished, the women 'went out and fled from the tomb. They said nothing to any one, for they were afraid.' Luke's gospel tells us that even though the women returned to tell the eleven what they had seen, the apostles 'did not believe them, their words seemed to them an idle tale.' John's gospel tells us that Mary Magdalene could only assume 'They have taken the Lord out of the tomb, and we don't know where they have laid him!'

Our Gospel accounts of that first Easter morning describe individuals struggling to overcome a predisposed understanding of our human condition. Death is death; our body eventually fails us and life comes to an end. Funeral arrangements are made for us, we are laid to rest, and our gravestone is marked with our birth and death dates. First-century funeral practices vary from our own, but this basic understanding of death wasn't much different for those first witnesses arriving at the empty tomb of Jesus – even though they had heard the promise of Jesus, that on the third day, he would be raised from the dead.

Given that, and hearing it from Jesus himself, they still came to the tomb Sunday morning expecting to complete his burial. Jesus had died on Friday, but because of Jewish custom – Friday being the day of Preparation, the day before the Sabbath – they had to wait until Sunday morning to complete the rite of burial. Bury him because he was dead. They – we – are not inclined to expect otherwise.

Most had witnessed, looking on from afar, the test performed by the soldier. No need to break the legs of Jesus to ensure his death before sundown on Friday, as was the case for the two thieves hanged beside him. Clearly, Jesus was already dead. One of the Roman soldiers pierced his side with a spear, and at once there came out blood and water. Convincing enough, and no reason to think anything else come Sunday morning – in spite of Jesus' promises. And yes, in spite of Jesus' promise, that because he lives, we too shall live, many of us come to our final days expecting death and the end –

convinced our life here on earth is all there is. The reality of death for someone we love can be so powerful an emotional force, leaving us so empty and distraught, we hardly think to question its finality.

But as a parish pastor, I have had the heartrending privilege to sit at the deathbed of those who have waited with faith and confidence for their Easter time. And I'm here to tell you their wait was more than worth it. An experience I cannot now explain to you, I don't have the words! But I could feel their long-awaited Easter moment as I held their hand in prayer and observed their weak, final breath."

My father then illustrated his point by sharing some stories about members of Our Savior's who had died the past year – members whose Easter time had finally come.

Bud waited until our catechism class the next day when we shared our sermon notes with each other. "So Andy, let me ask you somethin'. Why didn't those women in the movie *Ben-Hur* have to wait until it was their Easter time – wait until they died? Seems to me they got to live their Easter time right then and there, doesn't it?" I knew what Bud was up to before he had even asked me the question. Our sermon notes asked how the death and resurrection of Jesus assured us of new life when it was our Easter time. Bud reveled in any opportunity to question things about our Christian faith because he knew the questions bothered me; it was my father who was making this point. As our futures would parallel each other, this turned out to be our first debate salvo about God's Gift of Salvation: life in the hereafter when it's our Easter time versus abundant life in the here and now.

Suffering less disrespect for my father and what he did for a living gradually reinforced my own growing adoration for him. By the time I was thirteen, I had abandoned those embarrassing denials of his work. I was paying less attention to my peers at school and associating more with my fellow scouts – all of whom belonged to our church, the sponsor for Troop 316, San Gabriel Valley Council, Boy Scouts of America.

Those fellow scouts had become my gang – in the purest and most innocent tradition of that social system. It was a first-time feeling; it's where I belonged. By my baptism, of course, I also belonged to God – but being a PK is like belonging to the state church in a Scandinavian country where you're born.

We had named our Scout patrol after our favorite television show, Rod Serling's *The Twilight Zone*. We had designed our own patch, a white horizon line with a signpost and the initials TZ. We felt like we were "traveling through another dimension, a dimension not only of sight and sound but of mind; a journey into a wondrous land whose boundaries are that of imagination. That's the signpost up ahead – your next stop, the Twilight Zone!"

I'm sure it didn't hurt that this new "wondrous land" was located on Tuesday nights in the basement of the church where my father was the pastor. Hickory plaques with our wood-burned names hung under the appropriate rank designation. Bud Caine, Frank Gilbride, Brian Peaslee, Stan Orlander, Randy Fenske, Ted Edmonds, and I had watched our names advance from Tenderfoot to Second Class to First Class to Star to Life and then to Eagle – an achievement that meant more to each of us personally than it did to the rest of the world.

Took a four-day bicycle trip with Bud and his brother George during spring break of our junior year in high school, riding from San Gabriel out to the coast and then up to Santa Barbara, sleeping at Zuma Beach our first night and forgetting about the incoming high tide that woke us up in a panic around 11:00 PM. Eagle Scouts should have been prepared for that. Of all the timing, riding along Pacific Coast Highway 101 north of Ventura the next day, a Southern Pacific freight train barreled past us on the right as two cars crashed head-on to our left, throwing a hubcap that struck my rear wheel and sent me off into the ditch. I might have been more distraught about this than those accident victims who survived. We weren't prepared for such major repairs, so Bud fashioned a towrope out of his spare clothes to pull me north to a gas station. We finally realized, almost simultaneously, this was too long a haul, so Bud left George and me and rode ahead to borrow some wrenches.

"Son, I don't lend out any of my tools."

"Sir, I'll give you my Scout's honor I'll return these wrenches, and just so you know, I'm an Eagle Scout."

"Yeah, well, I don't care if you're George Washington, you ain't borrowing any of my tools."

By sundown, we eventually made it to another gas station south of Carpinteria.

The seven of us formed an Explorer Post of Eagle Scouts strictly dedicated to backpacking adventures, one of which almost cost me my life. We had hiked into a box canyon north of the Jet Propulsion Laboratory in Pasadena one weekend. Our post advisor Clarence Shurman had never earned the Eagle rank, but was an Army Ranger veteran of the Korean War. He liked to needle us by testing our skills to the limit. We liked to tease him about why he always combed his hair like the actor Ed Byrnes on 77 *Sunset Strip*. We called him "Kookie."

We discovered a way out by descending a narrow waterfall using a one-hundred-foot rope to lower each of us down. The last man would tie a sheepshank knot to hold the rope and then cut the middle section so it could be shaken loose when all of us were safely at the bottom. The sheepshank knot will become loose when not under strain, but it is not a stable knot and can fall apart quickly with any release of tension on the knot. That's what Bud and I had learned at Philmont Scout Ranch in Cimarron, New Mexico, where we heard the story about how Kit Carson had evaded capture by the Apaches when he faced a one hundred foot cliff. With only a fifty foot rope, but a small, convenient ledge about halfway down, he was able to lower himself to that ledge, dislodge the sheepshank knot, retie it around a convenient rock on that convenient ledge, and lower himself the remaining fifty feet.

When I couldn't find solid footing to continue my climb down, I stalled about fifteen feet from the top and yelled for help over the roar of the falls. As Bud waved from above to acknowledge my distress, I couldn't help myself swinging into the falls, the crushing pressure forcing me to lose my balance until I leaned my body into the rock surface behind the falls for some relief. But I was stuck there now and a little weary. Next thing I know, Bud offered me his hand and motioned with his head that we could move along a ledge to safety. I continued down from there, and we never made too much of the incident after that. We had to keep our composure to prove our bravery (Tenth Scout Law) in front of Kookie. It was a close call, though; I knew it, and so did Bud.

All of us daydreamed about our future life as soldiers. After all, that was one of the motivating forces behind the Scouting movement: the future defense of the British Empire. Why not provide middle-class boys with a much-needed head start to prepare them to serve their country in uniform someday? When General Robert Baden-Powell returned a popular hero in 1903 after defending the besieged city of Mafeking during South Africa's Second Boer War, he discovered young British boys were using his *Aid to*

Scouting manual as a guide for outdoor activities and comradeship. After applying his army scouting concepts and military drills to the training of boys – successfully field-tested on Brownsea Island in 1907 – he rewrote his manual and called it *Scouting for Boys*. This was my kind of outfit, preparing boys to become real men, like my hero Peter with his sword in the Garden of Gethsemane. No more wimpy Christianity for me!

Baden-Powell can't be credited with being the first organizer of a youth program dedicated to the character building of young boys, although he surely seized the moment on a grand scale. Across the Atlantic, his ideas merged with Ernest Seton's Woodcraft Indians and Daniel Beard's Sons of Daniel Boone to launch the Boy Scouts of America. William Smith's Boy's Brigade had limited its membership to those who would follow in the footsteps of Christ, as Smith personally defined those footsteps. This meant Jewish boys and those with beliefs other than Christian were excluded. The Boys Scouts of America tried to avoid such narrow-minded membership criteria, proclaiming a more racially progressive and non-discriminatory policy – as long as membership wasn't extended to certain individuals singled out by Baden-Powell, individuals like atheists and homosexuals. A simple acknowledgment that God existed was sufficient enough belief to qualify as reverent. As for homosexuality, that was another matter.

At first, it seemed like a short distance between our catechism class upstairs and our Boy Scout training in the church basement. Allegiance to God and Country could have served equally well as a banner for both rooms. But I quickly observed a significant distance between the two: God, Luther, the Bible, and my father upstairs, and the British Empire, Baden-Powell, *Scouting for Boys*, and me downstairs. Talk about two celebrated best-selling textbooks for our instruction – although our Bible upstairs was often replaced with Luther's *Small Catechism*, a condensed version of Christian doctrine that hardly could match the stories from the Bible or Baden-Powell's own version of the Bible, his *Scouting for Boys*.

Upstairs: My father adapted the ideals of Scouting to serve what he considered the true principle behind the Lutheran PRO DEO ET PATRIA award. He was making the same leap the Rev. R. L. Bellamy had made in Baden-Powell's day when he authored *Hints from Baden-Powell: A Book for Boys' Brigades*. Moral lessons could be read between the lines on every page of *Aids to Scouting*. So Bellamy spoke of a lone Christian boy living in a sinful society facing dangers no different from those faced by a solitary military scout behind enemy lines. Become a "Scout in Christ's Army," the invitation was extended. And so my father prepared us to follow Luther – always doing battle against sin and the devil. "Share in suffering like a good soldier of Christ Jesus."

Onward Christian soldiers, marching as to war,
With the cross of Jesus going on before.

Downstairs: Baden-Powell's Boy Scout movement was more than a recruiting program for the army. Prepare boys to become good citizens. And his definition of good citizenship included a spirit of self-sacrifice and patriotism. But his moral lessons in Scouting would be as helpful in combating hooliganism as they would be against the enemies of the British Empire.

Upstairs: I read in Luther's preface to his *Small Catechism* that he had found many common Christians woefully uninstructed in the faith. Sounds like Baden-Powell's assessment of the deplorable state of Britain's youth. So Luther had provided some guidance: For those who refuse to receive proper instructions, "they should be turned over to the pope and his officials, and even to the devil himself." And furthermore, "parents and employers should refuse to furnish them with food and drink and should notify them the prince is disposed to banish such rude people from his land."

After I read Luther's *Large Catechism* instructions for my father to follow as head of our household – that he should not give my two sisters and me anything to eat or drink until we had recited The Ten Commandments, The Apostles' Creed, and The Lord's Prayer daily when we rise in the morning, when we go to our meals, and when we go to bed at night – I had a newfound appreciation for my lapsed Lutheran father.

Downstairs: Baden-Powell's advice to scoutmasters sounded more reasonable. "Discipline is not gained by punishing a child for a bad habit, but by substituting a better occupation that will absorb his attention and gradually lead him to forget and abandon the old one." Threatening young boys won't lead to a responsible citizenry.

Upstairs: Luther's *Large Catechism* explained in detail how we risk God's wrath and punishment by our neglect of the poor. "Beware of this: those poor whom you neglect will cry to heaven, and their cries will have an effect too heavy for you and all the world to bear, for they will reach God, who watches over poor, sorrowful hearts, and He will not leave them unavenged."

Downstairs: Following the Scout Laws was a lot easier than following some of my father's teachings about why we should try to live a certain way because God had forgiven us for our rebellion against Him. With the Scouts, I just tried to do my best every day – no grave consequences like "the wages of sin is death." Baden-Powell's philosophy emphasized doing something good rather than not doing something bad. "A practical Christianity" would be Baden-Powell's term to describe his context for character building – "a spirit of manly self-reliance and of unselfishness. Scouting is nothing less than applied Christianity." Muscular Christianity, some would call it.

In his 1902 lecture ("Cultivating Habits of Observation") at the Wanderer's Hall in Johannesburg, Baden-Powell suggested our eyes turned outward away from self – in careful study of others and their daily concerns – will produce the kind of empathy and love of our fellowmen that is the one great principle for which we ought to live.

So I lived by a simple slogan – "Do a Good Turn Daily!" – asking me to help ease the burdens of others, asking me to make this world a better place. I was expected to keep working out so I wouldn't end up a wimp, to learn all I could and never stop asking questions, and to live morally straight (honest and strong of character) – even though I was slowly discovering I wasn't straight at all, and even though I felt morally straight about what I was discovering.

Following our twelve Scout laws – a Scout is trustworthy, loyal, helpful, friendly, courteous, kind, obedient, cheerful, thrifty, brave, clean, and reverent – seemed like a reasonable guide for living each day, kind of like that guide the pastor wrote, *All I Really Need to Know I Learned in Kindergarten.* The twelve Scout laws didn't feel anything like the Ten Commandments; the Scout laws described how to do our best because that's what was expected of us – nothing about breaking the Ten Commandments and threatened with eternal life in hell.

Upstairs: I loved my father the teacher of Christian doctrine, how he would try to explain to us that we had nothing to fear even though we recited those first few words of the meaning for every commandment: "We should fear and love God so we don't do this or don't do that." "A child-like fear is what Luther means here," he explained, "the fear of a little child who tightly holds his mother's hand, afraid he might lose her, that she will disappear from his side." So we sat and listened.

We had to memorize and then recite before the congregation on the day of our confirmation the answers to questions posed in Luther's *Small Catechism*. My father asked Bud Caine that day, "What gifts or benefits does Baptism bestow?" Bud answered correctly, "It effects forgiveness of sins, delivers from death and the devil, and grants eternal salvation to all who believe, as the Word and promise of God declare." My father asked this follow-up question, "What is this Word and promise of God?" Bud answered correctly again, "As recorded in Mark 16:16, our Lord Jesus said, 'He who believes and is baptized will be saved; but he who does not believe will be condemned.'" And then Bud raised his hand in front of everyone and asked my father, "Pastor Messner, what do you think *condemned* means?"

Downstairs: I don't remember anything about condemnation if I failed to follow one of the Scout Laws. I do remember learning about chivalry, Indian woodcraft (nature study, hunting, surviving in the wild, tracking), building a fire with only one match, judging distances, and providing first aid. I do remember sleeping on the ground under the stars, playing games, hiking, swimming, and exploring the woods.

Rudyard Kipling's novel, *Kim,* inspired Baden-Powell's *Scouting for Boys* – the adventures of a young boy thrown into a secret service mission for the British in India. In his manual, Baden-Powell's condensed version of *Kim* explained the famous observation game every spy should master. In 1908, this Kipling fictional character was every boy's hero. By becoming a Scout, a boy could live those adventures he had read about.

No surprise, of course, that Baden-Powell admired Sir Arthur Conan Doyle, creator of Sherlock Holmes. Power of observation and deductive reasoning! In *Scouting for Boys*, you can find half a dozen references to Sherlock Holmes, and even one to Dr. Joseph Bell, the Edinburgh professor upon whom Conan Doyle had based his legendary detective.

Upstairs: That twelfth Scout Law about being reverent can take on new meaning in the hands of a guardian of the faith like my father. He would have preferred "A Scout is Religious" – and he would not have apologized for the trace of Pharisaism inferred by such a term. Plus the fact, my father didn't like the twelfth law being the last – thought it should introduce the other eleven laws.

Downstairs: We never discussed this significant difference at the time, but I learned later the founder of the Boy Scout Movement in America had added that Twelfth Scout Law. Baden-Powell's Movement in England listed ten Scout Laws, the tenth – "A Scout is clean in thought and word and deed" – considered the most important. The American James West had served six years as the superintendent of the large progressive Sunday school of Mount Pleasant Congregationalist Church and was an active member of the Young Men's Christian Association. Because the YMCA did not consider Roman Catholics a Christian denomination, it prohibited them from serving in any capacity within the organization. And because the BSA had closely aligned itself with this strictly evangelical Protestant organization, the Catholic Church prohibited its boys from joining the Scouts. Baden-Powell's phrase "Duty to God" in his original Scout Oath apparently was not enough emphasis, so West revised the Scout Oath and Laws in *Scouting for Boys*.

Baden-Powell had rarely attended church and seldom mentioned religion in his letters. And yet he proclaimed religion to be the foundation underlying the ideals of Scouting. In 1900, Christian morality was considered the sole purpose for which religion existed. Bible interpretation made Jesus the teacher of the proper moral life. This liberal theology led the way for the Social Gospel that addressed issues of injustice.

Baden-Powell's unique connection with his father also helps explain some of his unpopularity with churchmen. His father, Professor Powell, an ordained cleric with a reputation for holding alarmingly advanced religious views, had written *The Order of Nature* (claiming that the only proof Christianity required was contained in the moral truth of the Gospels). After authorities condemned Baden-Powell's father as heretical, the Boy Scout founder grew up with a distrust of clergyman and theology that followed him all his life.

In 1921, Baden-Powell wrote an article, "The Religion of the Woods," in which he argued that our observation of Nature's wonders was the best way to apprehend God (a view influenced by his father's pantheistic book) and that no one religion held a monopoly on truth. His unique synthesis of camping adventures and religious experiences is not often acknowledged in Scouting circles today.

Baden-Powell's gravestone bears no cross or other religious symbols. Instead, along with the Boy Scout and Girl Guide Badges, a circle with a dot in the center is inscribed, the trail sign for "I have gone home."

Bud and I decided to take our Scouting careers to the next level by applying for summer staff positions at Camp Cherry Valley, located north of the isthmus on Catalina Island. We lived the Scouting life each day as if it had been passed down through the centuries from St. Peter himself. Scouting defined who we were and gave us purpose. By our service in Scouting, we were claiming a more honorable place in the ranks of humanity.

Imagine two dozen eighteen-to-twenty-year-old male staffers responsible for lifeguard duty every day, watching over a hundred young boys splash around in the translucent waters of Cherry Cove as the eighty-four-foot catamaran *Inception* dropped anchor every week with a fresh group of bikini-clad teenage girls ready to sunbath and party. Already feeling something different about these young female yacht guests moored in our cove, I honestly was amused but not distracted. I garnered exceptional praise for my disciplined refusal to pay attention to those sights – a source of constant trouble for the other staffers who strained to stay focused on the "buddy-system" pairs of scouts while trying to ignore the friendly gestures of those other pairs preparing their bodies with suntan lotion. It troubles me now to think that if anyone had known my reason, I would have been banned as a leader.

I had not paid close attention to this addendum to the Scout Oath, Laws, Motto, and Slogan; I was supposed to have read, "Homosexuality is not a positive male image. It's not something to hold up as a good role model for young boys." Excluding gays under its membership rules was a Scout guideline I had ignored. Specific tenets at that – a gay man should not be allowed to lead a Scout camping trip, a lesbian mother should not be allowed to lead a Cub Scout den, and a boy who has completed every step to earn his Eagle rank should be denied the award if he comes out as gay. If he comes out? We figured Kookie might have been gay, but since he wasn't openly gay, I guess it didn't matter. He never talked about it, that's all. So we didn't talk about it either.

My father had alerted me to a disturbing trend he had read about. Many United Church of Christ congregations were protesting the Boy Scout's policy of exclusion.

"Andy, what if such loose moral teachings pervade other denominations?"

"Father, are there denominations I'm not familiar with that teach prejudice, intolerance, and discrimination in the name of Christ? Are we called by Christ to shame and embarrass those whose sexual orientation we may not understand? Didn't Christ come for the downtrodden, the diminished, the invisible, and the marginalized? And aside from the teachings of Christ, what about the values embedded in the Scout Laws, values like helpful, friendly, courteous, and kind, respectful of others who may differ from us. What becomes of those young boys at Cherry Valley – what part will they play in society – if such bigotry is what I'm teaching them?"

Did my "wondrous 'Twilight Zone' land whose boundaries are that of imagination" have some specific homophobic boundaries about who I was? Maybe all God's critters don't have a place in the choir after all!

CHAPTER 7

Henry
9 April 1998
Maundy Thursday

After twenty-eight years together, Denise and I often find ourselves in like agreement without ever conferring with each other; but neither of us could explain the next day why we had chosen to remember our wedding day in this way. As we shared the photographs from our wedding album, we recounted the passing of family who had been part of our lives that day in 1970. We had never done that before. Some deaths expected, some unexpected, we both concluded. Whatever that's supposed to mean.

My German immigrant grandparents, already in their seventies when I made my two promises that spring day in Bend, Oregon, were content enough sitting in a Lutheran church for a traditional ceremony. Their promise of faithfulness had expanded to include my mother, her brother and sister, nine grandchildren, and five great-grandchildren at the time of our wedding. That's a lot of people to keep in your prayers. My grandfather was not a golfer – a baseball fan, National League, Chicago Cubs, in stark contrast to his son, my Uncle George, who was an American League fan, Chicago White Sox – but he may have understood my double ceremony if I had explained it to him. My grandparents both tried hard to understand things. Their deaths at ninety-three and eighty-five – expected.

My little nephew, Josey Martinez, always a brave and good-natured kid, had to fight for his life from the day he was born. My sister lost both her husband

75

and her son to the ravages of alcohol – the one at forty-four, the other at eleven, because his little body could not fend off the poison he had inherited from his father at conception. Both deaths – expected and unexpected.

My dad had his second heart attack the evening before my sister's wedding to Miguel Martinez – stress and strain of the machine shop business, but not wholly accepting of his daughter's choice of a husband. A Roman Catholic, after all, and part of another culture. Why couldn't she have found someone at the church where she had grown up? But she hadn't; she had fallen in love with this young sailor. Before her wedding at the San Gabriel Mission, the priest had to re-baptize her because her baptism in a Lutheran Church didn't count (that would be part of the fuss I'm talking about). I had the honor of walking her down the aisle while my dad recovered at Valley General. He did survive that round, but after two more attacks, my dad's heart finally failed the year after he retired. Factor in his cigarette smoking, his high blood pressure, and the daily burdens of life he faced with a Christian faith that declared his only consolation is the expectancy of life in the hereafter – his death expected.

Eva my mother-in-law never smoked a day in her life; she walked every day, took a handful of vitamins every morning, saw her doctor regularly, and ate the healthiest meals imaginable. During the final months before she died of throat cancer in 1986 at the age of sixty-five, she could only speak by using that artificial larynx held next to her throat. Listening to her before that was not easy, but such a device made it even worse. We had a lot of questions about her unexpected death, about how much attention she had paid to her health.

When her grandson Sean was killed three years later, most of my wife's family secretly expressed a trace of relief. Eva would have had a far more difficult time coping with Sean's unexpected death than with her own fate. After returning from a family-backpacking trip Labor Day weekend before his high school senior year, Sean was taking a friend home when a drunk driver ran a red light and slammed into the side of his compact car. His father sued the county sheriff's department responsible for the high-speed chase through a residential neighborhood and eventually received a settlement – after his twenty-five-year marriage to my wife's stepsister Melissa had ended in divorce over the whole tragedy. Max's career as a college professor of American history – in daily contact with young people his son's age – lost most of the luster it may have collected over the years. Max the professor, we called him, was responsible for serving alcoholic beverages at the family reception the evening of our wedding. He's that smiling guy in one of our photographs, a shot glass of Wild Turkey in one hand and a cigar in the other.

On that same Labor Day weekend, as if the night were not dark enough already, Denise received word of her Grandmother Genevieve's death. Family tragedies are stressful enough without compounding our grief and asking too much of our emotions. Her grandmother had only one child, Roberta Rouene, who had died of skin cancer at thirty-one; Denise was only seven years old when this happened, so her grandmother had served as both a mother and a grandmother all these years. Genevieve represented the last direct link to Denise's mom. When my wife's father remarried shortly after Roberta's death in 1957, feeling pressure by the family to provide a mother for his three children, the widowed Eva stepped into his life along with her two daughters – Melissa, Max's wife, and Diane, who was adopted when she was born. In her misguided attempt to help everyone start over fresh, Eva increasingly found ways to exclude Genevieve from the family, certain that such a reminder of their sad past could only cause further sadness for Gordon's three children. Denise's grandma did not sit in a front pew or a place of honor at our wedding; she chose to sit inconspicuously halfway back down the aisle. Sitting up front near Eva would have been too uncomfortable. The same for her attendance at the reception downstairs, so she had quietly slipped out the side door of the sanctuary right after the ceremony. We talk about that lapse in family protocol every anniversary; we should have insisted on a different arrangement. But we hadn't.

My Uncle David, my mom's Uncle Bob, my wife's Uncle Mare – all of these lives now fading memories as we shared their aging photographs from our wedding album. Twenty-eight years later. Expected and unexpected deaths.

Denise closed our album and set it off to the corner of our table. We both knew what the other was thinking now. We hadn't looked at our groom's party photograph.

I wish we had taken some photographs at the South Meadows course that morning. It took us most of the nine holes to recover from the night before. We weren't thinking photographs; we were having too much fun cursing whiffs and slices and chunks and misread putts. When we finally did pose for the groom's party official photograph later that afternoon, our faces before the camera now expressed what we had said to each other walking off the ninth green. We had all been thinking those thoughts during the days leading up to April 11.

Denise and I answered *Yes* to Rev. Roland Johansson's questions. We exchanged rings and then knelt before the altar for the traditional blessing, "Those whom God hath joined together, Let no one put asunder." After we were pronounced man and wife, we remained kneeling and silently held hands while my father-in-law sang "The Lord's Prayer" to conclude our wedding service, his confident baritone voice a welcome relief from the pastor's high-pitched nasal intonations.

After suffering the formalities of our receiving line, most wedding guests gathered in the church social hall for our reception. Our wedding party, our parents, and a few curious relatives returned to the sanctuary to record the marriage of Henry B. and Denise R. Caine. Every few minutes, a well-intentioned relative would interrupt the proceedings to remind us that guests were anxiously waiting. With each reminder and interruption, of course, the whole process took more time.

My radiant bride first, then the two of us, then a large group picture with flower girls, ring bearers, and acolytes, then the bridal party, then a few family photos for both sides, and finally, the groom's party. By this time, most everyone had moseyed into the social hall, so the four of us men stood there on the chancel steps – an odd site for anyone sneaking a peek. Like we had walked off the ninth green – I had my left arm around my brother's back; he had his left hand resting on Karl's right shoulder, giving the two-finger peace sign; and Karl and Andy had their arms around each other's neck.

All four of us were smiling with such heart and soul that our photographer paused for a moment and gazed at this foursome of little-boys-becoming-men. "What's with you guys, anyway? Glad it's over, hey? This will only take a second, and we're done." Obviously, he didn't have a clue about the picture he was taking. But we did.

Andy explained to the photographer what our foursome was up to that day, said we were hardly in a hurry. The photographer didn't get it. How could he?

I will say my best friend Andy looked the best of us in our rented tuxedos (white jackets and black trousers). Born with the ideal body proportions, he was that guy fashion designers called their model. Cross-Country in the fall and Track and Field in the spring were his two high school sports and he excelled at both, enough to earn self-respect but not enough for any scholarship. When he ran, he ran alone – always satisfied to compete against himself. At six foot two and 185 lbs., he always kept himself lean and fit.

Since we were kids, I remember him sweeping his long coal-black hair to his left side across his broad forehead, parting his hair on the right side. Inherited a distinctively darker complexion from his mother. His carefully trimmed RCMP mustache, high cheekbones, dark brown eyes, and thick eyebrows might give you the wrong first impression, a foreboding and stern look. But that would not be Andy. He was full of deep empathy for everyone he met. But his friendly smile didn't always serve him well in later years, regulated and restrained so often it lost its authenticity – can happen when your external expressions don't always match your internal emotions. Not a troubling stutter, but once in a while, it got the best of him.

One of our favorite photographs to talk about each year was taken by Max the professor. Denise and I were anxious to get underway in my father-in-law's '67 Chevy pea-green and white pickup truck – wedding gifts loaded in the camper shell, goodbyes exchanged, and tears wiped away. In the photograph, the viewer is looking at our pickup truck pulling away with my left hand waving out the window, still enough daylight for the viewer to barely see the detail in either side-view mirror. I can see Max in the driver's side-view mirror, snapping the shot, and I can see my three best men in the passenger side-view mirror – George with a thumbs up, Karl with a clenched you-did-it fist in the air, and Andy with a grand wave to royalty newly crowned as king and queen. With my left hand back on the steering wheel, I reached for Denise's hand. A kiss for luck, and we were off at last on our tight-budget honeymoon drive to Southern California. Our actual honeymoon took place at a crescent-moonlit highway rest stop on Interstate Five south of Redding, California, about 2:00 AM. It was an awkward night, and one we have tried to make up for on our anniversary.

Earlier that day, while my three best men and I were making our promise to each other, the unsuspecting crew of Apollo 13 was also making such a promise on their launch pad at Kennedy Space Center in Florida, to stand by each other in the darkness of night. And that night came two days later when an oxygen tank exploded on their Odyssey spacecraft 205,000 miles from Earth.

For Denise and me, we had just begun our new life together. We started out walking, but oh, how soon we would learn to run. We shared life, we watched for signs along the way, we talked things over just the two of us, and we worked together every day. And like my promise to George, Karl, and Andy, we promised to smile when the evening came; after all, come on, so much of life ahead. Why be afraid? We would stand by each other.

After twenty-eight years, Denise and I are still standing by each other. But what had happened to my foursome at South Meadows?

Our anniversary dinner conversation at the Trout House had lasted longer than either of us realized. We had to ride our bikes back in the darkness, but we weren't afraid. I had not remembered a flashlight because I was not thinking about darkness with my partner of twenty-eight years. And besides, our full moon was one night away. We rode along the north end of the airstrip and then paused at the turn leading us back to the lights of the resort lodge in the distant southeast.

We both stood silently astride our bikes beneath the vast reaches of the universe. Four, maybe five minutes passed. Don't know if the serenity of this Sunriver night heard Denise's whispered sigh, "I can't understand how it happened."

I heard it.

Some deaths expected, some unexpected – whatever that's supposed to mean.

CHAPTER 8

George

The year before my brother Bud was born, my mother and dad had loaded their two daughters into the back seat of a new Chevrolet Fleetline Sedan. Decided to follow the exodus moving west from the cold and snow of Chicago to the warmth and sunshine of California. A better climate for my sister Cath and her bronchial asthma, and a better job climate for my dad the tool and die maker.

He and his partner, Wayne Berg, had opened a machine shop after the War to produce tools, dies, jigs, molds, and fixtures. They worked out of a small rented garage on Fullerton Avenue. Since they rarely met monthly expenses, my dad's decision to pack up and leave home with his family was easy enough. He sold his half of the business to Wayne for fifteen hundred dollars and caravanned with my mother's Uncle Wally and Aunt Gertie across country to Alhambra. Within a week, he was working at the O'Keefe and Merritt plant on East Olympic Boulevard in Los Angeles. It was there on a lunch break one day that he spotted a four-line notice in a trade magazine about a Cragin Manufacturing Company moving its facility from Glendale to Anaheim.

Someone else in our family had preceded my dad out West, but no one had a clue about where Uncle Ed had finally settled. He had deserted his wife and children right after the War, had vanished without a word, and had set down residence in a growing community called Buena Park. My dad was always grateful to his Uncle Ed for teaching him the tool and die making trade and giving him his first real job. How could he ever forget his Uncle Ed's machine shop down on Kostner Avenue across from the West Chicago Railroad Yard, across from the Cragin Yard, to be exact?

Hard to say who was the most surprised when Hank Caine showed up at Ed's place, but my dad didn't hesitate to refuse his Uncle Ed's substantial offer of cash and property to keep his mouth shut and act like he had never found him. "Better pay that to your wife and kids back in Chicago, Uncle Ed," and the two never met up again. And so life for my dad the proud-to-be Chicago toolmaker began with a noble gesture and a promising career path in the burgeoning aerospace industry of postwar Southern California.

Within a year, my dad welcomed the opportunity to try his hand at management. After two months at the A.O. Smith Machine Company, he was appointed foreman. In September of 1949, Waste King Corporation's B.B.B. and Valley Air Division offered him a plant manager position. A subcontractor for North American Aviation, this B.B.B. division (Spanish for *bueno*, *bonito*, and *barato*, meaning *good*, *beautiful*, and *inexpensive*) manufactured components for military aircraft and weapons systems. My brother and I would end up with more pictures of the F-86 Sabre Jet posted around our bedroom than were displayed at the Pentagon. A year later, my parents purchased a larger home on Meridian Avenue, where Bud and I had our model train layout. I was born there on March 12 and named after my two grandfathers, George and William.

My dad's impressive climb up the corporate ladder didn't miss a step. To celebrate, he bought himself a new Torch Red 1956 T-Bird with portholes in the side of the removable hardtop. In 1957, he was promoted to Superintendent of Manufacturing for the Technical Products Division of Waste King Corp. He built a new home for our family on De Sales Street in San Gabriel, a few blocks away from the wealthy estates of San Marino. The next year, he bought a new vacation home overlooking the forest around Lake Arrowhead and the waterfront estate of Walter O'Malley, owner of the Los Angeles Dodgers. In 1960, my parents took advantage of the California real estate game and purchased a sprawling four-bedroom home on half an acre down the street from the San Gabriel Country Club, complete with a twenty-by-forty-foot swimming pool.

That country club would be where Bud and I first took up the game of golf, sneaking through the shrubbery and climbing the fence to play the number three hole over and over again. When we tired of golf, we would take turns jumping into the deep sand bunker marking mid-fairway. That's where we were late in the afternoon on the 23 of August 1963 when my dad's corporate ladder collapsed under the weight of his first major heart attack. Taking care of last minute church council obligations, packing gear for a weekend Boy Scout outing for Bud and me, and trying to repair the filter pump for our pool.

Grandpa Caine had taught my dad a simple rule for success in the corporate world. Regardless of whose name was on the building, act as though it's your own company, your own profit or loss, and your own money. My dad's employer sure appreciated that advice, and its bottom-line showed it. The more my dad managed the factory like he owned it, the more money the company banked. It consumed him, though, and our family never felt like anyone cared too much about my dad's health. People even bothered him at the hospital every day with questions about production problems. "If I'm going to work like that," my dad concluded after three months of recovery, "at least I'm going to reap the bottom-line."

From the first day, though, I was nervous about the location of his new machine shop. This bold endeavor of the American free enterprise system would be my dad's chance to test his father's advice for the good of his own company. This time, the fruit he would bear or not to make a living included his family name on the building.

I was fourteen years old when my dad opened Caine Precision Manufacturing on Troy Avenue in El Monte. This was only about two miles from our home in San Gabriel, but in a neighborhood that commanded less rent and even less respect. We didn't know it at the time, but my brother and I had a rendezvous with one of the great American dreams. Bud didn't daydream as much as I did, though, about becoming a tool and die maker like our dad.

"Is it just me, or does everything around here look gray?" Bud asked our dad one day when old-and-gray Howie Brunner and Ned Fuchs were unloading a steel-gray Bridgeport milling machine in our dad's aircraft-gray building between two charcoal-gray dilapidated warehouses. Of course, Bud had no problem pulling straight onto the drab gray cement floor of the shop when he needed some repairs for his British Racing Green '63 Austin Healey or, after he totaled that car, his Regency Red '48 MG TC. With my dad's help, old-and-gray Howie and Ned could produce a newly machined gray carburetor overnight if Bud asked them nicely enough.

I guess I saw gray-colored things differently. Gray-colored things settled my mind, seemed to relax me. As soon as I read our family name on my dad's new sign, I was anxious to begin my apprenticeship and share this American dream with him. He had designed his business card with a small gold-imprinted micrometer in the upper left corner to represent the pride and workmanship behind every precision-machined component. With Bud's lack of enthusiasm, I would eventually feel a slight shift of attention toward me for a change, a feeling often longed for but seldom felt.

After my high school graduation in 1968, I got my first taste of tool and die making and that new attention. A summer job at my dad's machine shop. I also got my first taste of what was happening in America outside the protective walls of high school.

Although I respected Howie and Ned and Vince, I refrained from sharing too much while visiting with those guys at my dad's shop. I tended to save my feelings for weekends with my buddies Richie and Kevin. Howie could get on my nerves. Was over thirty so he couldn't be trusted. He looked a lot like Christopher Plummer, that captain in *The Sound of Music*. He constantly ribbed me while we ate lunch together, more guarded, of course, when my dad was eating with us.

"So, you gonna end up one of those hippies, Georgie Boy?" he queried after a long drag on his after-lunch Camel. "Hey, did you hear that joke from Governor Reagan? 'We have some hippies in California,' Reagan had deadpanned. 'For those of you who don't know what a hippie is, he's a fellow who dresses like Tarzan, has hair like Jane, and smells like Cheetah.'" With a gentle fist nudge to my right shoulder, "I hear your dad's pretty good at givin' haircuts." My dad listened and took another bite, but Howie gave him a quick glance while he flipped his ashes into a Folgers coffee can. "Seriously, what have you guys got against America, anyway?"

"America ain't the problem, Howie. What we're claiming for all Americans is about as good as anyone could expect. Hard to beat our ideals, anywhere in the world. The problem is reality, Howie, what our country has become. Our system doesn't work equally for everybody. That's the problem."

This was straight from my senior year civics class with Mr. Scott, and Howie could only stare at me. "Well, nobody's claiming we're perfect here, Georgie Boy. Not that I know of, anyway."

"That's right, and that's what Kennedy said when he visited Berlin in 1963. 'Freedom has many difficulties and democracy is not perfect, but we have never had to put a wall up to keep our people in, to prevent them from leaving us.' The point, Howie, is that we're supposedly working toward a more perfect union, but many of us don't feel we're working hard enough."

"I don't ever miss a chance to vote," Howie quickly replied, "and I'm glad to pay my share of taxes. I try to be a good husband and father and neighbor and employee. What more?"

"Nothing, Howie. You're not the problem."

Of course, I knew better. Howie was the problem, and so were Ned and Vince and my dad and myself. Didn't want to threaten our comfortable daily existence. Not bold and daring enough, not outraged enough. All of us are the problem. The times they were a-changin', that's for sure, and maybe Howie didn't understand.

Should I bring ol' Howie up-to-date? Back in 1963, the word *hippie* was introduced in an article about real swingers switching from sniffin' glue or takin' peyote or swallowing a little Electric Kool-Aid, about real swingers switchin' to chewin' morning glory seeds. About a hundred of them will do, but be on alert for the investigation underway. Could there be that many flower lovers interested in morning glory seeds? A year later, *hippie* hit the BIG time. If you were hip, you let your hair grow long, you wore the opposite of whatever, and you couldn't get enough of groovy dancin' and folk music. I could have taken good ol' Howie down to Canter's Deli in the Fairfax District, but hangin' loose down there might have been too much for him.

Fans of jazz were called hipsters. Counterculture types who were hangin' out in the Haight-Ashbury district of San Francisco were called beatniks. Like most Americans, Howie was already behind the times when it came to the latest shift in derogatory labels for America's rebellious youth. He must have missed the coverage last year of that mock funeral in San Francisco. Hippies had grown tired of the term, so they organized "The Death of the Hippie," hoping to put an end to all of the media hype. Thanks to Richie's senior English class report about hippies, I knew about this stuff. As for ol' Howie, I decided to pass on the history lesson. And Howie passed on seeing *Easy Rider* when it came out the next year. Too uptight. John Wayne's *True Grit* would be Howie's movie.

My lunch visits with good ol' Howie provided a calm in the midst of a gathering storm. Richie and Kevin had talked me into enrolling with them at Cal State, East L.A. We were hoping that our fall term Twentieth Century U.S. history class would help us understand why it seemed like America was collapsing all around us.

As soon as I paid closer attention to what was happening around me, I was back with my Grandpa Koehler and Martin Luther. It wasn't the corrupt papacy in Rome this time, and it wasn't the invading Turks. It was 1968. You would think my Grandpa Koehler would have been smugly satisfied by what he witnessed this year. The deaths of heroes, protests and uprisings, the end of dreams, blood in the streets of Chicago and Paris and Saigon.

I remember my Grandpa Koehler predicting our country wouldn't be able to handle all of the chaos and turmoil if we kept turning our backs on God. He said he could feel it in his heart, a growing hostility to the Christian faith and all that he and my grandma trusted. Many people stayed home on Sunday because they thought churches behind the times and irrelevant. To my parents, grandparents, and many hard-working, middle and lower-middle class citizens, our nation was coming apart because religion had lost its influence on society. But maybe my grandpa had a different *Last Day* picture in his mind, different from the one slowly developing over the summer.

Our nation was coming apart, but my Grandpa Koehler's church attendance worries hardly scratched the surface. America's original ideals had finally decided to catch up with reality, and it wasn't going to be pretty. And I thought I was scared in the 1950s.

What Robert Kennedy felt compelled to say that dark day in April goes a long way in explaining 1968 and what was happening to our country. He said what he did because he was burdened with reporting the tragic news of Dr. Martin Luther King Jr.'s assassination earlier that evening in Memphis, Tennessee. Before a crowd of black supporters, in one of Indianapolis's poorest communities, Kennedy chose to set aside his campaign for the presidency and respectfully share his sorrow with those fellow Americans standing in his midst. King's death shocked our country, a country already in shock over riots, civil unrest, and a controversial war. "And let's dedicate ourselves," Kennedy concluded, "to what the Greeks wrote so many years ago: to tame the savageness of man and to make gentle the life of this world." Two months later, this gentle man would be assassinated himself after his victory in the California primary.

We desperately needed to tame the savageness of man and make gentle our life this side of death. But human progress boasted otherwise, that we had achieved a more humane existence, a unique community where fellow citizens could live in harmony and peace.

No, we had not. And the psychic impact of this on America's youth was about to erupt.

As I would learn, the tensions and division across our country that summer reminded many historians of an America one hundred years before. Who we would become seemed to hang in the balance of our presidential election.

I was only twelve years old when some young college students decided life this side of death needed some serious attention. Seemed like most Americans had lost their fervor for improving society. Were there that many Grandpa Koehler's around? "What reason is there to try and reform a society that is doomed to collapse sooner than later?" But enough college activists took the teachings of Jesus, Gandhi, and M.L.K. Jr. seriously – "to tame the savageness of man and to make gentle the life of this world." These Students for a Democratic Society based their manifesto for social change on the premise that change could take place within the system. So the early youth rebellion almost seemed mainstream.

Their initial confidence that government could eliminate poverty and racism was partly justified by President Johnson's efforts following Kennedy's assassination, vowing to carry on in the tradition of JFK. After his landslide election in 1964, LBJ had labeled his reform proposals the Great Society. His work with the fabulous eighty-ninth Congress set a new standard for government's role in tackling our social problems. This new nanny state was not a big hit with most conservatives who were worried about how we would pay for all of the federal programs. LBJ's reforms were popular, though, and our booming economy assured us that funding would not be a problem.

But whatever happened in the Gulf of Tonkin, within a year after Kennedy's assassination, LBJ faced the reality of a future commitment in Southeast Asia that would eventually shut down his Great Society and his presidency. Up until that moment, LBJ was prepared to follow JFK's policy that the South Vietnamese were responsible for defending themselves. By June of the following year, though, American troops were fighting alongside those South Vietnamese.

It didn't take long for opposition to organize against this new war policy. LBJ's own party included many who opposed the war, and many black leaders feared that the costs of war would jeopardize the Great Society proposals. Once Johnson requested a tax increase to help fund the war, any accolades for his domestic reforms were lost in the anti-war chants now blaming him for the mess.

"One, two, three, four, we don't want your lousy war."

"One, two, three, four, what are we fighting for? Five, six, seven, eight, we don't give a damn, we ain't going to Vietnam."

And as our war efforts escalated, "Hey, hey, LBJ, how many babies did you kill today?"

Good thing, though, we were spending so much on our military. We would eventually need it back home to help restore order after all the rioting about why we spent so much on our military!

Nothing like a child's innocence shattered by simply growing up. On two fronts, my faith in God and my faith in America. But the SDS Port Huron Statement was like my naive Sunday school faith. Not adequate for the task at hand. Still trusting in a government of, by, and for the people. But reality had become too troubling to ignore, so reforming society looked for fresh energy and a more radical approach.

Not all of America's youth were hanging onto the innocent hope of SDS. Stoned on drugs, many turned away from any responsibility for those circumstances too troubling to ignore. Some, like Bob Dylan, felt like a rolling stone, no longer at home with the folk movement, having lost hope in the power of that movement to change things. He had watched countless young people walk away from their families and their childhood with a fragile hope they could create a new society. It seemed to Dylan, though, such hope was too fragile after all. And however he had connected with this generation, he found himself more and more disconnected, unable to put his finger on the pulse of any new direction. Sometimes our most deeply held beliefs can't lead us to the place we want to be, can't sustain us in the battles of our day-to-day existence.

That same year, 1965, Julie Andrews was singing, "These Are a Few of My Favorite Things."

Those who were quick to realize their Sunday school faith and Port Huron Statement would not carry the day found their hope elsewhere. The 1960s had already provided enough evidence. Bringing about peaceful social reform wasn't going to happen. Most were figuring out the only answer was revolution.

In January of 1967, this new direction kicked off with the world's first *Human Be-In*, the latest version of the human being experiment. This love feast, this psychedelic picnic, took place at Golden Gate Park in San Francisco. An energized hippie movement challenged those traditional values of SDS. Once you have opened your mind to a cosmic consciousness, religious and social institutions lose much of their meaning and significance. A counterculture was coming to life.

Timothy Leary was there, dressed in white and wearing flowers in his hair. "Turn on, Tune In, Drop Out," said Leary, reciting his famous commercial for the synthetic hallucinogen LSD. Easy to take, easy to hide, difficult to detect, and compared to other drugs, cheap. Follow me, not Jesus, he preached. Quicksilver Messenger Service, Jefferson Airplane, and the Grateful Dead provided acid rock music for the occasion.

Sure helped if you were stoned. Did Indian peyote, or Huxley's mescaline, or Leary's shrooms, or Kesey's LSD provide a little courage for these Merry Pranksters? Hallucinogenic drugs did their best to break down most of the barriers holding back a psychedelic revolution aimed at altering the mind of America. Some claimed smoking pot and taking LSD were a means to an end, not the end itself. Looking for some meaning in life. Looking for something their Sunday school faith had not provided. Looking for something to fill the emptiness, the void in their soul. Whatever they were looking for, maybe drugs would help them find it.

And then, after this *Human Be-In*, the Summer of Love.

Had a hard time figuring out that new explanation of those gentle people going to San Francisco with flowers in their hair. Much of that SDS reform agenda can claim some roots in Western ideals we adopted as a nation two centuries ago. And yet, many of those gentle people you would meet in San Francisco, those people who were no longer inclined to settle for peaceful change, had turned to gurus and mentors steeped in Hinduism and Buddhism. But such counsel advised acceptance of reality, acknowledged that suffering and injustice were conditions of life we can't change, that we needed to endure. That sounds like my Grandpa Koehler and Luther. And that blows my mind!

Don't think for a moment that P. F. Sloan's song was out of touch. Here's what Representative Allard Lowenstein had to say while preparing for his "Dump Johnson" movement. "Let's make 1968 the year when students help change a society almost everyone agrees is headed for destruction."

America's youth had left behind the idealism of that original Port Huron Statement of six years ago. Now we rallied around Mark Rudd's letter to the president of Columbia University. No more safe and compliant. Our "society is sick and you and your capitalism are the sickness," he wrote. "We are ready for a war of liberation."

In August, the Democratic Convention met in Chicago for what can only be called another example of our savageness. I shouldn't have expected anything different. Doesn't matter too much about the guilt or innocence of Rubin and Hoffman and the rest of the Chicago Eight. So passionately against the war and President Johnson, thousands of hippies, yippies, and radicals chose to exercise their right to protest and break with the past. Our traditional political system no longer worked to achieve change.

Mayor Daley had already had enough of the counterculture long before this event. So when police confronted protestors throwing rocks and bottles, Daley unleashed his dogs. He had the National Guard standing by, ready to mobilize and, if necessary, ordered them "Shoot to kill."

Thanks to television, Americans witnessed two different events those hot and humid summer nights. Some watched Daley's violent response, his Chicago police bludgeoning, gassing, and arresting anti-war young people. It would be reported as a police riot, denounced as "gestapo tactics." Others watched Boss Daley's courageous response to a ruthless youth mob trying to disrupt America's political process. It would be applauded and respected. Same television camera for both. Over 1,500 people, both civilians and police, were injured.

Aside from Daley's affiliation with the Democratic Party, many who cheered for his law-and-order response would be "the great, quiet forgotten majority" ready to elect Richard Nixon in November. Couldn't wait for a return to traditional values and patriotism. Supporters like evangelist Billy Graham found a welcome ally in the fight to preserve our nation's morals. But when he learned about Nixon's darker side, he had to reevaluate his earlier enthusiasm.

Maybe Woodstock the following year was my generation trying to express our disillusionment about an America that was most likely hurtling toward a dead-end. Was the special delivery of emergency supplies of Thorazine needed for more than treating the epidemic of bad trips? Did America need such help because of inferior acid spiked with speed or because life in America had become such a bad trip? Had it come to this? "Drop out and do your own thing." Popular psychology had guided America's self-exploration, and we had become OK with "I'm Okay, You're Okay." Personally, I was feeling the opposite. "I'm not Okay, and neither are you!"

The Cold War threat of a nuclear winter reminded us every day of our common peril, thinking about death on such a scale. And for the first time, not only thinking about such death but supporting our military each day to prepare for it. While I'm hiding from my eve of destruction fears, our country is creating a permanent war economy, a military-industrial complex that could solve our economic problems by continuous spending to prepare for that eve of destruction. What the hell!

How many times could my generation be reminded of our own mortality before we questioned the promise of America? Our existence was defined by this democratic experiment slowly going bust. How many of the 58,194 Vietnam War dead had we watched die on live TV broadcasts? How do you set aside so much death when you are surrounded by it twenty-four seven? So our question that fall in our course at Cal State, "How will we respond to the changes America is facing?" The more I learned about America's real story, the more unsettled I became about my place in it. This was not the story of America I had learned about in the eighth grade. Kind of like realizing how sugarcoated your Sunday school faith was when compared with your doubt and questions growing up.

My dad's aerospace contacts had served him well. Old-balding-and-gray Howie and Ned were both proud of their small part in producing parts for this endeavor. Old-gray-shirt-and-pants-combo himself, Vince Brzezinski, however, had other things on his mind.

Maybe it was their shared entrepreneurial camaraderie, don't know for sure, but my dad agreed to stake Vince a small corner of the machine shop he could call his own. Such a financial arrangement allowed Vince to operate his own little piece of the American dream. Never satisfied with his cut or the amount of work my dad had contracted for him, Vince refused to accept payment after an argument about how he would have to absorb some of the higher costs of government-required material. The day after Armstrong and Aldrin landed on the moon in July of 1969, Vince sued my dad with a petition that left Caine Precision Mfg. with no other choice. Howie and I weren't talking with each other too much my second summer at the shop.

A week before I returned to school for my sophomore year, Caine Precision filed for Chapter Thirteen bankruptcy, forcing Vince to accept a repayment plan like all of my dad's other creditors. So now we could add to my grandfather's dictum about hard work and loyalty, "Sometimes the bottom line is zero." Paul Lynde used to answer his sit-com wife's question "How goes the rat-race?" with that devilish and annoying smirk, "The rats are winning!" Funny, but not when the rats are winning at your dad's expense.

So how does that work? My dad is as honest a businessman as they come, but still gets screwed. He had taught my brother and me that our country guaranteed the freedom to fail and the corresponding freedom to try again. But how does life get so sideways for people of faith like my parents? Struck down with heart attacks. What's the connection between such unfairness and my dad's high blood pressure? An equal counterpart, but an individual who does not live by my dad's Christian faith, accepts challenges and setbacks of life as normal. No one speaks of unfairness. My dad, on the other hand, has prayed each night for God's goodness, has prayed each night to a loving Heavenly Father who has counted all the hairs on his head. "Do not be afraid," Jesus said.

After a year and a half of college and enough dope to dull my unsettledness, I was ready to try my dad's trade full-time. My buddies Kevin and Richie envied my real job. I wore my new gray shirt with pride, even when I met them for Genaro's pizza on Friday night.

For my brother's wedding then, my dad had to borrow enough money from his in-laws for the trip north to Bend. I was my brother's best man. I remember golfing on his wedding day. We had made a promise to stand by each other in the darkness of night. Don't know what became of that. Maybe we were still too drunk from the night before to even realize what we were promising.

Three weeks after my brother's wedding in Bend, we watched President Nixon's announcement on television. The United States would invade Cambodia. To support this expansion of the Vietnam War effort, our country would need to draft 150,000 more soldiers. Massive protests erupted on college campuses around the country, and at Kent State University in Ohio, angry protestors set fire to the ROTC building. The governor called out 900 National Guardsmen to secure the campus. Instead of a firefight in some Southeast Asian rice field, twenty-eight soldiers opened fire on a crowd of unarmed college demonstrators. Body count: four students killed, nine wounded. The President's Commission on Campus Unrest finally acknowledged the action of the guardsmen had been "unnecessary, unwarranted, and inexcusable." But charges were eventually dismissed for lack of evidence. What the hell? Eleven days later, at Jackson State College in Mississippi, police killed two students who were protesting the war and the Kent State killings.

And my Grandpa Koehler was worried about declining church attendance.

We talked Richie out of heading up to Berkeley for the latest anti-war demonstration. Kevin's brother Arlen, too scared to face the draft, decided to give up who he was and leave for Canada. Couldn't even say goodbye to his parents.

Our dad was fifty-three years old, worn out and uncertain about what lay ahead. Faithful and true to my mother for thirty years, loving and giving to his four children, loyal and more to every employer (including himself), Hank Caine now found himself empty and spent. His Dr. Putler recommended an extra martini each night if it would help. He had little left to offer my two sisters in their hopeless struggles to survive marriages headed in the opposite direction of his marriage to my mother. She had begun working full-time at the local Hallmark Gift Shop to help make ends meet. My dad picked up the pieces of his business and relocated in an Orange County industrial park, not far from where his Uncle Ed had relocated his shop twenty years earlier.

I usually drove with my dad every day, at least an hour and a half with traffic. It was the two of us now, and most days, only me at the shop while my dad delivered parts and pursued new contracts. His bankruptcy felt like another stumbling block in my life because it proved the transitory nature of what I had first thought was so reliable. If not the stability of my dad's machine shop, the way he worked, his integrity, his grit, his pride, then what? I felt like one of those dominoes waiting down the line in a toppling arrangement over which I had no control or say. How many more dominoes to go before I fall?

Seems like I was forever visiting with my Grandpa Koehler and Martin Luther. "For as long as we live in this vale of sorrows we will have little peace and rest. Today we are plagued with one, tomorrow with another misfortune. Furthermore, the world is our bitter enemy and persecutes us cruelly. Such misery we cannot shed as long as this life lasts." How much does life this side of death have to suck before you figure that out?

CHAPTER 9

Henry
9 April 1998
Maundy Thursday

Never one to fiddle with her daily routines, Denise was off to bed by 9:00 PM. Always off to bed by 9:00 PM. I lay awake with photographs, both real and imagined, asking way more of my heart than I was prepared for this evening. I stared at that photograph Max had taken as we pulled away after our wedding, fixated on my brother George and his thumbs up. What was my brother thinking about at that moment? Was he thinking about our ninth-green promise to stand by each other?

I let my memory indulge in some of our yesteryears together as brothers. Like two interwoven strands of a rope, our lives often composed a single story.

George and I had shared adventures together. Johnny Weissmuller, a.k.a. Tarzan, had nothing on us in the jungle. We used to climb out of our bedroom window on Santa Ynez Lane to balance ourselves on a low-hanging branch of the expansive Avocado tree between our house and our backyard swimming pool. We could make it all the way to the pool without touching the ground, springing up and down on the last branch until it catapulted us over the cement walkway into the pool.

We had done stupid things together. That Avocado tree stunt wasn't our only jungle achievement. In our front yard stood a forty-foot Himalayan pine that we climbed to the top of and then straddled each branch as we slid backward onto each lower branch. We were tough enough to endure the whip in the face of each branch as we cleared away from it on our plunge to the ground – a slight annoyance that made us forget the severe pain in our crotch as we slid down.

We had fought each other. In an unfortunate wrestling match one summer day in July, George recovered from my smothering headlock a bit frustrated, pulled me in close enough to surprise me with his knee into my groin. I recovered enough to take a full haymaker swing at the side of his face, planting a severe bruise between his eye and ear. I would answer for that one, and of course, George's knee to my balls got lost in the reporting.

We shared a bedroom when we lived on Meridian Ave. in Alhambra. Our dad had built a first-rate model train layout for the both of us that could be lowered down from its hinged-vertical storage position against the wall to lie flat across our two beds. When I was seven, Santa Claus supplied the first Lionel O-gauge equipment for our ping-pong tabletop layout. I powered our new back-to-back red and silver Santa Fe diesel locomotives, so heavy and authentic-looking, around the oval until my brother finally fell asleep that Christmas Eve. I couldn't take my eyes off of them. George was all of five years old that year, and this set of locomotives was his big gift too. But he wasn't sure what to make of them; I at least had a clue. By the next Christmas, I was carefully off-loading barrels of milk from our new white refrigerated milk car by remotely operating a tiny laborer. George insisted on running the Santa Fe locomotives with all of our boxcars at full throttle around the oval until part of the train derailed and flew off the track. And I insisted on beating him up every time he did that. Merry Christmas!

We had blamed each other for our own mistakes. We both figured we knew what we were doing when it came to launching rockets; our dad, after all, was helping to build rockets for NASA. We prepared a random mixture of chemicals from our chemistry set – we figured the volatility increased the more stuff we mixed – and then placed a balsawood rocket over the test tube and struck a match. But the burning candle under our rocket paid no attention to our dramatic countdown.

"Why don't you raise the candle until the flame is touching the test tube?" George suggested.

That did it, all right! *KBOOM!* Both of our faces were covered with the shattered glass of the test tube; we had been watching the whole thing up close. I opened my eyes to see little red dots all over George's face; he apparently opened his eyes to see the same on my face. "What are you two boys up to out there?" my mother asked from the back porch. "Nothin', Mom!" we answered as we jumped into the swimming pool. Just a little explosion.

Later that evening with our Dad: "So which of you two boys is responsible for that foolish stunt?"

"The whole thing was Bud's idea."

"Yeah, but George came up with the great idea to put the candle right under the test tube."

We had argued with each other. George thought it was cool to roll up his short-sleeves; I thought it looked ridiculous.

"What does it matter to you, Bud?"

"It looks stupid, George, that's all."

"Why does it look stupid?"

"Because your sleeves are already short. What's the point?"

"You're just jealous."

"Now why would I be jealous of your short sleeves?"

"You don't do it because your arms are too skinny. You don't have any muscles in your arms. If you had any muscles in your arms, you would roll up your sleeves too."

"Oh, so you like to show off your arm muscles. Is that it?"

We had protected each other. I walked out front one Sunday afternoon to find George on the wrong end of a neighborhood kid scuffle that had spiraled out of control – an eighth-grade bully named Nathan Driscoll was throwing some punches to George's head. I wasn't any bigger than Nate, but I was a high school sophomore, and that made all the difference in the world. Our dad had to intervene as I altered Nat's face. No one does that to my kid brother, even if he does roll up his short sleeves.

We had laughed together. Our Dad was grooming us to join the diehard L.A. Dodger fan club, but we could never get past the names of shortstop Pee Wee Reese (#1) and center fielder Duke Snider (#4) without cracking up. A duke in our household was a turd, and Pee Wee was, well, it was peewee. Our Dad took us to a game the first year the Brooklyn Dodgers moved out West to become the Los Angeles Dodgers; this was at the Memorial Coliseum, four years before the Dodgers would play in their new ballpark at Chavez Ravine. All we could do was laugh our heads off every time Pee Wee and Duke were announced. It was embarrassing. Oddly enough, the nickname

"Pee Wee" had nothing to do with Harold Henry Reese's height; he was a champion marbles player when he was a kid (a "pee wee" is a small marble).

We had invented things together, like skateboarding with a two-by-four board about two feet long and wheels from our sister Cathy's skates; we assumed she didn't want them anymore since she hadn't used them in weeks.

We had supported each other in times of trial. Hoping to find some authentic and unique resources for my junior-year English report about Hitler's Germany, I decided to visit a Nazi Literature Center in Pasadena. All kinds of Nazi paraphernalia, and under surveillance by our government. George spotted the black sedan pulling into our driveway the next week when some official-looking men showed up to question our dad about his purchases at the Nazi Center. I had signed a register there so I could receive future resources. Henry B. Caine Jr., but the junior didn't matter. I wasn't home at the time, but George was clever enough to explain to our dad that my teacher had recommended I dig as deep as I could. That, of course, opened up a whole new can of worms. But at least he had tried.

We had covered for each other. I was born with an Edgar Allen Poe fear of water. Most of my kid nightmares were about swimming lessons and how I would drown. My parents understood this; my dad had the same fear when he was a kid. Our imminent move to our new home with the swimming pool, though, forced my mother to finally take action. "Buddy, you and your brother are taking swimming lessons at the YMCA every Saturday."

Our first lesson was simple: get used to submerging your head under water. Hold your breath, close your eyes, and slowly let the water cover the top of your head. Wouldn't do it. Couldn't do it. I sat on the side of the pool and asked everyone to leave me alone. My sister Cathy picked us up then every Saturday morning, but not before I had jumped in the shower to come out soaking wet. "So how were swim lessons today?" George didn't hesitate. "Great! We are having a blast."

Great, that is, until my birthday.

My mother invited everyone to the party where Bud and George would be showing off how much they had learned the past month at the YMCA. My Aunt Gertie and Uncle Wally had no idea how their gift had saved me from an embarrassing confession, how they had opened an exciting new world to me. A mask and fins. "Try them out, Buddy. They're supposed to help you go even faster." In one of those rare life-changing moments, I figured I wouldn't be drowning that day with everyone standing around the pool. I couldn't believe it when I lowered my head under water. I could see the whole pool so clearly, an underwater playground. Like a dolphin, my fins propelled me across the length of the pool, then under the water, then back across the surface, then under again, to cheers and whistles and applause. My brother was smiling at the other end when I removed my mask. I smiled back and then smiled at Aunt Gertie.

We competed with each other. So inspired by the Olympic diving events, we created Saturday diving contests that sometimes lasted for seven or eight hours. Every imaginable dive was attempted, but our judging system always left us tied at the end of the day. Wonder why? We were each other's only judge – another stupid thing – and we copied each other for every number we posted. I would give George an 8.5 for a half-twist, and he would give me the same for my dive; he would give me a 9.5 for my swan dive, and I would give him the same. We never bothered to break the tie, though. Why bother? We were brothers.

We have shared a love for dogs. No doubt in our minds, we were those two brothers Travis and Arliss in the story about Ol' Yeller. It didn't matter what name our dad gave our family dog; our dog was always Ol' Yeller to George and me. Our best Ol' Yeller (our family called him Sarge) was a big golden retriever that got away from us one summer evening and knocked one of my mother's Bible Study friends into our pool. We had to explain to Ol' Yeller why he was in trouble while we were laughing so hard. Mrs. Hinkle was not laughing when our dad pulled her out of the pool.

We had kept secrets from one another. George was a proud fisherman when he caught some six-inch trout outside Redmond, Oregon, on our summer vacation in 1957. My dad didn't have the heart to tell him his fish would not provide dinner for all of us. My brother was so disappointed, convinced his catch was worthless; so my dad and Uncle Bob figured out a way to make the best of it. I listened on the other side of the hallway door as they planned the evening switch. "We'll pull these good-sized trout out of the freezer, Hank, and tell George this was his catch. He'll never know the difference." I turned to see my brother sitting on the back porch, tossing pebbles out onto the driveway. I thought about telling him the truth, but when I saw that surprise grin on his face the next morning, I was glad I could be part of the cover-up.

We shared our fantasies with each other. I convinced George the two of us would have a better chance of test-driving a Silver Birch Aston Martin DB5 than if I tried such a stunt by myself. Our request, though, at Peter Satori's Rolls-Royce dealership in Pasadena was another matter. At least the British salesman didn't laugh in front of us. I was nineteen, George was seventeen, and I wore an ascot with my sport coat. "Honestly, gentlemen, even with your father's commitment you have told me about, the best I can offer you is a ride." Don't know how he managed, but George contorted himself enough to squeeze in behind me. We took a quick run up around the Rose Bowl and Brookside Golf Course, never did get out of third gear. A short ride, but satisfied our James Bond fancy.

And we have loved one another, as only brothers can.

A year before our wedding, George and I had outfitted ourselves for a major expedition into the High Sierra wilderness north of Mt. Whitney – a half-serious search for the legendary BIGFOOT. I had no actual data confirming any sightings in that area; like Tom Sawyer helping Jim to escape in *The Adventures of Huckleberry Finn*, I just wanted to add a little adventure to our otherwise everyday backpacking trek. I didn't need to clarify this, however, as my kid brother fully believed our search was genuine. His imagination was way more fertile than mine – leading to future fascinations with space travel, gun designs, missile systems, and exotic weapons to fight the good fight against an alien invasion. He could never be sure he was prepared enough for such an attack.

We both carried fifty-pound bows and hunting arrows purchased at the local Army-Navy Surplus Store in Alhambra. Neither one of us had ever hunted before. I brought our dad's .22 caliber Ruger revolver for backup, and George packed a thirteen-inch Bowie knife. We had a chessboard with plastic pieces and a deck of playing cards to pass the time, and we had enough snacks to last out an all-night dorm party. Appropriately, we hiked in from the Devil's Postpile National Monument and pitched our tent high above a small, tree-lined lake. By the time we had talked along the trail and devised our strategy while we waited for our slow-cooking Boy Scout foil dinners, we were convinced we might cross paths with BIGFOOT. Once the daylight forest had turned to night, we both took our search more seriously. We took turns keeping watch that night. The forest at night can be the most peaceful setting imaginable; it can also produce sounds you would prefer not to hear. Dark nights are funny that way; the grandeur of the Heavens is most breathtaking when it's dark and scary.

A sleepless night in the forest for both of us – way too dark, way too stressful.

The next day we were off to Twin Lakes west of Bridgeport off Highway 395 for some car camping and fishing. I provided the Budweiser and the Marlboros. Relaxing in the bow of our rented fishing boat, I remember my brother both disappointed and relieved. But he had that satisfied smile on his face. I was spending the weekend with him, and not with my girlfriend Denise. We talked about all kinds of stuff that day out on the lake. He had finished his first year at Cal State.

I asked him about girlfriends.

Nothing.

I had been away at college, so I had missed a lot of opportunities to connect with him during the school year. I was playing big brother catch-up, and that's never too effective. We talked about the "shadow" thing – guilt on my part, frustration on his. Two years younger, George constantly lived in my shadow: family, school, church, Scouts, the neighborhood.

That "shadow stuff" could have worked itself out under normal conditions, but George wasn't living under normal conditions.

We couldn't know at the time what awaited George and us as a family. It's not easy to diagnose the first stages of schizophrenia. Some first signs that might alert a family – so-and-so's not a good friend anymore, a poor grade doesn't seem to matter, crazy sleep habits, irritated about the littlest thing – are behaviors common to many teens. And George's alcohol and substance dependence can produce symptoms similar to those of schizophrenia.

George and I returned to our dad's gray machine shop on Troy Ave. This was not a good summer for Caine Precision Manufacturing. And I had a lot of things to figure out for myself in those days. A lot of questions to answer – questions like, "How serious should I take that promise Margaret Anita (a.k.a. Hannah) had made to God when I was six years old?" Seems like we all had plenty to think about.

Who would have thought, but after an early investment in a new company called Apple, Jerry Rubin of the Chicago Eight, Mr. "I don't own a suit or tie" yippie, settled down in Los Angeles and became a successful yuppie multimillionaire. Abbie Hoffman, one of those rare and powerful voices for social change, took the frustration of failed reform personally. When he finally emerged from hiding in 1980, his counterculture was dead. Must have felt like a full circle return to the complacency and indifference he had denounced in the first place. Grew despondent, but continued to write and speak about his convictions. His encouragement to young people: "You have what's vitally needed to make social change. You're impatient; you want it to happen now."

On a Wednesday in early April of 1989, Hoffman took his life, a massive overdose of phenobarbital tablets. His brother had only this to say: "He was fifty-two years old, and I think he gave up."

CHAPTER 10

Karl

The last place my grandfather Albert Benson figured he'd be sitting on a warm spring evening was the Good Friday Service at Ebenezer Lutheran Church. Last place, that is, until his wandering eyes caught a glimpse of his proper former confirmation classmate who had become the stunning young woman Alma Lundstrom. The congregation was singing an old Swedish melody, *"May we all thy loved ones be, All one holy family, Loving for the love of thee: hear us, holy Jesus,"* when he concluded on the spot that he was in love with Alma Lundstrom. Three months later, he turned that Good Friday conclusion into a question. Alma said yes.

After his parents, John and Brita Benson, had emigrated from Sweden when he was five years old, Albert wasted no time teaching himself everything he could about how mechanical things worked on his family's farm in Minnesota. He was eleven years old when his family moved to Central Oregon in 1900, and by the time he celebrated his twentieth birthday, he was already earning a good wage as an apprentice machinist at the Bend Company Sawmill. Worked there until the mill burned down in 1915.

The Rev. John Ekdahl performed my grandparents' wedding in 1912, and by 1921, Albert's millwright job at the Shevlin-Hixon Lumber Company was responsible for feeding five more mouths: Emmett, Hubert, Adeline, Marion, and my dad, Gordon. No problem though, as timber times were good. His mill was located on the west bank of the Deschutes, and the mill of the Brooks-Scanlon Lumber Company out of Minnesota was located on the east bank. Between them, the two mills could cut a million board feet of lumber each day. At their peak of production, two of the largest pine sawmills in the world, running around the clock. His buddies R. O. Kittelson and K. T. Hansen worked the millpond shared by the two mills, pond monkeys managing the floating logs. The timber industry sustaining Bend's growth was itself sustained for decades by Deschutes National Forest western yellow pines (called ponderosa pines after the 1930s).

By the end of the 1920s, though, lumber production was slowing down. These sawmills produced dimension lumber used for building, but people out of work weren't building new houses. The mills helped their workers by staggering the schedules for logging and manufacturing, so everyone received some work during the bleakest months. Many of the NIRA programs under President Roosevelt were unpopular with workers and mill owners, but regulation of lumber industry wages and prices from 1935 to 1937 helped stabilize the industry. By the end of the decade, Bend mills were increasing production, and new mills had opened in Gilchrist, Prineville, Redmond, and Sisters. Hard to compete with Oregon at that time for leading producer of lumber products. This sure looked promising for my dad after his graduation from Bend High School in 1940.

Until that date which will live in infamy. My dad and his buddies could hardly wait to enlist in the Marines and avenge the Japanese attack on Pearl Harbor. But when he was turned away because of color blindness and flat feet, he tried to commiserate with his best friend, good ol' Cecil Johnson. He figured good ol' Cecil had suffered the same fate because he had been sick almost every day in high school. But good ol' Cecil wasn't anywhere to be found, because good ol' Cecil had been classified 1-A and was on his way to the Solomon Islands.

Eating a bundle of carrots every day changed nothing for my dad. By August of 1942, though, he had been drafted by the Army and was serving in the Philippines as a combat medic in the 503rd Paratroop Regiment. He managed to spend considerable time in the brig for scuffling with fellow soldiers as well as considerable time in the field trying to save their lives. Ended up a corporal at his discharge, lucky not any lower.

A nightmarish three years later – and like most nightmares, impossible to make sense of once you wake up – my dad returned home to a job at a new sawmill in Prineville. Older and wiser, and tested some by a brief war-inspired marriage that ended when his new bride got confused and took a train to Portland, Maine, instead of Portland, Oregon, he began daydreaming about his own sawmill some day.

He was still daydreaming in 1947 when he married my mother, Roberta Rouene Sheldon, at the Court House in Coeur d'Alene, Idaho. He didn't exactly break the bank with his one-night honeymoon arrangements at the Lambert Hotel, but he knew how to make dreams come true, and if he could make this one come true, then he could make his other one come true too. And that swayed my mother's heart enough.

By the end of 1948, my dad had waited long enough for his dream to come true. Right after I was born on the sixth of February in 1949, he had nervously counted out seven hundred dollars as payment in full for Fred Rogers's old sawmill equipment. With one additional dollar, he secured a lease agreement for the land west of Prineville. To borrow this amount of money from the bank, he had to mortgage his 1941 Buick. Wisely, he borrowed seven hundred and fifty dollars so he would have fifty dollars left to buy his first load of logs.

His generous father-in-law Sam Sheldon had offered to loan him a thousand dollars to invest in this new venture, but my dad had some mixed feelings about the whole project and wanted to succeed or fail strictly on his own terms. As things turned out three days later, that was a good idea.

After the sawmill motor operating the head rig exploded in a coughing cloud of black smoke and spitting sparks, my dad turned to his brother Marion the mechanic, who had been nursing back to life a 1946 Ford flathead V-8. He offered to buy the repaired engine for twenty-five dollars down and five dollars a month for one year. "It'll never work, Gord," his brother and Pa advised. "You'll at least need a governor on that thing for what you're trying to do." But by mounting the one-hundred-horsepower engine directly to the rust-pitted forty-eight-inch head saw with a makeshift throttle chain, Benson Lumber was officially up and running.

Until the next day.

Old man Rogers had never worked at the pace my dad was setting, so no one had given much thought to a conveyor belt for removing the sawdust. But stopping production every twenty minutes to remove the sawdust pile with the wheelbarrow he had borrowed from his mother-in-law was hardly my dad's idea of efficiency. Maybe trying to turn Rogers's mill into Gordon Benson's dream was a long shot not worth the gamble.

His two older brothers, Emmett and Hubert, who were logging northeast of town, persuaded my dad to accept a lease offer for some of Harold Ofstey's property. By the end of the week, with the help of his first millwright, Everett Withrow, he had moved the head rig to this new location. With a borrowed Case tractor he dug out a trench, installed a sawdust conveyor belt, and placed under the end of the belt a large container box his Pa had built during the week. At the end of the working day, the sawdust box was raised and emptied by a cherry picker mounted on the front end of a 1943 International Harvester Army truck.

To celebrate both anniversaries, his first two years as husband of Roberta Rouene and his first two years as owner of Benson Lumber, he agreed to a second honeymoon trip. Drove all the way to New Orleans, checked out Camp Barkeley outside of Abilene, Texas (nothing left of the old barracks), and then hurried home to get back to work at his mill.

Not by choice but by destiny, Gordon Benson's dream was tied to the reckless disregard by those two big Deschutes River lumber mills built five years before he was born. Both had approved heavy cutting of the region's ponderosa pine forests to feed their frenzied mill production. After more than 20 years of nonstop logging and depletion of forest resources, both companies had been warned in the late 1930s of pending economic disaster if sustainable forestry was not practiced. They ignored these warnings and continued producing at full capacity.

Their dwindling timber supplies sounded a reality check in 1950. Shevlin-Hixon was swallowed up by Brooks-Scanlon and closed four months later. The sale included the firm's timber, production facilities, and logging equipment. In the long run, clear-cutting your own landholdings with no regard for replanting will eventually leave a mill at the mercy of the federal government for subsidized timber sales off public lands.

Any lessons learned by the big mill? Apparently not. Even as the privately held stands were diminishing, logging of the remaining old-growth ponderosa pine continued with no regard for tomorrow. And production at the sprawling Brooks-Scanlon complex along the Deschutes River continued with no regard for tomorrow. Unable to ignore the obvious, company loggers began cutting the commercially less valuable lodgepole pine in an attempt to extend the mill's log supplies. But tomorrow was coming.

Even though the postwar building boom created a demand for lumber during the early 1950s, many of the smaller sawmills with high expectations following the war were struggling to stay in business. Established family sawmill owners like Sam Johnson didn't have to worry as much about this. Johnson had seen the writing on the wall and had successfully negotiated timber sale contracts with the United States Forest Service. But many of the smaller family-owned outfits weren't trusted after they reneged on their payment for logs delivered but never sawed into lumber, so Benson Lumber was forced sometimes to pay for logs before the truck was even unloaded.

Undaunted by the discouraging fate suffered by some of his competitors, my dad talked his good friend and off-bearer Buel Smelcer into picking up the pace enough to outrun the difficult times. The two of them drove each other to record-setting production numbers every day, beginning at 4:00 AM in the summer, working straight through for eight hours, and then driving over to Johnson's mill in Redmond to work the 2:15 PM swing shift off-bearing lumber. Marion's rebuilt V-8 kept up with the two, used only fifty-five gallons of gas each week, and shut down early only when they ran out of logs to saw. Turning raw timber like ponderosa pine into marketable lumber – turning thirty-five dollars a thousand board feet of logs into sixty dollars a thousand board feet of pine cants – is a production goal easy to get excited about. And excited they got, producing on one remarkable day eighty-five hundred board feet.

My dad broke three peavey handles that day (a tool invented by Joseph Peavey to provide a little leverage for turning the log over on the carriage), stubbornly determined that either the log was going to turn for the next cut or the handle would break. Poor Buel needed help walking to his car that afternoon, his eyes nearly blinded by the swirling sawdust.

But such small-scale production rallies did not alter the facts. My dad remained a victim of the distrust plaguing so many of the local sawmills like his. Not easy to compete with the larger operations that were able to pay for logs when delivered. Ever the daydreamer, though, he offered Tom Lee a thousand dollars one day for an eight-acre section of land on the corner of Juniper Gin Road and Highway Twenty east of Bend. No more gypo logging for Gordon Benson. It was time to prove his mettle. The owner of the land hesitated at first, but a week later called to accept the offer.

My dad stood near the highway, gazing out over a field of sagebrush, bitterbrush, and one-thousand-year-old juniper trees, wondering what would become of his endeavor, his latest dream come true. And what would become of his family, his three children, now that my mom was suffering and sick with cancer. If only he could trade a new dream now for one already come true.

With a borrowed tractor from his brother Emmett, my dad kept himself busy digging up stumps whenever he was out of saw logs. He had to clear a path for the main P.U.D. line from town so he could hook up his seventy-five-horsepower electric motor, which was checked more often than usual because the bill always seemed so low. When he was out of stumps to clear away, he was off tracking log supply locations all over the county. Couldn't always keep busy enough, though, to forget his fear and distress. He was trying to build one dream while losing another. When my mom died a week before their tenth anniversary, my dad took a total of one week off to grieve, and then it was back to the mill. I suppose, though, he had been grieving for a long time leading up to her death. More than my mom died that Wednesday in 1957, but I don't think my dad bothered to reflect much about that. He didn't bother to reflect about much of anything after that.

Whenever I listened to conversations my dad had with family or friends, I was forever hopeful I might hear him interject something about my mom. Always hoping he might share some fond recollection of a moment from their past together. Didn't even have to share directly with my two sisters and me. We would have been satisfied with overhearing some affectionate memory he was thinking about.

Maybe some wise advice my mom had shared with him. "Having a drink with the boys on a Friday afternoon at the mill to toast a good week of production is one thing. Arriving here at home on Friday evening to eat dinner with your children and me is another thing. We're not the boys at the mill."

Maybe some laughter they shared together, like the time my mom got my dad's signals mixed up when he was guiding her back to unload our boat at the ramp. He had jumped up on the trailer fender while clenching his fist, was climbing into our boat while my mom kept backing up. "Well, I assumed you were climbing up into the boat to get out of the water. Didn't make much sense to me why you would keep standing in the water with an empty boat pulling up next to you." So she kept backing up until my dad shouted. At which point she jammed on her breaks, and my dad went flying backward, fortunately onto a stack of cushions against the outboard motor. He took a few seconds to compose himself in front of the crowd before he joined in the laughter with my mom. I would have loved to eavesdrop on their private conversation that night.

Maybe some decision they reached together after our family camping trip turned into a disaster. Like the time my mom talked our dad into a camping trip over Memorial Day weekend up at Paulina Lake that ended up with snow all night and not nearly enough firewood to keep us warm. My dad was up all night trying to remove the snow from our tent. "This will be our last camping trip," he declared, as he threw all of our wet stuff into the trunk.

Maybe some embarrassment they shared together, a remark or a look-on-the-face that the other could hardly imagine their spouse ever making.

Maybe some disagreement they shared about how to discipline their children.

Maybe some disappointment they managed to work through.

Maybe some holiday or birthday celebration that seemed to stir their emotions more than others.

I wanted so badly to hear about my dad and mom together because that would have momentarily brought their marriage back to life, would have brought her back to life, and therefore would have brought my sisters and me back to life. Was that too much to ask? Apparently so.

Which is why I found myself gradually following my dad's way of dealing with 1957. Had he figured out a way to separate himself from that Wednesday when God separated Himself from us? Deny his sorrow and pain by working seven days a week at the mill. I was hardly old enough to work productively at the mill, but I spent as much time there as I could. My other option was staying at home with five women. When I later claimed at my installation as Grand Snark of the Universe for Hoo-Hoo International that I had started in the sawmill business when I was just a kid, I wasn't kidding.

Of course, when I said that, my fellow Hoo-Hoo brothers probably pictured me as a kid sweeping out our A-Frame office or washing my dad's pickup truck. What I meant, though, is what I said. I started in the sawmill business when I was a kid. And I meant business. My dad's business. He would have had a difficult time understanding what I meant because that would have required him to think too much about my mom.

What I meant about "starting in the sawmill business when I was just a kid" is the way I ended up my dad's partner. Eva might have been his partner when he called it a day and arrived home for dinner. She might have been his partner for a Saturday night date, might have been his partner on Sunday morning at Ebenezer Lutheran, might have been his partner when it came to bills and how much money to spend. Was for sure his partner in bed now (having taken my place). But she wasn't his partner in the sawmill business, not like I was.

Dreams like my dad's dream about owning his own sawmill business have trouble adjusting for things like my mom's death. A new dream can be dreamt, but that can cause all kinds of heartache for someone like my dad. His dream had originated with himself and my mom as main characters, and in that old-world tradition of a family-owned business, I was supposed to dream someday that same dream.

I found myself forced to daydream about a life I couldn't even imagine or understand. I was fourteen years old, I was working the summer before my freshman year at Bend High School, and my dad has me sitting there with him for negotiations with Patrick, the lumber broker from Prineville. "Need another five bucks a thousand, Patrick, and you know we haven't talked about this for months." My dad tapped his cigar by the corner of his desk (I would sweep that up later after the meeting) and looked to me like I was some senior partner. His nod was clever, though, when I think back about that afternoon. At once, signaling to me to keep my damn mouth shut but indicating to Patrick that the two of us had outmaneuvered him.

But business partner aside, my dad stopped short of ever acknowledging my quest to restore my mother's honor, to detect and uncover those layers of secrecy surrounding her death. I shared with him one day my latest visit with Grandma Genevieve. She had tried to help me let go of some of my bitterness toward God, some of my need to blame God for my mother's death. Over the course of her lifetime, she had gradually adjusted her own faith after realizing that directing blame toward God had trapped her bitterness inside. Blaming God for my mother's death required my admission that God was in charge of the universe, was in charge over all of life, period. My grandmother wasn't so sure anymore about God being in charge of everything. She had refrained from connecting God's Will with her daughter's death almost immediately after that twenty-first of August. At first, this threw me off because I did not have the lifetime of experiences she had, whatever it was that had helped her distance herself from God altogether. I felt like a kid who finally learns there is no real Santa Claus. Once that myth is dispelled, thinking about presents and wishes at Christmas takes on new meaning.

Once you let go of God's power over all of life, His absolute control over all of creation, you think differently about His part in your daughter's death at thirty-one. It's odd in a way because I sensed some peace of heart when she spoke about all of this. "If I'm constrained by Grandpa Sheldon's Christian Science teachings or your dad's Lutheran church teachings, I have to think about your mother's death according to those constraints. If I step back from all of that, my heart is still broken, but I don't feel any anger or bitterness. I'm sad, of course, and I expect this sadness will keep me company for the rest of my days. And that feels like my daughter keeping me company."

My dad didn't say a thing. He had been listening, though, I could tell. But he didn't say a word. Had he and my Grandma Genevieve come to a similar place in their walk through life? Kind of like, if our faith in God isn't helping us honestly understand life and all its twists and turns, why should we persist in nurturing that relationship?

Losing your mom is different from losing your spouse (like for my dad) or your daughter (like for my grandma) because when you lose your mom, you lose your growing up, your childhood. So you lose two people. You don't have the emotional maturity to think about this loss, so you end up confronting your mother's death as you grow up and mature. And every time you confront her death, it feels like it just happened, over and over again.

When my dad and I did talk about his WW II days in the Philippines, I got the impression that he may have been thinking about all of this long before my mother's death. Accepting God's power over all of life versus the freedom to cope with life each day on your own terms.

Have never been able to figure this out. My dad has two favorite songs. Loved to sing Frank Sinatra's "My Way."

Gordon Benson was just as certain of his case. Ask anybody who knew him. He lived life his way. Oh, he had more than a few regrets. But his John Wayne "I did what I had to do" made up for any lack of memory about regrets. He carefully planned each step along life's byway, planned it all his way. Not God's plan, but Gordon Benson's plan. And hardly shy about it. From what my dad had figured out about life, it was best if he counted on himself. My dad wasn't about to kneel down before God the Creator, or anybody else. Hadn't always been easy on his own, sure had his share of losing, but at least he had done it his way.

But here's the thing. My dad's other favorite song was Elvis Presley's "Somebody Bigger Than You and I." Is it you, Dad, who plans each step along life's byway, or is it somebody bigger than you and I who lights the road along life's way? And if that somebody is keeping you company and guiding you and walking beside you, how is that doing it all your way? If you are always counting on yourself, why are you also seeking courage from somebody bigger than you and I?

I wasn't old enough at the time to put all this together like some psychiatrist. I've had to figure this out over the course of our tumultuous and tender years together as partners of Benson Lumber. I love my dad. But I believe he managed his grief by turning inward while puffing out his chest (not easy, just try it), by shielding himself from any questions, and by privately wrestling with the fact that such an approach left him feeling alone and small.

I was old enough to understand and appreciate the completion of our new mill in 1966 because I had taken our family business to heart. I no longer worked at Benson Lumber because that's what my dad had expected me to do. I now worked for Benson Lumber because that's what I wanted to do. For me, it had become our dream.

My dad had a way of expanding Benson Lumber that would confuse most oddsmakers, defying the long-accepted logic of the old time loggers with whom he shared the region and its timber. Cliff Baker, a master millwright who was heads above anyone else when it came to operating his equipment but heads below most everyone else when it came to making any money using his equipment, had offered to sell his more-up-to-date sawmill equipment for $12,000. Although my dad was excited to make this deal, he stood firmly by his low-ball, four-thousand-dollar counteroffer. Cliff finally accepted after my dad offered him a millwright job to make sure everything kept working. My dad didn't have a clue about how all of the stuff worked, but thanks to my mom, he did have a clue about how to make money.

Back in 1949, the two of them had devised a budget plan that first week after Fred Rogers's old head rig had exploded. My mom was a certified public accountant when it came to running her household, and she extended that expertise to the mill books. All costs were declared up front, including my dad's take-home pay each month, a realistic profit margin, a savings plan, taxes, and capital improvements. I can't count the number of times my dad and I have exchanged nervous glances over the years as we gambled on expected receivables for an extra load of logs. Mom would not have approved.

Fifteen years earlier, my dad and Buel had produced four to five thousand board feet per day. Now, with a third man, nine to twelve thousand board feet could be produced each day while my dad was out buying logs. Here's part of the story the *Redmond Spokesman* reported in a feature covering operations at our new mill, the new mill that had been built by Gordon and Robin Benson, Albert "Pa" Benson, Gordon's in-laws, the Sheldons, brothers Emmett, Hubert, and Marion, son Karl, millwrights Everett Withrow and Cliff Baker, and Buel Smelcer

And Eva.

> "From the time the logs are dumped on the log deck, the process begins. Power conveyors bring them up the head rig, air dogs sink their fangs into them immediately, the electric setter obeys the sawyer's order for the cut (pushing a button to set the thickness of next log on carriage), the electric chain turners flip the log, it moves through the saw and zips back for the next, while the slab rolls on its way on the power-operated conveyor to the automatic wood saw, the trimmers, and on to the yard or planer."

We had grown from three broken peavey handles in a single day in 1951 to pushing a button in 1966 that automatically set the thickness of the next cut on the log carriage. It was into this world of logs, lumber, and legacy that I was born and raised, and expected to preserve and protect all that had preceded me.

In the fall, I would begin my senior year at Bend High.

Like I said, I started in my dad's sawmill business when I was just a kid.

CHAPTER 11

Henry
9 April 1998
Maundy Thursday

Of the less-than-inspired photographs we had taken twenty-nine years ago to record our engagement memory, one picture always prompts that "What-was-I-thinking?" recollection. It provided our only genuine laugh earlier this evening. Maybe that's why I was staring at it again. After I had taken a photograph of Denise's hand on the rail of the sternwheeler *Mark Twain*, her engagement ring reflection shimmering on the still waters of the Rivers of America, we had asked a young man to take a picture of us.

A bright red Mickey Mouse balloon hovers overhead, casually dressed tourists behind us enjoying the cruise around Tom Sawyer's Island, and there we stand, clearly overdressed for that veiled overcast day at Disneyland, the thirteenth of June 1969. Denise looked like a Swedish model in her doubled-breasted yellow raincoat, and I'm modeling an OK combination of blue shirt, burgundy tie, and light tan sport coat. But my hair! My god, what had happened to my hair?

I had towel-dried it that morning with my regular rigor, creating a peculiarly snarled style of wild animal nest. Since my '63 VW Bug wasn't running too well that week, we had to borrow my Dad's '54 GMC pickup, a retired but reliable public works vehicle repainted light brown, used during the week to deliver parts for his machine shop. Seems we were driving a lot of borrowed pickup trucks in those days. A blast of warm air below the dashboard

– winter and summer – couldn't be regulated, so we had the windows wide open for our ride south on Interstate Five to Disneyland. Denise hadn't said a thing about it all morning; love, I guess, has a way of overlooking such a sight. But there I am, my right arm around my sweetheart, looking as though I've been electrocuted!

On that same note about how love has a way of overlooking things, driving my Dad's old delivery truck seemed like a good time to clarify something Denise had learned about me when we were dating in college. I had bragged about my dad's multi-million dollar manufacturing business in Southern California, how he was responsible for production of the Apollo spacecraft. The thing is, a person never knows for sure how far a relationship will go, so why not kick it off with an impressive claim you can always walk back from later if things should become serious? So clarify, I did. "Hey Denise, you do know my dad only produces the two hinges for the door of the Apollo spacecraft, right?"

The Rivers of America don't flow anywhere; it's a canal imagineered by Walt Disney to represent a river flowing somewhere. After the original attempt to fill the trench had disappeared into the sandy soil of this former orange grove in Anaheim, clay soil was trucked in to waterproof the leaking riverbed. As the *Mark Twain* steamboat followed its underwater guidance track past Cascade Peak and its beautiful waterfalls, I couldn't wait any longer. It wasn't getting any more romantic than this. Denise knew what was happening today, she just didn't know where or when. I told her how glad I was she had come into my life, how very happy she had made me. I asked her to marry me, I placed the ring on her finger, we kissed briefly amidst a small group of curious onlookers, and I took the photo of her left hand on that rail – a symbol of our engagement at Disneyland, the Happiest Place on Earth.

Our day at the Happiest Place on Earth cost us $4.95 each, although the actual "D" ticket for the *Mark Twain* Steamboat Ride was only seventy-five cents. Our coupon book to the Magic Kingdom included enough tickets for ten adventures – from an "A" coupon worth ten cents for a ride on the fire engine up and down Main Street to the "E" coupon worth eighty-five cents for the Jungle Cruise ride.

Disneyland had cost my friend Mark Buehler only fifty cents when he visited the park its first year in 1955. He was the first kid I ever knew to visit Disneyland; we were both seven years old, so waiting until the next day to hear his firsthand account was absolute agony for both of us. His uncle was almost mauled by lions and tigers on the jungle cruise from which you may not return. His description was believable enough. "Don't go on that ride," he warned. If Walt Disney had had his way, living wild animals would have populated this attraction; he was talked out of that proposal when experts reminded him such animals would be hiding or sleeping during daytime operation.

Mark did mention something about a genuine, ol' time shootin' gallery at the Penny Arcade on Main Street – that you could fire honest-to-goodness, real live ammunition .22 caliber rifles! He was right about the live ammunition, but this attraction was quickly removed after the first year.

It didn't take my brother George and me too long to figure out the truth about that jungle cruise ride. We didn't make it to Disneyland until the next year, but when we walked down Main Street, U.S.A., on my birthday that June, our mother securely holding our hands, we had only one thing on our minds: Tomorrowland, and those Grand Prix racing cars on the Autopia Freeway. Oh no, what if my kid brother isn't tall enough to drive his own car? It turned out he was, and I wisely stepped in front of him at the last minute to ensure my car would be behind his. We accelerated in no time to a screaming top speed (eleven mph), barely able to negotiate our turns (limited, of course, by the curbs on either side), my brother bumping the girls driving too slowly in front of us every time I bumped him, and finally screeching to an out-of-control halt at the finish line (a park attendant had mysterious control of my car by riding alongside on the running board).

I never understood the *free* guest pass I happened upon; I assumed my dad got them somehow. "Hey, how 'bout dinner at Disneyland tomorrow night?" I would usually play down the need to go on a lot of rides; that would have made it seem like I needed to justify using the pass. "I thought this would be a great place for dinner, don't you? If you wanna go on a ride or two, that's fine with me." Maybe fine with me, but this was not fine with my dad, who finally approached my mother about her distribution of these *free* passes to Disneyland. I guess she assumed like me that he got them somehow. Free to her and me, and my revolving girlfriends at San Gabriel High School – I sure didn't have any trouble getting a date that fall of my senior year – but not exactly free for Caine Precision Manufacturing. Reserved, I quickly learned, for people who provided contracts for my dad's business. Those free dates gave me the idea, though, about proposing to the right girl someday at Disneyland – while riding the *Mark Twain* sternwheeler around the Rivers of America.

Our high school senior class was not the first, nor the last, to celebrate our Grad Night at Disneyland in 1966; Walt Disney had introduced the idea five years earlier. "Hey, Andy, listen to me here. You and I won't be talkin' about any of our childhood 'Mr. Toad's Wild Ride' memories. You understand what I'm saying here, right? We'll let the girls have all that kind of fun." When Gail and Susan asked us to go on that little kid ride with them, we claimed first-time-ever for that experience and acted accordingly cool enough to impress them either way – real guys still "little boy" enough to enjoy the Magic Kingdom.

A strange night, though, because we had to reconcile our happiest-place-on-earth good times with a rumor that somebody had been killed trying to crash our party by sneaking into the park without paying. A nineteen-year-old guy from Northridge had climbed the park's sixteen-foot-high outer fence onto the Monorail track, had ignored a security guard's warning about an approaching train, and had thought he was safe by jumping onto a fiberglass canopy beneath the track. His body was dragged for forty feet. He was the first Grad Night fatality at Disneyland; he would not be the last. Later that year, Walt Disney died of cancer, after recovering from surgery a month earlier to remove one of his lungs.

Walt Disney had written on the back of our $4.95 coupon book: "We hope that your visit with us today will be a happy and memorable experience for you and your family. May your day at Disneyland be a pleasant one." When you have built a legacy like Disneyland, it's almost as if you don't ever die. A happy and memorable experience? By far, one of the best days of my life, wild animal hair nest and all! As we circled Tom Sawyer's Island onboard the riverboat *Mark Twain*, my daydream proposal had come true. I was ready to spend my whole life with Denise.

At least we had film in our camera that day at Disneyland. We talk about that every anniversary. We talk about that because Denise's brother Karl and his bride, Sharon, had visited Disneyland with us while on their honeymoon in 1972.

They had driven down in Karl's green '67 Camaro convertible with a calligraphic "Let It Be" on the side. Paul McCartney's words of wisdom were attributed at first to the biblical Mother of Jesus, but these words of wisdom were a tribute to his own mother who had died of cancer when he was fourteen. For Karl, this connection had helped him make it through to this point in his life, his mother whispering those words of wisdom, "Let It Be." Maybe that was as good as holding his hand. Whenever he found himself in times of trouble, his mother came to him; in any hour of darkness, she was standing right in front of him, speaking words of wisdom, "Let It Be." There will be an answer, she said. It will be all right.

Sharon's parents had given them a new super 8 movie camera. They had been using it for most of their trip down the coast of California and were now recording some footage of where we were engaged. "This oughta be good, Caine, the four of us here on the *Mark Twain* – you guys engaged here a few years ago, and now Sharon and I taking our honeymoon here."

I agreed, and I asked him about what else he had been filming.

"Oh, we've been using this contraption every day since we left, and you know what's incredible? I haven't had to put any new film in it yet. It's like it's endless."

"Let me see that thing a second," I took it in hand, inspecting the control panel for any indication of how much film remained. "Hey, Karl, you chucklehead, there isn't any film in this thing!"

"But my father-in-law told us it was all set and ready to go. I can't believe this. I figured he meant it was all ready to go. Can you believe this, Sharon?"

I couldn't help my insensitive remark, but I had to say something. "Hey, Karl, 'Let It Be,' right?"

Sharon had a look on her face that only Disneyland could change. Thank God we were at the Happiest Place on Earth, even though they would have no record of their honeymoon. Besides, nothing ever goes wrong at Disneyland.

Nothing ever does go wrong at Disneyland. Or, at least, that's the intended impression. An attendant isn't called to mop up a kid's vomit on the Mad Tea Party ride; the attendant is called to mop up a protein spill. Visitors to the park are always walking above an underground complex of facilities for security, for employee needs, for administrative offices, for garbage collection – a vast network of corridors all hidden from view. "I don't want the public to see the world they live in while they're in the Park," Walt Disney had said. "I want them to feel they are in another world."

But our 1969 world was not so easy to hide. Like body counts in Vietnam. Hard to think about another world when that world was so vividly portrayed on TV every day. The antiwar movement was shifting gears and picking up new energy and new leaders.

Four months after our wedding in 1970, on August 6, seven hundred and fifty hippies and yippie protestors had invaded the Park and taken over Fort Wilderness on Tom Sawyer's Island by yanking down the historic fifteen-star American flag and hoisting in its place a National Liberation Front Viet Cong flag. Passing out reefers to park guests didn't exactly help their cause. Imagine irate fathers covering the Mickey Mouse clad ears of their children to protect them from hearing the loud chants coming from across the Rivers of America: "Ho, Ho, Ho Chi Minh." When the protesters marched in a Main Street parade singing their own lyrics to "Zip-A-Dee-Doo-Dah" ("Ho, Ho, Ho Chi Minh, NLF is gonna win ..."), park guests tried to drown them out by singing "America the Beautiful."

The Magic Kingdom did not know how to respond. This was an amusement park that had initially refused entry to young men with beards (a common practice in some cities of Orange County in those days). Police arriving in full riot gear ordered the park closed at 7:00 PM and ushered out 30,000 guests with no rain checks offered. The remaining protestors set trash cans on fire and hurled rocks and debris at police blocking the main gate. The arrest of twenty-three protestors that Thursday evening did not fit the script for the Happiest Place on Earth. In the aftermath, Disneyland selectively enforced a dress code for many years, occasionally turning away visitors who resembled stereotypical hippies.

It was for this reason – that our world was not an easy thing to hide from our view – that the four of us stand-by-me boys had made our promise that day on the ninth green. The future scared the hell out of us! America had changed *big time*! The world we had been preparing to live in – the 1955 world of our fathers and mothers – was going to pot. Not even Disneyland could hide this reality from us.

"Why do we have to grow up?" Walt Disney had asked.

Good question!

A month after our engagement at the Happiest Place on Earth, Neil Armstrong and Buzz Aldrin sent America a gift from outer space – a short recess from reality here on earth by beating the Soviets to a landing on the moon. But when they returned, of course, it was the same old place.

On that Friday afternoon in June of 1969, though, Denise and I refused to think about the same old place. Every anniversary, we look forward to laughing about that photograph of us taken by the young man right after I had asked Denise to be the one. She made me so very happy. And that's all we care to remember about our world in 1969.

Almost forgot. Two weeks before, on Friday, the thirtieth of May, the actual date of Memorial Day, Mario Andretti had won the Indy 500. My dad and I always watched this race, even if we had to wait until the next Saturday when the broadcast aired on Wide World of Sports with Jim McKay. Our family tradition included a little Jim Beam whiskey with chasers to help dull the count of two hundred laps. My mom took this opportunity to initiate me (so she thought), offering me my first shot and a beer a few weeks shy of my twenty-first birthday. Served on a tray, no less. Margaret Anita was somethin' else.

CHAPTER 12

Andy

I felt those ambivalent Boy Scout feelings my freshman year at California Lutheran College in Thousand Oaks. Plenty of PKs to go around, a familiarity I appreciated. But not enough that I felt inclined to share my real self with anyone. I was growing more distrustful, and I realized CLC was not exactly a cutting-edge college campus of the sixties. Our most controversial protest claim was signing a petition to abolish compulsory chapel attendance twice a week, such required gathering nothing more than a rally to promote some opportunity to serve others. Compared with other college campuses in 1967, CLC was an innocent kid brother along for the ride, an underage teenager who hadn't been invited to the uptown frat party. Like most of my CLC friends, I was home visiting my family for spring break.

In Ft. Lauderdale, Florida, college students woke up Easter morning ready to carry on the shenanigans and rioting they had begun on Good Friday – five hundred arrests and hundreds of thousands of dollars in property damage amidst flying beer bottles and flailing batons. Christ has risen!

I remember sharing with my father a story from my freshman English Literature class. In a 1905 letter to a librarian who had asked Mark Twain to defend Huckleberry Finn and Tom Sawyer against an overzealous official's recommendations that such bad examples be removed from the children's department, Twain had written:

Dear Sir:

I am greatly troubled by what you say. I wrote Tom Sawyer & Huck Finn for adults exclusively, & it always distressed me when I find that boys and girls have been allowed access to them. The mind that becomes soiled in youth can never again be washed clean. I know this by my own experience, & to this day I cherish an unappeased bitterness against the unfaithful guardians of my young life, who not only permitted but compelled me to read an unexpurgated Bible through before I was 15 years old. None can do that and ever draw a clean sweet breath again on this side of the grave. Ask that young lady – she will tell you so.

Most honestly do I wish I could say a softening word or two in defense of Huck's character, since you wish it, but really in my opinion it is no better than God's (in the Ahab & 97 others), & the rest of the sacred brotherhood.

If there is an Unexpurgated Bible in the Children's Department, won't you please help that young woman remove Tom & Huck from that questionable companionship?

Sincerely yours,
S. L. Clemens

When my father was not amused, I knew we were turning another corner. As I think back now, we were turning a lot of corners about this time.

Confident my quiet and private sexual orientation would not interfere with my personal commitment to the ideals of Scouting, I became a Professional Scouter for the Chief Seattle Council after graduation from CLC.

Some leaders at Camp Parsons on the Olympic Peninsula had expressed concern about a scoutmaster suspected of being gay; they alerted my superior about a question I had posed. "If you've got to decide between a leader who is gay (but who also exhibits sound leadership qualities like integrity and who faithfully follows the Twelve Scout Laws) and a straight guy who cheats on his wife with no remorse, who are you inclined to choose for that position of leadership?"

It didn't take much in those days; someone was already writing on the wall. Four years later, gay scouts and gay leaders were officially banned from the Boy Scouts of America. In the meantime, I was asked to resign. For the first time in my adult life, I failed to fight back my tears as I drove home to my apartment in Kirkland. Your advice, Baden-Powell – "So when things look bad just smile and sing to yourself: 'Stick to it, stick to it, stick to it,' and you will come through it all right." – did not help. What was I supposed to resign from, the Scout Oath? From the Scout Laws, from the Motto, from the Slogan? My dedication to the higher principles of Scouting had left me ignorant of the lower principles that had infected Scouting.

Because my DNA strands included an inherited calling to serve others, and God surely knew this about me, I found myself thinking about seminary, following in my father's footsteps, a vocation I considered safe from such ignorance and bigotry.

I still included my father in that world I considered safe, but our theological differences would test that world halfway through my first year at Evangelical Lutheran Theological Seminary in Columbus, Ohio. I couldn't help question what my father had learned; I was not learning the same thing. Divinity school faculties had a challenging time keeping up with current scholarship.

I had waited until Sunday evening before I bothered to share my latest first-year seminary enlightenment. Visiting with my father any time leading up to Sunday morning wasn't too fruitful, his sermon preparation held captive by the expectations of his parishioners. Add the demands of Holy Week – Maundy Thursday and Good Friday sermons – and we had no choice but to accept his preoccupation. I felt fortunate to have this brief time with him before I returned to seminary. My sisters and I, and our mother, often felt no different from his parishioners; in some ways, we weren't so different. It didn't take long for our debate to sound like a major church schism – because it is a major church schism.

While I was learning how to use historical-critical methods to understand the ancient texts of the Bible, my father was formulating his own nervous inhibitions about this new approach – an approach slowly emerging over the past two centuries, but not yet recognized by my father's seminary faculty as formidable enough to alter the landscape of biblical studies. By the time my professors were preparing their lecture notes after the Second World War, this new method was already taken for granted by many biblical scholars. I was introduced to Wellhausen, Dibelius, and Bultmann in the same breath as Hosea, Amos, and Micah. Albert Schweitzer had already given popular voice to this new approach back in 1906 when he had written his *Quest of the Historical Jesus*, calling into question all of the sentimental and devotional accounts of Jesus.

My father rejected his fellow Lutheran Rudolf Bultmann's call to demythologize the New Testament. "Why," he asked me, "should we have to separate the Gospel from its ancient mythological trappings if your historical-critical method can simply extract the kerygma from its original setting?"

"That's the point! Thanks to the historical-critical method," I answered, "Bultmann acknowledged the difficulties faced by modern readers whose thinking is shaped by science. Not easy to take seriously a pre-scientific, mythical worldview that describes Jesus ascending into heaven above the earth. Without demythologizing the Gospel, God's decisive message of salvation through Jesus Christ can get lost in that mythical world."

"Well, Andy, if you don't mind, I prefer Karl Barth's more middle-of-the-road approach when it comes to honoring Scripture as it stands. I'll let your historical-critical method lay the groundwork to help me prepare for the task of explaining Scripture. But then a little Spirit-led discernment of the 'Word within the words' can lead the way to our understanding of a given text."

"Bultmann deserves more of your respect, Father. For some of the German liberal theologians like Harnack, we owe our greatest thanks to Jesus for his moral teachings. Such an interpretation, though, leaves the Easter proclamation in the past, hardly demanding an urgent and life-changing response. Bultmann speaks about an Easter proclamation of Christ crucified and risen that requires our decision one way or the other. The Kingdom of God is at hand! Do we want God's reign, or is it the world we want? Jesus' word invites us to decide for the reign of God breaking in. The Easter proclamation is not about an event in the past."

I paused for a moment and decided to offer an observation I thought he could accept as logical and reasonable. "It's fair to say, Father, that our better understanding of the historical settings and life situations of all biblical authors can help bridge that vast distance in time between their culture and ours. Before Scripture can shed relevance on our present, we need to connect with Scripture's meaning in the past by using all of the literary tools we can bring to bear. Why would we want to risk not making a connection between the power of the ancient story and those we now serve? Shouldn't we bring our best, Father, to the study of God's Word? How dare we bring anything less. No one volume could describe all the layers of interpretation propounded over the centuries of Christianity by countless theologians and denominations, but an historical-critical approach sets those accumulated layers aside to ask questions about the original text. I'll grant you this, a theological presupposition always exists; to approach the text with a neutral, detached, objective attitude is impossible. But what is possible is a critical study of the ancient texts unfettered by any such presuppositions. Making sense of these texts for modern listeners who live in a scientific age is always the true work of interpretation."

My father was staring at me, his exhaustion after a long Holy Week now rejuvenated by my opening assertion. In contrast to the historical-critical method I was using to understand God's Word, my father had lived by the historical-grammatical method he had been taught – accepting Holy Scripture as the verbally inspired and inerrant word of God.

"You know, Andy, I too take time to study each and every word of Scripture to determine what the original author meant to say. But I stand under the Word of God; I do not stand above it to pass judgment on what the original author might have meant. I do not submit divine revelation to human literary investigation, or criticism, as you call it."

"Father, let me give you an example of what I'm learning about at seminary, will you? Take Jesus' parable about the Prodigal Son. I remember your sermon for the Fourth Sunday of Lent, reading from your RSV. You read verses one to three, and then spent a lot of time talking about how those Pharisees and scribes were worrying too much about something they didn't need to worry about.

> 'Now the tax collectors and sinners were all drawing
> near to him. And the Pharisees and the scribes murmured,
> saying, 'This man receives sinners and eats with them.' So
> he told them this parable: . . .'

You had little time left to talk about the amazing grace God is prepared to offer us who are lost but trying to return home to his love. God has planned a celebration for us because 'this son of mine was dead and is alive again; he was lost and is found!' When the son 'was still far off, his father saw him and was filled with compassion; he ran and put his arms around him and kissed him.' The father *ran*! He didn't hesitate, he didn't saunter down to meet his son, and he didn't send a servant. The father ran to greet his son! Didn't you want your congregation to hear about this celebration?"

How will my father react when I return home after coming out as gay? Will his love surprise me? Will he welcome me home like that prodigal son? I'm always saddened by this thought because I predict he will measure his grace by the dogma and orthodoxy of the church.

"Luke used this parable sixty or seventy years after Jesus to address some different concerns," I continued, "and so that introduction is how he chose to frame its use as a parable. The Jewish religious leaders of Luke's day had some trouble understanding this kind of love and reception, resented the Gospel invitation to Gentiles without any strings attached. I'm not so sure, though, that the first hearers thought about sinners and IRS agents when they heard about how the father (God) had welcomed home the younger brother. Did they think about the righteous Pharisees when they heard about that older brother who begrudged this unconditional love? Or was this parable later used during the early church years to address issues about how some Jewish leaders were questioning Paul's openness to Gentiles?

So I'm learning, Father, that we ask about what forms or patterns the teachings and parables of Jesus took as they were orally circulated among the various hearers of the first century. We then ask about how those teachings and parables and sayings, once committed to writing and circulated, were selected by the authors to use for their gospel text. Next, we consider the editorial process, how an evangelist decided to use a source; maybe the source was modified to serve a particular purpose, as Luke did with that parable about the Prodigal Son. Since no original manuscript of any biblical book has survived, we ask questions about how the gospel text was copied many times by hand. Any additions or subtractions? Is the son's statement in that parable used by Luke – 'Treat me like one of your hired servants.' – a later addition to verse twenty-one?"

"Andy, listen, I'm the first to acknowledge the rich diversity of that collection of books we call the Bible. How our Jewish predecessors organized their scared writings testifies to that diversity: the Law, the Former and Later

Prophets, and the Writings. Our Bible is not sixty-six chapters of a single book. I can adhere one hundred percent to my belief that all Scripture is inerrant and inspired by God but still accept a story about Jonah as historical fiction. Scripture includes all kinds of literary genre, and we should expect each genre to guide our interpretation of its content. The Book of Jonah presents itself as a story, not as an incredulous miracle. I'm not wondering why it took Jonah three days to walk across that 'exceedingly large city' of Nineveh, estimated by historians to cover an area of only three square miles. Such an exaggeration helps me understand how God wants me to read this book. As a story, these historical inaccuracies don't matter. Does this genre demand historical accuracy before we consider it relevant?"

"I'm surprised to hear you say that, Father. There is uniform scholarly agreement that Jonah is historical fiction. The Book of Jonah is a midrash. But I remember reading in Bainton's *Here I Stand* that Luther, unlike you, treated the Book of Jonah as history. 'How could anyone imagine that a man could be three days and three nights in the belly of a fish without light, without food, absolutely alone, and come out alive? Who would not take this for a fairy tale if it were not in Scripture?' Since the book is in Scripture, Luther concluded, 'we can believe it as it is told.'"

"Look, Andy, I treat God's Word as just that: His Holy Word. I understand that God chose to reveal His plan of salvation over the course of centuries, from Genesis to Revelation, but all of Scripture is in harmony with one central theological theme, the Gospel of salvation through faith in Jesus Christ. The teachings of Moses and the Prophets became the foundation for the teachings of the apostles. You might be familiar with Augustine's maxim, 'The New Testament is concealed in the Old Testament, and the Old is revealed in the New.' I don't ignore the complexities behind our study of Scripture, Andy, but I allow God's Word to clarify for me how I'm supposed to interpret a particular passage. Take that last verse of Luke chapter three, where the evangelist traces the lineage of Jesus. Adam is described as a real person in that list of descendants, so I accept Genesis as a historical book. I also recognize that chapter twelve in the Book of Revelation uses symbols like the dragon, that ancient serpent, to represent Satan because the passage directs me to this conclusion by its opening line, 'And a great portent appeared in heaven, a woman clothed with the sun . . . .' I'll give you another example. I have no knowledge of any scriptural clarification for the prohibitions against homosexuality that Paul discusses in Romans. Your historical-critical method, however, relies on the human judgment of modern science and culture to declare Paul's admonition against homosexuality and other forms of sexual immorality in Romans is all a misunderstanding of what he meant to say."

How did I know this was coming? Of course, homosexuality. Honestly, I was waiting for this opportunity. Maybe broaching this subject now could help us connect as a father and son when I returned home someday to come out to my family. When you are gay, and you have accepted God's calling to serve Him, but your father believes God's Word condemns who you are, this conversation reaches deep into your soul and begs for love and understanding beyond the boundaries of dogma and orthodoxy.

"As you know, Father, the moment you identify any specifics in Paul's letters, you are acknowledging he wrote those letters for specific reasons and needs of the early Church. If we presume his time and place are identical to ours – that his historical situation is the same as ours – we nullify twenty centuries of history, including whatever Luther may have contributed to our interpretation of God's Word. Odd, isn't it, how we seem ready to acknowledge that Luther's interpretation and translation of Scripture reflect his sixteenth-century historical setting, but we are forever stuck in Paul's time and place?

Luther's 'Scripture dilemma' is a perfect example," I added, "of how his historical setting requires our modern historical-critical method. On the one hand, he admits, 'When discrepancies occur in the Holy Scriptures and we cannot harmonize them, let it pass, it does not endanger the articles of the Christian faith.' Luther's not suggesting it doesn't matter, but sometimes we may not be able to resolve those discrepancies. On the other hand, he declares, 'It is impossible that Scripture should contradict itself; it only appears so in senseless and obstinate hypocrites. But everyone, indeed, knows that at times the early Church Fathers have erred, as men will: therefore I am ready to trust them only when they prove their opinions from Scripture, which has never erred.' Never erred, but discrepancies do exist that we cannot harmonize. It seems Luther didn't hesitate using text criticism now and then to address some of those discrepancies."

Although my father was a self-proclaimed McCarthyite of Reformation truth, he did not, thankfully, join forces with those who conducted a veritable witch-hunt for church leaders persuaded by this historical-critical communist plot to undermine the sacred text and its truth. These voices warned of doctrinal decay and erosion of our faith. Once Biblical inerrancy is breached by the historical-critical method, the door swings wide open to abandon the doctrines of verbal inspiration, biblical authority, and acceptance of the Bible as the Word of God – spreading uncertainty and doubt in the church. These church leaders claim our faith in Christ Jesus and the confessional heritage of our Lutheran Church are incompatible with the use of the historical-critical method that dares to question the ancient voice of the Holy Spirit. This approach to Bible study, they claim, was invented by the devil to stir unbelief among modern Christians no less so than were those damnable heresies of old!

I'm not sure Luther's translation of Scripture into the language of the people implied an unquestioning trust in the ability of all lay people to interpret the Bible. Yes, everyone should be able to read it, but why bother then to educate clergy? Baptists are fervent believers in soul competency – the idea that each individual is equipped by the Holy Spirit to interpret the Bible for himself, as long as we're assured the inspired guidance of that same Holy Spirit of old is still at work.

But what if the inspired guidance of that same Holy Spirit of old isn't at work when some ardent believers interpret the Bible for themselves? What about believers who defend bloody crusades and cruel inquisitions? Believers who support slavery, apartheid, segregation, or the Ku Klux Klan? Believers who persecute Jews and other non-Christian people of faith? Believers who execute women as witches? Believers who conducted genocidal campaigns against Native Americans? Believers who oppose medical science? Believers who condemn interracial marriage? Are those believers equipped by the Holy Spirit to interpret the Bible for themselves? Shakespeare offered this: "Even the devil can cite Scripture for his purpose."

"By the way, Father, you might find it interesting that I used your historical-grammatical method to learn more about how homosexuality is understood in Scripture. The Bible contains only seven passages that refer directly to homosexual behavior, and none are connected with Jesus in the four Gospels. Why does Jesus himself never refer to it? For all the topics he covers, what lesson can we glean here by his choice not to cover that one? If we let the Gospels be our guide, as you propose, Father – nothing about homosexuality mentioned by Jesus, no questions asked him by his followers – shouldn't we be paying attention to that?

As you said before, Father, about letting Scripture shed light on its own meaning, consider Paul's mind at work here, the context of his letter to the Christians living in Rome. He knew what had happened to the Jewish people of old who practiced idolatry, and here he expanded this concern to include the Gentiles – since we're all sinners, both alike are in need of God's redeeming grace. He brought attention to an idolatrous practice common in the ancient world in which 'they exchanged the glory of the immortal God for images resembling a mortal human being or birds or four-footed animals or reptiles.' Paul declared that God had had enough of the ungodly and wicked – most especially those who had abandoned the one true God for idols – and He gave them up to degrading passions.

By studying Paul's historical setting, we know he was familiar with some temple cults that used men and women to perform same-gender sexual acts in devotion to an idol – acts we would classify as degrading passions. This is what God had given them up to, but this was not the original cause of God's anger; the original cause was idolatry.

A careful consideration of those verbs *exchanged* and *gave up* indicate that Paul was concerned about those heterosexually inclined who indulged voluntarily to act contrary to their ordinary sexual appetite – who chose to act contrary to their true nature. Their true nature, Paul understood, meant the customary way we think about humankind; it was not a natural law argument designating one lifestyle as sinful while another is not.

Using the Greek lexicon to see how other writers at this time were using these words *natural* vs. *unnatural* passions reveals the Greek term *para physin*, translated *unnatural*, is more often translated *atypical* or *unusual*. What would be Paul's intent if we could ask him now? In Romans 11:24, he uses this same Greek term to describe how God's grafting of a wild olive shoot (the Gentiles) into a cultivated olive tree (the Jewish people) is 'contrary to nature.' An unusual thing to do. Atypical, nothing more. No ethical condemnation.

In our discussions about human sexuality today, when we are talking about two people of the same gender who have committed themselves to a faithful, lifelong relationship with one another, are we talking about the same thing Paul is – about temple prostitutes in ancient Rome, or about male pederasty in ancient Greece? We do not know of a word in ancient Greece to describe homosexual practices; such practices were understood using the word *aphrodisiac* (love), which included men and women alike.

Please tell me, Father, how what I have said is a misunderstanding of what Paul meant to say in Romans chapter one. If I'm honoring your respect for Scripture, using it, as you said, to guide our interpretation of Scripture, then we had better pay closer attention to those two Old Testament passages. Genesis 19:1-11 is the story of Abraham's nephew Lot who was staying in Sodom. Men from the city wanted to have sex with Lot's guests whom he had welcomed in hospitality for the night. Lot refused, and when he was threatened by the townspeople the angels he has hosted protected him. Judges 19:16-30, a similar story, describes how a threat by the townspeople violated the tradition of hospitality. Same-sex acts or gang rape are not named as the sin of Sodom. The prophet Ezekiel clarified this passage for us; his reference to the sin of Sodom is about injustice, not sexual immorality or homosexuality as some have interpreted it. 'This was the guilt of your sister Sodom: she and her daughters had pride, excess of food, and prosperous ease, but did not aid the poor and needy.' In addition to the mention of Sodom and Gomorrah as first told in Genesis chapter nineteen, both are mentioned in about two-dozen different places in the Bible. In none of those passages is homosexuality associated with the Sodomites.

We had better pay closer attention to that Council of Jerusalem held around 50 AD and recorded in Acts chapter fifteen. It was decided Christians would not be bound by that holiness code in Leviticus, except for what was listed, and nothing related to homosexuality was listed. We can agree, right, that Paul vehemently argued on behalf of non-Jewish Christians, that they should not be forced to obey Jewish purity laws such as circumcision and diet before they would be welcomed as members of the Christian community. Could I extend his logic here, Father, and suggest homosexuals should not have to try to become heterosexuals to join our Christian community? In Christ there is neither Jew nor Greek, slave nor free, male nor female – neither is there gay or straight – but all are one in Christ."

While I was sharing all of this with my father, his tired eyes told me he would not be responding anymore this evening. It was almost midnight. Did he know who I was? Was he in denial about who I had become? I do not know. Did he think I had been dismissed from the Boy Scouts because of my DUI charge crossing the floating bridge over Lake Washington, coming home from a party in West Seattle where I had arrived still comfortable in my Scouter uniform because I had left Camp Parsons too late in the day?

According to those inexorable witch-hunters who aren't interested in asking any questions of Scripture, who only find condemnation in the Bible for homosexuality, I guess I need to repent of my sin, repent because I'm a homosexual child of God, and trust God will forgive me. But then, so does my hero Baden-Powell, who more than likely shared my struggle with homosexuality.

Didn't help that his father had died when he was only three years old, leaving him on his own to figure out his manhood, constantly agonizing over his childhood anxieties about what information his father might have passed on to him if he had lived. Didn't help that he had to break free from his overly possessive and controlling mother's opposition to any relationships with women that might lead to marriage – this for both his brothers and him.

Who can know how much his fear of *girlitis* – a sexual attraction to a girl, a condition he likened to a disease and a smear on any scout who fell victim to this perversion – complicated his denial and repression of his homosexual urges? Like me in a way, he finally chose marriage as a way out, reluctantly, at age fifty-five. And it was awkward and conflicted, like mine.

Didn't help that he grew up living with the guilt-laden taboos of the Victorian and Edwardian codes, attending an oldfangled public school system that conditioned boys to treat the opposite sex as obscene.

Didn't help that no one in Baden-Powell's day was trying to better understand homosexuality; it was publicly condemned as an abominable evil. Considered such a grievous crime that a war hero like General Hector McDonald, after he was accused of homosexual practices, killed himself not long after Baden-Powell's return home.

Didn't help that banishing evil thoughts was easier said than done – evil thoughts a self-mastering man should be able to defeat. No masturbation, no *girlitis*, and surely no such love that even he or his era refused to name. Did counseling and trying to reform young boys help him control his own sexual urges?

About marriage, I have read that Baden-Powell thought two men could be just as happy living together as any man and woman.

Maybe the good general and founder of the Boy Scouts could help me respond to what I heard from those Scout leaders at Camp Parsons: "The

Bible clearly tells us, homosexuality is a sin. The Scouts should be fair for all boys, but everybody has a right to feel comfortable, and a lot of people don't feel comfortable around homosexuals. How many parents are going to be comfortable sending their children into the woods with an openly gay scoutmaster?"

I wanted to ask them, "How many parents are going to be comfortable sending their children into the woods with Baden-Powell?"

But I didn't.

Have we helped or hindered those we claim to care about, Stephe, by our insistence on remaining quiet and private about who we are?

CHAPTER 13

Henry
9 April 1998
Maundy Thursday

With my thumbs and forefingers, I framed a photo of my dad and me taken before our groom's party photo. Our wedding plans hadn't considered my dad's difficulties in 1970, but his smile had fought the good fight against his underlying anxiety. By 1984, though, his smile was tired and ready to surrender. I can recall every summer day of that year, each day filled with constant reminders of his failing health. I thought about him every day, every week; I even thought about him when I took a break from thinking about him.

On the last Sunday in June that year, Pastors Messner and Larson presided at my ordination service at Our Savior's Lutheran Church. The next day, our family celebrated with a trip to Disneyland, my dad's treat. A Mason jar full of $127.30 in change covered most of the costs that day – $14.00 for an adult ticket passport and $9.00 for a child – even after twenty-eight years of steadily-rising prices to enjoy the Happiest Place On Earth. Happiness doesn't always come cheap. My dad established his headquarters on a bench near that circle at the end of Main Street. His grandkids reported to him throughout the day while my mother, Denise, and I took turns keeping him company.

Later that week, our family hurried home to prepare for the next big event. On Denise's birthday, the 11 of July, Bishop Landers officiated at my installation as pastor of Immanuel Lutheran Church east of Astoria, Oregon.

Karl and Sharon showed up in support of what I was doing – an odd transition from my vice-president of forklifts job to Lutheran minister. I think Karl wanted to see for himself if I was for real. Like his Uncle Spud, the cedar-shake-and-shingle inspector, who had come to visit us and attend a Sunday morning service, but who had called me from The Logger Tavern Saturday evening to announce his arrival and see if I would meet him there for an old times' sake drink, hoping I might refuse on the grounds I no longer lived such a lifestyle now that I was a minister. I met him there to the affectionate greetings of backroom bar patrons, and he could only grin and pat me on the back with a "Thank God, you haven't changed, have you?"

Karl had driven his 1981 black Ferrari 308 GTSi over from Central Oregon and asked me after the ceremony if I would like to take it for a quick spin on the way back to our home for the reception. As I barreled down old Hwy 30 past the local Grange Hall, I couldn't help but turn a donut in the parking lot across from the market as Pastor Jim Carper of the Friends' Church was walking out. Pastor Jim's salary was based each week on the collection plate receipts, unlike the more traditional budget arrangements of a Lutheran church.

"Bud, congratulations on your ordination," he mumbled as he leaned down against the driver's side door with a puzzled look on his face. "Everything going well, I take it."

"Jim, things couldn't be better. Have a swell evening." And off I sped down the road with a long screech of the tires. Always had fun when Karl was around.

It was a splendid evening, and the last night I would see my dad alive. We had enjoyed our short time together, spending the day before at the Cord antique car show on the beautiful campus of Pacific University in Forest Grove. I remember how anxious I was that day, watching him pass nitro from his pocket to his lips like a child eating candy. It was an uncomfortable day for him, but walking around all of those superbly restored automobiles was the best possible therapy. He was not feeling much better the next evening during my installation service, but the chance to witness that event for his son was a welcome distraction.

Within two months of that July night, the nitro was about as worthless as candy. It was a Friday morning, the seventh of September, when I received the phone call from Pastor Messner. I was preparing for Rally Day weekend and the Fall Program where I was serving. Translating seminary training into everyday life is one thing, but this was my dad who had died. Of all the people who had stood behind me that June 24 day for the laying-on of hands at my ordination, he and my mom were the only two who could truly feel that inner satisfaction when someone you love finds fulfillment in life.

My dad would have celebrated his sixty-seventh birthday in a few months, but surviving three major attacks the past twenty years had exacted too serious a toll on his ever-weakening heart. With plans underway to relocate from Southern California to Oregon, my parents had already made an offer to buy a house near us.

Death cheats us out of tomorrows we were looking forward to with the person who has died. But to this day, I feel more cheated by my dad's troubled years of life before death than by the tomorrows following his death. The years before his death were filled with endless worries and stress – living his life as a Christian with no sense of God's presence or peace in his life.

How do I know this profound insight about my dad?

I was his official biographer. When I became a father, I decided to preserve his memory for my children. So I set out to chronicle his life. As a gesture of my love for him, I wrote a small book, *A Portrait of My Father*. I wanted my children and grandchildren to know all about him, although I could see his disappointment the past few years when my children interrupted him mid-story to say they already knew about a memory he was recalling. I failed to anticipate that.

Whenever my dad and I visited during vacations or holidays, I interviewed him and recorded his many stories about growing up in Chicago in the 1920s and preparing for his tool and die maker trade in the 1930s. I learned all about his daily experiences, both personal and business, about his hopes and his disappointments, about his joys and his frustrations, about his self-employment endeavors and his bankruptcy, about his vision and his fears. I even sent away for his report card from Carl Schurz High School in Chicago, discovered incompletes he didn't care to remember. I learned as much as I could about him. And that's why I'm happier for him now than I was for him when he was alive. But how can this be?

The Church had taught him about God's gift of salvation – my mother's Easter. The gift of life in God's eternal presence. And he believed such a life would begin when Jesus Christ returned at the Second Coming for the Final

Judgment and the Resurrection of the Dead. Centuries of biblical interpretation, teaching, preaching, and worshiping, have defined salvation as a gift lived in the hereafter – saved from the wages of sin, saved from death and eternal separation from God. We know it is the central theme of all Scripture, and we know the name of Jesus means "God will save His people." (Hebrew: *Joshua*) The whole point of our faith is based on God's decision to save us.

But the church had not taught my dad that the Greek word meaning *to save* (*sozo*) also means to heal, to restore, to rescue from danger (dangers like despair and desolation). "And those who had seen it reported to them how the man who was demon-possessed had been made well." (*sozo*)." (Luke 8:36)

As a Lutheran pastor, I met others who reminded me of my dad. With a sure and certain hope of their eventual resurrection to life in the hereafter, they knew about the gift that awaits them someday when Christ returns. But what about their here and now? They struggle with themselves, with family, with their job, with co-workers, with meaning in life, with money, with addictions, with health problems, with trials and tribulations, with Monday mornings, and they struggle with God. They struggle in the here and now and see no meaningful connection between God's gift of salvation and their daily lives. *To be saved*, for many Christians, means to be saved from spending eternity in hell.

So I asked this question: "When do we begin living God's gift of salvation – the day we are baptized, or the day we die, or the day Jesus Christ finally returns for the Resurrection of the Dead?" My dad's answer: "The day Jesus Christ finally returns for the Resurrection of the Dead." But shouldn't God's gift of salvation be "Living in Peace" in the here and now, not just "Resting in Peace" in the hereafter?

As a pastor and counselor, I have shared my heart with countless people who recounted for me their experience of hell this side of death – depression, hopelessness, fear, loneliness, brokenness, physical and mental abuse, tired-of-it-all, guilt, shame, bitterness, emotional pain and anxiety that will not go away. Hell is not only possible in the here and now; for many, it is a daily reality. *To be saved* would mean to be saved from such a death-in-life existence.

I have also listened to countless people share their experience of heaven this side of death – a long-awaited wedding ceremony, the birth of a healthy child, a profound sense of forgiveness, a moment of restored hope, fulfillment as a human being, another passage in life safely negotiated, recovery after a threatening illness, watching a grandchild play baseball, laughing from your heels up because you are alive! Heaven can be daily experiences this side of death. My mother's Easter did not have a voice in these stories.

Where my seminary training had concluded in celebration earlier that summer was now a place of mourning and grief while I waited for Pastor Messner to begin my dad's memorial service. I was still mulling over my answers to the many questions my mother had asked me the night before.

"Bud, do you think Dad's soul is with God now? His body was cremated after the medical research at UCLA. He didn't want us burdened with any burial expenses. How will he be raised from the dead at Christ's Second Coming? How can his body be reunited with his soul? Is he in some kind of intermediate state? Or do you think Dad has gone home to our Lord? Is he there now with grandma and his family who have preceded him in death, already resurrected to eternal life? Can we think of him as though he is already in heaven? Do you think Dad ever knew heaven here on earth? Bud, what did your dad's baptism mean all those years?"

My mother's dying wish to go at last to heaven had paled over the years as she watched my dad's ER heart monitor tell a story – a story about what his Sunday faith had meant on Monday mornings all those years. Or had not meant. Pastor Messner had concluded his sermon every Sunday with those words of the apostle Paul in his letter to the church at Philippi: "May the peace of God, which surpasses all understanding, guard your hearts and your minds in Christ Jesus." Apparently, God's peace had eluded my dad most of his life and was in fact beyond his understanding. What exactly is a heart attack when understood in the context of the gospel? Jesus had said, "Peace I leave with you; My peace I give to you; not as the world gives do I give to you. Do not let your heart be troubled, nor let it be fearful." Do not let your heart be attacked.

What my mother was asking was not one of the questions she had asked. What, after all, does salvation mean? Is it what she had celebrated every Easter for all those years – to go at last to heaven? That definition of salvation had not helped my dad in the here and now.

In my Hebrew class at seminary, Rabbi Perelmuter had told us the old story about a rabbi who was asked by one of his students, "Why is it you rabbis so often present your teaching in the form of a question?" To which the rabbi had answered, "So what's wrong with a question?" What is wrong with a question? The grieving and questions about my dad's death led me directly to grieving and questions about his life and what the Church had taught him to believe about Easter and salvation.

To my mother's questions about my dad's whereabouts after death, I had provided a quick and confident answer. Having completed Lutheran seminary training, I dare not hesitate. Both of my parents had sacrificed and helped to support my family and me for those four years. I knew my mother was counting on me for some answers.

I couldn't have been more straightforward. "Oh Mom, no need to worry or wonder. Dad is part of God's time now – eternity – a time wherein all things occur now, including his resurrection. His heart is at peace – no more stress and struggle. He is with God now. As a matter of fact," I added, more for myself than for my mother, "his death never separated him from God in the first place!"

I said all this that evening before my dad's memorial service, but even then I knew my response would require some further reflection. I felt as though I had pitched a massive rock of reality into the middle of an otherwise calm pond of Christian piety. Ripples immediately circled out from the center, ripples and ripples of questions. Century after century, how many times had these questions been asked? And how had the Church been responding? Many people have wrestled with these questions when faced with the death of someone dearly loved. How many clergy and friends have offered similar words of comfort as I had, with the same confidence based on how they understood the Bible? And that's another question all by itself. How can there be such a difference in understanding death and the hereafter when it comes to this promise of the Christian faith? Is there a single, orthodox Christian belief about the afterlife?

Those questions my mother had asked reflected her quandary, the same dilemma faced by so many Christians. Her Easter faith was easy as long as she only had to think about it using the traditional words of worship. Every Sunday at church, my parents had recited the standard-bearer of our faith, The Apostles' Creed. At the end of the Second Article, they had declared their belief that Jesus would come again someday to preside at the Final Judgment and the Resurrection of the Dead.

But believing salvation is a gift we begin to live in the hereafter required my mom to think about that interval between my dad's death and the future

Second Coming. What state or condition was my dad in following his fatal heart attack? My mom intuitively knew – by her faith in a God who has promised to let nothing, not even death, separate us from Him – that God had already welcomed him home. If by his baptism my dad had become a child of God, then he merely continued life in God's eternal presence, having not been separated from God in death. But that is not what she had been declaring all those years in the words of The Apostles' Creed. So, her questions.

What the Church had taught my parents was far different from my seminary classes and personal insights as a pastor. While I half-listened to Pastor Messner's recitations and prayers, I began the further reflection I knew was necessary.

Following the service, I walked with my mom into the fellowship hall where her friends had prepared a light brunch. I spotted my best friend Andy. I did not tell him I had been protesting his father's affirmation of my mother's Easter. Every word uttered the past hour spoke about a future gift of salvation. Nothing about my dad continuing to enjoy God's eternal presence that he had been experiencing since his baptism. Of course not, because he had not been experiencing God's eternal presence in his here and now.

Andy, who knew intimately of my dad's heart problems, sat down across from me and shared these well-intentioned words: "Bud, I've been thinking about you all weekend. At least now your father is at peace and home with our Lord."

Wait a minute. Does Andy think my dad's immortal soul, separate from his body, is at least home with our Lord? Or does he have something else in mind?

"Andy, you know my dad had arranged for the donation of his body to the UCLA medical center for research, right? And you know he believed his body was nothing more than a mortal prison for his immortal soul. When he died, he believed his immortal soul would survive his death and would be kept safe in heaven until the Second Coming, at which time his immortal soul would be reunited with a new heavenly body. His Resurrection from the Dead would be God's gift of salvation, and by separating his soul from his body, my mom was able to reconcile that time gap between my dad's death and the Second Coming, knowing my dad's soul was at least in the company of Christ."

"I only know, Bud, we aren't able to fully understand all of this. Like the apostle Paul explained, 'Lo! I tell you a mystery. We shall not all sleep, but we shall be changed, in a moment, in the twinkling of an eye, at the last trumpet. For the trumpet will sound, and the dead will be raised imperishable, and we shall be changed. For this perishable nature must put on the imperishable, and this mortal nature must put on immortality.'"

My old friend Andy was forever quick to echo his father's tread-worn theological dogma and orthodoxy. And in the tradition of his father, Andy never wasted a chance to quote Scripture to support his point. Andy had completed seminary eight years ago while I was working a milling machine at my dad's machine shop and then working the yard at Benson Lumber. Maybe pastors resort to Scripture more often after they have been in a parish for a few years. I, on the other hand, had recently completed four years of theological study that raised more questions than answers about my mother's Easter.

"So Andy, back to your condolence, that my dad is at peace and home with our Lord. If our confession of faith directs us to a future day when that last trumpet will sound, how exactly do you explain that my dad is at least home with our Lord?"

Pastor Messner had pulled up his chair to hear what was going on. Out of sheer courtesy in the wake of my dad's death, Andy and his father listened to my theological ruminations. I desperately needed to understand why my dad's Christian faith had meant so little to him over the course of his life.

I wanted to clarify for Pastor Messner what we had been discussing. "Andy, I took your condolence to heart, but as soon as I tried to answer my mother's questions last night, tried to comfort her with some answers that challenged her confession of faith about the Last Day, I realized we have more to consider here than simple condolences we accept as mystery.

You and I both know, Andy, that even though this teaching about immortality has no biblical foundation, many who have questioned this separation of the soul from the body have been suspected of heresy. Didn't help much that the Hebrew concept of *nephesh* – the word for soul, but a word that embodies the fullness of a living being, as in flesh, body, soul, spirit, and heart – was distorted when forced into a Greek construct that described the human soul as our divine and immortal essence separate from the prison of our mortal body. 'An angel in a slot machine' someone once described this belief. That such a notion places less importance on life in the here and now, more importance on life in the hereafter once we have escaped from our body, is what troubles me now about my dad's life."

"I think I know where you're heading here, Bud, but let's be honest about how much sway our seminary study of that intertestamental literature has against Christian piety when it comes to our consoling the bereaved. I know this literature provides some background about how the Greek concept of an immortal soul influenced this Christian belief about the hereafter. But at the time of a loved one's death, Bud, do you think it's appropriate to question this non-biblical doctrine of the separation of body and soul? Who at such a time in their life will care about books found in The Apocrypha written under the widespread influence of Greek thought, books such as Enoch, Wisdom of Solomon, Second and Fourth Maccabees, books that refer to the soul as separate from the body? We do our best to respect the piety of those we serve when we are called to comfort and console them. Isn't always so clear, isn't always so easy."

"Andy, I understand that, but this belief about an immortal soul separate from his mortal body led my dad to think ahead to the hereafter whenever he thought about God. Immortality belonged to the realm of God; his mortal body could not experience any such thing as God's eternal presence. That's why my grandmother had taught my mother her prayer, 'Dear God, make me holy so I can go to heaven.' And many Christians of my dad's generation have shared with me that their here and now life is merely a preparation for the life that finally matters, the life hereafter. They are perfectly content to simply know where they will spend eternity. Our Lutheran tradition, Andy, includes a hymn that speaks about our resurrection '*From the cares which keep us still in prison, living still as in a dungeon, oppressed with sorrow and misgiving, our undertakings are but toils and heart-breakings. Who wouldn't be glad to depart this earthly sadness? Who would want to languish longer in bewailing and in anguish?*' Not exactly one of my favorite hymns."

I needed to memorialize my dad honestly, and I knew I had to revise my mother's Easter to do that. So I continued. "You know, Andy, early American theology contributed to this disconnect between the here and now and the hereafter. Puritans remained on the watch for anyone who may be happy in the here and now, God forbid, and questioned any consolations offered in this life that traditionally are advertised as belonging exclusively to the hereafter. If we focus on life in the here and now, are we, therefore, necessarily less close to God?"

I felt myself shift my energy now toward Pastor Messner. "The Church had taught my dad that God's gift of salvation is the destination, not the journey. My dad had a preliminary relationship with God; he did not have a living relationship with God. His life in the here and now often felt like a life lived in a dungeon, so beset was my dad with toils and troubles. Last night, my mother had asked, 'Do you think Dad has gone home to our Lord?' As if my dad, living in this prison and earthly sadness of the here and now, bewailing and in anguish, was living life away from home. Where is *Immanuel*, Pastor Messner? *God is with us.* Do we wait until death before we experience life with God? What about the Incarnation, God becoming flesh and setting up His tent-home, His tabernacle, living with us in the here and now?"

With every thought I expressed, how I could modify my mother's Easter was becoming clearer. Projecting our salvation out into the future (my dad's answer to my question "When do we begin living God's gift of salvation?") required explanations like that belief about an immortal soul. But I could resolve my mother's Easter quandary – believing in a God Who will not let us go, even in death, but also believing that we do not experience such a loving God until a future Second Coming – by redefining salvation.

"Andy, one of my first purchases at the GTU bookstore in Berkeley was Harvey's *A Handbook of Theological Terms*. This is where I had read that the resurrection of the dead can be spoken of as both a future event as well as one happening now. Our baptism incorporates us into the death and resurrection of Christ, so we are already sharing in the risen life, can already be said to have eternal life. Since my dad was united with God forever at his baptism, why was he waiting until death and some future day before he could live in God's eternal presence? Of course, the apostle Paul still cautioned that the present new life is but a guarantee of the future hope. This would be the already-but-not-yet tension of our baptized life in Christ."

Pastor Messner had been patiently waiting to ask, "Did you read that member's question in *The Lutheran*, Bud? A long-time Lutheran from Wisconsin had written to the section 'Since You Asked' in our denomination's monthly periodical asking the question, 'A member of another denomination said his pastor does not believe the Resurrection occurred or that there will be a Second Coming of Christ. This member says these teachings are not taught in seminaries today. Is this true at Lutheran seminaries?' No, was the reply. 'Our seminaries and pastors are bound by the Lutheran Confessions, which affirm both the Resurrection and God's raising of the dead on the last day. Lutheran seminaries teach that Christian ministry and mission flow from the resurrection of Jesus Christ. It is at the heart of Christian hope. The second coming of Christ also teaches us that we need not fear the decay of this world. Rather, we have confidence that God has the last word.' That is what you were taught at Berkeley, right, Bud?"

Pastor Messner liked to compare his son Andy's theological education at Trinity Lutheran Seminary in Ohio with mine at Pacific Lutheran Theological Seminary in Berkeley. For Pastor Messner, most of America's problems could be blamed on Berkeley and Woodstock. Of course, my dad had been taught about Christ's *Second* Coming, about a raising of the dead on the *last* day, about having confidence that God has the *last* word – all teachings that project God's gift of salvation into the future.

"No, not exactly, Pastor Messner," as I now found myself debating with our Lutheran Confessions. "Christian dogma and orthodoxy and personal piety do not always ask all the questions. How did Bonhoeffer say it? 'I'm afraid the Church has dragged first-century Christianity forward to today without making the necessary stops along the way to reconcile its teachings with contemporary learning.'

I was taught to ask questions about a chronological succession of events based on our concept of time that no longer has meaning beyond our death. A second coming implies an action in time; the word *second* suggests a specific moment in time – after the first, presumably before a third. And so, we end up, as did the apostle Paul when he wrote to the Thessalonians, struggling with the question about who will be around for the second coming. Can a person already dead – no longer in time, no longer part of its passage – experience an action in time? Thus the dead must be raised from the dead, out of their timelessness state, so they can be a part of time's passage again and experience a second coming.

A theologian has suggested, Pastor Messner, that the border of this life we know as death is the same as the border of time itself – beyond which is God's eternal presence, wherein all moments of time converge as one. When we as individuals cross the borderline of time (at different times according to our time-bound condition) and encounter this eternal presence of God, we will appear on the other side at the same moment as everyone else.

Everything in eternity occurs now – the Second Coming, the Final Judgment, and our Resurrection, last things my dad had associated with the Last Day far off in the future.

If my dad had been taught that his baptism had inaugurated life in God's eternal presence, I believe his relationship with God would have been more intimate, his here and now more dependent on a caring and loving God. Don't know, though, that he was ever taught that. My dad believed the only way he could live in God's eternal presence was for his soul to separate from his body after death and be with Christ in heaven until the Second Coming."

"Do you think your time borderline explanation, Bud, is comforting for those who grieve the loss of someone dearly loved?"

"Pastor Messner, you're expressing the same concern as Andy, how my inquiry this morning seems so insensitive when we're trying to console the bereaved. I'm not talking, though, about the *death* of someone dearly loved; I'm talking about the *life* of someone dearly loved! I'm talking about my dad!"

"But be careful, Bud, about erasing that borderline with one broad stroke! We don't cross over it until we die. Our life this side of death has not yet received the divine quality that unites us to God's eternal presence."

"With all due respect, Pastor Messner, in baptism we have received a divine quality that unites us to God's eternal presence in the here and now. Are you familiar with Father Pierre Benoit of the Biblical School of Jerusalem? Baptism, and not death, is what he considered the definitive moment, the reception of the fullness of God's promise. When we are united in baptism with the risen Christ, we begin living in God's eternal presence, a life that cannot be interrupted by death. Benoit insists on the efficacy of our already initiated union, our new life with Christ received by baptism."

"Bud, do you think adding this already-but-not-yet tension to peoples' lives is helping them find God's peace? As you said yourself, the apostle Paul cautioned us that our present new life is only a guarantee of the future hope."

"Can we live in God's eternal presence without resolving that tension? Yes, Andy, I believe we can. What about that old favorite Easter hymn we sing? *'The strife is o'er, the battle done; The victory of life is won; The song of triumph has begun. Alleluia!'* Has the victory been won or not? I think I'll share in my Easter sermon from now on Bonhoeffer's poem from prison, 'Who Am I?' Maybe you know that poem, Andy. I never heard about it growing up; I learned about it last year. Makes me think about all the questions my dad had in his daily battles with life in the here and now, all the questions that mocked him. I wish he could have found enough peace to share those final words with Bonhoeffer, to know God claimed him as His own. But my dad was never taught that about his baptism.

Bonhoeffer had asked, 'Or is something within me still like a beaten army, fleeing in disorder from victory already achieved?' Yes, I would answer. Victory already achieved is what my dad was baptized into – Easter! No qualifier to add here – no 'already, but not yet.' Victory already achieved!"

I was trying to rework my mother's Easter while still honoring the tradition that had authorized my ordination, the faith I had inherited. The day we are baptized, I was proposing, we begin to live God's gift of salvation. Not easy to set aside what I had inherited from my mother, so I was trying to find an acceptable Easter modification that stressed salvation in the here and now.

"Andy, I will never know if living in the tension of the already-but-not-yet would have been helpful for my dad. I believe though that the 'already' would have at least provided him with a closer relationship with God than his answer to my question – his belief that he would begin living God's gift of salvation the day Jesus Christ finally returned for the Resurrection of the Dead."

"Hey, didn't mean to debate with you now, Caine. Just wanted to offer my condolence, that's all. I sure loved your dad. What a fine gentleman he was."

Andy and I debated about a lot of things, but no debating about that.

12:45 AM. My evening with all of the photos and memories was wearing down my heart. But not knowing what Friday had in store for me, I still had trouble closing my eyes. What was that long ago night like for you, Jesus of Nazareth? You were wrestling with questions too.

Chapter 14

George

When I think about my dad's bankruptcy, I try to avoid using my grandmother's "Be Still, My Soul" language.

Disappointment.

Grief.

Fear.

Sorrow.

Tears.

Life can be miserable enough without thinking about those words to describe it. I should know.

I wish I wasn't so easily given to writing off my present life. But I find myself hoping less and less for some satisfaction in life this side of death, more and more for my grandfather's heavenly home. Sometimes Kennedy's voice still inspires me to think about taming the savageness of man and making gentle the life of this world. Most of the time, though, I'm listening to my Grandpa Koehler and Luther. We don't need to chase after temporary comforts or concerns, they remind me. We're pilgrims here on earth. We only need to think about our permanent home God has provided for us.

Like schizophrenia, two opposing thoughts, both acceptable and unacceptable at once.

My dad's contracts with the government are a small part of that military-industrial complex that had created so much fear in me. But I don't consider my job working for him a sellout. We're only making the parts.

I have asked myself, "So what difference does it make if you think about life like Grandpa Koehler and Luther?" I feel out of step, though, with my own generation. Everybody's obsessed with their own glorious selves, thinking only about themselves, and doing whatever they feel like doing. And I'm trying to figure out why I have to think so much each day about my self.

What's so troubling about feeling so troubled about my life right now is the sick frustration that I kind of know what's wrong with me but I can't do anything about it anyway. I'm told I'm supposed to accept this condition. That's what's so crazy. Could be worse, I'm told. Which isn't too helpful.

Here's a bad trip, reading Ward's novel, *The Snake Pit*, about how my disorder would have been treated by society thirty years ago. The old baseball guy, Mr. Thorazine shuffle himself, gave me a copy the last time I was at rehab. I couldn't get back to today fast enough! Agitation, shock treatment, therapies. What the hell? If you weren't already insane, living in one of those institutions, it was only a matter of time.

I didn't like doing this, but I was asked by some government people to tell them what I knew about some questionable stuff going on at Norwalk. Seems these documentary filmmakers decided to blow the whistle on hospital staff who were coercively drugging patients with the sedatives Chlorpromazine and Prolixin. My little interview was cut from their film, *Hurry Tomorrow*, although Walter Cronkite used parts of the film in his report about patient deaths at Metropolitan and Camarillo State Hospitals.

I can't think about God anymore the way I think I used to think about Him. My schizophrenia is a mental disorder, so thinking about God one day may not make too much sense the next. Maybe more people suffer from my disorder than we think!

Add to my schizophrenia my fear of living on the eve of destruction and my fear that we seem incapable of taming the savageness of man, and you're just asking for it! My schizophrenia has doubled my fears, but then I begin to fear that maybe I'm not afraid enough. Could it be?

I have relied on my beer and pot to provide a detour for such introspection, an alternate route around my daily existence. Whenever I think about my dad and my grandpa, I drink more beer and smoke more weed. I don't like thinking about their two viewpoints, and I don't like thinking about the fact that I hate thinking about them. I suffer from headaches when I'm not stoned.

Growing up, I had tried like crazy to make sense of my childhood faith that makes no sense in my adult world. I'm supposed to live with misery I cannot shed as long as this life lasts. And growing up, I had tried like crazy to make sense of my eighth-grade American history story that makes no sense in a country headed for destruction. Reality keeps updating my scrambled brain, but my schizophrenia won't let me adjust my life to accommodate those updates. Feeling kind of trapped most of the time. Like living in a straitjacket.

As my life this side of death grows scarier, though, what's the point of debating Luther against Kennedy? And if you are discovering you are too severely damaged to deal with life every day, and every year I live I'm discovering my country is also severely damaged (same disorder as me!), my mother's faith is not too helpful, seeing as how a Savior can't save me or my country from schizophrenia.

I remember that dark night in Shelton, Nebraska, traveling with Jack when that tall, lanky carnie fella in a gallon hat stopped his car on the wrong side of the road and came over to us. I remember him asking, "You boys going to get somewhere, or just going?" Jack and I didn't understand his question, but it was a damned good one. Jack wasn't much interested in his offer to work and make a buck, said that he was going as fast as he could and didn't think he had the time. Seems like I'm going as fast as I can too.

Like Jack said, though, we begin life so sweet and innocent accepting everything our mother tells us. Like when my mother introduced me to those ladies at the tomb of Jesus, holding my hand all the time so I would think Jesus was holding my hand. But then comes that goddamn day of the Laodiceans when you finally grow up, when you realize how messed up you are, living a nightmare life called schizophrenia from which you can't wake up and over which you have no control.

I was fourteen years old when my Old Testament prophet P. F. Sloan wrote his poem "Eve of Destruction." He was nineteen-years-old, and the poem he was writing was the prayer he was praying. But I'm not sure he expected God to answer.

The more I looked around me, the more it scared me. It scared me a lot. Growing up had been scary enough. By the time I turned twenty-five, I was too scared to keep looking around. Life was getting darker by the day. Only nobody was there to stand by me as promised.

I don't know how long this eve will last. Does anybody? Will I be living on the *eve of destruction* for the rest of my life? I know now that Daniel Ellsberg tried to convince America we were on the eve of destruction in 1973, ten years after JFK and the Cuban missile crisis. In spite of lies and deception, I learned that Nixon and Kissinger were ready to use nuclear weapons on China and Vietnam. Fortunately for the American public, Ellsberg courageously exposed the Pentagon Papers. In addition to that discussion about the possible use of nuclear weapons, we learned our leaders had discarded peace offers and intentionally escalated the war. How powerful was our military-industrial complex?

When your schizophrenic brain is full of *eve of destruction* fear and failed reforms to tame the savageness of man, the last thing you need to hear is news of your country's scandal and shame. "Dirty tricks" they were called. A break-in of the other party's offices, and even though the burglars were caught, the White House denied the allegations and proceeded to cover it all up. Our president refused to release secret tape recordings but was eventually forced by the Supreme Court to turn them over. In the middle of all this, the vice-president pleaded guilty to tax evasion on bribes he had taken while serving as governor of Maryland. Articles of impeachment were filed against the president, and the special prosecutor learned from one of those tape recordings that the president had known about the Watergate burglary long before he admitted it and was guilty of obstructing justice, a federal crime.

This is what I'm talking about when I'm talking about America's schizophrenia. Can our leaders honestly lay claim to logical thinking here? Was there some question about what was real and what was not? Nixon resigned in August of 1974, and his newly appointed Vice-President Gerald Ford quickly assured the American people that "our long national nightmare is over."

No, it wasn't. It wasn't over for me.

Ford named Nelson Rockefeller his vice president. For the first time in American history, neither our president nor our vice-president had been elected.

At least I had Sloan to thank for helping others understand what I was feeling about myself every day. Imagine the burden of a mental disorder like schizophrenia and trying to live every day in a world that's suffering from the same thing. Nothin' much seems real anymore if you and the world around you are both dislocated from reality.

Medical professionals like Dr. Cutlip told my mother I was losing touch with reality. "What the hell reality are you talking about?" I asked her and the psychiatrist. "How can my perception of reality be distorted if I'm paying more attention than most everybody else to the lies we all live with every day? What, am I the only person in America who is feeling a little frightened, anxious, and confused? My own little personal panic? Am I the only guy in America right now who depends on drugs and alcohol? Am I the only one self-medicating? You're worried about my bizarre behavior or irrational beliefs. Have you looked around here lately? 'It's bound to scare you boy.' And because people can't always make sense of where I'm coming from, I'm the one diagnosed with schizophrenia. And I can't be cured, right? How about America? Can America be cured?"

For America and me, drugs seemed like a good hiding place from our disorders. Some hiding places darker than others, some too dark. Too dark for my schizophrenic friend Emmett Grogan who walked the talk of his Digger Papers by feeding the hungry gathered around Haight-Ashbury. But at thirty-five years old, he collapsed on a New York subway car, had suffered from a heart attack most likely due to his chronic heroin use. Such a daily habit is pretty much committing suicide in slow motion.

Thanks to my schizophrenia, didn't need much more than my beer and pot. Had my own built-in trip every day just wakin' up. LSD's effects have nothing on a genuine disorder like schizophrenia. Altered thinking was my daily walk, hallucinations my companion, and time of day was anybody's guess. Hard to take my emotional temperature because my emotions refused to hang around for long in one place.

Of all the goddamn timing, our country's finally coming of age after two hundred plus years, apparently troubled by the onset of a schizophrenic disorder at the same time Dr. Cutlip is diagnosing me, and I'm supposed to figure out the best way to survive all this crap happening around me.

Jim Jones of Indianapolis had convinced his disenchanted followers to flee all of this crap for a new promised land in the sweltering hot jungle of Guyana. Finally a sanctuary from the torments of life in the states. Called this haven Jonestown. But in the end, it wasn't life in the states from which they had fled. It was life itself. And there was only one way to escape life. In November of 1978, some 914 followers poisoned themselves using cyanide mixed with Kool-Aid. So much for the promise of America.

155

It's always Luther's invading Turks or some variation. Year after year, our Cold War nuclear posturing with the Soviet Union reminds me those falling dominoes are getting closer to knocking me down.

In November of 1979, an Air Force technician inside Cheyenne Mountain had mistakenly transferred software that alerted NORAD's computers of a simulated Soviet offensive. Expect a massive missile attack from Soviet submarines off the West Coast, warheads beginning to hit American targets within five or six minutes. Our U.S. air-defense system launched fighters to look for signs of this Soviet aggression. An investigation following revealed hardcore drug abuse by some of the security force responsible for protecting our nerve center. This played right into the hands of an America fully convinced a nuclear war was conceivable.

While we took a breath, we learned of the Soviet Union military build up and invasion of Afghanistan. So we withdrew from the Salt II Agreement that limited nuclear missiles and launchers and then we boycotted the 1980 Olympic Games in Moscow.

I still can't figure out why we call the Cold War cold. What the hell, does anybody truly think that living in constant fear of war is any less stressful than war itself? In the autumn of 1983, the Soviets had shot down a South Korean civilian airliner. We were deploying intermediate-range and ground-launched cruise missiles in Europe. Earlier that year, President Reagan had called the Soviet Union an "evil empire." Nothing had changed since I was a kid.

Then, in November of 1983, the Soviet leadership suspected that a NATO nuclear weapons exercise was a cover for a nuclear surprise attack by the United States. A Soviet air force unit in Poland responded to those maneuvers by transferring nuclear weapons from storage to aircraft.

A year later, the Soviets boycotted our Olympic Games in Los Angeles. Seemed never ending.

Here's my diagnosis of America while I'm sittin' in Dr. Cutlip's office. When my brother Bud and I were visiting with those empty tomb ladies in the 1950s, America was taking a breather after weathering the Great Depression and the Second World War. But we're too restless a people to linger in recovery mode any longer than is necessary. Don't know which came first, but our American Empire was facing some internal upheaval at the same time as our American identity was undergoing a makeover. How

America was thinking about herself seemed disconnected. Like my mental disorder schizophrenia. Our 1960s activists had a difficult time changing an America so fearful of her future, and not nearly enough California sunshine to go around.

The measuring stick for figuring out how crazy I was becoming changed all the time according to how crazy the world around me was becoming.

My medication was supposed to help me climb back to the top of reality to escape from my dark hole of schizophrenia, and up on top, reality's as schizophrenic as I am. At least I could be treated for my schizophrenia. Treated, but not cured.

The crazy world described by P. F. Sloan lives in isolation from itself, and those who raise a voice of suspicion are silenced as mentally disordered themselves. Sloan's world has trouble thinking clearly enough to make reasonable decisions. So do I. Sloan's world can be unpredictable. So can I. The people of Sloan's world have trouble relating to one another. So do I. Sometimes Sloan's world believes things that are not real or true. So do I. I hate myself for living some of those hypocrisies of Sloan's world. Don't bother to care about your next-door neighbor but be sure you say grace before you eat. So I don't say grace anymore.

My medication, though, plays tricks on me, makes me think I'm independent and well, at which point I feel no further need for my antipsychotic drug. But my mother figured this out. So an injection every three to four weeks dispenses my Haloperidol over time. But even at that, it was a herculean task to convince me of the need for my shot. None of my family could understand the side effects, including myself. One day, leave me alone is all I wanted. The next, too lonely for my own good. I was gaining weight like crazy. Even I couldn't keep up with my changing moods each day.

Honest to God, I don't know which was worse. Accepting the reality that I could not cope with life without my medication, or when I felt better enough to self-adjust my medication which then threw me into a relapse. My symptoms came back or got worse. As things around me got more and more screwed up, sometimes I thought my condition was returning me to normal. But as that *eve of destruction* clock keeps ticking away, it's becoming clear to me I won't be experiencing any more normals in my life. I'm living in a cold, dark basement while everybody else is upstairs in the warm comfort of the family room.

How did we get to this national mental disorder? How come America had to unravel at the same time as me?

Reagan's election in 1980 had promised us a return to the good life, promised us we could make all the money we wanted. Like Gordon Gekko said, "Greed is good."

What the hell, I wasn't making any money. Most women, African-Americans, Hispanic Americans, Native Americans, and young Americans weren't making any money in the 1980s. And we hadn't made much progress when it came to taming the savageness of man.

Our country's history sure makes it easy on kids who are supposed to learn it. We keep repeating ourselves, so if you didn't understand what happened back then, chances are you can learn all about it when it happens again. And again, and again.

What I'm saying is, it's not easy to cope with my schizophrenia when I'm surrounded by America's schizophrenia on all sides. All day long, my reality feels disconnected from the way I think things should be, and my country's reality feels the same way. How many Americans have had to experience that same feeling? How they have been living is not how America had declared their lives should be.

Take what has happened to my friend Dwayne and his family. I worked with him at my dad's shop, along with Razman and Sam, all three young black men from local high schools who were interested in the tool and die making trade. I'm glad my dad decided to mentor these guys. I sure liked working with them.

I'm familiar with what happened to these guys' families. Talk about a disjointed foundation for our nation. I wrote a paper for one of my U.S. History classes at Cal State about how Jefferson had condemned slavery in his original draft of our Declaration of Independence. But South Carolina wasn't signing on to any such nonsense, its entire aristocratic economy built on slave labor. So those sections were omitted for the sake of all thirteen colonies coming together, knowing full well we'd have to address this eventually. Our Judeo-Christian tradition didn't exactly stand up against slavery at that time. Of course, that would catch up with us decades later when South Carolina opened fire on Ft. Sumter to begin the Civil War. The North smashed the South, but the South disguised slavery with Black Codes and Jim Crow laws. And then it's a hundred years later, it's 1965, and we're still looking to tame the savageness of man.

Dwayne's family can't win for losing. You're condemned for milking the welfare system, and you're condemned for making something of yourselves and moving into white neighborhoods and schools. Their lives don't seem any better since the Watts Riot in 1965, the worst urban riot in twenty years after two white policemen scuffled with a black motorist suspected of drunk driving. One more incident of racially motivated abuse by the police. Residents of Watts, embittered after years of economic and political isolation, took to looting stores, torching buildings, and beating whites as snipers fired at police and firefighters all over South Central Los Angeles. Five days of violence before the National Guardsmen could restore some temporary order. I say "temporary" because the rioting continued elsewhere, continues to this day.

I listened carefully when Dwayne explained to me why it was necessary to think beyond the non-violent protests. "I couldn't possibly get it," he said. I reminded him of Muhammad Ali's non-violent protest a year before the Watts Riot when the WBA stripped him of his title after he refused a call to serve in the United States Army. And Dwayne reminded me that, at the time, few sympathized with his defiance and opposition to the Vietnam War. I reminded Dwayne of that non-violent protest by Olympic medalists Tommie Smith and John Carlos in 1968, how they had raised their clenched fists above their heads in a black power salute while our national anthem played to honor their victory. He reminded me of the outrage that had followed against black protestors like them.

I reminded Dwayne about how third-grader Linda Brown and her family had tried to make a difference using the system. How Rosa Parks had tried to make a difference using the system. How black students all over the South have protested through sit-ins and kneel-ins.

"But has our life been made gentler by all of this?" Dwayne asked me. "For how long are people supposed to struggle and march against hatred and racism? 'Black pride,' George, is what it's all about. Like James Brown declared, 'Say it loud. I'm black and I'm proud.' I told you before, you can't possibly get it."

"A lot of Americans, Dwayne, are asking, 'Has anybody here seen my old friends Abraham, John, Martin, and Bobby?' Can anyone tell us where they've gone? We all loved the things they stood for. Didn't they try to tame the savageness of man and make gentle the life of this world? How come it seems the good die young?"

But Dwayne asked me, "How come no one's asking, 'Anybody here seen my old friend Malcolm X?' Two days before his assassination, he prophetically had proclaimed, 'It is a time for martyrs now, and if I am to be one, it will be for the cause of brotherhood. That's the only thing that can save this country.' In the fight against discrimination, violence might be necessary. Abraham thought the same thing, so why don't we ask about Malcolm X?

And why don't we ask about Amiri Baraka? Because his poem 'Black People' called for violence against those who were responsible for injustice and racism? Like the Newark Rebellion when twenty-six people died, twelve hundred injured. You know his infamous call to action, George. 'All the stores will open if you say the magic words, *Up against the wall, mother-fucker, this is a stick up!*'"

Dwayne was right. I couldn't possibly get it. How do people live in two different realities, I would like to know? I'm having some trouble myself.

This kind of fragmented and disjointed American story goes on and on for every group not included in that original group of white, male, over twenty-one, property owners who founded our country.

I'm forever updating those lyrics for Sloan's "Eve of Destruction." Seems like no shortage of frustratin' crazy stuff! Am I the only one? Don't think so.

How about this for crazy stuff? You're old enough to go to Vietnam and get killed, but not old enough to choose the president who might send you there. Well, we got that changed, right? The twenty-sixth amendment lowered the voting age to eighteen. Now you're old enough to kill and to vote. Now you can at least vote for the president who'll get you killed. Don't stop going to war, but lower the voting age to remove that crazy disconnect!

Lately, though, instead of "Eve of Destruction," I've been singing one of my mother's favorites. She even sings along with me sometimes.

> *Jesus loves the little children*
> *All the children of the world*
> *Black and yellow, red and white*
> *They're all precious in His sight*
> *Jesus loves the little children of the world*
>
> *Whether you're rich or whether you're poor*
> *It matters not to Him*

He remembers where you're going
Not where you've been

If your heart is troubled
Don't worry, don't you fret
He knows that you have heard His call
And he won't forget

All around the world tonight
His children rest assured
That He will watch and He will keep us
Safe and secure

Come to think of it, I don't want my mother to let go of my hand. I don't want Jesus to let go of my hand either. But that's the problem. Jesus loves the *little* children. Once you grow up, Good Fucking Luck!

CHAPTER 15

Henry
10 April 1998
Good Friday

After our coffee, bagels, and melon fruit bowl, Denise and I greeted other early risers walking the path south from the Great Hall, including the faunae living in habitat zones we seldom thought about outside of this place called Sunriver. Revisiting memories has a way of mending or breaking your heart – not much in between, it would seem.

We both knew this would not be an easy day.

This path runs parallel to the fairway of the ninth hole until it meanders around to a small bridge covering the Sun River tributary – the only way to get to the ninth tee from the tight par-three eighth hole tucked away between homes and towering ponderosa pines. This path hadn't changed much in twenty-eight years, a blink of the eye for Mother Nature. We paused to watch a family of geese take their morning swim across the pond-like stillness of this canal. Denise placed her left hand on the rail of the bridge, her wedding band reflection shimmering on the surface of the moss-colored water below.

"Hey, that's like the picture I took of your engagement ring at Disneyland. Ya' remember? We looked at it last night."

Of course she did.

How many times have I stood by this ninth hole at South Meadows imagining one more round of golf with my three best men? That we broke our ninth green promise to each other would be reason enough to refrain from talking about it over the course of our everyday lives. And so we hadn't, which exacerbated our feelings of betrayal. I will never know how much our failure to keep that promise contributed to what happened the past ten years. I only know we had promised each other we would never let such a thing happen. But it did.

Delivered a well-received eulogy once for an avid golfer who most likely had never stepped foot in a church other than on his wedding day. Had never stepped foot in the church I served. I had continued to adjust my theology and preaching – reading, reflecting, listening, studying – to emphasize less and less the promise of a life hereafter and more and more the possibility of a life fulfilled in the here and now. "Is there life after birth?" I kept asking.

The eulogies I prepared for families reflected this theological persuasion. I increasingly modified the Lutheran liturgy meant to provide consolation for the bereaved by spending the better part of the funeral recalling the life of the deceased. This often took hours and hours of interview time before the funeral – time I believe was helpful for the families I interviewed – and offered a more personal and lasting memory than any collection of prayer-book recitals or Scripture readings.

I credit my four years of debate team at San Gabriel High School. Individual competition like Impromptu Speaking, requiring students to deliver a credible speech after only thirty minutes to prepare a topic about some axiom or adage or proverb, helped me hone this skill for collecting information and then presenting it as though I had known it all my life. One of my better gifts for ministry, I was told, and before long, people outside of our regular church membership were asking if I could possibly officiate at their relative's funeral.

"Pastor Caine," a forty-something real estate broker asked, "you don't know me, but I attended a funeral a couple of weeks ago for a dear friend of mine, and the family can't thank you enough for your comforting eulogy. You have such a wonderful way of helping people deal with their loss, creating a personal remembrance for them. My father died yesterday morning after battling bone cancer for two years. He wasn't what you would call a churchgoer. I frankly don't know what he believed about God. All I know for sure is that he treated my mom and us with love and respect, and was about as good a friend as you could ever imagine. If there were any way you could deliver a eulogy for him, we would be so grateful to you."

"Yes, I could do that, and I'm sorry for your loss."

Ironic how my evolving theological emphasis on the here and now part of the Gospel has led me to create those keepsake biographies of the deceased. Celebrating a life lived in the here and now (what we know about) is a more honest ritual than our conjectures and speculations about life in the hereafter (what we don't know about). And so I found myself officiating at more and more funerals, often dealing intimately with death and final arrangements two or three times a week. As my clergy reputation grew for stressing the here and now, my calendar was filling up with dates at a cemetery!

Besides being a gentleman, a faithful husband, and a loving father, Wally Hastings was also a scratch golfer in his day and still claimed a four handicap even in his sixties. Wally adored the game of golf, I was told. From amateur tournaments when he was young, to men's tournaments all over the state of Oregon, to his own golf-club repair shop in his garage (but never charged his friends for any repairs), he could not get enough of golf. Wally didn't miss too many eighteen-hole days out at his club after retiring from an insurance company – until his chemotherapy appointments at sixty-seven. Within a year, all he had left of the game was a chance to talk about it, and his family just listened. And so did I as they shared his golf stories with me.

It didn't take me any Impromptu Speaking thirty minutes to settle on a theme for the eulogy I would deliver. I walked the over-flowing funeral chapel crowd around an eighteen-hole course of Wally's life, each hole representing some significant challenge or episode, some holes (especially when he birdied or drained a difficult putt) depicting the absolute delight with which he approached each day. A birdie four on the par-five longest hole was the result of a perfect fairway three-wood shot to the middle of the green – representing his valor and love of country serving in World War II. With his positive attitude and spirit in spite of the bone cancer that tried to interfere with his passion for life, he took a solid five on the final par-five hole. I remember that eulogy to this day, and so does his family.

I like the game of golf; the game, however, does not like me. The golf gods appreciate my faithfulness, but they seldom show me any favor. A round of golf imitates life. Walking eighteen holes is walking the ups and downs of life – some holes more difficult than others, some more deceptive than others, and some downright nasty, but each hole a reasonable facsimile of what we face in life each day, the course of life with all of its challenges, pitfalls, and accomplishments. Unfairness and bad breaks abound on both courses.

Ever since our wedding day, golf and Sunriver have been synonymous for me. Both stimulate reflection and perspective. Golf is a game that allows generous time to share life with each other. Playing a five-hour round of golf requires only about an hour of actual activity with a club in hand; the rest of the time is for walking, thinking, visiting, and thinking some more.

Most of the thoughtful axioms about golf also apply to life: attitude can make all the difference, some rounds (some days) are meant to turn out better than others, practice makes perfect (well, almost), and never, ever, give up! Golf is all about extreme focus; so also is life. Bobby Jones once quipped, "Competitive golf is played mainly on a five-and-a-half-inch course between your ears." One golf commentator likes to remind his listeners it's better to acknowledge an errant drive off the tee-box of a par four hole, take a short shot out of the rough back onto the middle of the fairway, accept the bogey five, and "Get out of Dodge!" Accept and learn from our mistakes, and move on.

Without a doubt over the years, I have more scorecards from the South Meadows course than any other. Renting a comfortable home here at Sunriver costs about the same as an hour with a therapist, but the rent is good for forty-eight hours. Our family brings everything to Sunriver. Here's our typical list:

- memories in a scrapbook from our previous visits
- Denise's one-of-a-kind potato salad for our BBQ
- a batch of her world-renowned chocolate chip cookies
- a good read
- our favorite board games (Yahtzee, Scrabble, Trivial Pursuit)
- movies: *Lonesome Dove*, *Legends of the Fall*, *Dances With Wolves*, and *The Mission*
- CDs: U-2, Oldies But Goodies (60s and 70s)
- bikes to ride on the miles and miles of paved bike paths (Sunriver *is* bicycling)
- swimming suits
- our golf clubs, of course

And whatever problem has been contributing to the latest headache in life, we bring that too, and miracle of miracles, whatever it is has lost its punch by the time we spend a few days here. Sunriver has become a kind of home for our family because we have moved too many times to call any other place home. We always feel healthier and at peace with ourselves after our visit here. We call Sunriver our sanctuary.

I can walk off the green of the short par three fourth hole with a three-putt bogey, convince myself I will never do that again, and feel wholly renewed as a person. Every time I golf here, I expect my score will be lower than the time before; of course, that seldom happens, as it rarely happens in life. Most often, I don't even land the ball on that green in one shot! That is why the game of golf is such a superb guide for reflection about life; golf mirrors the absurdity of our existence by its juxtaposition of extreme silliness (counting the number of times you swipe a stick at a ball until it goes in a hole!) with a long list of well-established rules and revered traditions. Example: even golf's *Caddyshack* exclusions tell us more about the snobbery behind our own mask of social niceties than about country-club life itself. One course I played had posted a sign high above its elaborate brick entrance gate: PUBLIC ONLY!

> Andy's favorite golf joke:
> A young man nervously closes the confessional booth door at St. Timothy's Catholic Church.
> Young man: "Father, forgive me, for I have sinned."
> Father O'Flaherty: "Yes, my son, tell me about this."
> Young man: "Playing golf with my buddies this morning, I broke the Second Commandment. I took the Lord's Name in vain."
> Father O'Flaherty: "How did this happen."
> Young man: "It happened on the first hole. I drove my ball, a terrible slice, deep into the woods beyond the out-of-bounds stakes."
> Father O'Flaherty: "Is that when you took the Lord's Name in vain?"
> Young man: "No, no, I couldn't believe it, but a squirrel came running out of the woods with my ball in its mouth and dropped it in the middle of the fairway."

Father O'Flaherty: "Wonderful, so when did you take the Lord's Name in vain?"

Young man: "Well, I struck my five iron well enough, plenty of club to carry the pond in front of the green, my ball arcing beautifully down to the middle of the green when a hawk swooped from high above, snatched my ball in mid-air, flew back over the pond and dropped it in the water."

Father O'Flaherty: "I can imagine your frustration. So that's when you took the Lord's Name in vain."

Young man: "No, Father, because almost miraculously, my ball emerged from the water on the back of an old turtle slowly making its way up onto the green where my ball rolled off to settle a foot from the hole."

Father O'Flaherty: "Don't tell me you missed a goddamn twelve-inch putt?"

Stopped playing golf with my two sons for a few years. Too much cussing and swearing, as if Jesus Christ had anything to do with their misread putt or their out-of-balance quick swing. They thought I was bluffing when I first mentioned my threat, but they came around to appreciate the creative designs of courses we had the privilege to play. Golf courses meant for our pleasure, not for our distress.

Our wedding anniversary weekend – and hoped for groom's reunion – falls every year on the same weekend as The Masters golf tournament from Augusta, Georgia, like it sometimes falls on the changing date of Easter weekend, like this weekend in 1998. That was a big deal on my wedding day, The Masters Golf Tournament.

The four of us had promised each other we would watch this tournament together every year as a way of preserving our own little corner of my wedding day – as if we thought the celebration of my wedding day could be parceled out into convenient little corners. Pat Summerall's CBS coverage in those days only included the last six holes at Augusta, but the whole tournament was grand enough that it lent a hint of grandness to our newly formed foursome. The Masters that year resulted in an eighteen-hole playoff on Monday after Billy Casper and Gene Littler both finished at nine under par Sunday afternoon. Casper shot a sixty-nine to win it, but the four of us were already off in our different directions by that time. Three-time winner Jack Nicklaus finished at minus four and four-time winner Arnold Palmer finished at plus seven. Last year, a twenty-one-year-old golfing phenomenon named Tiger Woods stunned the world of golf and Augusta country club life with a record-setting tournament victory of twelve strokes over his closest competitor.

I couldn't help overhearing the conversation of a foursome waiting for the frost delay, enjoying their breakfast outside the pro-shop. "Did we say OK to a front-nine mulligan (a breakfast mulligan), or are we taking a mulligan on both nines? Did we say a gimme putt was any putt exactly within a foot from the hole, or roughly within a foot from the hole?"

I can imagine a manual for the game of golf like that manual for mental disorders, the Diagnostic and Statistical Manual of Mental Disorders. Maybe the golf manual could evaluate all the crazy ways we play this crazy game of golf. I don't mean with our clubs; I mean with our heads. Like customer golf – a mulligan here, a mulligan there. A mulligan is a do-over that doesn't count toward your score. You don't have to tap in a gimme putt; you can pick it up as if it's a given you would have made it anyway. So many disorders. No wonder a foursome gathers for drinks at the nineteenth hole (bar) to celebrate and commiserate how they played their round. Golf is a crazy game.

Life can be just as crazy. According to the DSM-IV, if we've got a heartbeat, odds are good we're living with some undiagnosed mental disorder.

The psychiatric bible of mental diagnoses is one way we choose to define ourselves. Is that weird, or are we? If they want to get paid for treating us, shrinks use the codes to bill our insurance company. With each new edition, the number of mental disorders has multiplied. More than three hundred mental disorders are now listed, more than three times the number in the first edition published in 1952. It now includes the "Disorder of Written Expression" which afflicts people who can't write well. And a "Mathematics Disorder" (code 315.1) can now justify those low SAT math scores that kept you out of the Ivy League. Is crazy normal then? Is the DSM a reflection of the growing trend in our society to pathologize everything? Any human condition or behavior we can think of is a sign of a possible mental disorder. There is even a category for those occasions when no other category seems to apply – "Unspecified Mental Disorder, nonpsychotic" (Code 300.9).

What would such a manual look like for our Christian faith? How would we categorize our disorders? Is our reliance on a Sunday school faith to sustain us in the darkness of night a Christian disorder? Is our self-reliance a Christian disorder? What about our two different personalities – the one that expresses our true feelings, or the persona we present to the world?

That foursome I overheard outside the pro shop decided they could take a mulligan on both nines. What does "taking a mulligan" look like in real life? Is that called God's grace? Could taking a mulligan in life prevent someone from taking their own life?

CHAPTER 16

Karl

I don't know how those fine young men spent their Easter morning in Lam Dong Province. Some may have attended a worship service, some not. It doesn't matter, because what happened to them the next day didn't care either way. I attended a worship service, but I would not disparage their memories by suggesting the message I heard that morning had anything to do with their deaths at the hands of Viet Cong guerillas.

Our ultimate sacrifice in the war was compared with that of Jesus on the cross. Both sacrifices substituted one life for the lives of many. Couldn't help but ask, though, "Why is anyone's sacrifice in Jerusalem or Vietnam required to ensure life for others?" Seems kind of primitive and barbaric to me now, this whole idea of Christ our Passover lamb, hanged on a cross to die in my place, His blood shed for me so God would "pass over" and spare me from death, the penalty for my sins. All this is based on an ancient story about God slaughtering children in Egypt because the Pharaoh was so stubborn after nine plagues and would not let God's people go.

Those eleven soldiers who were slaughtered the day after Easter in 1969 were part of Company B, so I didn't know them well. I did visit with them years later at The Wall (Panel 27W, Lines 28 through 33) where I finally shared my doubts and questions about what we stood for and that sacrifice we were called to make. They didn't have any answers either. Nor did the other seventeen hundred soldiers of our 173rd Brigade whose names are inscribed on The Wall.

I have tried hard to avoid thinking about any of this. After Nam, most people didn't want to hear me think about it, and most everyone seemed pretty satisfied with how they already thought about it anyway. Finding a logical explanation for why some soldiers died and some did not reminds me of my quest to figure out why my mom died when she was only thirty-one. At least for my mom, I could suspect Mrs. Eddy's Christian Science might have had some unfortunate influence on how my mom sought treatment for her cancer. For my fellow eleven soldiers killed the day after Easter, I had to simply accept the insanity of our involvement in Vietnam. But here we go again. I was surrounded by death that got buried under layers of deceit and secrecy. And much like my quest to understand my mother's death, I didn't realize at the time how much I didn't know.

I'm grateful for those who dared to write about what we endured. I'd have no idea how little my ultimate sacrifice would have meant if I had not read Halberstam's *The Best and the Brightest*. Beginning with JFK's administration, our wrongheaded foreign policy had led us straight down a dead-end path to Vietnam. I'm grateful for Michael Herr's *Dispatches* because he brought home to America what many of us chose to leave behind in the Nam. I'm grateful for O'Brien, for Myers, and for Downs. These writers helped me remember what I was trying to forget about Vietnam.

Honoring a family legacy is not easy, especially when someone in the family doesn't believe you're capable enough. My mother would have supported me like she had believed in my dad when he did not always believe in himself. My enlistment meant I would be gone from the mill for two years. If things went well for Benson Lumber, Eva could use that as evidence to prove I wasn't needed after all. But I was gambling I could make up for that absence by enlisting in the same unit as my dad. To walk in his footsteps might prove my readiness as a young man to assume greater responsibility for our family business.

But that is not how I felt after my first week in the Nam. This was not my dad's regiment anymore, and this sure wasn't my dad's war. Still a young man's adventure, but maybe there's such a thing as too young. At nineteen years old, we were more gullible, more easily led, still inexperienced enough to buy into the required myths, still immature enough to buy into our own invincibility. Always plenty of volunteers. At nineteen, we didn't know any better. The danger we faced each day from one another was no less terrifying than the danger we faced from Charlie. Hand out a truckload of lethal ordnance to a bunch of teenagers? You're kidding, right? I was the average age of the American soldier in Vietnam. In my dad's war, the average age of an American soldier was twenty-six.

Hard to compare my dad's war with Vietnam. I'm trying to imagine him all gung-ho on his way to the Philippines in 1944 knowing the war's outcome was hopeless. Knowing that half of America was against the whole thing anyway, against fighting the Japanese who had attacked Pearl Harbor or against fighting Hitler who had attacked all of Europe. After the Tet Offensive in 1968, America began in earnest to prepare herself for the inevitable prospect that the whole Vietnam effort was all fucked up. Might have only been nineteen and gullible, but the senselessness of our sacrifice was turning Vietnam into a psychological quagmire. No space on the SITREP to account for the negligence and carelessness of soldiers stoned on marijuana or heroin supplied by Chinese traffickers and Saigon generals. How does a CO write up assassinations of officers and noncoms "accidentally" shot or fragged with grenades? Might have only been nineteen, but our invincibility did not extend to our morale. We were dying inside from the grinding fear and frustration of this war. I felt like Yossarian. Another *Catch-22* all over again.

Welcome to a daily routine of sitting and waiting and orders that made no sense, and simple pleasures to numb that boredom day after day after day. A little dew, a couple of Hamm's, and a whole lot of The Animals singing "We Gotta Get Out of This Place."

My dad's pride and excitement about my enlistment in his 3rd Battalion, 503rd Infantry, reorganized and redesignated countless times since WW II, had quickly turned sour before I ever shipped out to Vietnam. I was almost killed serving my country, but it wasn't in country, out in the middle of some Central Highlands hamlet fighting the Viet Cong. It was in our country, at Ft. Bragg in North Carolina, fighting some fellow soldiers who had helped themselves to the new stereo in my Camaro. Apparently, my buddy Fred Carson and I respected our brigade's esprit de corps more than the guys who stole my stereo, so we didn't hesitate to confront them right there in the barracks. All five of them. The knife wound to my stomach was severe enough to require the removal of my spleen and forced me to abandon any hopes of the OCS opportunity I had been notified about the day before the fight. And naturally, that fight was the first thing my CO read about me when I arrived in country. "Don't need any of that shit here in Nam, son!"

I didn't realize until years later that our presence in Vietnam was but a pawn's move in the much larger chess game of the Cold War, a pawn's move of over half a million American soldiers at its peak in the spring of 1969 when I was there. Nothing like saddlin' up to fight for nothin'. But newly elected President Nixon saw a way out of the mess that had forced President Johnson to refuse a second term. Nixon was not about to become the first American president to lose a war. Our entanglement in Southeast Asia, though, stretched far back before Nixon had become president in 1969, far back before Johnson had committed boo coo troops in 1965, and far back before Kennedy and our CIA had organized the military coup responsible for assassinating South Vietnam's tyrannical President Ngo Dinh Diem in 1963. It stretched back to the beginning of our military expansion to protect our American economy and interests. A chess game between the Free World and the Communist World.

President Johnson had had some help in reaching his decision. North Vietnam leaders knew what kind of political fallout they could create in America by upsetting the well-oiled propaganda machine in Washington, D.C. So the end of January 1968, in direct violation of a two-day cease-fire to celebrate their traditional new year holiday (a time of peace, brotherhood, and family reunion for all Vietnamese), the Viet Cong and North Vietnamese army inaugurated the year of the monkey by launching an unexpected wave of well-coordinated all-out military attacks against South Vietnam. In addition to stirring up the anti-war movement in America, this offensive might also stir up the oppressed people of South Vietnam to join the Communists in overthrowing the puppet regime supported by the United States.

Americans were not ready for this bold military campaign. Up until 1968, we had fought off the guerilla warfare tactics enough to maintain a stalemate that confidently was broadcast back home by General Westmoreland as a pending victory. The year before, the general had reported, "the end had begun to come into view." As a matter of fact, he declared, "The war would be over by the summer of 1967."

American reporters submitted a different opinion. "The Signs of Stalemate Are All Around Us." I remember that *LIFE* magazine editorial from 1967. The United States had gone into Vietnam "for honorable and sensible purposes," but the task "proved to be harder, longer, and more complicated than had been foreseen" and it was no longer vital enough "to ask young Americans to die for." Retired General James Gavin had returned to the United States in October of 1967 and declared of Vietnam, "We are in a tragedy."

But I was headed there anyway. And I learned quickly the politics back home didn't mean shit on most days. We bitched, and we kept track of our DEROS, but we knew it didn't matter what any of us grunts thought. Bitched more around major holidays like Easter, when a guy couldn't help but think on things back in the World, and no news about any peace talks or progress in ending the war.

Might have only been nineteen and invincible, but we didn't bitch for nothin' about General Westmoreland's self-devised, and eventually discredited, strategy of attrition warfare. Inflict on the North more casualties than they can tolerate, and they will abandon their efforts to overthrow the South. That's why the insane body count was so important. It's how we would know we had reached the crossover point, the point at which our forces were causing more casualties than the North could replace. We were on our way to victory as long as the "kill ratio" was comfortably above General Westmoreland's preferred rate of four to one. But the general had ignored the numbers, the overpopulated Orient. The 200,000 North Vietnamese who came of draft age every year could be sent down the Ho Chi Minh Trail to replace any losses against the U.S. We were fighting the insurmountable birthrate of Southeast Asia.

But this Tet wake-up call, especially the occupation of our U.S. embassy in Saigon for eight hours, provided a counterview of reality from what Westmoreland had been reporting. And was ordered to say the day after Tet's initial incursions to "reassure the public here that you have the situation under control." Americans were hearing a different side of the story now. Not only was that crossover point further down the road than we had thought, but the Communist forces had taken a step toward reaching their own psychological crossover point, a point at which America had had enough of Vietnam.

For the Communists, their Tet Offensive turned out to be far more successful in America than it did in country. Tet had stunned allied forces and had taken us by surprise, but back in the World, Tet had shocked the American public out of its casual superiority. Although many of our leaders still thought, "The only way to avert a catastrophe in Vietnam is to send out more men." Talk about stumbling through the fog of war! By June 10, General Abrams was in, Westmoreland out.

Meanwhile, American journalists were trying to understand My Lai, an American massacre of unarmed villagers a month and a half after Tet. One of many stains on our reputation as soldiers. Reporters thought they could understand it by interviewing both sides, hoped they could understand it by reviewing combat experiences leading up to it. But why would we pretend such understanding was possible when we could not understand this impossible war in the first place? I remember giving my dad a copy of Hammer's *One Morning In The War: The Tragedy At Son My (Pinkville)*. Handing it back to me, he mumbled, "I don't care to read this."

How many times do you avenge your buddy's death? How many times do you kill that fifteen-year-old girl who had detonated the mine? And her mother, and her father, and her sisters and brothers, and her village? I have read that the Old Testament axiom about "An eye for an eye" is not about justification or encouragement to take revenge. It's a call for limiting revenge because our human tendency to retaliate is prone to excess, like the savagery carried out by Charlie Company against hundreds of villagers.

After ten weeks of medical corpsman training at Fort Sam Houston, I was heading to the insanity of Vietnam. I had a tough time explaining my feelings to Bud and Denise that night in San Francisco before I shipped out. Already feeling uncomfortable in my uniform in this city where anti-war was all the fashion, I opted to wear my civvies.

I called home my second night at the Oakland Army Base. My dad liked hearing about all my paper processing. He just laughed. We left by bus from Oakland the third morning, caught a Continental jet out of Travis AFB, refueled in Honolulu and then Clark AFB in the Philippines, and after twenty-three hours, touched down at Bien Hoa AFB at 0530. A hot blonde stewardess named Melinda offered a warm smile, said "See you again soon," and I stepped off the plane into the hell of Vietnam. Exchanged my greenbacks for MPCs and piasters, was issued my clothing and TA-50 equipment, and I was off for a week of jungle school.

After three months in the Nam, premonitions lose some mystique. I had a bad feeling every day that something bad was going to happen to one of us, and guess what? As those premonitions turned into reality every day, a guy pays less and less attention. How a guy's supposed to get used to that shit, I haven't a clue.

But listening to our chaplain's Easter morning sermon in Bao Loc revived my belief in premonitions. As Christ has paid for our sins by his sacrifice on the cross, all of you are prepared to pay the ultimate sacrifice so that others may have life and live in freedom. I couldn't help but think to myself, "Why am I offering a sacrifice for others? Wasn't that God's job?" And I knew by then at least half of America didn't care about any sacrifice I might be making for them. Sacrificing for what? At least Jesus' sacrifice paid for our sins, paid for something.

That Sunday afternoon, we listened to the Fifth Dimension. The Age of Aquarius had dawned. Was it that simple? Had the time finally come for peace and love? Could the sunshine finally be shining on the falsehood that was this war in Vietnam?

Sometimes the more simple symbols stir our hearts the most. Those bayoneted M-16s stuck in the ground behind eleven pairs of boots with helmets balanced on each rifle stock will forever remain my most endearing Easter symbol. Not that cross the chaplain placed atop our makeshift altar constructed of wooden C-ration crates, and not the planet Jupiter aligned with Mars.

The next Sunday, our chaplain prayed for the souls of those eleven Sky Soldiers from Lima Platoon who had been ambushed by an estimated force of thirty-three NVA troops, those eleven soldiers who had made the ultimate sacrifice to ensure life for others. All eleven distinguished themselves that frightful night. An initial barrage of rocket, automatic weapons, and small arms fire took them by surprise. At one point, they momentarily halted the aggressors' assault, but the intense ground attack proved too much to resist when the communists attacked from all sides.

Peter, Paul, and Mary were asking, "Where Have All the Flowers Gone?" From young girls, to young men, to soldiers, to graveyards under flowers, and then picked again. Were we learning anything from this war?

Part of an answer to that question can be found in the aftermath of a futile battle at Hamburger Hill. In the wild A Shau Valley west of Hue, seventy-two American soldiers died during a fierce ten-day battle for a strategically worthless hill. After defeating the NVA, the hill was abandoned, and the enemy returned unopposed to take it back. Leaders in Washington erupted with outrage and disgust. Senator Ted Kennedy labeled the assault "senseless and irresponsible." Said another way, an American soldier in Vietnam was not killed there. He was "wasted." He was "blown away." Enough futility this time to force the Nixon administration to order the end of major tactical ground operations.

So we would no longer be chasing the Viet Cong and North Vietnamese Army troops in large-scale search and clear combat operations in unpopulated jungle and mountain areas. Instead, we would support the Vietnamese Government's pacification program to help bring all of the area's 300,000 people under government control and help them return to some kind of normalcy. The only body count that mattered now was the number of villagers we could protect. Securing the homes and farms of the South Vietnamese would deny the VC the support they needed from the hamlets.

This new mission in northern Binh Dinh Province was hardly in the tradition of the 1st and 2nd Battalions of our 503rd Parachute Infantry Regiment Sky Soldiers that were first committed to the war in 1965. We had been the first army units sent to the Republic of South Vietnam along with the 3rd Battalion of the 319th Artillery.

Hardly in the tradition of our regiment that had driven a battalion of the North Vietnamese Army's 1st Infantry Division off Hill 875 about 5 miles from the Cambodian border in November of 1967, and had captured the hill on Thanksgiving Day. But we had not expected the Viet Cong resistance, a far more formidable foe as often was the case. Eighty-one of the hundred and ten men in our company who went up that hill did not come back down. Some killed by the VC, others killed by a five-hundred-pound bomb mistakenly dropped on their position from an American plane. Those ninety-six hours at Dak To made enough of an impression to warrant a book written by Edward J. Murphy about some of the bitterest fighting of the war.

Hardly in the tradition of my 3rd Battalion, 503rd Parachute Infantry, when we joined the Brigade at Tuy Hoa in October of 1967 following our reactivation and training at Fort Bragg.

Hardly in the tradition of battle-hardened paratroopers.

Our support of pacification did not exactly send the VC packing. But Operation Washington-Green may have been a greater threat to our enemy than some of our direct assaults. By late summer, Charlie had been making quick and limited raids from the mountains to the west to disrupt pacification in the lowland hamlets. On a Monday morning in August, while Jimi Hendrix was playing his own version of "The Star-Spangled Banner" for the lingering crowd at Woodstock half a world away, a VC assassination and kidnap team had killed three key local officials, a Vietnamese soldier had found a mine the hard way, and VC and NVA troops had engaged a brigade patrol outside LZ English.

Here's the kind of thing they were trying to prevent. After constant fighting between VC and Allied forces had driven An Quang villagers to an open beach, their deserted hamlet had become a safe zone so the villagers could return to their homes from their temporary location on the beach. A safe zone thanks to the security provided by the 3/503rd Infantry and local Vietnamese forces.

You could feel some relief thanks to this new pacification mission. But problems arose for our brigade that had been used to fighting in dense jungles, rugged mountains, and mired rice paddies, used to always on the move, and used to constant bone-weary fatigue.

Problems like boredom.

Like monotony.

Platoons and companies training local forces and patrolling the same ground day after day remained in fixed positions for weeks. We always had to fight complacency, our best gift to the enemy.

In early September, our battalion traded places with the 1st of the 50th Infantry, taking over their pacification mission in the Phu My District while the 1/50th joined Task Force South at Phan Thiet. Brigadier General Cunningham had assumed command of our 173rd. Our battalion would eventually be freed up for combat operations in the Crow's Foot area in the southwestern corner of the AO.

The longer we remained in or near their hamlets, the more we learned about these people whose freedom might demand our ultimate sacrifice. We bonded with them in ways we had never thought possible. Ever since learning about Hue and My Lai when I arrived in country, I had felt differently about my sacrifice for these people. I wasn't the only one. But my growing empathy only made matters more complicated. What the fuck was this stinking war all about?

But out of this stinking war had survived a teenage girl named Tai, her haunting and regal beauty inherited from Hue's imperial past. Along with

Saigon, this ancient city of temples and palaces had endured a month of bitter fighting during the Tet Offensive in February of 1968. After-action reports indicate our forces were engaged with an unusually large enemy force in Hue, a presence of three unsuspected NVA regiments.

The invading Communists had arrested Tai's father, Pham Cong Lao, a South Vietnamese government bureaucrat. With three other officials, he was taken to a school playground and shot in the head, the beginning of an unimaginable bloodbath that claimed over five thousand men, women, and children. Many were shot like Tai's father, some clubbed to death, some stabbed to death, some buried alive. Tai had tried to escape with her mother but had to flee the city by herself after her mother was killed in an A-4 Sky-hawk bombing raid over the Citadel. To protect the historic structures of Hue, American airpower initially had been ordered to refrain, but after days had turned into weeks, that policy had been reevaluated and abandoned.

This atrocity on the school playground was not some hysterical reaction by an invading Communist army (like our massacre of civilians at My Lai the following month). This was a well-planned and systematic massacre of undesirables with lists prepared months beforehand targeting anyone linked to the South Vietnamese regime. Was this like my dad's war, after all, no less evil than Hitler's organized butchery against the Jews? But my dad had never heard about this atrocity until I returned home to tell him about it. My Lai, he had heard about. Hue, he didn't even know the city existed. Tai had refused to return to her home in Hue. I can't blame her.

Our most unforgettable night together was in Bong Son on the third of September 1969. Unforgettable because Uncle Ho had died that day, and we were under some spell that perhaps the world would change on our behalf. It didn't, and that was the last we ever saw of each other. The next day, Thursday, I was back with the Herd at LZ English north of Bong Son.

Don't know how much had changed since my dad's days as a combat medic. Like most, I had switched out my .45 pistol for an M-16. I only carried a bandolier of ammunition if we had been alerted to a high probability of action. I packed my C-rations for the day (beans and dicks my favorite) and my three canteens of water in my rucksack. But my dad had told me it would be a good idea to load up my pockets with medical items I would need quickly in the field. My medical aid bag I slung over my shoulder contained field dressings, bandages, IV tubing, and a small surgical kit with a scalpel, blades, sutures, and antibiotics. I taped heavy cans of blood volume expander to the outside of this battle bag. When faced with massive trauma and bleeding, we could use this extra serum albumin to buy a wounded soldier a little time before he could receive a transfusion. But pain relievers like Darvon (that was our motto, "Drive on with Darvon"), morphine Syrettes, salt pills, and extra DEET, I stuffed in my pockets.

Maybe I should have added a copy of Mrs. Eddy's *Science and Health* to my bag. Not sure though if I could have convinced any of my buddies that their frag wound from a grenade was just an illusion. Kind of like taking our standard criteria one step further. If it stops bleeding and no parts are missing, then it ain't serious.

After enemy gunners with 82mm mortars and recoilless rifles had shelled us at our brigade headquarters camp at LZ English, I stared into Rodriguez's eyes for a split second, reminded of that nonsense. As a medical corpsman, I often thought about my mom and Dr. Langer and Mrs. Eddy's religion. I could tell immediately, my brother Rodriguez wasn't interested in any such shit. A bullet had ripped into his lower leg, possibly shattering his fibula. For the moment, I applied a pressure dressing and bandage. We were all still nervous from the week before when sappers had overrun our perimeter. Next to God, I was Rodriguez's best friend. And out humping the boonies, he was my best friend, protecting my ass while I did my job.

But I did think about Grandpa Sheldon and his encouraging words. Seems like talk was often the only thing valuable I could provide. Most of the time, we could feel DOA before the arrival. Most thought my job was the worst job in the combat zone because I had to work alone to handle both the injury as well as the psychological burden of my buddy dealing with his injury. And this, often in the midst of enemy fire.

There is one thing, though, I know for sure. Diarrhea's not an illusion. Every Monday, we had to force down a large orange anti-malaria pill. Plan on diarrhea for two or three days, which didn't matter too much because much of the food at our mess caused diarrhea anyway, so always hard to tell the cause. Turns out, our Monday pill only protected us from one type of malaria. We had to pop a small white pill the other six days of the week for the other three types of malaria. This caused diarrhea every day. Wish I could have helped out some guys suffering from constipation. But never such a problem, thanks to our malaria pills and our chocolate version of reconstituted milk.

Replacing the policy of "de-Americanization" first announced by Nixon in June of 1969, Vietnamization, the official term for Nixon's exit strategy, would work out in the end to save a little American face. Our country was so deeply divided about this war, frustrated with our leaders and weary of the blunders. So Nixon proclaimed in November of 1969, "In the previous administration, we Americanized the war in Vietnam. In this administration, we are Vietnamizing the search for peace. The defense of freedom is everybody's business, not just America's business. And it is particularly the responsibility of the people whose freedom is threatened." For those of us in country who had to watch the AVRN watch us march out to battle on their behalf, well, we couldn't have said it better! As military responsibilities shifted to the South Vietnamese troops, America began a gradual, phased withdrawal of our combat forces.

So my plan to walk in the footsteps of my dad ended up as misguided as our country's efforts to end this tragedy. I'm still in country fighting a war that Washington, D.C. was trying to end with honor, but we were supposed to keep fighting while all of our leaders debated what "peace with honor" meant. I was expecting this to be my ticket to manhood and respect. So much for my sacrifice, and so much for the Age of Aquarius.

Six years later, in 1975, on the Friday before Memorial Day, I received the news. Sharon and I were expecting our first child. A certified letter from the State Department explained how research had turned up a connection between a young boy named Trinh and me. In the tragic crash of a C-5A used the week after Easter to baby lift orphans out of a collapsing South Vietnam, Trinh had been killed. Today, May 23, would have been his fifth birthday.

President Gerald R. Ford, himself an adoptee, had signed the "Operation Babylift" Executive Order to provide American military aircraft for the evacuation of over 2,500 Vietnamese war orphans. This evacuation would be the only way children assigned to overseas families could join their adoptive families. Three years after I had returned from Nam, Tai was running out of options for her Amerasian son. Life under Communist rule would have turned out to be a living hell for him because "in his veins flowed the blood of the enemy." The city of Saigon was collapsing, sounding a death knell for the whole country, and families desperate enough chose suicide together rather than live under the Communist regime. After the bloody and brutal

Communist takeover of Danang, witnessing the murder of children killed alongside their parents who were trying to escape, Tai had delivered him to an orphanage in Saigon.

What with the tense situation that existed at the end of March, the director of Friends For All Children, Rosemary Taylor, did not hesitate to accept the government's offer of the first evacuation flight. In the sweltering heat of April 4, fifteen minutes after takeoff, forty miles out of Saigon and 23,000 feet up in the air, the plane nearing the ocean and the first leg of its journey to America, an explosion suddenly rocked the aircraft. Later it was learned that the rear cargo doors had blown off because of a mechanical malfunction. The pilot lost rudder control and crashed into a rice paddy two miles from Tan Son Nhut airport. The pilot's heroic efforts saved the lives of nearly half of those on board the plane. Trinh was not one of them; he was one of the 78 of the 230 children on board who was killed. In the bottom cargo compartment, almost everyone was killed.

An embarrassing tide of relief immediately swept over my grief, the relief more painful than my grief. At least Trinh didn't have to grow up without his mom.

FTA!

Some of us would say we had been at war before Vietnam. Many of my fellow vets would say the war never ended for us.

I'm sure I returned to my life at the mill with a little extra bravado. I expected some respect after Sharon and I were married and began our family. But as much as the mill and my family filled up my present, I could feel the pain of my past constantly infringing on my right to find happiness. Maybe I was not up to the task of restoring my mother's honor and memory. That, after all, depended on my success in preserving our family legacy.

I gradually assumed more and more responsibility for the daily operations at the mill, although I still had to prove myself to Eva and my dad. Prove myself, that is, by making money. And the more money I made for Benson Lumber, the more money I was expected to make. In my personal battle to gain Eva's respect, I lavished a money-driven lifestyle on my family that required the same frenzied spiral. The more I could provide, the more I was expected to provide. Money problems plagued me all day long, and my pathetic solutions troubled me all night long. How much can I borrow? Who can I ask? How much will that end up costing? How much can I expect to make next month? How can I make more next month? How can I delay paying something back? What can I sell quickly if I have to? How much can I get for it? What if I hadn't spent so much last month? Have I got all the bills prioritized in the right order?

Like those days in the past when Brooks-Scanlon ignored the tomorrow that was coming, I took to expensive renovation and expansion of our mill like there was no tomorrow. If we were going to make it through these tough times, I didn't see a choice. Jesus, my dad and I argued every day about how to do this.

Few recognized the gradual decline of the lumber industry that required our extra attention through the 1970s. Our monthly Hoo-Hoo Meetings tried to keep us focused on the day-in-and-day-out market swings. But by the end of 1979, keeping up with the wood-products market was an impossible task. Over the next three years, lumber prices continued to plummet. In 1980, Diamond International swallowed up Brooks-Scanlon. By the end of the 1980s, the newly formed Crown Pacific Ltd. was in charge of what was left of lumber production. Even though our national economy was showing some signs of recovery by the mid-1980s, forty-eight thousand jobs in the Pacific Northwest lumber industry had been permanently lost.

Family legacy? You can have it.

CHAPTER 17

Henry
10 April 1998
Good Friday

This saying goodbye to half a century of life has asked my temporal lobes to work overtime – sorting through memories and forcing me to reexamine those past "might-have-beens" that have altered my destiny. Changed my fate enough so that whatever happened, or didn't happen, followed me at every turn in my life.

Denise and I were sitting now on the bench behind the tee box of the ninth fairway. We agreed: our most discussed "might-have-been" occurred four months before we were married twenty-eight years ago.

Much like his earlier days in Chicago with Wayne Berg, my dad spent most Sunday evenings trying to figure out how he could balance costs against revenue the coming week at Caine Precision Mfg. I didn't feel right about my college costs factoring into his Sunday evening stress, so I had decided to take a break from my studies halfway through my junior year at the University of Washington. Where my mother's Hannah promise fit into all of this, I didn't have a clue. I worked as a youth counselor for Alhambra Parks and Recreation, drove a truck for Industrial Contractor's Supply, and snagged a few hours in retail at California Outdoor Supplies – trying to avoid taking a paycheck from my dad. I did work for him whenever I could but didn't bother to clock any hours.

Reminiscing now with Denise, I couldn't help but ask her if she had had any doubts about me after my withdrawal from college. "No," she assured me, "because we had that plan." I would enlist in the Air Force, take advantage of any training I could, and then eventually complete my college courses on the GI Bill. Our plan sounded responsible, and we both felt proud of our new level of maturity.

On a Monday in early December of 1969, young men across America had gathered around radios and televisions to hear the odds of their birth date sending them to their death date. Hadn't happened since 1942, but Vietnam was still waitin', so the likelihood of a call to report for induction had to be determined for the year 1970. Three hundred and sixty-six blue plastic capsules containing birth dates were placed in a large glass container and drawn by hand to assign order-of-call numbers to all men within the 18-26 age range specified in Selective Service law.

The first capsule, drawn by Congressman Alexander Pirnie (R-NY) of the House Armed Services Committee, contained the date September 14, so all men born on that date in any year between 1944 and 1950 were assigned lottery number one. Congratulations! The drawing continued until all days of the year had been paired with sequence numbers. The date of June 8 was drawn last. Over 850,000 young men were affected by this first drawing. The highest lottery number eventually chosen for induction from this group was 195; all men assigned that lottery number or lower, and who were classified 1-A or 1-A-O, were called to report for possible induction.

If the first step, an Order to Report for Physical Exam, was followed by an Order to Report for Induction, a young man had been drafted. Of course, even with the winning lottery number of September 14, someone could still file for an exemption, deferment, or postponement based on his circumstances or beliefs. A seminary student preparing for ministry was classified 2-D and deferred from military service. Anyone who objected to military training and service based on his conscience was classified 1-O and could fulfill his service obligation as a civilian alternative service worker. A college student could have his induction postponed until he finished the current semester or, if a senior, the end of the academic year.

Young men could now rest assured that something more than a casino blackjack table determined their fate. At least the whole lottery-by-birthday drawing was opened with an invocation and closed with a benediction. God forbid that America would casually send off her young men – all based on a crapshoot – only to end up someday with their name on Maya Lin's black granite Wall!

Under the old system, a young man might wait for years with uncertainty over his draft status; under this new system, he could know with certainty within the year whether or not he might end up on that Wall some day. For those in the middle number range of the drawing, some uncertainty still existed. But they would know by the end of 1970 whether they would be inducted.

In spite of this system's fairness or impartiality, draft evasion and draft resistance quickly became a sophisticated business during the Vietnam War, including an underground railroad network to support AWOL soldiers fleeing to Canada. By providing an open forum for debate about America's unjust war involvement and a graduation cycle every year that produced a new batch of eligible, less-than-excited draftees, college campuses were ready-made centers for the antiwar protest movement. Selective Service Centers and campus ROTC programs became easy targets for protest – as did Disneyland and Tom Sawyer's Island that day in August after we were married.

In 1977, President Carter passed a general amnesty (his first official act as president) for all those in defiance of the draft who had fled abroad or to Canada or Mexico, allowing them to return to the United States. Out of over 200,000 accused war draft evaders, less than 9,000 were convicted – too many to prosecute and send to prison. Seemed like a disgusting blow-off, though, to those veterans who had honorably served in Vietnam.

The slip of paper with my birthdate of June 27 sealed in the blue plastic capsule was drawn after sixty-three other numbers – guaranteeing me free travel arrangements to Southeast Asia. Didn't matter though, because enlisting in the Air Force for me was not an escape from the draft. I had diligently maintained my college deferment II-S status and was still figuring out how to honor my mother's Hannah promise to God. Denise and I had come up with our plan, so I was ready to serve my country. After basic training at Lackland AFB in San Antonio, I looked forward to attending the USAF language school in Monterey, California.

The night before my physical exam at the downtown center in Los Angeles, my friend Tony Bracci got drunk enough to hold a snub-nose .38 caliber revolver next to his left ear and fire a shot into the ceiling above, resulting in permanent hearing loss and a probable get-out-of-the-army free pass (a IV-F classification). His older brother Vito wasn't so reckless; two years before, he had burned his draft card as an act of defiance and fled to Mexico.

I, however, was asked to bring a letter from our family physician, Dr. Putler, testifying that my brain concussion at age six when I rode my bicycle into that Childer's Nursery pickup truck would not impair my faculties. "Sorry, son, but you've got burr holes in your skull, and the Surgeon-General has determined you can't wear a helmet. Therefore you are rejected."

"But you don't understand. I don't want *out*; I want *in*! I had top scores on all of my written exams. I'm enlisting!" So drained by disappointment, I drove around for five hours contemplating the consequences of this might-have-been. My plans – our plans – denied because of six burr holes in my skull. Honest to the core like an Eagle Scout, I had recorded that accident and subsequent neurosurgery under the appropriate question on my physical exam form. I've second-guessed that decision more than once! Could have easily ignored the question.

Didn't feel much like dinner that night. Denise and I sat quietly rear-ranging our future. As if to compound my dismay, her brother Karl called from a 7-Eleven phone booth on Highway 39 to announce he had driven straight through to the West Coast from Ft. Bragg, North Carolina, finally on his way home from a war and a world he would never figure out. Karl hadn't bothered to wait for any lottery; he knew the year he graduated from high school that he wanted to serve as a paramedic like his father, hopefully in the same unit as his father had served in the Philippines during WW II.

"Hey Caine, how about a little Hollywood action to celebrate I'm still alive? Can you show me around? Maybe that famous 'Whisky a Go Go' out on the Sunset Strip."

"Yeah, where are you again?"

"It says here on my map I'm on Highway 39; I'm right close by. Tell me how to get to your place, man, I've been driving for forty-five hours solid, I need a shower."

"You idiot, that's Rosemead Blvd.; we don't call it Highway 39."

"Well, how should I know? That's what the map calls it."

"Okay, wait there at the store, I'll come and get you." I didn't have any trouble spotting Karl's dark-green '67 Camaro convertible.

Out to PJs, then, on Santa Monica Blvd., a popular and crowded night-club. Denise didn't seem to mind. This was her brother, after all, and be-sides, we were just having a few drinks. I tried to share my disappointment with Karl.

"What? Are you fuckin' crazy? You're out, man; IV-F, it's over, you're a free man." By midnight and a half-dozen Greyhounds, I had rearranged my emotions.

I wasn't crazy.

But I had found some direction in my life and felt ready for marriage. Now what? "Deemed unfit for military service." Like Baden-Powell in England had prepared boys to serve in the military, Scouting had prepared me. What happened?

Seemed like Karl was so ahead of me last year when we met him and his girlfriend Connie in San Francisco to see him off to President Johnson's "raggedy-ass, little fourth-rate country" in Southeast Asia. I could only imagine then what lie ahead for him, but at least he had something lying ahead of him. He belonged to something important; he wore a 173rd Airborne insignia on his shoulder that represented a long tradition of honor and service.

I was on Thanksgiving break first semester of my junior year, trying to make sense of a class schedule that wasn't making too much sense for where I was headed. How could it? I didn't know where I was headed. I was ready to put college on hold for a while (put college costs on hold, that is). How was I supposed to honor my mother's Hannah promise to God? How was I supposed to honor my dad's expectation that his sons would take over his tool and die making shop someday? All I knew for sure is that Denise and I were talking about marriage plans.

Our drive home from seeing Karl is not a bad metaphor for how I felt. Denise had decided to drive the first few hours back to Southern California in our tan 1963 VW Bug. I was so exhausted from our colorful night out at the colorful Old Spaghetti Factory in North Beach that I was already dosing before we hit Palo Alto on Highway 101. After she pulled into a Union 76 station for two bucks worth of gas, an attendant checked the oil and asked, "You want detergent or non-detergent?" Ever the cleaning lady, Denise opted for detergent, an excellent choice under some other circumstances, except for this one. Thanks to a quality brand of detergent oil, all of the built-up sludge of neglect now dislodged to expose any number of problems.

I couldn't help but wake up to the smoke now filling our small interior space, a direct result of our simple heating system. My dad had explained to me how this worked in a VW. Air was forced out of the fan housing through tubes into heater boxes that were wrapped around the exhaust pipes so that internal flappers could be activated by a lever to release the heated air – which was quickly becoming contaminated by our burning engine. Denise had that "Don't-ask-me" smile on her face when I asked what was going on, and responded with one of her typical Gracie Allen lines, "I don't know. Somethin' must be wrong. Maybe we should open the windows."

After we had pulled safely off the highway, I opened the rear cover, bent over slightly with my left hand still on the handle, and stared at the engine. I had seen lots of guys do that along the highway, including my dad, but the difference would be that most of them were looking for something. I was not, and after a couple of minutes, I was bright enough to realize my staring was entirely in vain. Even with my dad's explanation about those internal flappers, I didn't have a clue.

My dad would have had a clue; more than a clue, he would have torn down that engine during the night, created whatever parts were necessary, and by morning be on his way. It was in that moment of staring I finally recognized my general lack of mechanical aptitude. I was not my dad, and if I were not, then I would never be sharing Caine Precision Manufacturing with my brother. As much as the aerospace industry intrigued me – and what young boys aren't a little fascinated by airplanes and space exploration – I was not meant to become a tool and die maker like him.

While I was accepting this revelation, I was at the same time calling him to ask for some help with our situation, a broken down vehicle stuck north of San Jose. As if to confirm that which I already knew in my heart, he and I reached our first real impasse as a father and son. His Sunday evenings had not been too promising as of late, so he explained in as loving a way as only he could do. "Well, Bud, you'll just have to limp it home as best you can."

"Limp it home," I asked. "Whatta' ya' mean?"

That was the first time in my life my dad had not come to my rescue, an indication of what it means to finally grow-up. There was no limping it home. After we called Denise's father in Oregon to borrow some money for airline tickets to get back to L.A., we left that still smoldering Bug in the airport parking lot until we could return the following day to tow it home. My dad did let us use his old GMC pickup to drive up the coast and fetch our Bug. We visited about all of this both ways – seven hours up Highway 101, seven hours back, reevaluating our future plans and hopes, where we were headed.

Two years after our wedding, Denise and I were still in the middle of that conversation we had had while towing our VW back to L.A. – still unsure about how to fulfill my mother's Hannah promise, reasonably sure I wasn't meant to become a tool and die maker like my dad, and positively sure I had no career in the Air Force. Southern California felt different from a few years before, didn't seem to hold the same appeal anymore. We decided to move with our newborn son to Colorado, see if a change might help. As a courtesy to my wife's family in Oregon, we made a swing through Bend to say our goodbyes for the time being. That *time being* turned into being a long time after Gordon questioned me about our savings account. We didn't have much of a savings account, so it was easy to accept his offer to hang around awhile and work at the mill.

By the end of my first month at Benson Lumber, I had discovered my temporary job filling in around the yard and pulling green chain would demand considerable interpersonal skills, amateur counseling sessions and psychoanalysis, and careful choices of allegiance on any given day. Karl couldn't have returned home from war because his war was at his home. Three years after the U.S. had taken over the advisory role from the French in Indo-China, Karl's mother had died in August of 1957. At war then everyday, including battles with his mother-in-law Eva who often reminded him when he would come home from working at the mill that he need not hope or dream about any future management position at the family business. Since Karl was not his father, Eva decided, he didn't have what it took. And besides, she also reminded him, "You're too D-U-M-B to ever run the mill like your father."

This translated into a battle with his father. A volcano ready to erupt is the only way to describe their relationship, and this due in many ways to the absence of someone who could temper the love and jealousy and bickering between them – someone like Roberta Rouene. Without her, Gordon and Karl competed against one another sometimes more ruthlessly than two old neighboring sawmill owners – hubris against itself. Something about how brash Karl was, but so was Gordon in his day. Gordon had every right to speak up because he had built the mill from the ground up. He was handing Karl the great American dream, but sometimes, thanks to egos and fear of failure, the handing over can be complicated. So maybe Karl had some rights too. Working for Karl was way more exciting; working for Gordon was way more secure.

For Karl, I think life at the mill felt like a war every day; but this would not turn out to be another Vietnam. Everything he did, he did with a Broadway flare. No time for little things in his life. Didn't have to watch *Dallas* on Friday night after working with Karl all week. Even little things assumed epic proportions.

Karl would pull in late on Monday morning, he and his dad would be arguing by lunchtime about how much money Karl had spent, and this would escalate until Gordon was shoving his finger in Karl's chest, with Karl up and leaving at 2:30 in the afternoon. At which point, I was offered management of the mill because Gordon couldn't stand Karl any longer – until Tuesday at noon when CENORE called to confirm Karl's negotiated price hike that would cover the latest capital improvement. At which point, I was returned to the yard to load the next shipment of lumber with my forklift. Of course, by Wednesday, that could possibly have changed because Karl had bought a new piece of equipment that Gordon felt was hardly needed, so then I would be back at the top. "This mill could be all yours, Bud, if you want it." For the day at least, and then Karl would redeem himself by taking over Fred's bucking job the next day because Fred had called in sick, and then I would be reduced to pulling green chain to cover for someone else. "Who did I think I was?" This weekly yo-yo of who's-in-charge-of-Benson-Lumber became a game of some derision – gave the mill crew a chance to have some fun with me, which I took care of appropriately when I was in charge for the day. My business card reflected my all-purpose status with a short description of who I was at Benson Lumber: General Manager (when the owner and son are arguing), Vice-President in charge of forklift operations (when they are not arguing), and husband of the owner's daughter (all the time!).

Our little inside gang at the mill understood the Surgeon Generals' Warning on our pack of cigarettes, and we talked about that all the time, usually over a cigarette break in the office. But when Karl decided to quit by refusing to buy any more cigarettes for himself, we all got a little tired of him "borrowing one more" smoke from us every hour or so. "Come on, Benson, get real here, this isn't working." So, to Nancy in the office, to Fred out in the yard, to Larry the semi-truck driver, and to me, vice-president of forklifts, this wager on a late Friday afternoon: we all quit, and the first to light up pays everybody else $100.00! In the name of long life and happiness, we all agreed.

On Monday morning, Karl pulled in late, as usual, walked into the office with his Hollywood best-man smile, and handed over four one hundred dollar bills as he lit up his first Newport menthol for the day. Sucking on a menthol cigarette gave us all canker sores, but we figured it was worth it because we were taking in less tobacco and that would make the next time we tried to quit that much easier.

A vice-president at B.B.B. Manufacturing once bet my dad on New Year's Day a hundred bucks that he couldn't quit smoking for a year (assuming that would be a lasting fix). But my dad quit for the year, bought a carton on his birthday, the thirtieth of December, opened it on the thirty-first to unseal one of the packs, and enjoyed the Rose Bowl game with his gin martini and a smoke. And never offered a word of explanation.

When Karl was in charge, though, and on his game as a lumber broker, working at Benson Lumber felt like a step or two up the ladder – not this little family-owned outfit along Juniper Gin Road, but an international firm, a "Pacific" or a "Cascade International" Lumber Company. May as well have been working out a Middle East Peace Agreement the way he persevered on the phone with Greg and Drew at CENORE. He had a feel for what they were up to with anticipated higher retail prices, and they had a feel for what he was up to anticipating those higher retail prices with his little-anticipated increase in the wholesale price. What a game they played! He walked out to the yard one Friday morning about 9:00 AM, offered me a cigarette, and said, "Caine, you'll never guess what Greg is prepared to pay."

"Well?"

"A hundred and thirty bucks a thousand!"

His contagious wheelin' and dealin' excitement caught me off guard. I found myself arranging a killer week of work for myself and excited about it at that! "Then let's get busy and make some real money here. Maybe a record is in order, heh?"

In the tradition of Gordon and Buel, we began scheming our way to a week still remembered at Sid and Ethel's Cafe when Benson Lumber turned out nine truckloads of lumber, 125,000 board feet, the last load delivered to the Central Oregon yard at 4:55 Friday afternoon. I was in charge of the lumber tally by counting and averaging the length of each sling, and I tried to determine that average as honestly as I could. Karl asked me if I was maybe OK with a little stretching of the numbers to help make our mark that week. I replied, "Benson, if anything, let's go shorter on the averages this week, and you can remind Greg of that when he's screaming about the big check he's got to write out for this week's shipment. We can always stretch the numbers some week when no one is paying so much attention to the board footage we've shipped."

"I like the way you're thinking, Caine."

Karl had a way of building up people around him, myself included.

Eva didn't pay much attention to such weeks at Benson Lumber, so Karl accumulated conspicuous amenities and toys to impress her with his business acumen. Eva couldn't help but pay attention to his extravagant collection: his bright yellow ski-boat, his 47' yacht, his 1976 Cessna Turbo 210L, his black Ferrari, his Lincoln Continental, the ultimate Ford pickup, his cabin on the Metolius River, and snowmobiles. "All futile, and a dead-end, Caine. Makes me feel emptier than ever," he once confided in me. "But I don't know how else to prove myself to her and Dad. How do I win that battle? What, should I just 'Let it be' after Eva has told me all my life I'm too slow-witted to run the family lumber business?"

Karl couldn't resist calling the local newspaper for coverage of a hare-brained idea Larry Suthgate the semi-truck driver had concocted with me. Suthgate was a resident of some notoriety thanks to his heroic exploits in the Korean War. We had become good friends while visiting when I loaded his semi-trailer every day with eight slings of lumber. While the three of us were celebrating that Friday evening at Ann's Tavern after our big record-setting week, we decided to try a new sales angle at Benson Lumber. Suthgate thought I was the better everyday kind of salesman, teased Karl that he could only operate in the closed-door world of corporate buddies.

"Ya' think so, heh? Then prove it," Karl challenged him, and offered us both a cigarette.

"Caine and I will load up a semi-trailer full of odd-cuts of lumber, leave Thursday morning at 7:00 AM, drive to every retail yard in the area unannounced cold-turkey, and sell the entire load by sundown."

"I don't think so."

"What's our winnings when we do it?"

"I'll buy you both the most expensive steak dinner you can find."

"Deal!"

Most of the time, working with Karl felt more like fun than work.

Nothing more fun than our company-sanctioned boy's trip to Reno with Karl – Max driving the Chinook motorhome while Gordon, Karl, Tony, and I practiced our blackjack skills in the back. Like taking a trip with Jack Nicholson. Within one hour at the Eldorado, Karl had become a celebrity, and folktales of his blackjack playing swagger and winnings could only impress Eva even more. Lumber broker, high stakes gambler, and big man about town. Karl played at third base to wrest away as much control of the table as possible, would hit hands of twelve with the other casino guests holding their collective breath against the odds. A couple of Greyhounds to relax, and then one glass of milk after another, young ladies gathering in rows behind him around the table, extra pit bosses shifting their positions toward his dealer, hitting a crazy seventeen while the dealer was showing a face card, with two hundred in chips in front of his cards. A four! Of course! All this to a rousing hand of applause and cheers! My God, is it Jack Nicholson?

With a little over three-thousand dollars in winnings for the evening, we retired for an on-the-house dinner break, thanks to the hotel's guest Karl Benson. But he had to take a piss and was worried about a couple of guys who were following us toward the restroom. Gordon and I stood on either side of the urinal like a couple of mafia henchmen to protect our man, trying not to watch Karl too closely. We turned to the door. "Let's go eat some dinner."

Karl finally hit a streak of how the rest of us "enjoyed" Reno, what we called the regular guy's run of luck – too many IOUs from the casino showing up on Nancy's desk would not impress Eva or Gordon.

Oddest Christmas Eve I have ever spent in my life? That would be with Karl, of course. "Caine, whatta' ya' say we check out that new movie, *Apocalypse Now*? We'll get out of here early, do a little shopping for the wives before show-time."

"Benson, it's Christmas Eve, are you kidding? I've got some important people waiting for me at home."

"What, I'm not important?"

So with "Chestnuts Roasting on an Open Fire" playing in my heart, I'm watching American helicopters bomb a small Vietnamese village full of civilians and children while listening to "The Ride of the Valkyries." "And she gave birth to her firstborn son and wrapped him in bands of cloth, and laid him in a manger, because there was no place for them in the inn." And Captain Willard journeyed up river to hunt down and kill one of his own, a madman named Colonel Kurtz who had constructed a strange little kingdom of his own deep in the jungle.

I did buy Denise a new flannel nightgown, a *Little House on the Prairie* look, not exactly Victoria Secret. She said she liked it.

Sometimes, we had to figure out cheap ways on a Saturday afternoon to enjoy each other's company, like plinking around behind the log yard. I played a sophomoric prank once on Karl and Fred when they were downrange adjusting some glass bottles and tin cans for targets. A smart-ass decision, for sure, I fired off a .44 caliber round into the air with Karl's cap & ball revolver. They turned around all right. "What the fuck are you doing, Caine?"

I should have known better – two Vietnam vets, and one of them not home yet from the war. As if any soldier ever returns home from war.

CHAPTER 18

Andy

That debate with my father on Easter Sunday in 1973 almost seems recreational now in hindsight, hardly a significant hurdle on my journey to gay selfhood. But seminary had imposed on me a distressing schism between the Church I inherited from my father and the Church I was now supposed to serve. I needed a refuge for my soul, I needed the Church of my childhood; the Church I was supposed to serve needed parade participants to march on behalf of those whom the Gospel had ignored. I wasn't ready, though, to participate in any demonstrations, and I didn't feel prepared to reshape the future of the Church. I needed my father and his Church to accept me, but I wasn't prepared to change it. To change what? God's People? How we each interpret the Bible is one thing, but the Church had been around for two thousand years!

I didn't want to break down any barriers, and yet I had graduated to a position of church leadership and moral authority – an opportunity to effect change. Why was I so quiet and private about my homosexuality? Why so silent when I could be so vocal? While others were celebrating and welcoming a fresh understanding of the Gospel for our day, I found myself resisting their cause.

Why don't I celebrate that historic weekend in June of 1969 and claim it as the birthday of my self-discovery journey? Although I had just completed my junior year at CLC, I never visited with my family or friends about the rioting that followed the closing of the Stonewall Inn, a gay bar in the heart of New York's Greenwich Village. The patrons had refused to behave according to the Manhattan police officers' expectations. The graffiti proclaiming *Gay Power* scribbled on the walls and pavement announced the genesis of a powerful new social movement and the formation of the Gay Liberation Front. Shouldn't I have been seeking justice for homosexuals? Why don't I commemorate that event every year?

I'm still trying to understand why I retreated from another opportunity to have had real purpose in my life, to question the straights-only policy of the Boy Scouts. I could have mattered, I could have made a difference for so many young boys.

By repressing my homosexuality, by asking that I be left alone to my unacceptable sexual identity, I'm living a denial, I'm living a lie. And I'm ashamed of my cowardice. But by coming out to the growing public awareness and debates and gay pride marches, I would subject myself to a constant thousand-watt-industrial floodlight. Sometimes an outcast, scorned and ridiculed, and sometimes a tentative activist for gay rights, encouraged and befriended. But either way, no longer private and quiet. And that also would feel like a denial, like a lie.

Thanks to my father's Southern California connections in the American Lutheran Church, I received a call from Christ Lutheran Church out in Simi Valley the end of July 1976. Graduating from seminary is only a first step. A candidate for ordination must first be hired – receive a call, that is, from a congregational search committee working in conjunction with the Holy Spirit, the president of the American Lutheran Church, and any phone calls that may have been made behind the scenes on behalf of the candidate.

I had met Julie at First Lutheran Church in Des Moines, Iowa, where I was serving my third-year internship. Our friendship suited me well as I worked through my sexual identity – not yet a crisis because I honestly couldn't tell if God was leading me to some kind of celibate life and I didn't understand what that meant or how I was supposed to feel. Julie had completed her training at the Immanuel Deaconess Motherhouse in Omaha and considered herself a Lutheran nun when it came to serving God, although she no longer was bound by the requirement to remain unmarried. I think we fell in love – not with each other – but with what each of us was doing with our life. Make-up was not her thing, although she carefully braided her hair each day in different styles. I couldn't help but be drawn to her kind eyes, a window into an even kinder soul, and a smile to match that soul.

We were married at First Lutheran two weeks before my ordination at Our Savior's, where my father assisted The Rev. Rudy Lundquist who was representing our ALC president David Prescott. Julie's family had never been to Southern California, so we rolled out the red carpet for the standard tours and hosted her parents and two younger brothers. They stayed long enough to worship at Christ Lutheran my first Sunday as a pastor. My father had offered to help me prepare my sermon for the Fourteenth Sunday after Pentecost, but he was gracious enough to accept my I-can-handle-this-on-my-own response.

Christ Lutheran's search committee didn't know it at the time, but they had pulled off the ultimate two-for-one deal. A pastor's wife typically attends to all kinds of loose ends and congregational needs, not always willingly, and not always appreciated; with her professional training, though, Julie looked for every opportunity to serve.

Even with our busy schedules, trying to build on the few younger families that called Christ Lutheran their church home, my sexual inhibitions soon became our private counseling session. I love her to this day for her Christ-like empathy for what I was discovering about myself. For a marriage destined to fall apart, ours was a model of mutual trust – honestly sharing our feelings and our fears, listening to each other with respect as we both acknowledged the impossibility of our continuing relationship. With love and acceptance of who I was, Julie encouraged those conversations I had feared – with myself, with my father, and with God.

Apart from our private conversations, she could point to some support I should heed. Liberal Protestant denominations were revisiting centuries-old teachings about homosexuality. Lesbians and gay men had decided to come out to their family and their communities, surprising many who then found themselves rethinking their stereotypical images and attitudes. Although society's fear of homosexuality was not turned around by these developments, at least the gay movement had challenged America's sexual mores.

She could also point to some so-called support I should suspect. Exodus International had recently announced its mission: a Christian ministry to help people reclaim their heterosexuality. Homosexuality is not a gift from God, they proclaimed; heterosexuality is God's plan for humanity. But they were ready to admit that their evangelical churches had not put their best foot forward when dealing with this issue. Research psychologist Elizabeth Moberly from Cambridge, England, questioned the traditional view that homosexual behavior was perverse or unnatural. Once we understand the cause of such behavior, she exclaimed, the homosexual urge seems natural. Aborted development in same-sex relationships, especially between parent and child, is the problem. Homosexuals do not crave abnormal needs, she explained, but seek normal needs that have been denied in their youth.

John Evans wasn't buying any of this, could be found outside the Exodus conference center handing out tracts declaring that Christianity and homosexual practice are compatible. Speaking from experience, having returned to a homosexual lifestyle two years after he helped found Love in Action, Evans refuted the possibility that a true homosexual could ever change to heterosexuality.

"Julie, I long for a love I can never experience," I shared with her one Sunday afternoon in early January, "a love I can only imagine but will never embrace." We both had read Goethe's *The Sorrows of Young Werther*, and we both shared with this eighteenth-century German author our Lutheran heritage. "Being my father's son, being a Lutheran pastor, a servant of God, finding true love with another man feels like Werther's dilemma – it's an impossible arrangement, Julie, and I know it. I've been living Werther's sorrows since my freshman year in high school, daydreaming of tender moments of what could never be, and then waking up to my life of denial. My love for another man would be like Werther's love for Lotte, a relationship I know will never come to pass. When I was in college, I thought more than once about suicide, about how I could end my sorrows once and for all.

But then I discovered a way out of my wretched predicament after I graduated from seminary. Goethe had experienced his own version of Young Werther's love for Lotte; by writing about Werther's suicide in the novel, though, Goethe was able to save himself. To save myself, I chose to marry a woman, hoping foolishly and selfishly my celibate life might be accepted as a priest-like calling I had received from God. I am so sorry, Julie, and I can't possibly expect you to forgive me for my sins of abuse, denial, and deception."

Arranging for our divorce was the most difficult task I have ever faced. But given Julie's acceptance of who I was, I had fallen in love with her in a way I find hard to explain. She was my little Christ, and much like we self-ishly abuse the love of Christ to atone for our human condition, I had self-ishly abused Julie's love to help resolve my dilemma.

We continued serving Christ Lutheran for two more years. And then in 1980, I accepted another call while Julie began her studies at Pacific Lutheran Theological Seminary in Berkeley and was ordained the same year as my friend Bud Caine. She became a passionate spokeswoman for the direction our Church could take in the future on behalf of those children of God who differed from the majority in their sexual orientation.

I think my father suspected Julie might be a lesbian, what with her going to P.L.T.S. in Berkeley after all! What's so ludicrous – besides the fact my father suspected Julie and not me – is that straight women like Julie, let alone lesbians, had to fight for their right to be ordained! Objections were clearly stated like canon law. Even the Lutheran Church in America (the liberal synod among the big three) voiced its opposition. "God forbid!" declared the Slovak Zion president, arguing, "Jesus had many women helping him, but only men were sent out to preach and teach." The Caribbean president stated flatly, "I will not ordain a woman." He declared that women should not be ordained because, among other reasons, they "cannot keep secrets" (although he acknowledged "many men act likewise") and the ordination of women would create congregational vacancies "because of nervous break-downs they would have." Some bishops wondered "whether the men of the church would go to a woman, a 'weaker vessel,' for counseling as readily as they would to a man." One ALC president believed women could not fulfill all of the requirements of ministry because "I would hate to see my wife be called out to some lonely outpost at 3:00 in the morning." All of this about women gave me some idea of what a gay Lutheran pastor might expect.

We Lutherans share a common psychological disorder: *schismatism*. Our nickname: *schismatics*. It has been that way since the 1600s when we first arrived in New Amsterdam from Germany, Norway, Sweden, and Denmark. A merger amongst different Lutheran church organizations is no guarantee a schism won't follow when some group decides it has too hastily accepted the tenets of the body at large. Of course, Father Martin Luther didn't invent this divisive impulse. Long before our Reformation schism with the Holy Roman Catholic Church during the sixteenth century, the East had set an example with its split in the eleventh century to form the

Greek Orthodox Church. So you are the rock, St. Peter, the foundation upon which to build Christ's Church. How many more times will you be shattered and scattered apart?

The seminary my father attended is the result of a schism in Ohio between two Lutheran groups; my father's church, where I was ordained, is the result of a merger and subsequent schism. The Church may have one foundation, but be sure to check with the latest architect before trying to figure it all out. Staring into a bowl of alphabet soup would make more sense than the collection of acronyms and initialisms representing Lutheran church organizations. Thanks to some controversy about predestination, we can even lay claim to the formation of an Anti-Missourian Brotherhood back in the 1880s. By all means, if we disagree about something, let's at least be clear about which fellow Lutherans we're against so we can then form a splinter group!

Whenever you meet another Lutheran outside of your own church, you usually ask the question, "What alphabet?" Ethnicity is a major factor, and each group claims differences about social issues (liberal vs. conservative), about worship practices (low church vs. high church, even using the word *Mass*), and about personal piety and regard for Scripture (a critical study of the Bible vs. literalness and infallibility of Scripture).

Serving Peace Lutheran now, I had no trouble going through the motions of being a pastor. But according to my standards (I should say, my father's standards of ordained ministry), this hardly translated into effective pastoral care for those I was called to serve. My preaching, my visitation priorities, my leadership initiatives all suffered as I withdrew from my work – too confused and too broken. I was supposed to touch lives with the love of Christ, a love I was not feeling at the time. I was supposed to hide my vulnerability and handle things on my own. I drifted through the motions, time passed without meaning or fulfillment, seemingly accepted as an average pastor no one was complaining about, but who clearly wasn't proclaiming the Good News with any enthusiasm. How could I if I wasn't sure God loved me as I am?

And then in 1988, my Lutheran heritage of schisms merged with the Gay Liberation Movement to expose my personal schism between the Church I had inherited from my father and the Church I was now serving, a private world I had tried to maintain for myself. My father's Church had to answer the questions the Church I now served was asking.

I could still be an effective Scout leader even though I was gay; it was the Boy Scouts of America that had determined otherwise. But could I still be an effective pastor even though I was gay? Was it church policy that had determined otherwise? Was it God's People? Was it God? How I felt rejected or loved by God's People was how I felt rejected or loved by God.

While I was working on a draft for our Church's Suicide Prevention social statement – suggesting we speak further "about the data that attempted suicide rates among youth struggling with questions about their sexual orientation are higher than among others of the same age," emphasizing that we must address our Church's failure to acknowledge despair and brokenness as root causes of suicide – my Church is telling me I can't be an *openly* gay pastor. Was this the Scouts all over again – I wasn't morally straight enough because I wasn't straight?

The congregation I currently served, arguing that the proposed merger of Lutheran churches would be too liberal in its interpretation of Scripture, chose to join with my father's church and fifty-two other American Lutheran Church congregations to protest the formation of the new Evangelical Lutheran Church in America.

So thanks to my new profession I was sure would be a refuge for my quiet and private homosexual orientation, safe from the ignorance and bigotry of the Boy Scouts, I'm finding myself exposed under that floodlight. My privacy had shielded me from the gay movement sweeping our country, a collective coming out of the closet demanding a full embrace of our identity. I was now supposed to proclaim to all the world that I'm gay and proud of it.

Did I have a choice? What if I didn't want to proclaim to all the world?

Should have been the opposite, you would think, but the more that lesbians and gays demanded public attention, the more troubling for me. The flurry of energy and defiance and activism felt like an assault against my quiet and private self.

The gay liberation parade asked for private "coming out" confessions to step forward into the public forum, to boldly reject the stigma attached to homosexuality, calling for resistance against an oppressive society. Pride and self-acceptance was the lead banner. "Come Out For Freedom! Come Out Now! Come Out of the Closet Before the Door Is Nailed Shut!" This coming out, I was told, would help me shed much of the self-hatred I have internalized. Maybe I am unable to accept myself. Was I afraid of my own sexuality? What if I didn't want my sexuality to publicly define me?

My personal misgivings turned into nightmares too real to leave uninterpreted. I found myself designated the grand marshal of a Gay Freedom Day Parade marching in front of throngs of Lutherans from my father's church and Peace Lutheran. The communal human spirit of gay and lesbian activists marching in this parade was brave enough to ask the question, "When does a new life in Christ begin for a gay or lesbian? Now, or in the fullness of time?" Like the Rose Parade in Pasadena, Eagle Scouts carried banners to introduce each entry in this parade, but the banners also proclaimed these Eagle Scouts were all openly gay!

While my father's church was rejecting the merger, a Lutheran seminarian decided to open his closet door in preparation for ordained service to God. He was asking "Why can't I feel as strongly about my calling and gift from God for being gay as I do about my calling and gift from God for ministry? How could I serve Christ from within a closet? How could the Church condone such dishonesty? Why should I be treated any differently when it comes to seeking employment as a parish pastor?" He not only constituted a dilemma for the Church, but for me as well.

This seminarian was assured God would not withhold His grace from him based on his sexual orientation, but his profession expected him to lead a morally exemplary life. Here we go again – *morally straight*, like the Boy Scouts. Although church leaders declared there was nothing to keep those who are homosexual in orientation from seeking ordination, the bishops claimed they were unaware of any Scriptures that approve of homosexuality as a lifestyle for religious leaders; so a practicing homosexual could not be ordained. The same rule applied to unmarried heterosexuals since the Church considered traditional marriage as the only acceptable framework for sex. According to our denomination's policies, homosexuals could be ordained only if they promise lifelong celibacy – a promise this seminarian was not willing to make.

The more I felt dismissed by the Church I served, the brighter that industrial strength floodlight shined on what I wanted to remain so private.

Shined brighter still when James Dale, a nineteen-year-old Eagle Scout and unpaid assistant scoutmaster, bravely shared with a conference of high school teachers his struggles as a gay youth growing up in New Jersey. No sooner had his comments been reported in a local newspaper, the Scouts fired him. The Scouts had issued this formal position statement in 1991: "Homosexual conduct is inconsistent with the requirement in the Scout Oath that a Scout be morally straight and in the Scout Law that a Scout be clean in word and deed, and that homosexuals do not provide a desirable role model for Scouts." A rising conservative movement in America commanded considerable attention from the private and non-profit BSA organization, declaring Baden-Powell's *morally straight* portion of the Scout Oath as its justification for condemning gays in Scouting. When the BSA was founded in 1910, of course, *straight* was not considered a synonym for heterosexual; it was more closely associated with *righteous* or *honorable*.

And never mind the serious risk this posed for gay youth. I didn't know what to do about reports describing the anguish and despair that drove young scouts to attempt suicide. They can find no reason for living. They feel doubly tormented because they are victimized by hurtful gay bashing but can't do anything to change who they are.

Shined even brighter when two Lutheran churches in San Francisco chose to defy our denomination's policy and ordain openly practicing homosexuals. Their suspension for five years was viewed as a compromise. The seminarians in this unauthorized ceremony in 1990 were informed they would not be recognized as valid clergy. So apparently, I'm only valid if I keep my mouth shut!

Shined brighter when thirteen Evangelical Lutheran churches in San Francisco adopted a resolution refusing to break fellowship with the two congregations if they were expelled. Letters of support had come in from around the country. This would further test whether practicing homosexuals would be considered suitable for ordained ministry within a historic Christian denomination – considered middle-of-the-road in mainline Protestantism, neither liberal nor conservative in its theology and social stances. This question was also now under study by Presbyterian and Episcopal churches. The United Church of Christ already permitted the ordination of homosexuals.

Shined brightest when the new ELCA released that October 1993 twenty-one-page report, "The Church and Human Sexuality: A Lutheran Perspective." This social statement was supposed to offer guidance for members of our Church and serve as a public witness in the broader society. You would think the first draft might have provided some relief for me, but I knew better. It didn't take long before God's People had spoken.

The study confessed that the Church had too often overlooked "the created goodness of sexuality." A task force suggested heterosexual marriage is not the only legitimate form of commitment, the Bible supports homosexual unions, masturbation can be considered healthy, and teaching teenagers how to use condoms to prevent disease is a moral imperative. The Church should re-examine traditional disapproval of committed gay and lesbian couples.

The report attacked adultery, promiscuity, sexual abuse, prostitution, anti-gay violence, pornography and the exploitation of sexuality in advertising and entertainment. Homosexuals, in particular, have felt condemned by the Church, have not felt the life-giving Gospel was addressed to them. This draft recognized that many Lutherans take the biblical condemnations of homosexuality in the books of Leviticus and Romans literally and reject homosexual activity as prescribed by God's law. But Lutherans were asked to challenge such attitudes. Always, we begin with the preeminent biblical command – to "love your neighbor as yourself." That passage in the thirteenth chapter of Paul's Letter to the Romans continues, "Love does no wrong to a neighbor; therefore, love is the fulfilling of the law." Gays and lesbians are among the neighbors Christ calls us to love.

Four years in the making, this statement declared the core of human sexuality should be loving, committed relationships and not limited to heterosexual marriages. Local churches had until June to consider the draft and respond. Unfortunately, before ELCA pastors had received their copies – so that they could prepare themselves for the questions and objections raised by their parishioners – it had been released to the press. Many outraged church members mistakenly thought the draft was a new Church policy. A second draft, taking the responses into account, would be prepared for a church-wide assembly of lay and clergy delegates in 1995. But the Lutheran Church's sixty-seven member Conference of Bishops had already expressed reservations about the report. Bishop Richard Foss of the Synod of Eastern North Dakota said many Lutherans would be confused and dismayed by the challenge to the traditional biblical understanding of homosexuality.

The brighter that industrial floodlight shined on the gay movement challenging the Church I served, the more I retreated from my role as a pastor, uneasy because I knew how offensive the gay movement was to so many people of God I served.

The election of our new bishop in November of 1994 surprised even me; but his bold leadership could not allay my restlessness, judged unfit for ministry as I was by God's people. Well-known for his continuing education work at my alma mater in Thousand Oaks, Pastor Peter Nordquist had also served part-time for two years at St. Luke's Lutheran Church in North Hollywood where he had publicly welcomed gay and lesbian congregants since 1985. He now advocated for the ordination of gays and lesbians. He had conducted three wedding-like blessings for gay couples ("holy union services") – contrary to our denomination's stated official opposition to such ceremonies. He claimed these blessings were done with dignity and reverence, not as publicity stunts to change people's minds. And he was familiar with several other pastors and bishops who had performed such rites in quiet defiance of church policies. The church's bishops had adopted a statement in 1993 saying there is no basis in Scripture or church tradition "for the blessing of a homosexual relationship," ruling out their approval for "an official ceremony."

A conflicted feeling that last Saturday in January of 1995, sitting alongside my colleagues at Bishop Nordquist's installation, trying to support this new leader after our denomination had rejected the first draft of that human sexuality proposal. As we sang "The Church's One Foundation," my mind drifted off to an image of the reported, angry parish reactions that had overwhelmed the Chicago headquarters of the ELCA.

Those reactions had led to preparation of a second, more traditional draft, declaring Scripture teaches us that sex between people of the same gender is not following God's will. Nevertheless, the draft also called for respect for gay and lesbian people and for their civil rights. While continuing present policies, the church will further study and discuss the issues, the draft said.

Nordquist questioned the extent to which our best biblical and theological scholarship had participated in the preparation of the first draft of this social statement. In an interview, he had said that divisions within the denomination are too significant to change church positions on sexuality at present.

Bishop Nordquist's son, Michael, had already come out to his family long before he graduated from Pacific Lutheran Theological Seminary the year before Julie and Bud began their studies there. He hardly expected that his Church would suddenly modify its criteria for ordination, that his Church would change for him its official policy barring non-celibate homosexuals from the ministry. But he had changed the way his parents thought about homosexuality. I remember Nordquist saying, "Most people change their minds on the gay issues, not on logic, but from personal experience and acquaintance with gay people."

Most people, Bishop Nordquist. But you have never met my father, have you?

That bright, shining floodlight had revealed what I had tried so hard to conceal, the reality I would continue to face in spite of courageous Scout leaders, seminarians, and church leaders. Curiously, my privacy had been turned-inside-out by the actual forces hoping to liberate all gays and lesbians from the bonds of discrimination. That bright, shining light did not change my unacceptability in the eyes of the people I served. God's People had rejected me; God had rejected me.

By our baptism, we are joined to God's new creation inaugurated by Easter. As Christ was raised, so we walk in newness of life. Unless we're gay. If we're gay, we are still walking in the old age of sin, bondage, and death. I don't think my friend Bud Caine has this in mind when he emphasizes the here and now, walking in newness of life, a new creation. A new creation means what Paul declared: we are all one in Christ.

Apparently, we gays need to wait for the fullness of God's reign someday. In the meantime, God's people are supposed to respect us. Our peculiar relationships should be honored, but marriage is clearly understood as a life-long covenant of faithfulness between a man and a woman.

At least who I am was not directly listed under the misuses of sexuality, along with adultery, abuse, promiscuity, prostitution, practices that spread sexually transmitted diseases, pornography, and manipulation of sexuality in media and advertising.

Here's what the ELCA, the Church I was supposed to serve, was concluding: "On some matters of sexuality, there are strong and continuing differences among us. As we discuss areas where we differ, the power of the Holy Spirit can guide and unite us. Trust in the Gospel brings together people whose differences over sexuality ought not to be a basis for division."

"Ought not to be a basis for division?" We're still talking here about schismatic Lutherans, right? Here's the position of those with whom I'm supposed to unite: "We are convinced that same-gender sexual behavior is sinful, contrary to biblical teaching and our understanding of natural law. The Bible could not be any clearer. We are supposed to agree with God that the practice of homosexuality is wrong. It undermines the basis of God's created order where God made Adam, a man, and Eve, a woman – not two men, not two women – to carry out his command to fill and subdue the earth (Gen. 1:28). Homosexuality cannot carry out that command. It also undermines the basic family unit of husband and wife, the God-ordained means of procreation. It is also dangerous to society."

How am I supposed to unite with you? For you, this is about God's Word. For me, this is about my life. I'm dangerous to society? I'M YOUR PASTOR!

Would God's People, my father's Church, ever recognize the needs of same-gender-oriented individuals to seek relationships of lifelong companionship and commitment? Or will there always be differing and conscience-bound understandings about the place of such relationships within the Christian community? Can we ever reach a consensus about how we regard same-gender committed relationships, even after many years of thoughtful, respectful, and faithful study and conversation?

To protect my privacy, I had quietly walked away from the Boy Scouts. But now I was facing my fellow Christians who were prepared to use God's Word to condemn who I was. How could I accept myself if God's People couldn't accept me? Didn't matter how I interpreted those seven passages of Scripture; what mattered was how they understood it. Why did I have to fight for God's acceptance? What was Easter all about? I thought Easter was supposed to have settled all this two thousand years ago. If God's Love for us is determined by however people decide to interpret the Bible, then what's the point? Is living out the Gospel supposed to include a constant quarrel about what the Gospel means?

Of all the schisms plaguing the Lutheran Church over the centuries and the BSA over the past decade, the only one that mattered was the schism between my father and me – because that ultimately had become a schism between God and me. I had become anathema to my father, an insult to what he had taught his family and preached to his congregation.

So who can separate me from the love of Christ? Apparently my father, the fourth person of the Holy Trinity, and the Church he serves!

CHAPTER 19

Henry
10 April 1998
Good Friday

After our morning together discussing life's "might-have-beens," Denise left me to my Good Friday trials. Meditating on those stations of Jesus' final day did not help me understand what had happened to our foursome. I opted for an alternate VIA DOLOROSA while I walked the paths of Sunriver – a walk through the centuries to review all of the interrogations following that first trial long ago when Jesus of Nazareth stood before Pontius Pilate, the governor of Judaea. My own extended version of the First Station, when Christ was condemned to death.

I could not utter those words "It is finished!" – I could not cast aside my mother's Easter and complete what I had planned – until I had responded one more time to those four eternal words that ask every generation to at least acknowledge and ponder. Two words in Latin: ECCE HOMO!

"Here is the man!" Pontius Pilate had declared, as he presented Jesus to the chief priests and the crowds. That was Pilate's little world, but he was presenting this man to all people, for all time. His wife had warned him, "You must have nothing to do with this innocent man." After his first questions of Jesus, he had said, "I find no basis for an accusation against this man. You brought him to me as one who was perverting the people; and here I have examined him in your presence and have not found this man guilty of any of your charges against him. Neither has Herod, for he sent him back to us. Indeed, he has done nothing to deserve death. I will therefore have him flogged and release him."

Pilate had hoped Herod might relieve him of this matter. Like many of us, Pilate was confused. During the interrogation, Jesus had responded, "Everyone who belongs to the truth listens to my voice." And Pilate had asked him in return, "What is the truth?"

That would be the question, Pontius Pilate. "What is the truth?" What is the truth about this man, Jesus of Nazareth?

To avoid a riot that was fomenting, Pilot had washed his hands before the agitated crowds and exclaimed, "I am innocent of this man's blood. See to his crucifixion yourselves." Little did he know then that this man would be tried over and over again through twenty centuries. Even Jesus had asked the question, "Who do people say that I am?"

Who do people say that you are? My dad, my three best men, my children – who do they say that you are, Jesus of Nazareth? Who do I say that you are?

Jesus on trial, one more time.

I remember asking Professor Mumm one day at seminary, "After twenty centuries, doesn't it seem reasonable to you that we would have a satisfactory answer to Jesus' question by now?"

"Yes, Henry, it does seem reasonable. But we don't, and most likely never will this side of His Second Coming."

The Q community ("Q" is short for *Quelle*, the German word for *source*) had tried this Nazarene. Before the apostle Paul's letters had shaped the identity of the Jesus we now read about in the New Testament, there was a community of followers who offered a different answer to Jesus' question. The Q writings of the earliest Jesus movement, the first writings following his life and crucifixion, do not include any stories about an empty tomb or a doctrine of atonement. Jesus addressed the social injustices of his time, was venerated as a roving sage who preached full acceptance of all people no matter how disreputable or marginal. Such a champion of multiculturalism with no real claim to divinity might be welcomed in many parts of America today. But in the first century, early Christianity had a different direction in mind.

The four evangelists had tried this Nazarene. Mark chose to answer the question differently from John. Matthew and Luke borrowed from Mark, but they each responded to that question in their own way. And none of the four gospels is a biography of Jesus. But all four would agree with John, the last to write his gospel: "Now Jesus did many other signs in the presence of his disciples, which are not written in this book. But these are written so that you may come to believe that Jesus is the Christ, the Son of God, and that through believing you may have life in his name."

But what does that phrase "life in his name" mean? Did John mean life in the here and now, or life in the hereafter, or both?

Church councils wrestling with doctrines about this man who claimed to be the Son of God had tried this Nazarene. Those creeds my mom and dad had recited were developed in the early days of Christianity to settle arguments incited by heresies and false doctrines (the controversies from which the creeds arose). Some would argue that the creeds protect our understanding of Christ. I believe the creeds are part of that stone we need to roll away – museum relics of ancient dogma and doctrine and tradition and orthodoxy. The Nicene Creed partially answered the question this way:

For us and for our salvation
he came down from heaven;

But that does not answer the question for my dad and his troubled heart, or for my brother George and his confusion living with schizophrenia, or for Karl and his constant heartache following his mother's death, or for Andy and his torment serving a Church that condemned him.

For us and for our salvation. What does that mean? Does it mean my mother's Easter – deliverance from the here and now, the promise of eternal life in the hereafter? When Paul told the Philippian jailer what he must do to be saved, he was talking about the jailer's eternal destiny. For my three best men, it did not mean salvation from what cheated them out of abundant life in the here and now.

The medieval Church – ruled by superstitions, subjected to abuses of power, anxious about a second coming in 1000 CE, divided apart into West and East – had tried this Nazarene. Not too sure if those first Easter women would have recognized their Jesus of Nazareth a millennium hence.

Reformation thinkers like Luther and Calvin had tried this Nazarene after the Holy Roman Catholic Church had spent fourteen hundred years competing with the Kingdom of God for authority and power. These Reformation thinkers were trying to separate the kerygma (the Gospel of Jesus Christ) from the Roman state of the fourth century with which it had formed an alliance.

Doubt has tried Jesus. In the seventeenth century, the philosopher-scientist René Descartes began his trial of Jesus by casting doubt on everything he had ever learned about the man from Nazareth. How does our common sense, our daily life experiences, answer your question, Jesus? Maybe there is no answer. Challenging others in his day about how we know what we know, Descartes called into question everything anyone had ever learned about anything. Human reason had found its latest champion, and now the modern world could debate the relationship between faith and reason without the prejudices of the past.

Descartes nervously called into the courtroom a co-defendant – the Holy Eucharist, the Catholic sacrament of Communion. Nervous because Descartes knew of the church's condemnation of scientists like Galileo, convicted for publishing his heliocentric views. At stake in this trial was the truth of Catholic doctrine. How could Descartes reconcile his way of knowing with the Catholic doctrine of *transubstantiation*? This twenty-five cent word described how the underlying substances of the bread and wine, once consecrated by the priest (and only a priest) changed into the substances of the flesh and blood of Jesus Christ (Christ's Real Presence) – even though the color, odor, and taste of the bread and wine (their appearance) were left unchanged. Transubstantiation is about a real conversion, a miracle, and a sacred mystery, beyond human words to explain; but for Descartes, beyond human words to explain was unacceptable. Protestants spoke about symbolism, how the bread and wine represented the body and blood of Christ. Any assault, like that of Descartes or the Protestant Reformation, on this doctrine of transubstantiation threatened the real-world power it gave the Catholic Church, its franchise on salvation. But most likely, Descartes did not intend to open the door as his philosophy did to supplanting faith with reason, although his doubt helped to shift our attention to the here and now and promote those principles which underlie our individual liberty and equality.

In this tradition, learned thinkers of the Enlightenment across Europe and the newly founded United States of America had tried this Nazarene. Benjamin Franklin got away with this heretical claim: "As to Jesus of Nazareth, my opinion of whom you particularly desire, I think the system of Morals and his Religion, as he left them to us, the best the World ever saw or is likely to see; but I apprehend it has received various corrupting Changes; and I have, with most of the present Dissenters in England, some doubts as to his divinity."

Deeply troubled writers like Tolstoy had tried this Nazarene by questioning his own Russian Orthodox Church's support of the state's use of violence in waging war as well as policing its own citizens. The Christian Church preached the principles of Jesus but did not follow them, he lamented. Either you stand by the moral teachings of Jesus (gentleness, meekness, peace-making, turning the other cheek when you are struck, love of enemies), or you stand by the use of force, an indispensable instrument of authority. Tolstoy was confident we could begin to establish the Kingdom of God in the here and now by serving humanity (although he did acknowledge our limitations in fully achieving such blessedness). He could not understand why our modern world had not embraced more enthusiastically the possibility of living out the teachings of Christ.

Theologians of every persuasion have tried this Nazarene. An answer to Jesus' question can be based on his teachings, on his death and resurrection, or on his proclamation that the Kingdom of God is at hand.

Social Gospel theologians like Charles Sheldon (*In His Steps: What Would Jesus Do?*) have tried this Nazarene based on his teachings. Sheldon claimed walking in the steps of Jesus provided the most favorable path forward to find fulfillment in life and a respectable community. Liberation theologians like Father Gutiérrez of Peru have tried this Nazarene, and have found support for their involvement in the political struggles of the poor. Some priests, bearing the cross of Jesus and a sword to fight oppression, have even joined the ranks of violent revolutionists. Some find little or no contradiction between Marxism and Christianity.

Even the definition of atonement itself has tried Jesus of Nazareth. How can it be that this man's death and resurrection achieved at-one-ment for us, what we are incapable of attaining ourselves? Proclaiming those words "He gave his life for us" hardly represents a summary of the theological debates of the last twenty centuries. At its most basic level, when we think about God, we think about who we are and who we are not. That's how the old priest responded to Rudy of Notre Dame football fame: "Son, I only know two things for certain. One, there is a God; and two, I'm not Him." God is defined by otherness. And the way we tend to live our lives (our disobedience and sin) doesn't draw us closer to that otherness; in fact, we confess, the gap between God and us seems to be widening. So we are always hoping for reconciliation with God, for at-one-ment with God.

Theologians could fill a library with their explanations about how Jesus' death and resurrection has achieved atonement for us.

Alluding to the Old Testament Jewish practice of animal sacrifice, theologians explain that Jesus served as our Passover Lamb. Because Jesus was innocent, His blood paid the penalty for our human sin. Some theologians refer to a court of law to explain how Christ paid the penalty for our sin, how his death on the cross is accepted by God as payment for our death penalty. Some theologians claim Satan has kidnapped us, and Jesus' death is a ransom paid to Satan, releasing sinners from their captivity.

In the Middle Ages, theologians like Anselm offered a different explanation. The devil wasn't owed anything; we were the ones who owed God a ransom of satisfaction because we had insulted God by our sin. Jesus' death satisfied God's wrath against us. Like a feudal arrangement between a lowly serf and a great lord – since we did not have the means to pay the debt ourselves, Christ stepped in, substituted for us, to pay our debt.

Theologians like Peter Abelard believed that God so overwhelmed us with His love (by giving of His only Son to die for us) that we can't help but turn our lives around and express our gratitude by obeying His commandments. "Love answers love's appeal," Abelard wrote.

And theologians point out that Christ's death offers so much more than reconciliation. For African-Americans, Christ's death delivered them from sin and death, but his suffering taught them how to stand up to oppressive powers.

Not all Christians have fallen in line with these explanations about atonement. In many Protestant churches, pastors can prepare for Easter Sunday right after their Palm Sunday service the week before. Many Christians, in addition to the historical Protestant aversion to crucifixes featuring Jesus' body, choose to spend as little time as possible reflecting on the agony of Jesus. If we're not bothered with too many cares – because Jesus is a friend of ours – then we're not thinking too much about atonement.

Aside from the teachings about Jesus' death and resurrection, theologians will try to answer that question about who Jesus is by debating about his proclamation that God's kingdom was at hand. Did he mean – considering God's time isn't what we experience as the passage of time – that the kingdom was just around the corner, would appear suddenly bringing an end to history, trumpets sounding at the last day? Or did he mean God's kingdom was dawning like the sunrise, but not here until the full light of day? Or did Jesus mean God's kingdom had arrived in the here and now, was already in our midst? Could all three be true?

One theologian will explain that Jesus considered his own life's work the prelude to God's decisive intervention to establish His reign. The end is near. The present age, the here and now, was beyond any hope of reform. The Day of the Lord, a terrifying day of destruction and judgment, has arrived; the last days have now begun, a climax of history that would come within Jesus' own lifetime. But given the events in Jerusalem two millennia ago, Jesus apparently was wrong about the timing! Albert Schweitzer was convinced Jesus recognized his error before he died.

Another will explain that Jesus considered his own life's work the kingdom of God. The end is here. The kingdom of God wasn't at hand; it was already happening. "For, in fact, the kingdom of God is among you," Jesus had said. God is acting now, in our midst. Unlike John the Baptist, Jesus stood in the tradition of a prophet, expecting in this world the establishment of God's kingdom. Unlike my Grandpa Koehler and Martin Luther, this here and now could be reformed and transformed if enough committed people took action and were willing to die for their convictions. The prophet believes in history.

Jesus' proclamation that the Kingdom of God is within us can be troubling for an institution like the One Holy Catholic and Apostolic Church. Who needs it to establish a relationship with God? Who needs a priest?

Another theologian will explain that the two beliefs ("The end is near" and "The end is here") can be reconciled by accepting this premise: In the ministry of Jesus, God's Kingdom has been inaugurated; but its complete fulfillment is still in the future. The tension between realized and future ("already, but not yet"). Maybe Jesus's ministry was simply trying to offer an alternative vision of how the world could work.

Some theologians worry about how the emphases on Jesus' teachings and proclamation about God's kingdom can be redefined to accommodate progressive political values. Some people have lost sight of the truth, these theologians warn. Get back to the basic truth here, they caution. Jesus is our Savior from sin, delivering us from the wrath to come, renewing us in righteousness, and opening heaven to us. Most assuredly, we are called to oppose social evils and to love our neighbor. But we march to that call knowing full well our practical good works are but a preparation for life eternal; this life in the here and now, this moral and spiritual training ground, is not God's kingdom.

Albert Schweitzer's trial of Jesus may be one of the most authentic and revealing, but not because of this Lutheran theologian's scholarship – like his study, *The Quest of the Historical Jesus,* that challenged so many of the traditional answers to Jesus' question. What could be more authentic than Schweitzer's sacramental life work as a physician at the hospital he and his wife Helene founded in Lambaréné, Gabon (then a province of French Equatorial Africa)? Meeting the desperate medical needs of his African patients – this is how we experience God in our lives. That's who Jesus is: Love. Active love. A practical Christianity. Schweitzer spoke about a "Reverence for Life" to imitate Jesus' religion of love proclaimed in his Sermon on the Mount. Matthew 25:40 was Schweitzer's favorite verse: "Whatever you do unto the least of these my brethren, you have done it unto me." This was Schweitzer's image of the Kingdom of God. "Who do people say that I am?" Jesus is our neighbor in need, answered Schweitzer. And such simple service to others in the name of Christ does not require our contempt for reason and rational thinking – such attributes are welcomed if you are joining Schweitzer on his journey of faith.

Spirituality has tried Jesus. In the American tradition, this trial answers Jesus' question differently depending on who's sitting in the courtroom. New Age animists, James Redfield and *The Celestine Prophecy,* traditional American writers like Emerson, Whitman, and Thoreau – these have not, are not, journeying down the same road. If finding oneself no longer requires the Church than it surely no longer requires Jesus' atoning sacrifice. Finding oneself may not even require being at one with the divine. Being at one with one's self may be all that's necessary. Variations on solipsism usually don't include any reference to the agony suffered by Jesus on Good Friday.

The Jesus Seminar has tried the man from Nazareth. Maybe we didn't know who you were, Jesus. Maybe if some media-savvy scholars could recover the real Jesus – what he said, what he did – we would have a satisfactory answer to his question. Not the biblical Jesus, not the creedal Jesus of dogma and church tradition, but the continuing quest for the historical Jesus. The authenticity of the words and deeds attributed to Jesus in the gospels came up for a vote. Using social anthropology, history, and textual analysis, these scholars used colored beads to cast their vote. Conclusion: We aren't supposed to prepare for the end of the world; we're supposed to prepare for our part in making the world right in the here and now. Like the "Q" community, when we think about Jesus, we should think about a wandering Jewish sage who spoke to the injustices of his time. These scholars challenged traditional Christian beliefs, but did their reorientation to the here and now make any difference to my three best men?

Modernity has tried Jesus.

Atheists and humanists have tried Jesus.

How many people, struggling with daily hardships and sorrows, have tried this Easter Jesus? Searching, hoping for a better day, a better day *now*. Not too interested in that spiritual training ground stuff! Wracked by pain from which no escape seems possible. If Jesus of Nazareth is the man, then why do so many people mask their suffering with alcohol and drug abuse, many of whom have heard the Good News of this Savior?

For us and our salvation, he came down from heaven. My dad was looking for more than salvation defined by the resurrection of the dead and the life of the world to come. He was looking for peace and assurance, for a light in the darkness. "Jesus, my dad struggled in the here and now to walk with you, to talk with you, to know that he was truly your own. You, Jesus, after all, had promised him so, that he is your own."

My three best men were searching for a here and now that could do battle against their perceived valueless life. They were looking for salvation that could lead them through the darkness of night to a new day.

And I, with my efforts to reinvent my mother's Easter, have tried this Nazarene. By devaluing the here and now, my mother's Easter had failed to help George, Karl, and Andy endure the pain and confusion and depression they faced in life. I had redefined my mother's Easter promise of eternal life – God's gift of salvation – to begin the day we are baptized. And my redefinition did not naively presume that living in God's eternal presence each day protected us from every affliction and tribulation. It did expect, however, a relationship with God that did not concede unbearable pain and fear and desolation and depression in this here and now by promising life in the hereafter.

Who are you, Jesus of Nazareth, King of the Jews, the Christ, the Son of God?

A lot of trials this Good Friday, Jesus standing before my dad, my three best men, and me. Both Jesus of Nazareth and Jesus of my mother's Easter. Either, or, it didn't matter to my three best men. None of my trials shed any light on the darkness that had engulfed them.

By late afternoon, I was tired enough of trials, so I slowly began my walk back to the lodge. I had reviewed enough answers to Jesus' question, "Who do people say that I am?" Now I found myself reciting Bonhoeffer's poem from prison, "Who Am I?" Weary and empty at asking questions.

I have tried to remain faithful to the Gospel of Mark scholarship that preserves the original ending of chapter 16:1-8. Mark 16:9-20 is most likely a later addition. This Gospel ends abruptly with no resurrection appearance at all. Written years later, the other three Gospels are already serving Christian communities with a story about Jesus' crucifixion and resurrection ready for the first-stage of theological councils and creeds. No such discussions, though, could be based on Mark's gospel, because this gospel requires the reader to finish the story; we are left to tell the rest of this story, to conclude it one way or the other. Only the reader can provide the closing verses. "He is going ahead of you to Galilee." Always going ahead of us into the Galilees of our life. Who knows when or where or how we will meet him? A Gospel of expectations still unfilled. The Gospel of Mark requires Christians to live a life of expectancy.

But after all of my trials today, I'm tired of expectancy. For us (my dad, my brother George, by brother-in-law Karl, and my best friend Andy), and for our salvation, Jesus, you came down from heaven. And then what? Your light did not shine bright enough in the darkness for them; in fact, their darkness overcame your light.

Not satisfied with any of the answers to Jesus' question, I took a bench on the path north of the Cardinal Landing Bridge, overlooking the Deschutes. Nature's reminder all around me: what is important and what is not.

The more I had reworked my mother's Easter, the more I felt like Descartes, trying to stay true to my value system while revising it to better serve the here and now needs of people I loved. Staying true to my value system required me to accept the relationship with God I had inherited from my mother. We are, I had been taught, finite before our infinite God. "Woe to you who strive with your Maker, earthen vessels with the potter! Does the clay say to the one who fashions it, 'What are you making'? or 'Your work has no handles.'" St. Paul made the same point. "But who indeed are you, a human being, to argue with God? Will what is molded say to the one who molds it, 'Why have you made me like this?'" We are finite, God is infinite – no matter when we begin living in His eternal presence. We aren't supposed to ask, "Why did God let this unfairness befall me?"

But my value system also expects me to ask questions about the reality I experience every day – what my three best men experienced every day. I'm supposed to ask questions about what we had inherited, questions about what we had been taught. I consider asking questions a core value of what it means to be a human being.

Kierkegaard would disagree. Our refusal to be the clay pot is our refusal to become what God had in mind for us as our Creator. That's why the Church's proscription against suicide is based on the belief that, as children of God, we are not our own. Voluntary death usurps God's prerogative. A collapse of our values does not cause despair, Kierkegaard argued; it's our refusal to become what God expects of us that leads to despair.

I met Denise on the path leading west from the lodge, between the front and back nines of the South Meadows course. She had spotted me in the distance walking south along the airstrip.

"I'm tired," I took Denise's hand. "Had hoped to answer Jesus' question, 'Who do people say that I am?' On trial all day long, my mother's Easter and what I'm doing to myself today. I'm more troubled today than I've ever been about their deaths. I can't imagine how those followers of Jesus must have felt that Friday evening long ago. All three of my best men baptized, but what did that mean? How could my brother reconcile his mental illness with the faith he had inherited? He couldn't even decode the confusion he faced each day. I have some idea about your brother's forsakenness after your mother's death because you have shared this same grief with me. How was he supposed to mend his broken relationship with God? And I can only imagine Andy's anguish trying to serve a Church that condemned him for his homosexuality, his torment doubly painful because his father the pastor did not accept him. But I thought Christ died for all people, so that all people may live."

Denise had patiently waited to respond. "You're still trying to stay true to that value system you inherited from your mother. I thought you were dying to that; I thought you were burying that this weekend."

We spent our Good Friday evening much like those first Easter women – full of questions, sullen with heartache, and trying to make sense of what had happened.

CHAPTER 20

George
10 April 1988
Good Friday

My mother preferred to worship her Resurrected Lord and Savior. Her Easter Jesus, she used to say. Wouldn't dare miss any details of Holy Week, but showing up at that empty tomb with the other women was what she waited for all year long. She forced herself to worship the Good Friday Jesus, the helpless and suffering Son of God who died on a cross to save the world. "To save the world from what exactly" is a concern my mother didn't care to think about too much. Like a twelve-year-old catechism student, she accepted the belief that some sacrificial offering must be presented on our behalf to satisfy God's demand that payment be made for our sinful and unclean nature. A sacrificial offering, like a lamb, pure and holy. Jesus died to take away our sins, to pay the price we were unable to pay. My mother didn't care about anthropological studies describing ancient practices of human sacrifice to appease the gods. She just looked forward to hearing that news about the empty tomb.

But all the linens, paraments, and candles had been stripped from the altar the night before to symbolize Jesus's capture and humiliation at the hands of the soldiers. No flowers, no banners, no adornments. So her place of worship was cold, lifeless, and uncomfortable this Good Friday evening in 1988. And like so many Holy Week Thursday nights, she had lain awake questioning what the sacrifice of God's Son on a cross meant for her son and his schizophrenia. For all of her faithful years worshiping in a Lutheran church, she had never once heard anyone say the word *schizophrenia*. At her weekly Bible Study group, she had boldly inquired about it; she was quickly redirected to the more generic question about why God allows human suffering. Once again this year, her heart was troubled, and she was tired.

I'm tired too. I've been sitting down here since early this morning, in the cold, lifeless, and uncomfortable garage below my apartment in Astoria, sitting on a faded yellow wooden kitchen chair, trying to understand how the death of a Savior named Jesus could possibly save me. Save me from what? From my schizophrenia? From what I'm about to do?

A visitor at rehab handed me this little leaflet yesterday from Everlasting Life Ministries:

> *"The million dollar question: Will you go to heaven when you die? Here is a quick test. Have you ever told a lie, stolen anything, or used God's name in vain? Jesus said, 'Whoever looks at a woman to lust for her has already committed adultery with her in his heart.' Have you looked with lust? Will you be guilty on Judgment Day? If you have done those things, God sees you as a lying, thieving, blasphemous, adulterer at heart. The Bible warns that if you are guilty you will end up in Hell. God is not willing that any perish. He sent his Son to suffer and die on the cross for sinners. We broke God's Law, but Jesus paid our fine. That means He can legally dismiss our case. He can commute our death sentence. 'For God so loved the world that He gave His only Begotten Son, that whoever believes in Him should not perish but have everlasting life.' Then He rose from the dead and defeated death. Please repent (Turn from sin) today, and God will grant everlasting life to all who trust in Jesus. Then read your Bible daily and obey it."*

Let me see now. Will my schizophrenia, which has led me off the right path so many times, leave me guilty on Judgment Day? Am I guilty because of my schizophrenia? If God knows my hair count, He also knows of my mental disorder, which leaves me incapable of thinking about Him as He prefers. So will He still legally dismiss His case against me?

How can I remove the self-stigma I feel about my mental illness? I'm forced to deal with the stigma and the mental disorder. I haven't isolated myself from my family and my friends. My family and my friends have isolated themselves from me. Seems like my mother and dad were always paying attention to troubles that had nothing to do with me. I was getting used to it, but they had trouble understanding my troubles. I can't be fixed, and my schizophrenic headache is a headache for even the professionals. I can't imagine how it must be for people like my parents.

When my dad died after his fourth heart attack in 1984, on a Friday morning in early September, I figured my mother and the rest of my family would gather around me. I figured wrong. As if my schizophrenia prevented me from realizing what had happened. Come on, people, read some literature about this stuff, would ya'! That was my dad who died. What the hell!

I was born for a troubled life. I was born with schizophrenia, something wrong with my brain that patiently waited to wreak its havoc on my life. But that makes no sense. Apparently, God missed this one when he declared His creation GOOD. Although my troubles in life are not entirely God's fault. The drugs and alcohol I have abused have altered His creation. I suppose that could be a case God has against me.

The trouble is, my troubles trouble other people besides me, people like my mother, people like my brother. But I have found salvation, a way out of this mental disorder that I'm trapped in, and a way out of these troubles. I can put an end to it. The trouble is, putting an end to it also puts an end to me.

I chose Good Friday to end my troubles because I knew this would be least hurtful to my mother. It will be a bad Good Friday for her, but she's only two days away from her Easter promise. Although I'm not sure if my mother can make sense of her Easter promise after what I'm about to do.

I was talking about this last week at rehab with Crystal and Manny. Crystal thinks she's Manny's girlfriend, but he doesn't feel the same about her. She was asking him about what had happened to his older brother, Vincent. How had he ended his life last week? Out of hope and out of dope, so decided to blow his brains out too.

"Ya' know, Manny, I was surprised your brother could be buried by a priest in the Catholic cemetery." I think Crystal meant well, was curious, that's all, but Manny quickly cleared up any misunderstanding.

"You don't know what you're talking about, Crystal. My brother wasn't right in his mind, and if you're not right, God's not condemning you for taking your own life. I'm not holding my brother responsible for what he did. He wasn't capable of such a responsibility. It's not as if he even knew what he was goin' through every day."

Like Crystal, I was curious too. "Is that what you and your mother think, Manny? Or is that what the priest told you?"

"It's what my mom and I think, and it's what our priest told us the Church believes. What my brother did can be a mortal sin, can cost you your salvation. But God knew his suffering, and does not hold it against him."

I felt some relief when Manny explained this, found myself kind of preoccupied for a moment while I thought more about this and what I was going to do. They were both staring at me when I acknowledged my relief. "Seems to me that maybe your brother, Manny, knew this too in his heart, and felt closer to God than he had ever felt before. I think a lot of people who take their life think they are separating themselves from God forever. I don't. I'm with Holden Caulfield on this one. Jesus isn't sending anyone to Hell for taking their life." Neither of them knew where I was coming from, so they kept staring at me.

But then again, maybe there's something about taking your own life that puts you in a category all by yourself. Maybe all that talk about Vincent only applies to him, so someone else who takes their life should be judged apart from Vincent's suicide. I'm hoping, though, that my mother will understand my misery and trust that I just wanted to head home. If I believe such a possibility still awaits me, I don't think the way I'm preparing to head home cancels out such a possibility.

I can't help but ask, "Who will care about what I'm doing?" My neighbor, my landlord, the police? Word at rehab is that our president won't care. Won't care because he doesn't understand mental illness. Pretty much decided to set mentally ill people out on the streets. Well, kicked them out of the state hospitals and moved them into lousy board-and-care facilities in rundown parts of the city. Same difference.

Here we go again with another injustice, another stain on who we are in America, failing to take care of those who cannot care for themselves.

Homeless mentally ill wandering aimlessly in the streets. Worse yet, untreated mentally ill committing violent crimes. Like the murder of former Congressman Allard Lowenstein, like the murder of John Lennon – the guilty individuals dealing with untreated schizophrenia.

John Hinckley, the same, tried to assassinate President Reagan in 1981. Two years later, Reagan requested an opportunity to visit John Hinckley so that he could personally forgive him. Authorities had to explain reality to the president. He didn't get it. Nobody gets it. The president showed no interest in the need for research or better treatment for severe mental illness, even though he was personally connected with families dealing with untreated schizophrenia and suicide.

I'm sure my television cable channel music won't miss a beat. It'll keep on playing hour after hour like it does now, with or without me. My mother will care, and so will my brother, I guess. He decided to block out my troubles once by refusing any phone calls I tried to make to him. His phone number would not work from my phone. He warned me he would do this. Like everyone, he has troubles of his own, and he's the kind of father who helps bear the troubles of his three kids, and he's the pastor right now of a Lutheran congregation with troubles of its own. I think he still loves me, but I think he can't be his brother's keeper right now. He's the keeper for too many other people. I don't know if God will care. If He did, I wouldn't be doing what I'm about to do. To tell you the truth, I feel forsaken by Him, like Jesus must have felt that long night before His death.

My mother returned to Southern California three months ago, closer now to her sister and my two sisters. A month later, my brother moved away to serve a church in Portland. I'm not so good on my own. Never have been. Honest to God, I don't know what the hell they were all thinking. I'm left here with a brain that works off and on, and when it is working, I can't be sure what it's even working on. I'm thinking about one thing, and all of a sudden, it dawns on me that my brain is thinking about something else.

I'm more scared of life than I've ever been.

The Cold War will never end.

Now we're talking about a nerve-gas arms race with the Soviet Union. So at the Army's Pine Bluff, Arkansas, arsenal, we have resumed chemical weapons production with an updated generation of toxins to deter an attack in Europe by the Soviet Union's more current and extensive stockpile.

I'm trying to hold steady a photograph of my mother and me at the airport. I had picked her up at LAX once after she had flown up to Oregon to see my brother and his family. We hadn't moved up there yet, and I remember looking forward to that after I heard her tell me all about it. I didn't want to stay in San Gabriel where I had grown up. I needed to move away from that place. In the photograph, my mother looks so thin, and I look so fat. She was always thin, though, and I was once thin like her. I don't know what happened. My mother hardly looks her age. This photograph was taken a week after her sixty-seventh birthday on the eighteenth of July. She always seems so happy to see me. I've got my arm around her shoulder, but she can barely touch the middle of my back with her hand.

I've already smoked two packs of Benson & Hedges today, but that's not unusual for me. Always Benson & Hedges, like my dad. I sure loved him. I pretty much keep this lonely place of mine in a state of sustained second-hand tobacco smoke. I'm smoking when I'm not even smoking. I wish I had a gun, but I don't. And besides, my mother would kill me if I ever shot myself with a gun. For the trouble I've caused everyone, hanging is what I deserve. I do have this backpacking rope my brother used to carry. Bud had fashioned a waist-size loop with a bowline knot at one end of his rope so he would be prepared with a ready-made rescue line.

My brother once saved me with this rope when we were climbing Mt. Whitney with Andy, smoking our Marlboro cigarettes while we whistled the theme song from *The Magnificent Seven*. I hadn't smoked much until then, and I grew lightheaded at 13,000 feet. Below the ridge that leads to the summit, I shifted my spot on the narrow trail, lost my footing along the steep switch-back, and tumbled down the talus slope about twenty feet, barely able to hold my fall. My brother had that loop down to me in a second, I secured it around my chest, and he and Andy pulled together as I crawled over the broken rocks back up to the trail.

Now this rope will save me a second time, save me from a life no longer worth living.

It has taken me most of the day to figure this out. One of the two-by-eight floor trusses in this single stall garage should hold my weight. I position the old wooden kitchen chair directly beneath a floor truss that has an oversized, electrical conduit cutout between the truss and the ceiling. Standing on the chair, I barely reach high enough to thread the end of the rope through that cutout. I stepped down, placed a sturdy five-gallon metal bucket on the chair, and carefully lifted myself up again using the dangling rope to support me. This metal bucket should provide the extra height I need to ensure a quick and certain death. After I secure the rope over the truss, I step off the bucket and chair while pulling down on the rope. A little creaking worried me, but this would have to do. I should be able to place the noose around my neck by using the truss to balance myself. All that's left, then, is to kick the back of the chair out from beneath me. This is a lot of trouble, though. I didn't think it would be so much trouble. What the hell.

I should be sad as I walk around my apartment for the last time. But I'm not. I'm just leaving, after all, and I've left places before. I sit on my bed and stare at that photograph of my mother and me. I stare at it as though I could take it with me. Maybe I will. Looking at her smiling face in that photograph, I try to imagine her face when she hears the news of my death. She will be mad at me at first, but then, she has been mad at me plenty of times before and has recovered from it. I'm not so sure about this time though. I know she has a difficult time ever feeling any anger toward God. She can usually figure out a way to justify how God has answered her prayers, even when it is apparent to me that God has not. This will be confusing for her, but then my mental disorder has been confusing for her all these years. I think she'll put the two together, my schizophrenia and my suicide, and that will let God off the hook. And that's what's so crazy. That's pretty much the reason why I'm hanging myself.

I'll take this photograph with me.

Lighting another cigarette makes me think I'm merely on a mission to take care of something. I don't think about which cigarette will be my last because I don't want to think about the last. For the first time in a long time, I refrained from drinking any beer last night because I didn't want my mother to think I was drunk when I did this. I hesitate for a moment before taking off my tennis shoes and then realize I'll need them on to help support my climb up onto that metal bucket. I find myself arranging the chair one more time, although I can't account for how I got back down here in the garage. But I've got the photograph with me.

My mother is attending the 7:00 PM Good Friday service today at Christ Lutheran Church in Monterey Park, and I suspect by Easter Sunday she'll be forced to reconcile the news about my suicide with her news about Jesus and the empty tomb. Maybe from my brother, who will figure this out. He's usually good at figuring out things like this, but he'll be too late this time. He'll be calling me about our Sunriver Reunion. He always calls the week before his anniversary. We were supposed to meet there every year after his wedding. We had made this promise to each other back then in 1970 to stand by each other for life. Maybe we weren't as serious as we thought. I don't feel a need to write any note. Most of my adult life has been a note. Besides, I've got the photograph with me.

I'm not waiting any longer. The night is not exactly my best friend.

From Psalm 22, my mother's pastor raises his voice slightly to proclaim Jesus' protest from the cross, "My God, my God, why have you forsaken me?" As each verse of the Psalm is recited, my mother uses her favorite bookmark to follow the reading. It's the same photograph I'm staring at, the two of us at the airport. I can hear my mother singing while I tightly clench the rope to climb up onto the chair and the metal bucket.

Beneath the cross of Jesus I long to take my stand;
The shadow of a mighty rock Within a weary land,
A Home within a wilderness, A rest upon the way,
From the burning of the noontide heat And troubles of the day.

I want the troubles to end, that's all. Only way I know how. No more Haldol, no more Norwalk, no more rehab, no more dope, no more beer. I carefully position the photograph in between the metal bucket and the back of the chair. Like the one thief hanged with Jesus today on Golgotha, I murmur, "Jesus, remember me when you come into your kingdom." Why did I wait until now to say that? My brother always preached that God's Kingdom was at hand. What does *at hand* mean?

Like my mother, I had been taught that God would never let me go. So I don't know what the hell happened. What I wouldn't do right now to hold my mother's hand. Nobody's holding my hand anymore. I've been afraid of life all my life, so holding someone's hand would have been helpful. My mother's hand. God's hand. Thinking about my Grandpa Koehler's world this side of death, waitin' for God to take us to where we have our permanent home, holding hands through those thorny ways would seem like a good idea. Most of my life has reinforced Grandpa Koehler's disdain for this earthly existence.

No thanks to my parents and grandparents, I was already on high alert, so not easy to diagnose my schizophrenia. Not exactly what I needed, an extra dose of paranoia and fear. Don't know about the other three, but I wish now we had kept our ninth-green promise.

As I step from the seat-edge of the chair to the top of the metal bucket, I let go of the rope with one hand and grab hold of the two-by-eight truss. I'm surprised my hands are shaking so much when I brace my forearms against the truss so I can secure the noose around my neck.

Our Father, who art in heaven, I mumble to myself,
hallowed be thy name, thy kingdom come,
thy will be done, on earth as it is in heaven.
Give us this day our daily bread;

I'm feeling a little dizzy now, and my shaking hands are making me more nervous. My eyes are filling up with tears and sweat and starting to burn. With my forearms still braced against the truss, I instinctively finish The Lord's Prayer, closing my eyes, hoping to stop the burning.

and forgive us our trespasses,
as we forgive those who trespass against us;
and lead us not into temptation, but deliver us from evil.
For thine is the kingdom, and the power, and the glory,
forever and ever. Amen

I keep my eyes shut as if I could avoid witnessing my death.

CHAPTER 21

Henry
11 April 1998
Saturday

On that Good Friday ten years ago, my mother had slowly risen to her feet and watched the usher pass by in procession carrying a rough-hewn wooden cross. Old Simon Loeffelbein measured each step to the altar, trying to imitate and honor the footsteps of his Savior. "Behold, the life-giving cross on which was hung the salvation of the whole world," Pastor Messner uttered in a clear but sacred tone. My mother responded with the rest of the congregation, "Oh, come, let us worship him." And after a short period of silence, the congregation had sung,

Ah, Holy Jesus
Who was the guilty?
Who brought this upon thee?
Alas, my treason, Jesus, hath undone thee.
'Twas I, Lord Jesus, I it was denied thee;
I crucified thee.

Behold, the bloodstained garage floor and broken wooden chair that salvation and the life-giving cross of Jesus had missed that Friday. Baptized in our mother's cradled arms on a Sunday morning in March of 1950 at Our Savior's Lutheran Church, George's life was already headed for this. Did my mother have a clue?

My brother's body was not discovered until the next morning. The police had responded to my early Saturday morning phone call. George need not have worried about any extra height with the metal bucket to ensure enough of a drop for a quick and certain death. Must have lost his balance when he tried to place that noose around his neck. When he came crashing down, the force of his weight drove a splintered spindle of the broken wooden chair into his neck and carotid artery. He lay bleeding to death on the cold cement floor until his long night had ended – his long night with no one standing by him. Except for that photograph of our mom and him.

While he lay bleeding to death on that cold cement floor, my mother was sitting silently in prayer in her cold, lifeless, and uncomfortable church, for over an hour, gently holding the hand of her good Lutheran friend Delores, as if she were holding the hand of Jesus. She took responsibility for my brother's suicide to her deathbed – as if she had denied him and his mental illness. Was that my treason too? And was it the Church's treason?

> *Lamb of God, who takest away the sins of the world, have mercy on us.*
> *Grant us peace.*

Never imagined such a thing, my brother completing suicide. Should have, I know now. I will say *completing suicide* because I do not think of him committing a crime, committing self-murder. He completed an act of self-surrender to a crippling mental disorder. More than likely to occur in those individuals who are not adequately treated. My mother and I did not know if George had been avoiding his medication. People like my brother are not likely to share their suicidal intentions with others, leaving us at a disadvantage when it came to any life-saving intervention. We knew of no antidepressants or mood stabilizers.

Living life with this statistic has not made it any easier: "Nearly one-third of those diagnosed with schizophrenia will attempt suicide." How am I supposed to reconcile church orthodoxy and creeds and my mother's Easter with that statistic and my brother's decision to end his life?

At George's funeral, I read from I Timothy 6:12, those words about fighting the good fight of the faith. Could the apostle Paul understand what that might look like for someone with a mental illness like schizophrenia?

In his *Cliffs of Despair: A Journey to the Edge*, Tom Hunt spoke about such a fight that a healthy mind could hardly imagine. We share a similar story about losing a loved one to schizophrenia and suicide. The experience of living, he concluded – for my brother, for his brother-in-law – might feel like dying. We should not be surprised that mental illness raises the suicide risk more than physical illness.

So did my brother win the good fight or lose it? I share my loss with another pastor who sees the hand of God in his brother's decision to end his suffering from schizophrenia on his own terms, a victory achieved, taking control of his own life by ending it. I could only think about how my brother felt abandoned by God's hand, how the light had failed to overcome his darkness. George and I had grown up holding our mother's Easter hand. This theologian and his brother had grown up in a good Western secular humanist home, an environment in marked contrast to our home. This theologian had rebelled in college, choosing at last to major in religion, a direct challenge to his father, an avowed atheist. Given our different backgrounds, questions, and grief, it is conceivable that we might think differently about God's hand in our brother's schizophrenia and suicide.

Golfing together on my wedding day had been a way for me to reconnect with my brother. As happens so often for close siblings, a wedding day is a mixed bag of emotions. Even as I had assumed my new role as Denise's spouse, I had tried hard to explain to George what he still meant to me. I don't know that he understood.

When George hit a golf ball, it would disappear into the sky. He usually outdrove me, and this made for a welcome respite from the usual shadow thing he endured. And George was a much better Little League player than I ever was, hitting out-of-the-park home runs at least once a week. When it came time to watch my brother George play baseball, it took half a bleacher to provide enough seating for our family. To bug him though, as brothers will do, I called him "Duke" whenever I watched him play.

But for most everything else, he seemed to live just a step behind me.

A step behind most everyone else.

But we didn't know about his mental illness when he was growing up; we didn't know about his paranoid schizophrenia. Nor did he. His self-awareness of this chronic, severe brain disorder emerged slowly during the years following my wedding in 1970. Slowly enough that we failed to respond sooner than we did. A clever thief in the night, that schizophrenia – stole into my parent's home every night and little by little kidnapped my brother. We didn't bother to wait for a ransom note; a mental illness like schizophrenia does not return its victim. Our denial, shame, and amateur psychology had left the back door unlocked; our support and treatment efforts were hindered by those same shortcomings. The diagnosis and acceptance of my brother's schizophrenia was a long-term process for our family.

Norman Vincent Peale wasn't talking about my brother George when he assured us that a simple childlike faith could overcome any complexities that might trouble us. My brother's schizophrenia was not a complexity of life over which George could prevail with a simple childlike faith because his complexity of life was incapable of reverting back to a simple childlike faith.

How exactly does a family pay attention to early warning signs for schizophrenia? In an attempt to self-medicate, increased reliance on drugs and alcohol might leave a person less motivated, less emotional, less likely to interact with others. Was my brother losing sight of his goals in his early twenties because he was relying on drugs and alcohol, or was his reliance an escape from a life without any goals? My brother had grown up paranoid of his era, afraid of life and the *eve of destruction*. He had felt anxious and confused since he was a kid. He could sit quietly sometimes for an entire day. How much was such behavior his personality or his schizophrenia? Until he talked about what he might be thinking, we couldn't be sure.

George couldn't be expected to understand that his marijuana reduced the effectiveness of his medication; that would have required clearer thinking than his schizophrenia allowed. Unfortunately, drugs like Haldol, which can be effective in treating specific symptoms, particularly hallucinations and delusions, may not be as helpful with other symptoms like reduced motivation and the inability to communicate one's emotions.

But the George I knew on my wedding day, his second year at Cal State, was hardly tormented by any of the delusions and bizarre behavior he would exhibit the next few years. Had smoked his share of pot with our cousin and with a neighborhood kid named Nick Arlotti, had confessed to stealing real estate *For Sale* signs around town and unloading all of them late one night on the unsuspecting front lawn of Sally Rollinger's house, and had blown off a couple of poor grades during his high school sophomore year. Big deal. Blessed with an ageless youthful look, an understated sense of humor, and a genuinely winsome personality, my brother had super destiny written all over his future.

Three weeks before my family arrived for a vacation at our parent's home, George had been arrested for hiding naked in the community park two blocks away – no explanation given. This left Denise and me in a quandary, thinking about the safety of our three little children but still trying to support my parents. How were we to make sense of my brother's behavior? My parents had alerted us: "Your brother, Bud, seems so different these days, hardly speaking with us, and when he does, talking in a dull and monotonous voice. Dad's not so sure he can keep him working at the machine shop. He seems so lazy these days."

George usually protested with anger and fear our parents' loving pleas for him to seek clinical help. Why would he think he needed help? He believed his delusions or hallucinations were real.

When our mother walked into our room the next afternoon with a bruised and swollen left cheek to report George had struck her, I was left with no choice but to confront my sick brother. And confront him I did! "What's goin' on here, George?"

All George could offer was a garbled explanation about how sick and tired he was of people spying on him. I tried to refocus his thinking by asking again about why he had struck our mother. I might as well have been talking to the empty bottle of Budweiser.

Unfortunately, we fought for real this time, which brothers should never do. Our eyes exchanged a hundred childhood memories in that single moment, our souls laid bare to emotions brothers should not have to feel. Not a fair match, of course, given his drunken condition – a dreadful mix that day of twenty-four-ounce bottles of Budweiser on top of his Haldol medication. I called the police to arrest my brother, driving a wedge further between us.

What might be everyday sights and sounds for me might be high-priority alien invasion warnings for my brother. He had grown increasingly suspicious of our military authorities, not convinced they were representing the United States. Maybe they were representing some alien force. I'm surprised George Lucas never consulted with my brother George, making use of some of his sophisticated designs for space-age weapons and defense systems – some more credible than others, but all designed with genuine anticipation of alien invaders. Maybe Lucas did, and George never bothered to tell us about it. I know my brother eventually submitted some of his drawings to the Air Force but was politely told that his designs did not fit current military criteria.

Schizophrenia is living a life on the *eve of destruction*, but our family treated my brother like America treated the songwriter P. F. Sloan. Sloan would later tell of his rejection, first by his writing partner after he had put a melody to the words, and then by the publishing company representatives. He was told not to write any more songs like that and was attacked as a communist dupe for his unpatriotic poem about our country's fears and anxieties. Ironically, as for trying to stir up any kind of revolution here, the only reason we even have his song today is that somewhere in the Great Midwest of America a DJ played the wrong side of Barry McGuire's latest release!

In many ways, my brother suffered the same misfortune that Sloan suffered. It would seem both tried praying, but to no avail. I'm sure they had to wonder if God was paying any attention to them.

I don't think now that my reinvented version of my mother's Easter would have made any difference for my brother George. Ten years after his death, I sometimes think my mother's Easter – along with Grandpa Koehler and Luther – served as a perfect guide along his schizophrenic path to that Good Friday in 1988.

CHAPTER 22

Karl

25 August 1990

Benson Lumber Company

It's over.

I can't believe it.

I can't believe it's over. ·

I thought our millwright, Lou Rokowski, might have spotted me this morning. I avoided most of my Hoo-Hoo buddies, my favorite locals, and the curiosity seekers, by parking half a mile past our mill entrance on Juniper Gin Road. Our six-foot-high chain link fence along this county access road running south off the main highway ended in the woods there, about fifty yards from our actual property line. I had walked slowly around the last pile of pecker poles, getting close enough so I could hear what was going on. Our diminished log inventory didn't afford much cover. Lou was standing toward the rear of the crowd, and to help manage his emotions I think, he kept looking up to the sky and to his left and right. He hesitated for a moment after looking in my direction. I wasn't supposed to be there today.

My dad didn't get out of his pickup. He had parked it past the corner of the old A-Frame office next to the main entrance so he could watch and listen from there without much bother from anyone. I was too far off in the distance for him to see me.

My heart ached for both of these men, one more than the other, I do not know. My dad had traded his whole life to build Benson Lumber, and on this August 25 Saturday morning, he had to witness over forty years of dreams and toil and pride dissipate into the air like the cloud of sawdust on our last day of production two weeks ago. Lou our millwright, though, was the genius who had hand-built the head-saw, the edger, the log deck, the green-chain, the Swedish gang saw, and our new fencing mill, all of the equipment that made us who we are.

At five minutes past 9:00 AM, the husky voice of seasoned auctioneer Ralph Maynard from Maynard Brothers Liquidation summoned the crowd to attention. "Good morning," his portable crackling speaker system announced, loud enough to hear from the highway. "Welcome to the public auction of Benson Lumber machinery and equipment," his voice dramatically fluctuating like a ring announcer for the main event at a Saturday night fight.

"Public," I thought. Yeah, that's fine, but does that mean everyone in the vicinity is entitled to hear these proceedings? And I didn't like his choice of language to explain the sale of our family's lumber business, started by my dad the year I was born. Our family name is not for sale, asshole, so you might want to clarify what exactly is available for purchase. If I'm gone, if I don't exist anymore, then the mill doesn't exist anymore either. You're just selling some machinery and equipment.

"Whatever you can unbolt, dismantle, and truck away from this property, we are prepared to sell you. We'll give you two weeks to arrange transport for the larger pieces of machinery, but our goal is to clear out everything from this place."

This place?

That's it? This place?

This place is where nineteen-year-old Tommy Gilwood was killed last year when a two-by-six board kicked back from the edger like a missile into his face. Maybe he hadn't listened to Dave's instructions and warnings, or maybe he didn't understand, or maybe he wasn't paying close enough attention when he tried to release the jammed board from the turning blades. His hard hat was useless, that much is clear, and his coffin remained closed to conceal his disfiguration. Tommy's death is what had set in motion the spiraling events leading to today, the end of Benson Lumber and the end of my life. There was nothing I could do for him as I cradled his head in my lap on the floor of the mill. Like in the Nam when I cradled Sgt. Pete Lachman, his shoulder torn off by a grenade he tried to smother. And like Nam, I could feel DOA before the arrival.

The IRS had already secured our property to ensure satisfaction of its lien, and the property included most of the buildings. My dad was playing John Wayne when the armed federal agents paid their first visit three months ago.

"I'm prepared to call the authorities if you don't get off of our property immediately."

"Mr. Benson, sir, we are the authorities."

"Well, there's no way I can identify what's already been sold and what is strictly our current inventory. I'll have to get back to you."

"Mr. Benson, we are not leaving today until all assets are determined and properly recorded. We are asking for your cooperation here to show us around."

"Over my dead body I'll show you around," Gordon stepped toward the young agent and jabbed his thumb into his own chest.

"Mr. Benson, this is going to happen with or without your cooperation. I'm asking you, please." With both hands raised outward, the agent signaled his this-is-the-best-I-can-do offer.

With that, my dad stomped out of the office, ordered Nancy our secretary to hand over nothing to these people, slammed the door in the agent's face, climbed into his pickup and headed for home.

Having interrogated myself over the past couple of months to explore any options I may have missed, I thought I was drained of all emotions by now. But with each piece of machinery and equipment sold, I was forced to recall the day we first added that to our mill, a day we celebrated with pride. Today I was admitting my failure, void of any vision that had once driven those acquisitions and improvements.

Hoping for a higher opening bid, the auctioneer explained in detail how Lou and I had rebuilt the edger three years ago. He didn't mention our efforts had not made it any safer for Tommy Gilwood. Working last month to dismantle this piece of machinery had little effect on me at the time because operating a mill is a daily cycle of disassembling and assembling. The auctioneer's explanation ended up having little impact on an opening bid because an old competitor named Harold Brandt turned out to be the only guy interested.

"And finally, for sale this afternoon," the auctioneer shuffled through his paperwork, "is the goodwill and pending revenue of Benson Lumber, including all existing and prospective lumber orders and sales. All of you who registered for this auction have been provided a schedule of orders and confirmed sales to date."

My heartache now forced me to breathe more deeply. I would never betray our family business, but in trying to fend off creditors, I had created pending deals with a phone conversation that would now surface as empty business promises. Hardly worth a second thought under normal day-to-day operations, but now publicly an embarrassment to acknowledge. My dad had done it, and I had done it, but it was always lost in the overall scheme of operations. When my mom had kept the first books for our company, she demanded my dad's integrity over his casual and indifferent regard for the IRS and credit applications and county regulations and building permits. He liked to think of himself as one of those first settlers moving West who tried to cut out a living in territory not yet established. I walked in his shoes when it came to all of that business, but Roberta Rouene had been determined to operate our company on a higher road, like a certified public accountant responsible to city, county, state, and federal rules and regulations.

The past few days following the twenty-first of August have never been easy for me. I can't count the times I have asked that question, "If my mother were still alive, how different would things be?" Our sawmill wouldn't be shut down right now if she were still alive. I wouldn't be doing this right now if she hadn't died.

My cap and ball black powder revolver felt so heavy now, laying it across my lap and staring at its beauty and fine craftsmanship, an Italian-made replica of the Colt Army model .44 caliber handgun. Nothing more than a small piece of machinery designed to take away life.

Machinery failed sometimes, and that is how I calmed my nerves for the moment. I had other handguns, but I chose this one because I needed to make this a process that I could evaluate slowly as I prepared to take my life. If it didn't work, if it misfired, I was ready to accept that omen.

My dad had taught me to respect machinery. "It talks to you all the time," he said. "But we don't always listen." How many mill accidents could have been avoided, he often mused, if the worker had been listening to his machinery? Tommy Gilwood wasn't listening to his machinery.

The head sawyer Orville Williams knew how to listen to his machinery, knew enough one morning to detect a large metal spike in the ponderosa pine log. Dave Hutchins, the off-bearer, who was saved from serious injury if he had been struck by that flying shrapnel, wasn't listening to the machinery. Orville had grazed the rusty spike enough to sound off the slightest high-pitched screech, enough to back off the log on the carriage for a careful inspection.

I was prepared to accept my fate, however this small piece of killing machinery would determine it. Almost a dare, a gamble. On purpose? Maybe so. Twice before, while shooting at cans behind this same pile of logs, the percussion caps had failed to ignite the black powder. Maybe this was my way to take my self-destruction partially out of my own hands. Maybe I couldn't do this. Maybe I wanted fate to be my accomplice. So I felt compelled to create the projectile that would end my life. A store-bought cartridge seemed like a bad idea, involving some innocent assembly worker in my dire scheme to end my life.

Don't know how much the carnage of Vietnam had eroded away my sensitivities to death, the daily sound and smell and feel of death. If not on a particular day at LZ English, then at least some report of death from another AO. Since those days twenty years ago, I have not feared death. Doesn't have anything to do with God or Easter and the resurrection of Jesus Christ. I have thought about my mom's death every day of my life. As of late, I think about death more than I think about life. But like Blood, Sweat & Tears sang, "And When I Die," I don't want death to come uneasy. If you're already feeling DOA, then you're just packin' up your equipment and stuffing it back into your battle bag. My mom didn't die uneasy. Sgt. Pete didn't die uneasy. Trinh didn't die uneasy.

Sitting on the tabletop surface of an old stump, I placed all of the necessary pieces of this machinery on a red shop rag to my left side. I pulled the hammer to the half-cock position, a safety feature that allowed the six-shot cylinder to turn freely for loading. Feeling how close the end was, I suddenly became aware of this crazy image. A photograph of me serving as the Grand Snark of the Universe for Hoo-Hoo International with notice of my suicide written below, describing how the responsibilities of that post had driven me to despair. That made me smile. It was the other way around.

"If you gave half-as-much attention to our mill as you give to that Hoo-Hoo job of yours, we wouldn't be in such trouble right now," my dad had complained.

"Dad, I've explained this to you a hundred times before. My Hoo-Hoo job helps the reputation of our mill, helps us to stand out above the others and gives us some respect we might not otherwise have when we need to buy logs or sell lumber in a depressed market. I'm watching out for our business every time I take one of my trips for Hoo-Hoo."

"Every time you take one of your trips for Hoo-Hoo is another time you're gone from the mill."

"Yeah, that's how you see it because you never bothered to build any trust with the people around you, including me. You've spent more time spying on your workers than I have ever spent traveling for Hoo-Hoo. If you had a little trust in me, if you had defended me once in a while when Eva or Agnes were questioning my ability to run this business."

"Trust you, when all you ever do is spend money like there's no tomorrow?"

Funny thing is, a guy had to get beyond the lighter side of Hoo-Hoo to appreciate what my dad refused to understand. The premise was simple. Promote good fellowship and goodwill among lumbermen that would then serve their companies and the industry. In 1892, some lumbermen had met in New Orleans to organize a club that would be unique and welcoming. So they called their new fraternal organization the "Concatenated Order of Hoo-Hoo" (a word coined to describe a most peculiar tuft of hair, greased and twisted to a point, atop the otherwise bald head of a Chicago lumberman by the name of Charles McCarer). Hoo-Hoo means anything unusual or out of the ordinary. Why not adopt a black cat as a mascot seeing as how it's usually associated with bad luck? And in honor of the legendary nine lives of a cat, why not use the number nine for everything Hoo-Hoo? Nine men on the Board of Directors (the "Supreme Nine"), the annual meeting would be held on the ninth day of the ninth month beginning at nine minutes after nine, the annual dues would be ninety-nine cents, and the initiation fee would be $9.99. One of the founders had read Lewis Carroll's "Hunting of the Snark" and suggested the directors be given peculiar names like "snark" and "bojum." Better yet, how about Grand Snark and Holy Bojum? Talk about grown men acting like a bunch of little rascals, but the intent and single aim rose above all that Hoo-Hoo silliness: To foster the health, happiness, and long life of its members.

To foster the long life of its members, heh? How has that worked out for me?

I poured a powder charge into the one cylinder I would use for this mission, and placed the round lead ball atop the charge. I turned the cylinder so this chamber was in line with the rammer, unhooked the rammer from its lug under the barrel, and drove the ball down into the chamber. Because I was only loading for one shot, no need to apply grease over this chamber opening to prevent a chain-fire where the flash from the burning powder ignites an adjacent chamber.

"Do you even remember, Dad, our big record week of nine truckloads hauled off to Redmond?"

"Yeah, grandstanding they call that. What about good ol' consistent production numbers?"

Under normal circumstances, the tiny percussion caps are a pain-in-the-neck to install over the nipple of each chamber. I wasn't exactly feeling normal circumstances here. I pressed it too hard off center, and it fumbled out of my reach onto the bark-and-chip-covered ground between my legs.

"Goddamn it," I regretted the whole idea of preparing my own death squad.

"Goddamn it, Dad, I've earned the right to make the big decisions about our mill. I've got as much invested in this now as you do. Do you have any idea what I had to do to satisfy our bank obligations and the IRS? Do you know how much I mortgaged my home for to help make payroll this past year?"

"I'm not discussing this anymore if you're going to use that kind of language. And you forget what your mother invested in the mill when I married her. She doesn't feel it's fair to Melissa and Diane to turn over her share now. It's all they've got."

"There's your first mistake! Eva is not my mother! And your second mistake will be to hesitate. If she's so worried about her share, she might want to sign these papers tonight, and hope there's any kind of share still left at the end of the year."

"How much are you prepared to pay us now if we turn over to you outright control of the mill?"

"I already told you. We'll work out a percentage of monthly receivables. I'm thirty-six years old, Dad, for Christ's sake. I've been working at the mill for over twenty years. When was it you thought I might finally be entitled to run our company?"

"I always figured we would run it together, but that obviously wasn't meant to be."

"Nothing seems meant to be anymore," I mumbled to myself as I worked the cap down over the nipple holding it around the sides instead of forcing it down from the top.

As things were deteriorating in our industry anyway, I was doing my dad a big favor by assuming the entire headache for our eventual collapse. After Eva's death in 1986, I gave my dad's partnership offer a little more consideration. Feeling our legacy slipping away was turning out to be a lonely experience.

I remember talking with my buddy Fred after we had arrived in the Nam. He had told me about why he had left his family ranch southeast of Alturas. Loved his dad but couldn't stand him and what he expected of Fred. Had come to blows with him after their Thanksgiving dinner a week before he left home for basic. I said, "Whatta' ya' mean, you came to blows?" He said, "I shoved my dad against the wall after he had punched me in the face." I could tell he wasn't kidding, so I didn't ask him anything more.

"I gotta ask ya, dad, what in the world were you thinkin' when you took a swing at me last year? So fed up with me because I told you that your old way of operatin' our mill kept interfering with how we were trying to climb out of a hole. We've been arguin' and debatin' about that for years. Usually walked away from each other when we couldn't settle anything. Who were you takin' a swing at that day? Me? Life? God? Agnes? Who were you so mad at?"

Within a year and a half after Eva's death, my dad had walked away from me again. Agnes is her name. Couldn't live without a woman in his life. My dad kept walking away from us. Denise and Kristin, I don't know how you take it. With Agnes in the mix, I began living through it all over again. "Is Karl capable enough? Seems like money is all Karl is interested in."

Seemed to me that money was all she was interested in! Wasted no time spending money to develop some land my dad owned around his home but she refused any advice. Almost insulted that anyone thought she needed any advice. Her project quickly failed.

And here's the worst part of it all. We were supposed to accept Agnes as a grandma for our kids, but we had no input about her suitability for our dad. Always the double standard. His children could be shunned like some disease, but God forbid we should show any disrespect toward our latest stepmom. Here's a question I'm having trouble answering. What's the official cutoff age for finally getting to ignore your dad's latest partner? At what point is his most recent wife no longer my stepmom? I figured that had happened long ago when I no longer lived in the house with Eva. For my dad, it seems, it's forever, because his latest wife automatically qualifies as my mom.

My mother not only gone but a replacement mom who can hardly stand me! How many times had my dad walked out on me, setting up this fantasy family that only he took seriously?

After I turned the cylinder, I carefully released the hammer to safely rest it on an uncapped nipple, the loaded chamber now rotated to next in line for firing. I was thinking now about my dad driving through the mill every morning to check up on me. What a thought to wake up to, that I would be late and not at the mill whenever he pulled in at 5:30 AM.

"Who did you think was going to unload that log truck this morning at 6:00 AM? You don't have Fred come in until 7:00."

"Well, feel free to unload any trucks you want at that time of the morning!"

"I thought you wanted complete control of the mill. Holy Mackerel, Karl, I don't know if you even realize what all that means."

I knew what it all meant. What had happened to our mill was compared with the plight of other mills throughout the timber industry. Heartbreaking and regrettable, but one of many. The *Bend Bulletin* reported that after forty-one years in business, hard times in the timber industry had closed the family-owned Benson Lumber, a major employer in the area. Hard times? We were a stable business and steady employer for decades. I told the reporter I thought our closure was temporary. "Tight money and the recession combined to cause the closure. We will not file for bankruptcy reorganization, and we expect to reopen when conditions in the industry improve. We're taking a breather right now. We're not done. I would compare our situation now to a puzzle that's been dropped on the floor. We need time to get the pieces of the puzzle back together. This shutdown will give me time to sit down and look at our options. Time is all we need. All these things just snowballed. I'm regrouping. I'm getting a handle on it."

Who was all of that bullshit for? My dad, I guess. My mother would have seen right through it. Keeping Benson Lumber alive in the face of timber market difficulties had been my latest attempt to restore my mother's honor and memory. Seems like I was letting her down again.

This single shot revolver required me to cock the hammer back once again to half, and then to full as it brought the capped nipple of the loaded chamber in line with the hammer.

I love my dad so much, but I hate how he's treated me, how he has treated me from the day my mother died. I've been at war with him, with myself, and with God ever since. I'm feeling like a blood trail, wounded the day my mother died, that no one ever bothered to follow. I've had no one to start my night and day.

Growing up after my mother's death, I had figured I would make good on the legacy she and my dad had passed on to me. I feel less guilt when it comes to my dad because he has chosen to muddy the waters with his screwed up loyalty to Eva and Agnes and his towering ego that I apparently threatened. Which makes my guilt, when it comes to my mom, feel that much more painful, for she would have loved me all these years without muddying the waters and without protecting her ego.

I don't have to feel this guilt anymore. I know a way out.

I covered my arm and head with my gold and burgundy Benson Lumber Company jacket, hoping to contain the splatter and mess I was about to make, and minimize the sound of the exploding discharge.

Mom, I'm thinkin' you'll forgive me.

Chapter 23

Henry
11 April 1998
Saturday

Karl's mother had come to him with an answer, whispering words of wisdom. Over and over again, she had said, "Let It Be." For her, such advice had meant one thing; for her son Karl, it had meant something else. He was forty-one years old, and he wanted the long war to finally end. He had had enough of war. He just wanted to let it be, and to do that, he had to raise the revolver to his head and pull the trigger. That's how he would let it be.

No one took notice of the muffled explosion, a distance far enough away to separate Karl once and for all from the death of Benson Lumber. Plinkers playing with their latest killing machinery could be heard all day long a quarter mile down the road from the mill.

The year before his suicide, Karl and his family had visited us for Easter. It had been only a year since my brother's death, his decision to end his life that Good Friday a daily reminder of my failure as a brother and a pastor. What had happened to our ninth-green promise? Shortly after his death, I began imagining his face on Sunday mornings while I preached my latest here and now revision of my mother's Easter. I saw his face in the faces of my parishioners; I could never know how much my words might have meant to him, how much my words meant to them. I had George on my mind again this Easter Sunday – wishing he could be here to think through one more time his fateful decision, hoping I might have one more chance to stand by him. Like Camus's protagonist in his novel, *The Fall*.

In my pretending that George was still here, that I did have one more chance, I took advantage of my pulpit to acknowledge my brother's pain, to articulate some of the hard questions I know he had asked of our mother's Easter, to assure him of my love. All in vain now, of course, but at least I was rehearsing that one more chance in case my wish ever came true. Perhaps on some Sunday mornings, someone else needed to hear their pain acknowledged, needed to hear their faith questions and doubts raised, needed to hear they were loved.

So perhaps my wish did come true sometimes.

Karl's presence commanded my attention this March 26 Easter morning, his face appearing now where I had imagined my brother's face. He and Sharon were sitting with their three children right behind my family. I found myself speaking with urgency and foreboding I had not felt before. Maybe we were all feeling a sense of urgency and foreboding about Karl – but not, apparently, feeling that way enough. Those who study such sadness tell us that our shock after the suicide of someone we love must often acknowledge the sadder truth that our loved one had shared their suicidal intentions well before they had acted on their decision.

I chose Eugene O'Neill's play, *Lazarus Laughed*, for my sermon illustration that Easter morning.

"Here is O'Neill's version of what happened after Jesus had raised the brother of Mary and Martha from the dead. (Jn. 11:1-44). Shrouded in grave clothes, softly laughing to himself in a kind of trance, Lazarus had returned to life from the dead – and he now knew the secret. O'Neill believed we can attribute most of our unhappiness to a fear of death. Lazarus had been re-born without that fear so he could live differently in the here and now. He knows death has been defeated. I doubt he would ever think about suicide at this point. Why would he?

At the dinner party following the miracle, one of the guests had remarked about how the look of Lazarus's face had changed, appearing like a stranger from a far off land, his eyes showing no sorrow, as if his sorrow had been left behind in the grave. For Lazarus, death no longer loomed on the horizon.

Lazarus offered the critical line in this play, though, when he politely corrected his father at the dinner table celebrating the miracle. Lazarus's father had risen to his feet to offer a toast, a goblet in his hand, expressing his thankfulness that his son had been brought back from death. But Lazarus, speaking with a strange unearthly calm in a voice that is like a loving whisper of hope and confidence, countered his father by declaring, 'There is no death.' That, after all, is what Jesus had said to Lazarus's sister, Martha, right? 'Those who believe in me, even though they die, will live, and everyone who lives and believes in me will never die.' (Jn.11:25-26) In the play, we are told that Lazarus began to laugh – a kind of laughter never heard before that announced to all the world what it means to love life, what it means to discover such a truth. His laugh filled the room and cast on his listeners a spell they could not ignore."

I then read a passage from O'Neill's play because it spoke to our fear and reluctance to believe such a glorious victory has been achieved for us. I wanted to stress how we forget the God in us. How we live by denying life. So I described fictitious characters who represented such a forgetting, hoping those listening might find a familiar example to think about it.

I concluded my sermon. "May I suggest that the raising of Lazarus is a metaphor for our baptism, to live as a child of God? But are we too timid, too afraid, to live out this gift of baptism – a way of living which is filled with joy and laughter? In baptism, aren't we reborn without the fear of death? Do we forget because our baptism then calls us to live a life we are too afraid to live? To live as a child of God?

O'Neill, by the way, wrote this play after his own resurrection experience following his attempted suicide in 1912 at the age of twenty-three. Always in O'Neill, suffering precedes rebirth and resurrection.

But to the obvious. Lazarus, of course, eventually died. We are not immortal, but thanks to our baptism, death does not separate us from God. The poet John Donne said it another way:

'Death be not proud, though some have called thee
Mighty and dreadful, for thou art not so;
. . .
One short sleep past, we wake eternally,
And Death shall be no more: Death, thou shalt die! (Holy Sonnet X)'

Like a soldier: once almost-certain death is faced, the battlefield loses some of its terror. As in battle, so also in life: death once confronted can lead to a life more fully lived.

Some of you have noticed how excited I get on Sunday mornings when a baptism is scheduled. How excited I get about making that connection between our baptism and Easter – when death itself died early that Sunday morning. God's eternal presence breaks into our here and now at baptism in much the same way His eternal presence broke into the death and resurrection of His Son Jesus of Nazareth. By our baptism, we can participate in a death like His, and a resurrection to newness of life in the here and now.

In O'Neill's play, Lazarus's home in Bethany would become known as the House of Laughter.

Have you ever laughed like Lazarus?"

We sat that afternoon out front of the parsonage. Sharon asked me about my sermon, trying to reconcile my reinvented version of Easter with her inherited background. Karl waited for a pause. "I heard what you said this morning about soldiers. In Vietnam, I've held death in my arms. And last month at the mill, Caine, I held death in my arms again. I've held DOA in my arms. After you read that passage from the play, I thought to myself, this sounds like we're trading one fear for another – our fear of death replaced now by our fear of life. What have we gained?"

I shared with Karl my latest efforts to help people experience God in the here and now, and I admitted that as of late I had been relying less on my mother's Easter – the faith we had both inherited.

"O'Neill's Lazarus is talking about living the life we are called to live as children of God, not the old life we die to in baptism. We are trading our fear of death, Karl, for a different way of living from the way we have lived life before. Otherwise, you're right in asking, 'What have we gained?' Baptism is our Lazarus experience, opening the door to this new way of life. A new way of life we don't need to fear after all."

I was still constrained by the Lutheran pastor boundaries of my inherited faith, and I could see in Karl's eyes I had wasted an opportunity to meet him where he was at that moment. Thinking now about that Sunday afternoon, I could have offered, "Karl, I'm not sure our inherited faith is enough for life's journey. Each of us must figure out, each of us in our own way, how to interpret what O'Neill's talking about here. What would a Lazarus experience look like for you? You may have to find that new life in spite of the faith you inherited, Karl, because the Church has failed to help many of us find the way to that new life."

I can remember my dad and George and Karl and Andy laughing on different occasions, but I'm sure they never laughed like Lazarus laughed.

Suicidologists have pondered this question: Why do we try to understand a suicide's fatal decision at the point when that decision is made? If someone completes suicide after losing all of their wealth, why don't we ask some questions about why that wealth meant so much to the person in the first place? How did the person lose it? How was it made? What was sacrificed to make it? Why so driven to make all that money? Any guilt feelings associated with making it? How far back should our inquiry take us?

Karl had managed to suppress some of his grief by interacting with Denise and Kristin at family gatherings where enough else was going on that he didn't have to talk too much about his feelings, about their shared sorrow, about their incomplete mourning. His two sisters accepted this as his willful independence, a trait he had been nurturing since his return to take charge of Benson Lumber. A trait Karl shared with his dad.

In his *Darkness Visible: A Memoir of Madness*, William Styron, who was thirteen when his mother died, explained that such early sorrow as the death of your mother before or during puberty can leave an emotional wound that never heals. And for Karl, Denise, and Kristin, their wound had been compounded by their father's denial – for Karl, hopelessly compounded.

On a Friday in early May, Karl had made an unexpected stop at Kristin's on his way home from the mill. Not feeling so independent these days. Stopped by for some lunch, hadn't done that in years. His eyes begged for a hug. Seemed so troubled, kept looking at the sky like he was searching for some help. "I'll fix ya' a fried-egg sandwich, like Grandma used to fix. Hey, since you're headed that way, can you drop Roberta off at soccer practice?" Karl didn't offer a reply, just ate his sandwich and then got up to leave. He took his time releasing Kristin from his embrace, and he whispered, "Everything's gonna be O.K." Both Kristin and Karl were thinking about their mother Robin today, the eleventh, her birthday.

This was an unnerving change for Kristin, who had relied on her older brother whenever she needed a hug. The next month, Karl stopped by again on his way home, this time for dinner. Didn't cry, but gritted his teeth. Had committed himself, but then had checked himself out. "I'm getting to be like Dad, and I don't like it," he exclaimed. "Didn't want to spend the forty dollars an hour to see the psychiatrist, didn't have it to spend." He talked about the accident at the mill last year, about the young man killed by a board from the edger. "Felt like Vietnam all over again, Kristin, holding him that morning. Hard to stop the bleeding. I've got to figure out a way to protect my family from the lawsuit. A lot of stuff these days feels like Vietnam all over again."

Our family has talked about how difficult it was to understand Karl's indescribable pain, like a foreign language we did not speak. Did Karl even know this foreign language? Does someone suffering from depression have the vocabulary to effectively share their unbearable pain? If Karl was unable to comprehend his desolation, how could we?

Is that our best excuse?

I can't watch Frank Capra's *It's a Wonderful Life* without thinking about Karl. All of us had been praying for him, so where was his guardian angel Clarence to show him the way back to life? The senior angel had told Clarence, "A man down on earth needs our help." "Is he sick?" Clarence asked. "No," the angel replied. "Worse. He's discouraged."

So was Karl.

Before his funeral service, I had scribbled around the margins of my eulogy notes the phrase, *heart attack*. I was thinking about my dad and what he had endured as a Christian, trying to figure out what salvation meant, what Jesus had come down from heaven to provide for us. How was Karl's already weakened heart – weakened by the years of incomplete mourning of his mother's death – supposed to cope with the failure of his family's lumber mill? He was losing his battle with guilt, having betrayed his mother by betraying his partnership in the family legacy. Even in his futile attempts to understand her death, he was letting his mother down. In my remarks at First Baptist Church in Bend, I never once spoke about suicide because I did not think about Karl taking his life. For me, he had found an escape from heart pain no physician could treat.

Thinking about his family, and all who loved him, was his escape a selfish act? Or was his escape from this tormenting heart pain in some way equivalent to our basic human instinct for survival. "I can only 'survive' this pain by escaping it." George Minois has reminded us: As impossible as it is to comprehend the *why* of someone's suicide, how much more impossible must it be to *judge* it.

After Karl's service, Gordon Benson had retreated quickly to his car, trying to avoid as many people as he could. Heartbroken, embarrassed, confused, angry. Kristin's kids walked up to his car to say goodbye. He rolled down his window halfway and said, "Who are you?"

We've talked about that a few times, still don't know what that was all about.

Why don't families discuss suicide risk factors like we talk about unhealthy diets or bad habits like smoking? Why didn't our family talk about the suicide risk factor for veterans? When are soldier suicides considered casualties of war – during or after the war? And does that matter when counting? And why is counseling in the military such a sign of weakness? Does a vet change his mind about that because he has returned to civilian life?

Kay Redfield Jamison has told of her objection to a story in the *Washington Post*, a story about disinterring the remains of the courageous and accomplished explorer Meriwether Lewis. Someone wanted to prove once and for all that he had been murdered, so the blot associated with his name could then be removed. Jamison explained that there was compelling evidence that Lewis had suffered from manic-depression and had killed himself. We need not think about Lewis's suicide as a blot associated with his name, she concluded; we need to think about his suicide as a tragedy.

CHAPTER 24

Andy
16 April 1995
Easter Sunday

I owe you this explanation, Father, though I doubt you'll understand anyway. I've tried to think of you as my dad, or as my pa, the way you spoke about your own father. Neither works for me. I can't help thinking of you in any other way but *Father*, much in the same way as I think about God my Heavenly Father. For better or for worse, I think of you fulfilling God's Fatherly role for me here on earth – for the worse, I'm sorry to say.

How I have experienced your love is how I have experienced God's love. Don't remember who asked it, but it's a thoughtful question. "What manner of God is He Who must be proved?" God's not a fact; God is experienced. So how have I experienced you, Father? How have I experienced the Church you serve? How have I experienced God's People? Hardly the infinite majesty we yearn to love.

I wish I could feel such a desperate longing for God, like Professor Lambert's longing in Updike's novel, *Roger's Version*. Even after his night of incest, adultery, and child abuse, laying on the floor with his niece Verna, his partner in sin, he gazed upward to the impalpable ceiling. He could hardly describe his newfound closeness to the Almighty, his longing for God now strangely reawakened after his night of sin. Maybe such longing is proof, after all, of God's existence. But that would be a problem for me: Since I experience God by how His people have condemned and reviled me for who I am, what exactly would I be longing for?

I remember the first time I ever thought about suicide. I was sitting in church listening to your sermon about the suicide of Israel's King Saul, about why he had chosen to fall on his sword. To prepare the congregation for your message, you had read the entire thirty-first chapter of I Samuel.

I listened to that story of Saul's tragic defeat fighting valiantly against the Philistines on Mount Gilboa. First, they killed his sons, Jonathan, Abinadab, and Malki-Shua. Then the Philistines pressed hard after Saul, and the fighting grew fierce around him. When the archers overtook Saul, they critically wounded him. He turned to his armor-bearer, "Draw your sword and run me through." He knew how his enemies would abuse him as the leader of the Israelites. Too afraid, his armor-bearer had refused. So Saul took his own sword and fell on it. He, with all of his men, died together that day. After their victory, the Philistines did cut off Saul's head, stripped him of his armor, and fastened his body to the wall of Beth Shan.

You couldn't know it at the time, but your sermon would turn out to presage my own suicide. You couldn't know it at the time because the fighting had not yet grown so fierce around me, the Philistines had not yet pressed hard upon my life. No doubt, you'll question my right to a self-willed death, as you questioned Saul's right because God had anointed him.

How dare he!

How dare I!

Yet you spoke about how God's people are expected to contend with life's trials and tribulations like everyone else. God's people are still vulnerable to life's hardships. "He makes His sun rise on the evil and on the good, and sends rain on the just and on the unjust." What's the advantage, then, if God anoints you?

I remember this background you shared with the congregation that morning. Saul grew up a simple shepherd boy, much like David who would succeed him. God's people soon faced what all theocracies must face. Certain tribes demanded a king so they could be like other nation-states – this, even after God had returned the ark of the covenant which had been lost to the Philistines at Shiloh. This artifact is how God symbolized His presence in their midst. In effect, the people Israel had rejected God by their demand for a king; they did not believe God and His Ark were adequate enough to rule the people.

A courageous and handsome man, taller than any of the people, Saul had quelled the voices of discontent and had reestablished Israel as a formidable kingdom. But he also refused to rule within the prescriptions of leadership established by God through Samuel – even assuming at one point the prophet Samuel's office by performing a ritual war sacrifice. He had momentarily forgotten who had chosen him to be the first king of Israel. Samuel would be that son born to Hannah, the previously barren mother who had promised God she would turn over her son to serve the Lord.

Again, Saul disobeyed Samuel – disobeyed God, that is – when he chose to spare the life of a conquered Amalekite ruler. These transgressions led to fits of depression, and Saul's moody, suspicious temperament had no time for the young lad named David whom Samuel had chosen to serve the royal court as a harp-player – hoping to soothe Saul's troubled spirit by playing music.

Meanwhile, the Philistines had been standing by for another opportunity – aren't they always – and this time they boasted of a nine-foot-tall giant warrior named Goliath. Most know this story: Saul and the Israelites trembling in fear while the young David marched out with his slingshot to confront and kill this fearsome Philistine with a single stone. Already near the edge, Saul grew insanely jealous of David. Who wouldn't, right? Feeling ever more depressed, and without the support of David, Saul ended up consulting a witch of Endor, who advised him of his pending doom. You would be surprised, Father, to hear of the many witches I have consulted.

"Why couldn't I be more like David?" you asked. David was God's ideal king. He triumphed over Goliath because he trusted in God's protection rather than the physical protection of the king's armor. A simple prayer was his only hope, and that, you have reminded me over and over again, was enough. Unlike Saul, David was satisfied with patiently waiting on God. Saul could hardly wait on himself sometimes, so quick to turn to himself and rely on human strengths and qualities to establish and maintain his leadership. Saul lived too much in and of this world to ever warrant God's favor. So his rebellion against God culminated in his loss of hope when faced with insuperable odds; surrounded by his advancing enemies, he chose a way out that he could arrange.

"Why couldn't you be less like Samuel?" I asked in return. And you have never answered my question.

I do not fear the wages of sin. Philistines, yes, but not the wages of sin. Maybe if you had helped me in my battle against the gathering Philistines in my life, we could have emerged victorious as father and son – like God and David. But you have rejected my style of ministry and my way of life, like God rejected Saul and his style of kingship. The Philistines have surrounded me, and I stand atop Mount Gilboa now by myself; you have failed, in all of your training so well applied in official service to others, to come to my aid. I felt at times you were waiting far off to see how I would fare, fearful of the embarrassment I might bring upon you as a son.

Like those advancing Philistines, my fear surrounds me. Fearful that I would become more and more like you, so attached to the dogma of our Church. But of course, I felt guilty for even thinking such a thing.

Like those advancing Philistines, my divorce surrounds me in shame. You chose to ignore what Julie meant to me, how she loved me.

Like those advancing Philistines, your denial surrounds me. You denied your emerging awareness of my homosexuality, what I have discovered about myself and what you think about that – doubly wounded, the more so because of your rejection and your Church's condemnation. It would have helped if you and I could have worked together to understand who I am. But you refused such a relationship. You could have read, on your own, without me ever asking, Boswell's *Christianity, Social Tolerance, and Homosexuality.*

We might have returned to our debate about those supposed passages of condemnation in Scripture. For centuries following those passages, we don't find much evidence about the birthplace of Christianity, the Roman world, declaring homosexuality abnormal or undesirable. In fact, there is no word for *homosexual* in Latin; the word was unknown in the ancient world. Sounds Latin, but a Hungarian physician coined the word in the late nineteenth century. Preferring his or her own gender in the early Roman world was no more a topic of discussion than preferring someone with blue eyes or who was short.

After the twelfth century, these ancient attitudes changed, and Christianity must accept some responsibility for the growing suspicion of certain individuals and groups. Among the popular prejudices of this time, gay people and Jews became the target of such intolerance. Gay culture was no longer acceptable – gays were accused of molesting children, violating God's natural law, and bringing harm to those people who tolerated them. By the late fourteenth century, almost every European state had passed civil laws demanding death for a single homosexual act. Theologians like Thomas

Aquinas took up the pen to portray homosexuality as one of the worst sins, second only to murder.

Like those advancing Philistines, my threatened exposure surrounds me. That bright shining floodlight of the Gay Liberation Movement would not leave me alone, would not let me be who I am.

Like those advancing Philistines, my faith questions surround me. I have failed to find a faith that could help me cope with what I was discovering about myself. What you taught me in catechism class – about a childlike fear that God might leave us, not a fear that He would come to judge us – was not adequate for adulthood. I didn't grow up ever fearing that you would leave me; as I grew into manhood, I feared that you would judge me like Samuel judged Saul. And I have lived every day in fear of that.

Like those advancing Philistines, my failure surrounds me. I was destined to fail as a pastor because what you bequeathed to me as a father-to-son profession was not what the Church of my generation was expecting. You and I, Father, remind me of Pastor Jung and his son Carl. Not sure why Carl's father refused to share his work with his son, why he refused to answer his son's questions about religion. Carl found himself more alone than he could sometimes endure, alone even in the presence of his father. I have felt that same loneliness, having no one who understands me or seems to care about my concerns. I think Carl expected much more of his confirmation than I ever did, and his later scholarship is a search to replace what he had lost.

Like those advancing Philistines, that goddamned DUI right after Christmas in 1971 surrounds me. How embarrassing that was for you.

My life has not been a struggle against homosexual impulses. And I don't think about reconciling my Christian faith with my homosexual feelings. My agony is my doubt. I'm gay. Am I still worthy of God's love? Would not be asking such a question if you had been accepting of me.

Like Sylvia Plath, I too have thought about changing over to the Catholic Church. Knowing that the Catholics think killing yourself is such an awful sin, she figured they might have a good way to talk her out of it. The only trouble is, church, even the Catholic Church, doesn't take up the whole of your life. For me, even worse – because the Church I served condemned me daily, and when I wasn't living with that, I was living with society's condemnation of who I am.

Having lived within this system all my life, I'm guessing that religion could be counted either way for me. If I'm still thinking about Young Werther, I'm boldly embracing Christianity's derogation of this earthly life, looking to that glorious promise of the afterlife. During his difficult days, Werther felt that religion served to tranquilize his fear of death. I'm joining with Werther in his prayer before his suicide. "I am back, my father! Don't be angry because I am cutting short the journey which you expected me to endure longer."

And having lived within this system all my life, I can find sufficient blame for religion leading me to this day. Did Jefferson's friend, the novelist, Charles Brown, get it right in 1798? Based on a true story in colonial times, Brown's novel explored the extent to which religious enthusiasm contributes to melancholy and suicide. What was the cause of Theodore Wieland's madness and suicide – Satan, or Wieland's own religious fanaticism? Questions were asked of the Christian faith, once considered a defense against the temptation to self-murder. Without the Biblical condemnation I have struggled with, would my sexual identity have led me to this day?

Either way, religion is my companion. But the more accepting I am of the person I have become, the more alienated I feel from God. We all must deal with alienation from God, but a homosexual must also deal with alienation from society.

If we accept our human limitation to endure extreme suffering, can't suicide be considered as natural an end as death is from sickness? "What's wrong with self-capitulation to death, the wages of sin?" I might ask of C. S. Lewis. "Is that not the ultimate acknowledgment of our fallen creaturehood?"

In your old copy of Chesterton's *Orthodoxy*, I read his scathing condemnation of suicide, what he considered such an evil crime. Even spoke about how the suicide should be buried apart at the crossroads with a stake driven through the body.

Like Werther, I'm not about to show off and pretend that death tastes anything but bitter. Even the Son of man prayed that the cup pass from him, Werther noted. "So why," he asked, "should I feel ashamed in that dreadful moment when my entire self trembles on the edge of being and not-being?"

Saul, if you did it, so can I. You fell on your sword to avoid what? Your inevitable death? Martyrdom? Why can't I choose to avoid what's ahead?

How did a fourteen-year-old come to write that theme song from *M*A*S*H*, "Suicide Is Painless"? I guess I have the option to take it or leave it.

Every glass of scotch and every pill I take, Father, deliver me closer to my rendezvous with death no less than does the Christian dogma and doctrine I inherited from you. This destruction of my physical being is nothing compared to the destruction of my spiritual being at the hands of orthodoxy and Church doctrine.

Thanks to Harriet Rothberger and her son, I had three full bottles of Valium; she had begged me to take away her son's prescription. I saved him by taking it, and now I'll use it to save me. Save me, that is, from the Philistines pressing hard upon my life.

I don't live in King Saul's world so I won't pretend I can turn this whole thing over to an armor-bearer. Besides, who would be my armor-bearer? You, Father? Maybe my best friend Bud because we made that promise to stand by one another. Would he consider such a request now, to stand by me on my Mount Gilboa? I have exhausted my options – like you said, Werther, my reason has failed to satisfy me – but I'm not sure I can complete such a task.

If I lived in London in 1878, I wouldn't hesitate for a moment to join Robert Stevenson's Suicide Club. And I would argue vehemently with Prince Florizal of Bohemia and his confidant Colonel Geraldine about their objection to this secret society. Was it the actual act of murder perpetrated by the one who was dealt the ace of clubs that was so disdainful? Or was it the idea itself, a last indulgence to avoid any shame by taking this easy and irresponsible path? Prince Florizal apparently had no objection to anyone seeking refuge in death. If a man has made up his mind, he added, at least let him do it like a gentleman. But he did have an objection to the President of the Club, and in his righteous indignation, chose to play the part of God in eliminating the scoundrel and his club.

For an entry fee of forty pounds, the Suicide Club unlocked a private door to death, a backdoor that provided an easy and convenient way to quit the stage (effectively an assisted-suicide service). With no elaborate background check or profile, the club arranged for the accidental deaths of its members. Might be for the family – to avoid the shock and blame and scandal. Might be for the self – unable to play the role of murderer, like me. Whatever the consideration, though, the deed is fulfilled by a pack of fifty-two cards played out each evening. Death's high priest for the evening is dealt the ace of clubs, his victim the ace of spades – a new arrangement played out every evening. Soliciting members is an easier task than one might first think.

Baden-Powell, I honestly wish I could have kept smiling and whistling under the circumstances.

So I go gently into the night, Dear Father, so drowsy now, my breathing more labored with each passing minute, into the darkness without anyone standing by me, save my trusted fifth of Black Label Scotch and my plastic container of valium – which I now discover are both empty. Unlike you, my old friend Werther, I guess I required more than one glass.

Oh, yeah, and my two ace cards. Which is which, I can't remember. And it doesn't matter anymore.

Alas! Would the deed be done by the questionable means I have used to avoid doing it? Now that, Mr. Stevenson, is a backdoor to death. I would like to think I have done my dying well, like my friend Sylvia. At least, I haven't laid violent hands upon myself, Father; I would have been excluded from *The Book of Common Prayer's* Burial Order. Another archaic taboo.

"May the Lord bless you and keep you, Father. May the Lord make his . . ."

CHAPTER 25

Henry
11 April 1998
Saturday

Couldn't help it once the setting sun had signaled the onset of the Sabbath. Every year it's the same routine. Having delivered my Maundy Thursday sermon and Good Friday meditation, my mind shifts to preparation of my Easter sermon. Since I had none to prepare, my memory recalled my Easter sermon from three years ago. While I was trying to inspire my parishioners to live new life in the here and now, I did not yet know my best friend Andy was trying at that precise moment to end his life in the here and now.

I had stepped into the myrtle wood pulpit of Trinity Lutheran Church that April morning in 1995 still hoping those I served could make some connection between God's gift of salvation and their everyday life. I was still trying, even after my brother's death, even after Karl's suicide. Still wishing for one more chance. I had thought about both of them every Sunday morning, about what words might have changed their mind.

"Let the words of my mouth and the meditation of my heart be acceptable to you, O Lord, my rock and my redeemer. Amen."

I focused on my family sitting in the front pew.

"Last Sunday afternoon, my youngest son Trevor and I watched The Masters Golf Tournament held in Augusta, Georgia. What a beautiful setting, this former nursery now eighteen fairways still lined with lime-green dogwoods

265

and pinkish-magenta azaleas. We were especially impressed with the introductory coverage.

Before the final Sunday afternoon round of golf was played, NBC treated us to some archival footage of two great names in golf, Arnold Palmer and Jack Nicklaus. Remembering those by-gone years of magical golf performances was set to the stirring theme music from the movie *Jurassic Park*. We could hardly turn away from the screen, so enraptured by this background music. When it was finished, I turned to Trevor and asked, 'How impressive was that?' Trevor replied with one of his assured grins, 'Well, few have played the game like those two guys, so how they've played sure lends something extra to that music.' And I agreed with him, the music more captivating because of what it was accompanying. I've been thinking about that all week, and about how wondrous an event this is today. And so for you, instead of trying to describe it further, I ask you, please, listen for a moment."

My request to "listen for a moment" was Denise's cue, who, like so many pastors' wives, also directed the adult vocal choir and the bell choir (had to play a few of the bells as she directed, three or more hands required!), also provided for the coffee hour when no one else had signed up, also taught the second and third grade Sunday school class, also cleaned up the kitchen when others had forgotten, also subbed for the organist, although that was way out of her comfort zone, also was expected to cover for me on occasion with a word of prayer, or counsel a troubled parishioner when I was unavailable. Also AD NAUSEUM. She had already slipped away from the front pew, had positioned herself in the sacristy where our sound system equipment was stored, and perfectly on cue, pushed the *Play* button for the CD's number two selection, "Theme From Jurassic Park."

I had slipped out the side door of the chancel during the second hymn, had hurried down the steps, practically running through the basement where our church youth group was preparing for their annual Easter morning breakfast, and climbed the stairs to the narthex and main door of our sanctuary. I was standing there, at the back of the church, when I began with the line, "Last Sunday afternoon, ..." Everyone could hear me with our new upgraded sound system, but no one knew where I was standing. I patiently waited for the opening anticipatory notes – French horn, clarinet, and flute – and when John Williams' magnificent score shifted to violins, I told the Gospel story for Easter morning as I walked up the aisle toward the altar.

"Early on the first day of the week, a hint of sunrise still hiding behind the hills east of Bethany, the women set out for the tomb of Jesus of Nazareth who had been crucified the Friday before. Mary Magdalene, Joanna, Mary the mother of James, and Salome had spices and ointment to prepare his body for burial. They were nervous, they were afraid, and they asked one another, 'Who will roll away the large stone in front of his tomb when we get there?' They walked into the garden to find a surprising answer to their question. The stone already had been rolled away from the tomb. They stepped into the darkness of this cave, this sepulcher, to discover their dead Jesus was not there. They were terrified and amazed. Two men standing nearby in dazzling apparel proclaimed to the women, 'Why do you look for the living among the dead? He is not here, but has risen.' The women fell to their knees and bowed their heads."

At which point, as the theme music rose to that crescendo when the paleontologist fell to his knees in absolute shock, I too fell to my knees at the altar and waited there until the selection ended. I returned to the pulpit.

"This music was the background last week for Arnold Palmer sinking a twenty-five-foot putt. And now you have heard it as background for the Easter Gospel this Sunday morning. Jurassic Park is a revolutionary idea – Disneyland in comparison seems like an old-fashioned swing-set at the local park – the brainstorm of a wealthy entrepreneur and DNA cloning scientists who have brought to life on a remote island the dinosaurs of our primeval past. Take a ride in a jeep and be prepared to drop your jaw! To be sure everything is safe and in place before the public is invited, this creator (Richard Attenborough) invites a paleontologist (Sam Neill) to inspect the project. All of a sudden, this paleontologist who has studied the bones of dinosaurs long dead is confronted with a sight not unlike that of those women who first visited the empty tomb of Jesus. With this theme music in the background, he is dropped to his knees by the sight of a brontosaurus walking among the trees. He could not stand up. What he had been studying for so many years – the fossilized bones of these Mesozoic creatures – was now walking in front of him. What was dead was now alive!

I must tell you, I had second thoughts about my introduction this morning – big dramatic entrance, theme music from a popular motion picture. Does this Gospel need anything else to enhance it? 'Why do you look for the living among the dead? He is not here, but has risen.' So why the Steven Spielberg movie and John Williams musical score?

Why?

Because I believe many of us live in anticipation of Easter, a future resurrection of the dead when Jesus comes again to judge the living and the dead. That, after all, is what we confessed in the words of The Apostles' Creed. But why don't we live Easter in the here and now? Why don't we think about living God's gift of salvation in the here and now, in the midst of life?

When I described for you the reaction of that paleontologist dropping to his knees at the sight of what was once dead but now walking alive in front of him, I wanted you to think about such an event happening in the midst of your life in the here and now. I don't want you thinking about some historical event of long ago that promises you life eternal in the hereafter someday after you die.

Not to put too fine a point on my reference to the movie *Jurassic Park*, but I didn't choose a film about primeval life in the distant past. Nor did I choose a film about some distant future when prehistoric life mysteriously returns to earth. *Jurassic Park's* 'what was dead is now alive' happened in the midst of life, and that is why John Williams' score takes your breath away. He has captured with this music a resurrection to new life in the middle of life. Now. Here and now. Today.

When you hear those words 'once dead but now alive,' I want you to think about your life here and now. What can we die to that subtracts from the life God intended for us – abundant life that's worth celebrating every day? We celebrate birthdays because birthdays recall the day we began life; we don't conduct solemn prayer vigils because we have finished off another lap of a losing race against time.

Could we die to our petty grievances that consume so much of our emotional energy?

Could we die to our self-absorption that ultimately diminishes our self?

Could we die to our stubbornness to confront the brokenness in our lives that threatens our psychological health?

Could we die to our fear of facing head-on those life challenges we keep trying to avoid?

Could we die to our indecision to change course out of that daily rut that keeps growing deeper?

Could we die to wearing the mask that hides our true self from others? Have we been pretending all is well?

Could we die to the pain of our past that continues to burden our soul?

Could we die to our worries that continually prove to be of little value for our well being?

Could we die to old habits that litter our path forward to a more productive and fulfilling life?

What is it that we can die to in the here and now so we can rise then to newness of life in the midst of life? Our Easter baptism joins us to the Easter event of long ago – Christ's death and resurrection – so we can participate in his death and resurrection to newness of life right now in the present. We can live God's gift of salvation today.

Don't misunderstand me here. This is a powerful message from Pope John Paul II, but here's the irony I'll share with you. In his encyclical, the Gospel of Life (EVANGELIUM VITAE), he speaks about all aspects of life: about birth and abortion, about the way we treat one another in our daily lives, about capital punishment, about how we take care of our aging parents (as in euthanasia, Measure 16). He's addressed all of life here. He talks about a Gospel of Life in contrast to what he describes as a culture of death. And he, as the leader of the Roman Catholic Church, is concerned and alarmed about this culture of violence and death. We condemn people to death who have bombed abortion clinics to murder people who weren't pro-life like them. The pope wants us to think about life.

Except here's what I found troubling and ironic about his newly published book, *Crossing the Threshold of Hope*. I read it, and I reread it. This Christian leader issued an encyclical about living life in the here and now, and then turned right around and declared that our death is the necessary first step toward salvation. Nothing about connecting our salvation secured by God's Son with the life we live each day. Salvation, defined by Pope John Paul II, is that which we attain to after we die.

With all due respect, Your Holiness, there's another understanding of salvation. Living out our baptism every day – Easter every day, dying to the old self and then raised to newness of life in the here and now – is living a relationship with God that cannot be broken by death. Salvation is not about life in the hereafter after you die; it's about life this afternoon and tomorrow morning.

Do you remember Truman Capote's short story, *A Christmas Memory*, that I read for all of you at our Thanksgiving Service last year? Remember what that elderly lady said to her seven-year-old cousin named Buddy? She would be on her deathbed, she had always thought, before she would ever see the Lord. And it would be a sight to see, like looking at a stained-glass window at church. But she wagered it never happens that way, that a person realizes at the end they have already seen the Lord in the here and now. From this, she found great comfort and peace.

For many of us, it takes half or more of a lifetime to figure out that which could have made all the difference in our living! At least she figured it out though: that long before she ever faced sickness and death, she had been seeing the Lord.

Have you figured that out?

Do you remember that conversation between two friends on the road to Emmaus later that first Easter Sunday afternoon? One of their names was Cleopas. They didn't recognize the risen Jesus at first but urged him to stay with them as the day was nearly over. When he was at table with them, he took bread, blessed and broke it, and gave it to them. Then they recognized him. They said to each other, 'Were not our hearts burning within us, while he was talking to us on the road, while he was opening the Scriptures to us?'

Aren't we always on the road to Emmaus? Isn't Jesus always with us? We experience his presence when we worship ('For where two or three are gathered in my name, I am there among them.'). We experience his presence in the words of Scripture. And we experience his presence in the bread and wine of the Eucharist. Jesus is always walking with us, whether we recognize him or not.

You may be familiar with the poem, 'Footprints In The Sand.' This man felt connected with the Lord most of his life but is bothered now in his last days about seeing only one set of footprints behind him. Happened at the lowest and saddest times in his life. So he asked the Lord why it was that he only saw one set of footprints during the most troublesome times in his life, why it was that the Lord who had promised to always walk with him had decided to abandon him. You remember the Lord's reply? It was during those troublesome times, the Lord explained, that He had carried the man, and that's why the man saw only one set of footprints.

Count those moments when you have come to know him and have recognized his presence. Was your heart not burning within you? Were you dropping to your knees in adoration and worship?

Theologian John Walvoord wants so desperately to assure us of the Second Coming that he cites Jesus' daily intervention in our lives as proof that he is able to fulfill his promise of a Second Coming. So let me get this right: the proof that Jesus will return someday is based on the fact that he intervenes daily in our lives! Should I bother to ask, 'Why does he need to come back if, in fact, he is intervening daily?' The time continuum has literalist preachers meeting themselves coming and going!

Our lectionary this morning, by the way, calls for only eleven verses from Luke 24. Some like to point out that at least Peter and an unnamed disciple rose up and ran to check out things for themselves. I'll read that verse for you. First, though, verse eleven, after the women had told this news to the disciples: '... but these words seemed to them an idle tale, and they did not believe them.' Other ancient authorities add verse twelve: 'But Peter rose and ran to the tomb; stooping and looking in, he saw the linen cloths by themselves; and he went home wondering at what had happened.' I'm not so certain that returning home after seeing the empty tomb and 'wondering at what had happened' could be considered falling to your knees.

The resurrected Jesus appeared to these people in the midst of life so his death and resurrection would have meaning in the midst of their life! Not as a promise of something realized in the future, but as a gift of something lived in the present.

How will you respond to this Gospel? We have a choice to make today.

We can be one of the disciples for whom these words reported by the women were nothing but an idle tale, or, slightly better, at least run to check things out. Or we can live Easter in the here and now. Live the fullness of the Gospel – living Easter every day, dying to the old self and then raised to newness of life in the here and now, living in God's eternal presence now and forever, never separated from Him, even in death.

Next time we play golf, I'm asking Trevor to bring a copy of that *Jurassic Park* music and something to play it on; I want to hear it while I'm lining up my twenty-five-foot putt. 'Do you think it'll make any difference, Dad?' He knows my game pretty well.

'But I thought you said our golf game sure lends something extra to that music.'

'Only if you make the putt,' he replied. 'The music is captivating because you make the putt.'

What was dead is now alive inspired this John Williams' musical score, not the other way around. This music is so stirring because it's the background for how *What was dead is now alive* actually sounds!

Can I order a copy of the CD for you this week?"

Later that Sunday evening in 1995, I received the call from Andy's father. His words sounded like a rebuttal to my words from this morning – what Andy had done to himself a *Negative* response to my *Affirmative* Easter sermon. With a weak voice, the most strained I have ever heard, he identified himself: "Bud, this is Pastor Messner, Andy's dad." I waited through the silence. "Bud, Andy died early this morning." Pastor Messner would not let himself say the word *suicide*.

After resigning from his parish the first of the year, Andy had spent the last three months coming to terms with the latest bigotry in his church – in such sodden despair, he had isolated himself, fearful of further persecution.

I sat at the kitchen table, my hands folded in front of me. Denise sat across from me.

"Andy and I debated about most everything," I softly mused.

"We once spent an entire night debating about how much we should tranquilize an injured hawk while we tried to repair its wing. We were Boy Scout counselors at Camp Cherry Valley on Catalina Island during the summer of 1965, and we had promised a group of young scouts who had found the bird that we would take care of it. Not enough, and the bird would suffer needlessly, so claimed Andy; too much, and we would end up killing it, so said I.

We once walked out of a movie theatre to commence an all-night debate about which one of us was Butch and which one of us was the Sundance Kid. We both wanted to be the Sundance Kid, but neither of us minded if we were Butch.

Remember when we debated that entire ride home from Las Vegas after you had invited your new roommate at the YWCA to join us? You were working at Ingram Pipe and Supply in Pasadena. Andy, you, and I were driving back without Vicki because she had disappeared in Vegas the night before after we had watched Elvis on stage at The International. We later discovered the FBI wanted her for armed robbery and interstate flight; we didn't know this at the time, so we were debating about her disappearance and possible whereabouts and our negligence if something horrible had happened to her. I was convinced we had no need to worry about her; Andy was convinced that something awful might have happened to her, and you should be turning our Bug around. But we had no need to worry about Vicki Forshetti; we had every need to worry about what we had done, driving her across state lines to help her meet up with some old friends and escape her parole obligations.

We debated about that movie, *The Big Chill*. What could they have done to prevent Alex's death by suicide?

We debated about Marilynne Robinson's novel, *Housekeeping*. Did Aunt Sylvie and Ruthie commit a kind of suicide by crossing that bridge to escape a life that would be good as dead, leaving all to believe they had committed suicide? Did they die that night to their old self in Fingerbone so they could find life? Ruthie's mom Helen had committed suicide in that lake below the bridge. 'But they didn't know at the time their disappearance would be considered that way,' so said Andy. 'Did they need to know? Maybe we are all transients, one suicide after another for the sake of life,' I countered.

We debated about our Boy Scout patch-trading business, a twelve-foot-diameter tepee my mother had helped us make that we set up at major BSA events to trade patches and neckerchiefs. Drove my Dad's '54 GMC pickup the summer of 1969 to Farragut State Park on the southern tip of Lake Pend Oreille north of Coeur d'Alene, Idaho, for the National Scout Jamboree. Non-stop most of the way. To switch drivers, I would climb around the back of the cab and position myself on the running board, open the door, and Andy would slide over. Hit a deer on Highway 97 south of Bend right after we had switched drivers. Caromed off the front fender and left us both a little dazed. We did stop then and watched that deer awkwardly run off into the woods.

We were master traders, serious enough about our craft that we trusted no one – I suppose because we hardly trusted ourselves. Where does *Trustworthy* end and *Thrifty* begin? How far would we go in besting the other Scout in one of our trades? Two for one a good deal? Three for one a better deal? Like trading my neckerchief for the first Jamboree scheduled in 1935 in Washington, D.C., but rescheduled for 1937 because of a polio epidemic.

Extremely rare! 'So I'll need at least five of your neckerchiefs if you want it,' I offered to a fellow trader. Andy said I was too greedy. I asked him, 'Andy, how else are you gonna build up your collection?'

Those were sure good times we had at the Jamboree in Idaho. Neil Armstrong, an Eagle Scout from Ohio, had greeted all of us personally while his Apollo 11 spacecraft zoomed through space to a landing on the moon.

Thinking back now, there's not much we didn't debate about. You know what, though? I don't remember ever debating with him about homosexuality."

CHAPTER 26

George
12 April 1998

CHAPTER 27

Henry
12 April 1998
Easter Sunday

So on this first day of the week, the ridge of Newberry Caldera now silhouetted against a new Easter dawn, I'm ready to bury my dead a second time – my three best men along with the burial of my mother's Easter. A new Easter dawn without my mother's Easter, so I'm also burying the person who no longer abides by that inherited faith.

I began planning my death and burial months ago. Such a decision requires patience sometimes, is not always a spontaneous reaction to a temporary problem. Long sleepless nights this past month as I lay awake double-checking the reality of my plan.

How can I know this is the right thing to do?

Is this my only option?

Am I even capable of carrying out such a plan?

How can I do this to Denise and our three children? What will they think of me? What will they think of God?

What will God think of me?

And how much does that question even matter? Is the death of my mother's Easter also the death of God for me?

How can I resolve such nihilism?

Is this how I want people to remember me?

Why do I still have so many questions?

Dear Easter women of long ago, maybe we do share the same space and time – at least, since late Friday night. Like a borderland between this world and the Other, a place where suicide is contemplated before the imminent act itself, a dimension shared with all spirits, past, present, and future. Like a strange dream world that temporarily interrupts a person's decision to snuff out their existence.

Suicide is both contemplation and action. While preparing to complete the actual act of voluntary death, a suicidal person is forced to think about how a victim of murder must feel. Before a trigger is ever pulled, or a pill swallowed, or a noose placed around one's neck, the victim has already quit this life. For a brief time, then – or perhaps hours and days – the victim can rethink their decision one last time. After rehearsing their ending so many times, some suicides have talked themselves out of it. This is what Schneidman called the acute suicidal crisis – when a person begins to experience his death by suicide but is either helped, talks himself out of it, or is dead. Some will spend more time than others contemplating this experience of death by suicide, Schneidman said, but no one can delay indefinitely the outcome of this experience, one way or the other.

Over twenty suicide attempts jumping from the Golden Gate Bridge have survived, most often by landing feet first. Some have later claimed they regretted their decision as soon as they stepped off the bridge two-hundred-and-twenty feet above the ocean. Of the over five hundred people who have attempted suicide, but who have been restrained by bridge police or by-standers, most have lived many years after their only suicide attempt.

Life is a dialogue with our conscience – inner and outer, sometimes both at once. In Graham Greene's novel, *The Heart of the Matter*, Major Scobie's borderland monologue sooner or later becomes a conversation with God. God pleads with him, but Scobie refuses to continue living.

We are always in conversation with ourselves about what we are thinking, about how we are answering Hamlet's question, "To be, or not to be." We enter the borderland once we answer that question with "not to be"; once we complete the act of voluntary death, we've departed that borderland for the "undiscover'd country" from which "no traveller returns."

Before I departed the borderland this morning, I decided, like Hamlet, to take one more look. Shakespeare's "Must give us pause" sounds like my borderland. "What dreams may come" is a frightening thought. A brief moment to weigh our two choices: to continue bearing "those troubles we have or to fly to others that we know not of."

So Hello REASON, my old friend, I've come to talk with you again.

Nietzsche, I credit you with the most contentious answer to Jesus' question about who people say that he is. After you put Jesus on trial – after you put the Christ of the creeds, contemporary Christianity, on trial – you declared, "In truth, there was only one Christian, and he died on the cross."

I am familiar, Nietzsche, with the path you took to walk away from Easter. However those historical-critical methods of interpreting Scripture led you away from the Lutheran catechism of your youth, you eventually rejected the heartfelt faith you had inherited from your father the pastor. I must say, you left no doubt about your rejection when you deliberately used that blasphemous title ECCE HOMO for a book about yourself. I guess you forced the Prussian censorship laws to put Jesus on trial too.

Following the teachings of Jesus, a practical way of life inscribed in our hearts, is what you had in mind when you spoke about the Kingdom of God. You said we betray Jesus' proclamation about the Kingdom of God whenever we seek it in the hereafter. Such seeking deprecates this life by accepting our human inability to fulfill Jesus' teachings. As you might have said it, Jesus did not command us to give it our best try. Once our here and now is deprecated, of what value, you asked, are any of our actions? Instead of daily becoming more and more like Christ, we only need faith that Christ was perfect and therefore paid the price we could not.

So you had no time for theologians trying to answer Jesus' question. Whatever a theologian considers true, you claimed, must of necessity be false. Including the apostle Paul. In fact, you considered Paul's theology a sellout. Unable to fulfill the Jewish Law – let alone the extraordinary demands of Jesus – you argued that Paul escaped this impossible task by substituting faith in Christ for the Christ-like life. I believe you thought the same about Luther.

You did introduce me, Nietzsche, to that word nihilism, the word I am using to describe this crisis I am facing with the death of my mother's Easter. As I failed to find here and now meaning for those I love and for myself, I began acknowledging Easter's death. But I have struggled to accept this because the death of Easter then has left me without the God-foundation upon which I have built my life.

You resolved your persistent problem of nihilism by rejecting God, a traditional worldview of how we understand reality. But once you had denied God, you immediately forced the question, "Does life have meaning at all?" If I answer *No*, I forgo my inquiry and can fall into despair. If I answer *Yes*, I'm led to the next question. If life does have meaning, who or what provides it? Who or what now provides our value system, our foundation, our understanding of reality, and our understanding of what it means to be human?

Can I provide my own meaning?

Or can I merely ascribe value to life in spite of it having no meaning?

At least, Mr. Camus, you confronted Nietzsche's nihilism with an alternative option. "Futile," you said of your search for life's meaning. The "absurd" you called it – our search to make sense of life in a universe that makes no sense. But then you asked, "If life has no meaning, does that mean life is not worth living?" Unlike Nietzsche, you conceded we can find meaning by taking a leap of faith and accepting God as our meaning provider (like Kierkegaard). Or, you conceded, our conviction that life is meaningless is so unacceptable we complete suicide.

Or, you boldly suggested, there is a third possibility. Living with the awareness that we are all condemned to death, life is given value by its daily uprising against this inevitability. By not completing suicide, we stage an existential rebellion against the absurdity of life. "Yes, I admit, life is absurd because the world around me makes no sense, but I choose to embrace life anyway as a revolt against that absurdity!" Choosing to live life each day is defiance of death's inevitability.

You retold the story of Sisyphus to make your point – a hero of the absurd struggling without any hope of success. According to Greek myth, Sisyphus was forced to watch the rock he had rolled up to the top of a mountain roll right back down to the bottom, over and over again. How familiar should this sound to us, representing as it does our human condition? But so long as Sisyphus accepts this absurd struggle as his lot in life, you claimed, he can embrace his life as it is.

What about Quentin Compson, Mr. Camus? Could he have walked away from suicide? Could he have chosen life in spite of his despair – despair because he could not accept the collapse of his moral values? You have suggested that our choice to live in constant awareness of this collapse of values, that continuing to live in spite of life's absurdity, is the more profound objection to that absurdity. Far more profound than suicide. You have also suggested that making a choice is answering the fundamental question of philosophy – judging whether life is or is not worth living.

With your alternative, I don't need someone or something to provide meaning.

With your alternative, Mr. Camus, I only need to accept the inexplicable universe and take my existential stand against the absurdity of it all. Are we all just *Waiting For Godot*? How is Luther's "Here below all is incomprehensible" any different, Mr. Camus, from "the absurd" you speak about?

So REASON, my old friend, help me out here. Why does my task this morning still feel complicated? Until I have accepted life without my mother's Easter – no more revisions, no more hedging like Pascal – until I'm prepared to live without a value system that has directed my life since birth, I have not conducted Easter's funeral.

And if I have not yet conducted Easter's funeral, I have not yet buried my three best men a second time. The first time I buried them I had not disavowed my mother's Easter. Clergy brain ON, broken heart OFF. Burying them a second time requires my complete disavowal of my mother's Easter because that Easter – devoid of any meaning for their here and now – had failed them in their darkest nights.

Although psychological autopsies of my three best men resist any simple connection between my mother's Easter and their suicides, the faith we had inherited did not help them sort out the options before them. I cannot say their Christian faith led to their suicides, that my mother's Easter is to blame for their self-destruction; I can only say that their Sunday school faith did not shine in their darkness. By their suicides, their darkness had overcome the light.

I have tried to learn about why their darkness was so powerful. No simple explanation can be had. Multiple factors have been proposed by those who research and study the "Why?" question about suicide. Some suggest that whatever unfulfilled needs we may be troubled about, we may remain at low risk for suicide if we have not acquired the ability to carry out self-harm.

For all of my post-mortem reflection about their lives, I cannot understand how their basic survival impulse to preserve life fell victim to their death wish. In each of their lives, I have tried to imagine a more powerful reason for remaining in this world than their conclusions for quitting it. Does Luther's denigration of our earthly existence – "the world is our bitter enemy and persecutes us cruelly. Such misery we cannot shed as long as this life lasts" – lend aid to such a death wish?

In his poem, "Statues in the Park," Billy Collins considers the different ways we remember our dead – death of the famous and not so famous, death of those without a horse, a saddle, or a sword, death of the sickly, death of the suicide, death of the accident victim, death of the murder victim. What do their statues look like? He describes his own: a figure on his knees, praying to the sky above, humbly pleading for one more day.

Please, let me have one more day.

Sheer logic, then, begs the question: Is your life no longer worth preserving? If the answer to that question is "My life is no longer worth preserving," then follow-up questions must be asked. "Why not? What has happened that brought you to this point? Unbearable physical suffering? An endless night of darkness? A here and now that offers no reason for living? A screaming psychache that will not subside?"

By creating the word *psychache* to describe the unendurable psychological pain from which we feel our only means of escape is suicide, Edwin Schneidman also created one of the most profound and sincerest ways to help those thinking that suicide will stop their intolerable pain. Two most critical questions we can ask a suicidal person: "Where do you hurt?" and "How can I help you?" For my three best men, I would have added this question: "How did your inherited Christian faith fail to meet your most vital psychological needs?"

Maybe some people are more disposed to self-destruction, and that instinct to preserve life is not their first step each day on life's journey. Like you Mr. Hemingway, maybe it's the instinct to survive that must meet the challenge.

Recovering from that war wound you suffered in October of 1918, you expressed a belief that you held until the end of your life: Why not avoid the ravages of old age and take one's exit in a self-determined instant while still enjoying youth's innocence? Nineteen years old, facing the nihilism of your generation, and you came up with that.

Your code of honor – formulated in your youth, based on a stoic self-independence – did not account for your lingering death. So your code failed you at the end. When you were younger, you had condemned your father for his cowardly suicide at age fifty-nine; your father couldn't bear the burden of his incurable illness any longer. But when faced with the same, you put a shotgun in your mouth and chose the same kind of death.

Countless times this question has been asked about you: "How does someone like Ernest Hemingway – good looks, sporting skills, friends, women, wealth, fame, recipient of Nobel and Pulitzer prizes – end up taking his own life?" But maybe this question doesn't account for your life-long escape from the nihilism that sabotaged your coming of age innocence, the nihilism you described in *The Sun Also Rises*.

World War I had called into question your long-accepted notions of morality, faith, and justice. "Things fall apart; the centre cannot hold." So Yeats warned in his 1921 poem, "The Second Coming." With your traditional beliefs and values now shattered, you joined the psychologically and morally lost generation wandering aimlessly in a world that no longer made sense. You created your own option to resolve Nietzsche's nihilism – escape by distracting yourself with enough drinking and dancing and carousing.

In the war, Mr. Hemingway, you had discovered that survival depended far more on luck than upon bravery. So you were already questioning your masculine code of courage long before your decadent lifestyle began to take its toll on your health. How did you define manhood then after the war? You tried so hard to hold fast to your lifelong scorn of psychiatrists and their belief that every man has a breaking point.

But escaping from nihilism by self-indulgence works only so long before we are pushed over the edge by our declining health – declining because our self-destructive lifestyle is not thinking about our health. Add to this your suspected hemochromatosis, and maybe your instinct to survive had lost the battle long ago.

But at least you tried to see your self-destruction from a survivor's point of view, admitting later in life that such a decision requires a bit of egotism and indifference to others. Was your mental breakdown that November before you took your life in 1961 the beginning of your borderland? You had already abandoned hope for an alternative. You considered your suicide a remedy, not a bargain you could make with life's misery. Which suggests to me that you were predisposed to self-destruction. I do appreciate your tribute to Ecclesiastes, though, how you concluded your suicide note with, "The sun also sets."

Your fascination, Mr. Hemingway, with the book of Ecclesiastes fascinates me because you apparently didn't read it the way Jewish commentators would suggest. In the context of a Christian Bible, Ecclesiastes speaks to life's hopelessness without a savior to redeem us. In Hebrew Scripture, Ecclesiastes offers us a guide to embracing life in the here and now in spite of its impermanence.

Dear REASON, I believe you and FAITH met a long time ago. Before Pontius Pilate had declared Jesus' innocence before the crowds in Jerusalem, Qoheleth the author of Ecclesiastes had already tried Jesus of Nazareth.

Many of us, dear Qoheleth, try to explain our reality using our inherited faith in God as a guide. You accepted reality as it is and then tried to understand how a belief in God could still make sense. Your book reminds me of Michener's novel, *The Source*. You began with a personal search for life's meaning, not with God's revelation made known in the biblical narrative. And your search for meaning does not require an act of atonement because your search is not predicated on Paul's essential premise: "For the wages of sin is death." This premise is the reason we look to Jesus' death and resurrection for our atonement. But according to you, Qoheleth, all of human existence is subject to time and chance; our fate is not dependent on good behavior or bad behavior. Swapping out a Christian commentary on your book for a Jewish analysis feels like swapping out the book itself for a different read.

As you explained, Qoheleth, we die because we are part of the animal kingdom, part of a biological system. "A time to be born, and a time to die." A guy by the name of Pete Seeger wrote a song, "To Everything There Is a Season," adopting word-for-word the first eight verses of your chapter three. But then in verses nineteen to twenty-one, you made this so clear: "For the fate of humans and the fate of animals is the same; as one dies, so dies the other. They all have the same breath, and humans have no advantage over the animals; for all is vanity. All go to one place; all are from the dust, and all turn to dust again." You may not know this, Qoheleth, but a psalmist said the same thing: "Mortals cannot abide in their pomp; they are like the animals that perish."

By returning to the Bible's first book, Qoheleth, your search for meaning settled on a different understanding of death. The Hebrew word *hevel* appears thirty-eight times in your book, and it is most commonly understood to mean futility or meaninglessness. In Christian Scripture, it is usually translated as *vanity*. If I die anyway, why does anything matter?

But *Hevel* is also the Hebrew name of Abel, son of Adam and Eve, first human being to die, killed by his brother Cain – but not before he had turned his shortened life into an offering to God (which offering, by the way, was not based on any achievements). Your clever reference, Qoheleth, to Abel's death underscores life's transience, not its futility. Even though Abel's life was cut short, his life still had a purpose. "Fleeting transience (*hevel havalim*)," you said. "All is fleeting." How swiftly life passes us by and comes to an end.

But our transience can motivate us to live life with urgency and renewed spirit, to experience every moment free from death's ominous threat. Since we cannot know our fate, why not accept life's uncertainty by appreciating God's gift of life while we can? And such uncertainty is not Nietzsche's nihilism. Even though this here and now world often made no sense to you, Qoheleth, you still believed life could be purposeful. You have provided, Qoheleth, another alternative to resolve Nietzsche's nihilism. And I think you might have understood why I have tried so hard to revise my mother's Easter.

I wish we had known of your Old Testament voice when my three best men and I were searching for an adult faith. Your here and now emphasis to counter my mother's "eternal life" Easter emphasis. Your voice of wisdom that spoke of living life in spite of its uncertainty – a life that could not answer all of our questions about mental illness, a mother's untimely death, or discrimination in God's name. Living life like playing golf – quit trying to figure it out. Our impermanence is our only certainty, and our denial of that was our first misstep into adulthood. How long does it take before we acknowledge the hopelessness of our quest for certainty? You had provided a practical guidebook for us to follow: a life based on moderation, fulfilling work, and meaningful relationships.

Dear Easter women, could it be that our acceptance of death's inevitability leads to an enhanced appreciation of life in the here and now? To honestly struggle with nihilism, with the absurd, and to make of that struggle a renewed dedication to embracing every moment of life in the here and now. Death doesn't follow life; death precedes life. "Oh my soul, do not aspire to immortal life, but exhaust the limits of the possible." So said Pindar.

Can psychache be traced to an expectation that life should be other than what it is, an expectation that life's certainty has eluded us? Are people who contemplate suicide living in a state of unrealistic certainty, agitated by failed assurances that bear no resemblance to reality? Qoheleth, those first two premises of theodicy, God is perfectly good and God is all-powerful, were not your first step toward understanding life. Your first step was that third premise: Sometimes evil wins the day. Uncertainty. Senselessness. It is what it is.

My early morning footsteps crossing the wooden bridge over the Sun River tributary startled four geese floating beneath; their frantic fluttering wings across the water then startled me. I was not prepared for the uncomfortable chill at this time of the morning; I didn't remember it so cold on my wedding day, but I wasn't up at this hour of the day back in 1970. A bright, full moon said good-morning before it finished its illumination duties for the night, no longer bright enough to compete with the glory of this new Easter dawn.

Of course, the moon was bright. About three hundred years after the first Easter, Church leaders had asked astronomers to approximate dates for the first full moon that occurs on or after March 20, which was the equinox date back then. Since 326 CE, these Ecclesiastical Full Moon dates have always corresponded with Paschal Full Moon dates. To guarantee a bright night sky for those pilgrims venturing to Jerusalem to celebrate the Resurrection of Our Lord, the Council of Nicaea declared that Easter should fall on the first Sunday following the ecclesiastical full moon date, anywhere from March 22 to April 25.

Most of Mother Nature was already awake – croaking frogs no match for the squawking geese overhead – and this abundant life around me, as it always did at Sunriver, helped to ease my apprehension about the unknown I now faced.

Already the Resort Lodge lights behind me revealed a flurry of 6:00 AM preparations for the Easter Brunch, but that activity seemed miles away as I walked along the short path to the ninth green. I don't know how it started, and I don't know for how long, but I could hardly stop weeping to answer the question posed by a shadowy figure walking toward me down the path along the ninth fairway.

"Sir, why are you weeping?"

A gardener, I thought, a grounds-keeper making his early rounds.

"Not easy to explain," I said, answering myself more than that gardener. "I've lost my brother, my brother-in-law, and my childhood best friend."

This sounded as though they had just died, so I offered to clarify further what had happened.

"We hadn't stood by each other over the years like we had promised. I managed to conduct their funerals, but now I must come to terms with their choice of voluntary death. Each of their deaths has struck a death blow to my Christian faith, so I'm hoping this morning for something beyond Easter's death."

My head was down as I spoke, so I hadn't noticed that this gardener had continued walking around the practice-putting surface to the first tee-box. I quickly walked in his direction, but the more I quickened my pace, the more he faded out of sight down the path along the first fairway, and was gone.

I followed anyway, talking to myself as I walked for an hour and a half along the cart path of the front nine. Maybe I was trying to avoid the task before me, what I had come to take care of this morning. Maybe I wasn't ready yet to depart the borderland.

CHAPTER 28

Karl
12 April 1998

CHAPTER 29

Henry
12 April 1998
Easter Sunday

"You and Dad spent Friday afternoon sitting by that ninth green?"

"Friday afternoon and evening."

"You've had a lot to talk about lately, haven't you?"

"We have. Uncle George, Uncle Karl, and Dad's best friend Andy – their suicides made no sense, you know that, but for your dad, their suicides have called into question his Christian faith and how he understood life."

"What about your anniversary yesterday?" Our daughter Kendra kept close tabs on our happiness.

"I've let Dad to himself since Friday night. He'll be surprised to see you this morning. I'm grateful you came. He's out walking around the golf course right now."

My three best men and I had pledged to each other the morning of my wedding day that we would never lose track of each other, that we would be there for each other when one of us stumbled and fell, that each of us would make it through the darkest of nights.

But we had not. Even though our wedding photograph shows four guys with smiles that could light up the darkest night imaginable. This groom's party was a memory now. Their deaths, both expected and unexpected.

291

Denise and I have been working through our heartache for ten years now, the depth of our sorrow sinking deeper with each passing year. We had canceled our Sunriver anniversary weekend back in 1988 following my brother's death on Good Friday. Denise became my pastor for those weeks after my brother's funeral, weeks turning into months until one warm Saturday evening in 1990, on the twenty-fifth of August, she took a call from a Deschutes County sheriff who had to report how her brother had shot himself earlier that day. Each without our brother now, each without a pastor. Church life felt more abusive than ever because now we were wounded healers expected to serve unselfishly the wounded lives of others. On Easter Sunday in 1995, we received word of Andy's suicide in Los Angeles; we sat in tormented silence for days after his funeral. We both have struggled to accept the reality of their suicides; we chose to ignore our anniversary the past two years, hardly in the mood to celebrate anything.

My walk this morning has forced me to recall my earnest efforts to revise my mother's Easter. With respect for her – and not because she had made that Hannah promise to God when I was six years old, but because I love her – I was determined to find my here-and-now-friendly version of Easter within the faith boundaries I had inherited from her. I believed that if I could roll away that stone of ancient dogma and doctrine and orthodoxy and tradition protecting twenty centuries of my mother's hereafter Easter, I would discover an Easter that could speak to my three best men. I had proposed this answer to my question about when we begin living God's gift of salvation: We begin living God's gift the day we are baptized. I proclaimed that answer from the pulpit, I wrote a book explaining that answer, and that answer guided my counseling every day.

The Sunday after my father's fatal heart attack in 1984, two months after my ordination, I had begun to emphasize in my preaching the other half of the Gospel – the here and now half. My mother's Easter covered the hereafter half. My father had never heard about the here and now half, so I was determined, by way of honoring him, to make sure others did – in part a frustrated reaction to my inadequate childhood faith, trying to salvage it for myself and the many I served in parish ministry who were yearning for a word of hope and comfort and support in their here and now.

Many Christians call on their pastor when they or a loved one are facing a major illness, a condition that may soon lead to death and the promised hereafter. Meanwhile, substance abuse, despair, distress, emptiness, seemingly endless troubles, heartrending emotions, daily setbacks, loneliness, and bitterness – all take their toll. My mother's Easter did not speak of this here and now half of the Gospel. Self-help groups like Alcoholics Anonymous speak of it, afternoon TV Talk Shows speak of it, and pop-psychology gurus dressed in clergy attire speak of it (sometimes with enough answers about life that you wonder what it is you need to be saved from!). At least my mother's Easter – concerned about a place to go after the here and now – offered a reason for our atonement. She had taught my brother and me what her father had taught her: "In our sad condition, our only consolation is the expectancy of another life. Here below all is incomprehensible."

"How relevant for your here and now is this Good News?" was my preacher's guiding question on Sunday morning. I never asked, "What does the Easter Proclamation mean for you when you die?" I never asked, "Do you know where you're headed after you die?" I kept asking, "Do you know where you're headed tomorrow and the next day and the next?"

My father's death had left me with a lot of questions. "What had the Easter Proclamation meant for him in his daily struggles to cope with such a sea of troubles?" What I had inherited from my mother and him was not serving me too well as I ventured out into the real world where I encountered all kinds of life stories that longed for the here and now half of the Gospel. My Sunday school faith, although much more sophisticated in language now after four years of seminary, was coming up short more often than not. I sensed failure as a pastor if I didn't acknowledge this.

I spent ten years writing a book about my new Easter thinking. Living out our Easter baptism every day means living in God's eternal presence from the day we are baptized, never separated from Him, even in death. And if we are never spiritually separated from Him in our here and now, I proposed, our relationship with Him could challenge any of our everyday trials and tribulations. I had Luther's famous hymn in mind, "A Mighty Fortress Is Our God." Relying on our own strength and striving, we will lose the battles; but relying on the Man of God's own choosing, we cannot lose. I cited examples like Armando Valladares, describing in his book, *Against All Hope*, how his faith had daily "set him free" during his tortuous twenty-two years in the political prisons of Castro's Cuba.

So crucial for me to stay in bounds with all of this – that's how comfortable and at home my childhood faith had made itself in my soul. Who I was, every system of my being, could be traced back to those voices of my mother's Easter. So I was surprised when my denomination's publishing house rejected my book proposal (*Salvation: God's Gift for the Here and Now*). Something about my new understanding of Easter not being a good fit for their publishing goals at the time. Even as my book was rejected, I kept trying to stay within my calling as a Lutheran pastor.

I field-tested my here and now revisions of my mother's Easter as I counseled and consoled and encouraged those whom I served. Easter is not about life after death; it's about renewal, a new creation, and a new approach to living life. That was my constant invitation – a new way to understand Christ's life, death, and resurrection. Recall your baptism every day. Die to your old self every day – to your weariness, to your frustrations, to your worries, to your fears, to your grievances. And rise up to new life every day, sustained by the love of God, a God who will never let you go, even in death. Instead of my mother's Easter, I was turning to some advice in the Talmud. The question was posed, "Why should we trust in God's Love, given all that we are struggling with now?" Rashi had answered, "Because He will not let us go." God will never quit us.

But my revision of my mother's Easter – faithfully staying within my inherited boundaries – was not enough to keep my part of our ninth green promise to stand by each other. As I worked on my new understanding of Easter and salvation – emphasizing a here and now friendly version of salvation from anything that subtracts from abundant life – my three best men were taking their own lives, unable to suffer any longer the psychache that subtracted from an abundant life.

The suicides of my three best men reminded me of my father's tragic story – being "Easter baptized" ended up meaning nothing at all. In their borderland, why hadn't George and Karl and Andy found any strength from their baptism? Luther spoke about "appreciating and using Baptism aright, drawing strength and comfort from it." At life's most oppressive and troubling moments, Luther, like Bonhoeffer, was prepared to affirm the power of his baptism, to shout back at that oppression, "But I am baptized!"

When I conducted their public services and delivered their eulogies, I had to switch OFF my broken heart so my clergy brain could be switched ON for the sake of those who gathered in bereavement – like my mother, like my father-in-law, like Andy's parents. I chose to ignore the impact of their deaths on my inherited Christian faith (that I was desperately trying to revise). I had no right at that moment to share my deepest feelings. What my three best men had done made no sense in a world where Jesus has promised abundant life, but they had done it. What had happened to my three best men should not have happened in the world I was proclaiming to be the object of God's love.

I'm sprinkling pixie dust on my watch hoping to slow down time's passage while my three best men had been rushing toward death like a speeding bullet. Why am I? Why were they? If I had faced similar circumstances, had faced their experiences, can I honestly claim I would have done differently?

A hangman's noose and a broken wooden chair, a meticulously self-loaded cap-and-ball revolver, and an overdose mix of scotch and Valium – this is not the stuff of the Easter message I had been proclaiming, the "glad tidings" announced by that host of angels.

But oh how quick the theological rebuttal sounds: "That is precisely the stuff of the Easter message!" The story is told about a Jewish prisoner asking his fellow captive – as both stared in cold bewilderment at a Christian prisoner hanging from the gallows – "So, where is your Christian God now?" The answer was simple enough. "Right there," the Christian answered, as he pointed to the prisoner hanging from a rope. As if to remind us that whatever figurative prison we may be stuck in, God suffers with us.

When I first heard this, I imagined that Jewish prisoner scratching his head. And thinking to himself what his friend Elie Wiesel had said when he observed a Jewish prisoner hanging from the gallows. "He (God) is hanging here on this gallows. God is dead for me, given what I'm experiencing."

I've heard more than one preacher exclaim, "We can find comfort in knowing Jesus has experienced whatever suffering we have experienced, whatever pain, distress, rejection, betrayal, and death." I don't know how this would have abated the psychache my three best men suffered.

I now realize how long and hard Easter's death has been for me. For one thing, my mother's Easter wouldn't let go of my hand. But she's home with her Lord now, died this past fall on All Saint's Day, November 1. Appropriately, All Saint's Day!

So I wasn't looking for Jesus' empty tomb this morning. I already knew that story as if I had been there.

And I wasn't looking to die. I was looking for life. I'm always looking for life – the main reason why I have questioned my mother's hereafter Easter. I've been looking for life all my life. Even my three best men were looking for life and not death, because what they were living sure as hell wasn't life!

Maybe like Joseph of Arimathea, I was also looking for the Kingdom of God – on earth as it is in heaven. Who isn't, right? That empty tomb promise, though – that promise my mother had introduced to my brother and me a long time ago, the same promise Andy and Karl had inherited from their families – had turned into a massive stone blocking my way whenever I was searching for life in the here and now. I fear it may have been blocking the way for my father and my three best men as well.

My disenchantment felt lonely for a time, but when an Episcopal bishop chose to practice his Christian faith in exile, I learned that the forces of reason were asking questions about my mother's Easter, prompting followers to challenge traditional ways of thinking about God. In the spirit of the Reformation, theologians like Crossan and Borg were opening the door to questions like the ones I was asking, like the ones my children were asking. "How can we reconcile the idea of God's Goodness with the apparent lack of His Goodness in our world?"

Acknowledging and processing the suicide of someone we love lasts a lifetime, and we never stop asking the "Why" question. The death by suicide of someone we love assumes a life of its own. However it continues to break our heart, their death never dies for us.

My three best men are not with me this morning for any more conversations about life. And one of our conversations may have prevailed against the last conversation they had with themselves in that borderland between decision and death.

Conversations can change minds. Our last conversation with someone who has then completed suicide was the last chance we had.

As I walked the cart path around the front nine of South Meadows, I could feel my pace slowing down. But now here I was, Easter morning, staring at that ninth green. I didn't appreciate, though, how the ninth green was staring back at me. I flipped it the finger, a far more convenient emotion to express than flipping off myself.

So I decided to play that reunion round of golf here at Sunriver that the four of us had never managed to play after that Saturday in April of 1970. That's how I would bury my dead a second time – golfing on Easter morning. A first for me. That's how I would finally bury Easter. Like Qoheleth said, "So I commend enjoyment, for there is nothing better for people under the sun than to play a round of golf on an Easter Sunday morning with three of their favorite people."

I patiently waited outside the southwest corner of the resort lodge until the pro-shop opened. I checked with the starter to confirm what I already knew about the frost delay. I didn't bother to explain I would be playing golf by myself; I would straighten that out later when I teed off.

CHAPTER 30

Andy
12 April 1998

CHAPTER 31

Henry
12 April 1998
Easter Sunday

Like my wedding day twenty-eight years ago, I had to wait.

I had to wait for the frost-covered fairways and greens to thaw before our groom's party could play golf that morning. Reminds me of those ladies at Ebenezer Lutheran – always restrictions and regulations.

This typical thirty-one degree Central Oregon sunrise was no different. From lava-flow-created lake and marshland to World War II army camp to high desert golf resort, the sacred terrain of Sunriver had earned a little respect. Ready for my broken heart, the South Meadows Course would serve as the resting place for the second time I'm burying my dead. So I waited.

"Yeah, you're fine to play now, Mr. Caine. I've got a father and son who are joining you this morning; they're out on the putting green."

"No," I firmly replied, "you don't understand. I scheduled this starting time for the Caine foursome."

With a puzzled look on his face, the starter expected some explanation. "But Mr. Caine, there's no one else here with you this morning. What do you mean?"

I liken my face at that moment to an IRS agent's face conducting a required audit of someone's questionable income tax return. "The Caine foursome is here; no one else will be joining us."

I had barely finished my sentence before my three children responded in unison behind me. "We're here!"

"You didn't think we would miss this, did ya' Dad?"

"Golfing with you on an Easter Sunday morning is too historical to pass up!"

"We're not intruding or anything, are we?"

"No, not at all, I appreciate you showing up." I was surprised, but I wasn't surprised. "When did you get here?"

"Late last night. We wanted to share this morning with you, your first Easter Sunday not in church."

"Yeah, my first Easter Sunday not in church!"

Those same four geese passed quietly overhead, I could hardly hear their effortless flight as we crossed the wooden bridge to the first tee. No wind or breeze, so the water surface of this canal-like tributary, built by that Army Corps of Engineers for training purposes, provided a natural mirror to reflect the grandeur of this park-like setting. Big Leaf Lupine blooming off to my left, Green-Leaf Manzanita coming to life again, the leaves of the Quaking Aspens ready to dance again with the slightest breeze, and the Belding Ground Squirrels (sometimes mistakenly called prairie dogs) were already playing the holes of the Great Meadow's grasslands. They did not have to wait for any thaw this morning.

By counting the number of needles per cluster, I can distinguish between the lodgepole pine and the ponderosa pine that border the fairways of the South Meadows course. Lodgepole (also called jack pine), with two syllables, has two short, stiff needles per bundle (the only pine with bunches of two needles). Lewis and Clark had observed the Native Americans using these trees to support their lodges. Ponderosa, derived from the word *ponderous* (three syllables, meaning "of great weight") has three long, evergreen needles per bundle. The ponderosa pine can grow to over two hundred feet in height. The bark of the older stately trees evolves from a dull brown to pumpkin orange or yellowish brown with deep furrows. Sniff the bark and discover a scent similar to butterscotch or vanilla.

Beyond a saddle ridge to the west, snow-covered Mt. Bachelor already basked in the high-desert sunrise, but it took until mid-morning before the rising temperature relieved any concerns about course damage. By noon, the thermometer would read seventy-three degrees.

I placed my Titleist #3 ball on the first tee, stepped back to take a casual practice swing, addressed the ball and readied myself for the first hole – par four, 395 yards from the blue tees. I could feel my hesitation. I was resting the clubhead on the ground, balancing myself with the shaft of my driver. Like vertigo, I felt unsteady, unsure of the distance between my eyes and the ground. I raised the clubhead, but my blurry eyes told me I would never connect with the ball. I quickly settled the golf club behind my teed up ball and took another glance down the undulating first fairway.

Standing over my golf ball, I recalled a similar feeling from twenty-eight years ago. I tried to focus again on my teed-up golf ball. I could hardly see through the dense layer of film accumulating over my eyes. When I blinked, the watery layer streamed down my cheek in the shape of tears, dropping onto my hands and shaft. I momentarily released my grip and rubbed my eyes with the back of my right hand. I know my children felt my heartache.

I finally took an awkward swing and sliced the ball past that ponderosa pine two hundred and thirty yards out, bouncing it off the cart path and rolling it into a clump of Idaho fescue. Like twenty-eight years ago, as if nothing had changed.

Only everything had changed.

As soon as my ball bounced into that grass to the right of the cart path, I turned around to face the lodge behind the first tee box. I knew Denise would be smiling. Smiling because I often sliced the ball, and I had come to accept that about my golf game. She appreciated that about me. Smiling because she knew I must tend to my broken heart by playing this reunion round of golf, and smiling because our three children had joined me. For twenty-eight years, I have imagined playing a round of golf with my three best men again here at the resort's South Meadows course. She knew what I was up to today. Smiling because it was our anniversary, and she loved me.

I placed my driver back in its slot, turned around and blew Denise a kiss. I turned around twice more before I reached that ponderosa pine. She was still smiling.

Out of the cart now, I walked past that tree, trying to judge how far my ball would have bounced away from the paved path. Lightly dragging my five-iron through the grass, about fifteen feet from the path along the fairway, I felt a slight nudge against the face of my club. Well, whatta' ya' know,

I found my ball. My god, what are the odds of that? I had to use both hands to free my ball from the long strands of tangled grass.

"Yep, Slazenger #2. That's it, all right. I'm gonna take an unplayable, George," I declared after dropping my ball on the fairway side of the path. "I'm lying two now, right?"

"Don't worry about that," my brother laughed. He had walked over to help me find my ball. He put his hand on my shoulder like a gentle hug. "It's your wedding day, Buddy. Drop your ball over here and try to put your second shot on the green."

We waited for Andy to take his shot, which he caught a little heavy, and watched his ball roll up ten yards short of the green. "What a shot, you chowderhead," I shouted across the fairway. Andy was used to my teasing. After George and I had both pushed our seven-iron shots out to the right of the first green, we instinctively merged together to walk up the first fairway with Karl and Andy.

Our golfing together the morning of my wedding felt like a groom's party team-building activity to prepare each of us for our role that afternoon. Who were we? Who were we becoming? What was this moment in time all about, this April Saturday in 1970? Where were we headed?

I had declared last night's bachelor party off-limits for any discussion. So we talked about family, about friendship, about marriage, about how best to handle life's ups and downs, about our anxieties, about America and the world we shared with others, about how we had grown up, and about the Christian faith we had inherited from our parents. Maybe the solemn nature of this day lent some gravity to our conversations. One of those turning-point days when you know life will be starkly different from the way it was lived the day before.

After our tee shots on the second hole, we walked along that tributary-canal water hazard on our left. Each of us had driven safely up to the bend on this par five, 555-yard dogleg to the left.

"Hey, Caine," Andy asked, "Did you take a double on that first hole, what with your unplayable lie?"

"Shut up, Messner," my brother quickly came to my defense.

"What if we abandoned our customer golf privileges?" Andy shrugged. "Seeing as how life itself seldom works out if played that way, and we have talked about how the game of golf mirrors the game of life, how would that affect our approach to a seemingly unfair turn of events? Would we react with a different resolve and perseverance not usually called upon? You can't rearrange that turn of events like you rearrange the lie of your golf ball."

"You're saying rules are rules, right? Either you follow them, or you don't. Maybe our golf game ultimately suffers from such a casual approach to the game, and maybe so does our life."

"Yeah, you might have somethin' there, Karl. But we all know that golf is a perplexing game. And some might argue that life can be the same. Maybe we play customer golf because coping with life feels less stressful if we live it that way."

All of us had questions about what our Sunday school faith now meant as we faced the challenges of adulthood. How do we step outside of what has been passed on from generation to generation (like my mother's Easter) and lay claim to what will work for us? What would such a rite of passage, a ritual born of our basic humanity, look like? Eternal verities, yes. But is questioning those verities off limits?

"Take God's goodness," I suggested after we took our approach shots to the green. "If we have been taught to expect God's goodness and never have to find excuses for Him, why are we so anxious about our future?"

"I'll tell you why," Karl quickly answered. "My time in Vietnam packed a lot of human life that wasn't so good into a single year. And I know now we've got plenty we should be anxious about. Andy, I figure you must feel pretty secure with your faith and all, being your dad's a preacher. So I'm not trying to argue with you here, but that faith all of us inherited doesn't mean jack shit once you hear how guys relied on their faith all for nothin'. Man, the stuff you see. The stories you hear. A lot of Sunday school faiths got lost in Vietnam."

"We already figured that out, Dad. Long before you decided to share some of your faith struggles with us, we have been experiencing our own. And no thanks to Grandma's Easter, we've got more questions than answers. What with being PKs and all, we ended up giving our Christian faith more latitude than most in our generation. Like most of our friends, though, we've resigned ourselves to a world that doesn't make a whole lot of sense. But we choose every day to fight the good fight anyway."

"Sounds like Camus and Qoheleth to me," I mumbled.

We had to wait for the group in front of us before we could tee off on the par 4, 448-yard third hole, another dogleg to the left.

"Forgive us for asking, Dad, but what happened to your ninth-green promise you made on your wedding day? You and Mom sure kept yours all right. We don't mean to be insensitive, but what happened to you, Uncle George, Uncle Karl, and Pastor Andy? What happened to your promise to each other?"

"It's OK you're asking. I wish you didn't have to though. I wish life had turned out differently for them. Know what I mean?"

After we had teed off, I walked down the right side of the fairway, thinking to myself for a moment.

The death of my mother's Easter isn't only about my broken heart.

My three children. Like apostolic succession, the laying-on-of-hands tradition, we often pass on our values and traditions by when and where we hold hands, from one generation to the next. Holding hands is a signal we send to those we love, a message saying that I'm with you, I have no intention of letting go, and with my not letting go comes my values and traditions. They are worth passing on. Our physical connection lays the groundwork for the more significant spiritual connection.

One of my most troubling days this past Lent was a panic button I pushed when I contemplated their life journey without holding my hand. Was I prepared to let them determine their own life course without passing on what I am experiencing? Just slowly drift away from their grandmother's Easter without the reflection with which I have struggled.

Of course, they are entitled to answer this essential question on their own: To what extent does a particular generation's understanding of God shape the course of their lives? But wasn't I also entitled to pass on my personal journey trying to escape from nihilism? And since our psychological development is continually evolving, so also must be our understanding of God or Goddess or Spirit. My children had been heading in the opposite direction from the hereafter God of my mother's Easter. Heading more toward a rational God, a demythologized Ground of Being for which more questions exist than answers.

From the day each was born, I have always promised my children that I would stand by them. They know this, and they value this more than Jesus dying for their sins. That Jesus died for their sins is hardly a game changer. Isn't for me either anymore.

After half a century, it seemed reasonable I could offer an acceptable answer to my children's questions. "Why is our messed up world like this if there's supposed to be a God? How do we make sense of life when the world around us makes no sense?" I'm trying to provide some wisdom here at the same time I'm burying Easter because it doesn't make sense in the world I'm living. How do I share this with them? Do I share all of my questions with them, how those questions have brought me to this Easter weekend?

In his movie, *Contact*, Carl Sagan questioned the likelihood of an all-powerful, mysterious God creating the Universe and then deciding not to give any proof of His existence. We could ask a similar question: "Why would an all-powerful, mysterious God create the Universe and then decide to leave so many questions unanswered?" Or is it we have no right to those many questions if we have accepted Qoheleth's claim that all we can be certain of is uncertainty? Maybe "It is what it is" is the only answer we deserve.

This much I know is true: Part of my legacy for my three children, what I leave them as a father, is an Easter Proclamation passed down through the centuries, passed onto me from my grandmother to my mother, holding Easter hands from one generation to the next. But now, each of my three children has cast off their Easter baptism, consider it a childhood ritual remembered by a date, a photo, and a parchment certificate that ends up in a manila folder between fourth-grade spelling bee and most improved soccer player.

Brandon had walked over to check out my lie and club selection to the green.

"Dad, you brought us up to believe our Heavenly Father loves us in the same way you love us. So when things happen to us that seem unfair and hardly in line with what we expect from a caring father, we who were taught to believe in God's Goodness are supposed to dismiss the caring part and accept that God's ways are different from ours. Or accept that God is testing us. Are people who don't feel so loved by God supposed to just deal with it? Can't ever imagine you treating us that way. So why do we excuse God sometimes? Why should we have to do that? Or accept that God can't be all-powerful because He created us with free will?"

"You and I wouldn't be talking about this without our Sunday school faith teaching us about God's goodness. Only when the concept of righteousness has been introduced can we then ask the question, 'How can God let this happen?' There is no unfairness in life if we don't introduce this concept. Shit happens, that's all. The rabbi's premise (*When Bad Things Happen to Good People*) only makes sense once a God of Righteousness has been introduced. Otherwise, we're left with Qoheleth's explanation for life's misfortunes, 'It is what it is.' From Ecclesiastes 1:9, by the way, his exact words. 'What has been is what will be, and what has been done is what will be done.' Or, we're just left with Vonnegut's favorite: 'So it goes.' Or, with one of your mother's favorites: 'And this too shall pass.'"

"Or Tupac. 'Life goes on.'"

"Yes. But some might argue," I continued, "that it's not all God's fault. Remember that ending to our movie, *The Mission*? After the disgraceful annihilation of the Guarani by the Portuguese government, a representative explained to the pope's emissary, who had lent his approval to the annihilation, that we are left with accepting the world as it is. The pope's emissary quickly made it clear that we are responsible for the world as it is.

In the beginning, so the story goes, God created Adam and Eve along with every basic human need fulfilled for them, caring for them like a mother cares for her newborn baby. But we grow up and long to become independent. To maintain fellowship with God, to live a spiritual life as God intended, Adam and Eve had to depend entirely on God."

"But are we made to live like that, Dad? According to your creation story, I guess, but is that the human spirit?"

"Hey, doesn't Satan get blamed in that story? Tempted Adam and Eve to rebel against God, to eat fruit from that tree of the knowledge of good and evil, to live independently of God, in control, on their own, seeking fulfillment apart from Him."

"Well, the point of the story is not about blame. Christian theology would argue that our basic human condition, our alienation from God, can be traced back to this story. We were created to live in continual fellowship with God, all of our contentment and fulfillment derives from Him."

"Why doesn't God let us grow up? Like a loving, caring father, a father like you. You have accepted that about your role. We are made to grow up. It's part of who we are. Why is it considered rebellion against God? We aren't rebelling against you by becoming independent and grown-up; we are honoring you, and how you brought us up."

"Isn't a father supposed to be kind of a life coach?"

"The analogy doesn't always serve us so well – Heavenly Father compared with biological father. But I'll concede your point. God is depicted in all kinds of loving ways as a Heavenly Father. The prophet Jeremiah speaks of a caring Father when he says, 'For surely I know the plans I have for you, says the LORD, plans for your welfare and not for harm, to give you a future with hope.'"

"Did Uncle Karl ever feel like his stepmom Eva was a future with hope?"

"I don't see how replacing your mom when you're eight years old could ever be considered 'not for harm.'"

"Yeah, and you always taught us that Old Testament people had a way of honestly confronting God, questioning Him, wrestling with Him, and doubting Him."

"Like Gideon, you mean, when he asked, 'But sir, if the LORD is with us, why then has all this happened to us? And where are all his wonderful deeds that our ancestors recounted to us, saying, 'Did not the LORD bring us up from Egypt?' But now the LORD has cast us off, and given us into the hand of Midian.'

I did, yes. God's Old Testament people once declared, 'The Lord has forsaken me, my Lord has forgotten me.' But to this God replied through the prophet Isaiah,

'Can a woman forget her nursing child,
or show no compassion for the child of her womb?
Even these may forget, yet I will not forget you.'

That does seem at odds with 'My ways aren't your ways. Just deal with it.'"

"So Dad, obviously anyone who commits suicide has felt abandoned by a caring Heavenly Father. Can a person who feels deeply loved and cared about by a mother or father end up committing suicide?"

"You wouldn't think so, and that is one of the mitigating factors considered by psychologists who search for the causes behind suicide, that someone who feels so deeply loved by a caring parent may be less at risk for suicide."

We had to wait on the tee-box of the fourth hole, a deceiving little par 3, only 161 yards from the blue tees. I found myself watching and thinking about the two-couple foursome still putting on the green ahead of us, twenty-somethings like my children, maybe married, maybe not. Thoroughly enjoying themselves, following Qoheleth's advice this Easter morning. I kept watching them while I listened to my children.

"Dad, what about your Easter Jurassic Park sermon a few years ago? What did you mean by that, trying to disguise your quasi-secular version of Easter? We still talk about that one."

"I don't remember what I said until you tell me what you heard."

"Ah, yeah, we've heard that before. One of your favorite ways to test us on how closely we were listening."

"I know what Dad meant. The music only matters if you make the putt!"

"Yup, there you go, the music only matters if we live the Gospel every day, live it as though death leads to life in the here and now. Based on an Easter paradigm, I referred to this as a transformational suicide, a voluntary death of who we are in favor now of the person we could become. Letting go of life so that you can live life."

"Like that movie the three of us saw last year, right? *The Game.* You've gotta see it, Dad, it's what you're talking about. This successful and self-centered businessman, Michael Douglas is Nicholas Van Orton, had accumulated all of his wealth at the expense of his family and those around him. He lives in the family estate where he lived as a kid, where he watched his father leap from the rooftop to his death at the age of forty-eight. Nicholas's brother, Sean Penn is Conrad, is worried about him, so he arranges for his brother's forty-eighth birthday an elaborate live-action role-playing scheme to help his brother recognize what is truly important after all."

"Oh come on, here you go, telling Dad all about the movie. Hey, maybe Dad would like to see it for himself."

"Anyway, this unusual birthday gift is a ruse, a way to make Nicholas think he has lost his business and all of his money, a virtual attack on everything Nicholas values. As his business and carefully ordered life collapses around him, he figures out the scam, but it's too late. He's been duped, and he wakes up to find himself buried alive in a cemetery in Mexico from which he quickly escapes. Dead, but not dead, right?

In a panic, he manages to retrieve a hidden handgun, and after he apologizes for his neglect and mistreatment, asks his ex-wife to help him. I think she's in on it too.

So finally, on the roof of the game company's skyscraper, Nicholas is losing it and demands some answers from the woman, Deborah Kara Unger is Christine, who had helped to set him up. She frantically explains the game. Everything that has happened has been one grand hoax, all an elaborate con; everyone's waiting to greet him. But Nicholas isn't buying her explanation. When the door bursts open, he's so disturbed and rattled, he shoots the first person in sight, his brother Conrad, holding a bottle of champagne.

Nicholas takes a step to the edge, in his father's footsteps now on his own forty-eighth birthday, and leaps to his death.

Or so you think.

Welcome to The Game! After Nicholas smashes through a simulated-glass ceiling and lands safely on a giant airbag, he is revived by medical technicians in front of his family and friends gathered in the ballroom, including his brother Conrad. The gun had been replaced with a gun that fired blanks. Conrad didn't want his brother to end up like their father. He wanted to bring Nicholas back from a dead-end, to live a life different from their father. Happy Birthday, Nicholas!"

"But on that skyscraper roof-top, Nicholas didn't know his physical suicide would turn into a transformational suicide, did he? Could someone contemplating suicide convince themselves to role-play such an event?"

"Maybe it's not necessary to role-play your suicide. Maybe some other kind of ritual could serve that purpose. Could it have happened another way? Transformational suicide, I mean." I didn't say it, but I was thinking about my borderland. "Remember Ishmael in *Moby Dick*? He spoke about quietly taking to the ship, his 'substitute for pistol and ball,' whenever 'it is a damp, drizzly November in his soul.'"

"So, Dad, how different from your new Easter thinking revisions is our American ideal about reinvention, always a 'second chance' to work through our problems? We are always looking to the future, optimistic and hopeful."

"Dad, come on, one of our favorite movies, *City Slickers*, is about the great American do-over. You can always reinvent yourself, right? Never stop believing in possibility, right? Out of our defeats and despair, we rise again to a better life."

"Wasn't that two-week cattle drive from New Mexico to Colorado a transformational suicide? Maybe we can't always be certain at the outset exactly what will come of our 'cattle drive' experiences. Remember how Phil confronted those two drunk cowhands in charge of the cattle drive, how angry and tired he was, how hopeless he felt about his life? But his friend Mitch had a different take, reminding him of when they were kids playing baseball and their ball would land up in a tree. They would agree to a do-over. And the same with life, he reminded Phil."

"Not a do-over, though," I clarified. "Reinventing yourself implies retention of some of the old, like a marriage when the two become four. The Easter paradigm is different: die to the old self."

"Dad, my good friend Meyer invited me to his home for their Seder Meal last night. You met him when I graduated. Seems like celebrants of Passover have more on their mind than the biblical story of their exodus from bondage in Egypt. Seems like it's more about the here and now. Meyer talked about God leading us out of own personal Egypts, our own personal houses of bondage, like our preconceptions and ignorance, like our fear to let go of the past, like our faith that shuns any trust in reason, like our abusive habits, like our petty gripes, like our destructive relationships. The exchanges – the questions and the answers – are about our own time, not the past. About us, not the ancient Hebrews. Why couldn't our Easter be more like the Jewish Seder?"

"How might such an emphasis dissuade someone from ending their own life? I believe the Jewish suicide rate is lower than our national average. Maybe hearing the Haggadah read is a salvation event of no less significance than their ancient story of salvation. Jewish people don't have to worry about that already-but-not-yet tension. Grandma's Easter is founded on an event that promises us life in the hereafter while Judaism is founded on an event that promises fulfillment in the here and now."

"You always talked so much, Dad, about how our belief in a life hereafter developed over time when Greek influence was more prevalent. You always talked so much about how the Old Testament people focused more on life in the here and now."

"Yeah, I did. Ya' know my *Minister's Edition of Lutheran Worship* suggests a reading of the Twenty-third Psalm to conclude a funeral service. Those attending often joined with me while I recited it. But a close examination of the original Hebrew offers a different interpretation of this beloved psalm from the one Christians most often assign to it. This psalm is more about life than about death, more about gratitude than about fear, and more concerned about the here and now than about the life hereafter.

In the KJV, the speaker 'walks through the valley of the shadow of death.' But the word here is *darkness, deep darkness,* like that darkness which prompted my wedding-day foursome to stand by each other. A translation from Hebrew excludes the word *death.*

The speaker is more interested in recounting God's gifts for life in the here and now. 'I lack nothing' for my life in the here and now. This psalm ends with the Hebrew word meaning *days,* which does not mean *forever* like the KJV translation 'and I will dwell in the house of the Lord forever.' It's not talking about life in the hereafter or about eternal salvation. The Hebrew is translated, 'And I shall dwell in the house of the Lord for many long days (for many years).'

But the persecution of faithful Jews in the middle of the second century BCE called into question this traditional Old Testament emphasis on the here and now. Hope that a better world was coming someday didn't help those who had died as martyrs for the faith; hope for a better world did not make right the injustice of their sufferings. So the Jews looked to a life after death when God would remedy this grave injustice. Before long, this hope for a life hereafter had become the central tenet of a new concern – our personal destiny after death.

For the ancient Israelites, their savior expectation about rebuilding Jerusalem had the here and now in mind; the Book of Genesis wasn't about the Fall, about our broken relationship with God. Our expectation of a savior figure can be traced to the Greek influence about the immortality of the soul – ironically, the transgression at the heart of the creation story in Genesis, wanting to be immortal like God."

"Dad, remember that ancient epitaph you alluded to once in a sermon, about how most of the ancient pagan world thought little if at all about the idea of a resurrection and a hereafter? *'I wasn't, I was, I am not, I don't care.'* This epitaph was so well known that it was often reduced on tombstones to its initial letters, in Latin as well as in Greek. I'm guessin' some might think such a thought is cold and hopeless. But Dad, listen, that epitaph's kind of how we see things – the way a lot of people see things. Why the fear of death and the need for a savior to save us from death?"

"You know, Dad, Seneca's not the only philosopher to figure that one out. How did he say it? Something about 'Be my guest, Death, you don't bother me. Besides, we met a long time ago, before I was born. I already know what you're like. It'll be the same after me as it was before me.' Our here and now life is such a short interlude between oblivions. Does such a thought lend encouragement to suicide, or does such a thought protest against it?"

"So what has happened to Grandma's Easter? What's this weekend been about for you and Mom?"

"I'm burying Easter this morning," I declared, sounding each word slowly and separately. "I'm figuring it out – why their three suicides have troubled me so. Grandma's Easter did not shine in the darkness for us. With each of their suicides, Easter has died a slow death for me. I tried to revise it, to render it more here-and-now friendly. But the suicides of Uncle George, Uncle Karl, and Pastor Andy proclaimed a loud and convincing rejection of my Easter revisions."

"Honestly, Dad, we don't know exactly what happened to the Christian faith we inherited from you and Mom; we only know it no longer helps us make sense of our reality."

"Dad, you remember my good friend Traci at college? Grew up Lutheran, has always considered herself Lutheran, but found herself open to ideas that sometimes run contrary to what she grew up believing. I can tell ya', she's not thinking about her personal salvation or atonement or an afterlife. She's focused on living her best life every day. Commitments to herself, to her family, to her students, to her community – that's what she's thinking about. She fully respects others who think differently from her. She can't fix everything she thinks is wrong. She accepts the limits of her here and now. She defines human progress as three steps forward and two back. She opens her school year with Michael Jackson's song 'We Are the World,' celebrities gathered to promote aid for Africa. We are the ones, after all, who can make a better day.

I would say Traci is a humanist agnostic. She's got more questions than I've got. Who is God, now that I know God is not what I learned about in Sunday school? Why has God been used to support the oppression of people? How can one religious tradition claim to have the truth when others claim the same thing? Who's right? Without Constantine's proclamation in the fourth century, how worldwide would Christianity be today? Some Christians declare, 'We believe the Bible is the Word of God as far as it is translated correctly.' Who gets to say that?

Is Traci living in rebellion against God because she has made such choices and asks those questions? She's been accused of selling out our American moral values by encouraging her eighth-grade students to discover their own identities, to learn how to express their true selves and to clarify their values for themselves, asking questions about what they have inherited."

"You know, Dad, we've been on this spiritual journey with you, and we're perfectly content to file away Easter with our other childhood memories."

"We're trying to face each day as best we can, Dad. Trying to get through the territory, that's all, like Jake Spoon in *Lonesome Dove* before his friends hanged him from a tree for falling in with those horse thieves and murderers."

"We're all trying to get through the territory, right?"

"The wisdom ol' Gus McCrae shared with Lorie darlin' sounds a lot like the wisdom of Qoheleth. Don't get your hopes up too much about moving to some place new. Life there will still just be life. Settle for the little things in life – a simple meal, a sip of whiskey, a comfortable bed, a day of satisfying work, some time with someone who matters to ya'."

"Dad, our study of developmental psychology helps us understand human behavior, not the theological premise of the Fall recorded in Genesis. We accept our shortcomings and try each day to become the kind of people you and Mom expect of us – how you raised us to care about ourselves, about others, and about our planet."

"Ya' gotta remember, Dad, we're coming home from college at Christmas having taken a final exam on Freud and Jung and psychotherapy, and you've got us helping with distribution for Holy Communion, 'The body and blood of Christ shed for you.' Shed for what? Why? We do not spend our time thinking about that basic premise of Christianity – 'the wages of sin is death.'"

If our life experiences shape the kind of relationship we have with God – or don't have – how had the faith and theology of my children evolved to this point over the years? I had encouraged each of them in their own way to never stop asking questions. And they had not.

"We've asked you this before, Dad, but why are there so many perfectly happy, independent, purpose-filled human beings who do not believe in God like Grandma did? Who truly care about the welfare of others and the welfare of our planet. And of course, we know, we've heard your debates before with Pastor Andy, how he argued that there's something they're hiding, that deep within, they aren't so perfectly happy after all. You used to argue the opposite, and you were honest enough to admit you didn't know why there were so many perfectly happy, purpose-filled human beings who do not believe in God like Grandma."

"You're right, I don't. I'm guessing these people figured out some things on their own about life and how to live it."

"Well, Dad, we've figured out some things on our own about life and how to live it. We try to die to our old self, always looking for new life in the here and now. We try to recognize and confront the living death, the death in life that steals away life. Like Andy Dufresne in *Shawshank Redemption*, we try to keep busy living."

I spotted Denise in the distance, standing behind the ninth green. Par 4, 403 yards. "Remember, Dad, ya' gotta stay clear of the water on the right and that bunker in the center about 250 yards out. So aim a little left, but don't hug the left side too much and land behind one of those pines." I always appreciated well-meant golf advice from my two sons, even though it hardly mattered to my game.

I was pleased with my drive down the left side of the fairway, although that left me with a shot that had to clear two bunkers guarding the left-front corner of the green. My six-iron scuffed the grass enough to fly my dimpled little orb across those bunkers. But it kicked off to the left across the cart path, leaving me with a shot out of the rough staring at water directly behind the flag. A timid chip to the edge of the green and two putts later, I raised my arms to celebrate my bogey five. I celebrated bogeys like many golfers celebrate pars.

Brandon had already sunk his straight-in eight-foot par putt, and Kendra had rolled her seven-foot bogey putt perfectly along the slight break. Trevor tapped in his two-foot par putt, reached into the cup to retrieve our golf balls, and handed me my Slazenger #2. "Not a bad front nine, Pops. Hey, we are watching The Masters this afternoon, right? Fred Couples had a two-stroke lead this morning."

I knew Denise was waiting to hear about my troubled heart. "Easter dead and buried?" she asked. I could only smile. Of course, she already knew my answer.

"Thinking about you, Dad, about how you keep trying to come to terms with their suicides, about how you have been revising Grandma's Easter over the years – trying to make sense of it all. Why do you keep looking for life among the dead trappings of your past? Look at you! You have risen to new life in the here and now."

"Can't believe Dad's playing golf on Easter Sunday!"

"Played golf on his wedding day."

"Yep, that he did. Happy Easter, Dad."

"Hey, Happy Easter to you."

"So, like we asked earlier, Dad, where do you go from here?"

"Teaching. I'm going back to school to get my teaching credentials. Always wanted to be a teacher."

"Gotta hand it to you, Dad. How many times have you died to your old self and been raised to new life? How many transformational suicides?"

"Still counting. How about you?"

CHAPTER 32

Henry
10 April 2009
Good Friday

Eleven years later, I'm still living with the suicides of my three best men, still searching for some consolation to ease my suffering – my suffering caused by their decisions to end their suffering.

My brother George.

My brother-in-law Karl.

My best friend Andy.

My three best men.

Their suicides haunt me to this day as if I have just received news of their deaths.

Celebrated my sixtieth birthday last year, a gentle reminder of life's transience but also an appreciated reminder of life lived thus far. Looking forward to our thirty-ninth anniversary tomorrow at Sunriver, Easter weekend like 1998.

I'll be thinking about my dad and mom this Easter Sunday, always do. I imagined visiting with my mom a couple of years ago at a Sunriver Community Church sunrise service. She held my hand; it was 1955 all over again. The preacher's sermon title: "What Are You Expecting When This Life Is Over?" She would have loved it.

And I'll be thinking about my three children, about that Easter morning round of golf we played. We share a questioning and free spirit these days, trying to live our lives with a simpler path before us. All three are married now and living out of state – and must share our grandchildren on holidays – so not expecting them Easter morning.

With each passing year, I think less and less about how my inherited faith has repackaged this springtime of renewal to accommodate its sacramental theology. Isn't this life-affirming gift from Nature sacred enough without all of our cosmological explanations? So why the suicide rate peaks in the spring still puzzles me.

In the days and weeks following my transformational suicide in 1998, I realized my escape from nihilism had ironically depended on that Easter baptism paradigm I had promoted for those revisions of my mother's Easter. But I have since learned, am learning still, of Easter death and resurrection variations that transcend my inherited Christian faith boundaries. Which is why the suicides of my three best men are still so heartbreaking for me. What if together we had questioned our Christian faith boundaries sooner?

Like Jack Kerouac figured out, transformational suicides are so ghostly easy, we may not even realize how many times we have transitioned from life to death and back to life. The utter casualness of it.

My children's life choices were not the only examples of how Easter has morphed into a metaphor for renewal and transformation. I discovered that Easter theology is convenient for renewal and transformation without nary a mention of the wages of sin and atonement. No need to think about a life hereafter.

Long before the suicides of my three best men had challenged me to confront the death of my mother's Easter and all of my revision attempts, others had been busy rethinking Easter theology. Some hardly restrained at all by that stone of ancient dogma and doctrine and orthodoxy and tradition protecting twenty centuries of my mother's Easter.

What did you have in mind, Goethe, when you used Easter morning to introduce your story about Heinrich Faust? We know of your preference for stressing renewal – about recurring death and resurrection in the here and now, about your disdain for otherworldliness and hereafter beliefs. The last lines of your poem, "Blessed Longing," say it best:

So long as you have not lived this:
To die is to become new,

You remain a gloomy guest
On the dark earth.

Given your preference for thinking about renewal in the here and now, we know something more is going on than a retelling of the biblical story of Job. Your protagonist chose suicide to escape the nihilism he faced – all of his knowledge had still left him frustrated because he could not share in the spirit world as he wished. But a chorus of angels announced Easter morning, saved him from his concoction of poison, and presented him with a second chance – albeit a second chance by making a pact with the devil. We may conclude that the choices he then made did not render him *new*.

You clearly had Easter theology in mind, Tolstoy, when you wrote your last novel, *Resurrection*. Your protagonist, Prince Nekhlyudov, discovered that our best efforts to redeem ourselves, our Good Friday deaths and Easter resurrections in the here and now, do not always turn out the way we first planned or hoped. We anticipate one outcome while reality throws another at us. Hoping to atone for his abandonment of Katusha Maslova, a young servant girl with whom he had fallen in love when he was a university student, the prince sought to reverse the wrong she now endured under the judicial system of nineteenth-century Russia. He could not have imagined, though, what he would discover.

You left little doubt, August Strindberg, as to what you had in mind when you wrote your three-act play, *Easter*. Act One opens the afternoon of Holy Thursday when we are introduced to a Swedish family on the brink of ruin thanks to the father's scandal. Living with this family shame had exacted a daily emotional toll. "Can you understand this?" the son Elis Heyst asked. "The Redeemer suffered for our iniquities, yet we continue to pay." But hope abides because it's Easter Eve, and they live out in the midst of everyday life a gift of redemption. Sometimes accepting forgiveness is harder than the act of forgiving.

Like Goethe, Tolstoy, and Strindberg, Mr. Faulkner, you took advantage of Easter symbolism and themes to write your novel, *The Sound and the Fury*. If any family could use an Easter experience, it would be the Compsons. This story of the southern aristocratic Compson family ends on Easter Sunday with Dilsey Gibson, the matriarch of the Compson family black servants, attending church. A Christ-like figure herself, Dilsey is the only possible hope for an Easter resurrection for the Compsons.

I have a good idea, Walker Percy, what you had in mind when you wrote your novel, *The Second Coming*. You had trouble making sense of our world, so you projected that onto your protagonist, widowed attorney Will Barrett. Why do our churches talk so much about death, Will mused, if Christ came so that all may have life?

You also projected onto him your own thinking about how to escape from such senselessness. Your cynical father had failed to make sense of this world, thought you would fail the same way; in his frustration and despair, your father had committed suicide. You did find yourself contemplating suicide in the desert of New Mexico, carrying the Luger your father had used. And so also your main character, Will Barrett. The father's suicide in your novel is a frightening recreation of your own father's suicide in the attic of your Birmingham home.

But Will Barrett finally realized in mid-life that his father was trying to warn him, trying to tell him that one day it would happen to him too, that he would reach the same conclusion. As Barrett silently studied the gun he was holding, he had one last thought. What if there is a God who can save me from my meaningless life in the here and now, and you missed that, father? What if your suicide was a waste? Is there a transformational death that leads to life in the here and now – our own Second Coming experience?

Never would have imagined this when I returned to graduate school for my teaching credentials. Assigned to a reading from Brazilian educator Paulo Freire's book, *Pedagogy of the Oppressed*, I learned that the gap between teachers and learners must be transcended through the "class suicide" or "Easter experience" of the teacher. A transformational suicide whereby the teacher dies as the unilateral educator to be born again as a teacher-learner along with his/her learner-teachers. One of my younger cohort colleagues asked me if I had any idea what Freire meant by "Easter experience."

I have since read Michael Patrick MacDonald's novel, *Easter Rising*, his follow up to *All Souls*, his story about losing four siblings to the horrid conditions of Irish South Boston. *Easter Rising* is his story about how he fled from Southie by reinventing himself. At nineteen, he escaped further, to Paris and then to London. Out of money, his Irish immigrant grandfather offered a loan, but only if Michael would visit Ireland. It is this reluctant journey home that gave MacDonald a chance at reconciliation – with his heritage, his neighborhood, and his family – and a way forward. Would Michael consider using the phrase "transformational suicide" to describe the incarnations he went through to become his new self? Maybe we can miss Easter Mass at Grandpa's church but still experience an Easter rising on our personal journey.

So Easter, long before 1998, had you been dying to your old self and raised to newness of life, a metaphor for recurring death and rebirth in the here and now?

My death to the person I had prepared a lifetime to become forced me to reevaluate what my life could mean. A teaching legacy can touch and change so many lives, can shape the future instead of it shaping us. I've been teaching middle school social studies; that is to say, I've been using the broad context of social studies to help seventh and eighth graders grow up as human beings, to find fulfillment and become conscientious and mature shapers of history. It's my small contribution to the questioning of our American narrative (sugar-coated vs. Howard Zinn). Is our striving toward a more perfect union one Easter experience after another for our country? A dying to the old to make way for the new?

Suicidology, though, still all around me, younger versions of my three best men. Life's not easy. The battles seem endless. How quickly we can tire of it all.

Not too practical sharing the philosophy of Nietzsche or Camus or Qoheleth with an eighth grader. They have left the planet for a time, will return at some future date. Which isn't a bad metaphor for Camus's whole point about the absurd. The life of a thirteen-year-old makes no sense; accept it, live with it, don't try to escape from it. It is what it is. Qoheleth again.

We gathered at 8:00 AM for our Friday morning eighth-grade staff meeting at East Lake Middle School.

1) After 15 minutes of deliberation about a new student who had been transferred to our school, our principal concluded, "I think Nathan hates his parents!"

2) Anarchist wannabe Monica, pink hair, piercings all over, outlandish outfits, feels targeted by teachers and staff every day.

3) Kyle's mom called, her son on suicide watch, sending him to school anyway.

4) Our counselor produced the Que file on a new student from Southern Oregon. OAKS math score: 192; reading: 188. Rachel has had some serious problems with her stepdad; she reported problems, so now she fears retribution.

5) "Had to see it to believe it. Zach had the room turned upside down when Jackie had a sub yesterday. Has anyone talked to our district autism specialist yet?"

6) Karlie, a new student who transferred from Riverview MS last fall because of multiple learning difficulties, is representative of the data that describes how deficiencies in learning proportionately multiply each year by our neglect from grade level to grade level.

Our counselor, Pam Calkins, the most caring individual in our school of exceptionally caring teachers, offered a few words of explanation. I had shared with her the day before what Kyle had turned in for his assignment. She asked me to share this with our group.

After our assembly on Wednesday – a dramatic presentation about Anne Frank – I had asked students to share their personal thoughts using a six-word summary. "What connections did you make with Anne Frank? Any feelings you share with her?" I modeled a six-word summary I thought Anne Frank might have written: "Had every right to be scared." After thinking about this during our class discussion, Kyle had turned in his summary at the end of class: "Scared to be yourself, nothing's changed."

When I visited with Kyle after school, I learned he too had every right to be scared. What assails us as adults every day – chaos at home, a marriage falling apart, having to move every year – gets magnified for an eighth grader who is struggling to sort out who he is becoming.

Our staff meeting adjourned at 8:55 AM. By 9:10 AM during my first-period eighth-grade humanities class, I'm distributing a handout about how a Venn diagram can help us compare and contrast two different accounts of Native Americans' reaction to the invasion of white settlers. We'll read both accounts at least twice, the traditional textbook account versus Howard Zinn's *People's History*. We need to know the basic approach of both before we can determine the differences. We'll be concentrating on how this graphic organizer helps our brain sort out the differences.

But I've got Kyle in my thoughts, thinking about a Venn diagram with him on one side and another student (less troubled, less scared) on the other. Differences and similarities?

My mind was yanked back to 9:20 AM as Rachel shyly raised her hand, "I don't know what you mean. How am I supposed to know what to put in that middle section?" I should have known better. We teachers have little choice but to operate by a guiding axiom that ninety percent of our energy must be spent on helping eighth graders become students (in many cases, human beings first) and the remaining energy devoted to content area. This obligation is pretty much by default. Most teachers try to integrate their content into that ninety percent task.

Could all of our recent attention paid to social-emotional learning be traced back to Descartes? Helping our students learn how to learn must take seriously into account their most pressing concerns – their parents' morning argument and pending separation, the prospect of having to put their sick dog to sleep, misplacing a cherished note from a best friend, disappointed about a Sunday visit from Grandma that she canceled, anxiety over an upcoming school dance, a bad day at baseball practice, dealing with an online school bully. Such is the stuff of our human consciousness, and any theory of knowledge that does not recognize such stuff is flawed.

With a nod to Descartes's expanded definition of knowledge, we now pay closer attention to the non-cognitive competencies, attributes, and feelings of our students. "How do we cope with life?" is as important as any question. "What about uncertainty? What do we make of that?"

Some Professional Learning Community meetings seem productive and energizing, some seem a questionable use of valuable morning time before students arrive, and some seem downright disconcerting – like last Friday's morning meeting when we were asked to evaluate all 250 of our eighth graders for a report the high school counselors had requested. A color-coded highlighting system was used to identify behavioral and emotional concerns, study habits and academic concerns, attitude concerns, and attendance and tardy concerns. Our administrator provided appropriate labels, but as we shared around the table, it became clear how little consensus we were providing for our high school. Math teacher: "Oh, Kyle's trouble! Low production, if I get any work at all turned in. And his mother won't even speak with me anymore." Science teacher: "Well, I'm wondering if Kyle's parents' divorce last year so unsettled him that he can hardly function this year. Did I hear right, was that his second stepdad?" Humanities teacher (that would be me): "I'm pleased with his writing lately. He's interested in pro and con issues and participates in our classroom debates."

Our feedback for all of the students covered the entire A-Z range, sometimes each of us weighing in on a single eighth grader as if we were talking about two different students. Clearly, all of us teachers experience students like Kyle differently. Which would probably scare Kyle even more if he knew of this.

Before Kyle reached the door at the end of first period this morning, the last to leave my classroom, I wanted to acknowledge a connection with him, a subtle "I'll be thinking about you." I instinctively said, "Hey, Kyle, Happy *Good* Friday!" Couldn't help it, adding *Good* to my usual "Happy Friday." Always treaded carefully, though, to avoid any reference to a personal religious belief.

I thought about him the rest of the day, thought about his life and what he had written. "Scared to be yourself, nothing's changed."

Nothing had changed.

I tried to imagine how his cognitive awareness of the trials of Jesus I had conducted could have provided any relief for him. How my revised versions of my mother's Easter, Camus's third alternative to living in "the absurd," and Qoheleth's lessons about life's impermanence and uncertainty, could have helped him through his darkest night.

Could the poet Galway Kinnell be right, Kyle? If you'll wait, time's passage will prove your waiting was worth it. At fourteen years old, Kyle, feeling scared, abandoned, and bullied, has life so far convinced you of such a truth?

My brother George felt scared.

My brother-in-law Karl felt abandoned.

My best friend Andy felt bullied by the Church.

Kyle must have been thinking all day about how I had said goodbye this morning. He stopped by my classroom at the end of the day.

"Happy *Good* Friday," he repeated what I had said. "What's so good about it?"

I have never dismissed my theological underpinnings so quickly. Wages of sin, cross, atonement, the mystery of redemption - never came to mind. "'What's so good about Good Friday?' you ask. It's what we've got."

"So what's that supposed to mean? 'It's what we've got.' That's it? Today is good because it's what we've got."

"We can't be certain about what tomorrow will bring, Kyle. So to make up for that, today invites us to live every moment to the fullest."

Kyle was thinking about that while I continued. "I've got a favor to ask of you. I know you walk home every afternoon, that you don't have to worry about riding the bus. Any chance you could help me get ready for our role-play Monday morning? You seem to have a good understanding of what Native Americans would feel like expressing at our mock Westward Expansion Conference we're holding."

"Yeah, I guess so."

Kyle and I worked together for forty-five minutes. Of course he had a good understanding of what Native Americans might have expressed at a conference about their destiny in the direct path of someone else's Manifest Destiny.

"Thanks for your help today, Kyle."

"Yeah, sure. See you later, Mr. Caine."

Listening to an eighth grader who is feeling scared and abandoned and bullied made me think about my three best men and my Easter death weekend in 1998. I'm more aware of conversations I have now, more sensitive to their ultimate significance. To this day, I cannot recall my last conversation with George, or with Karl, or with Andy.

I won't let that happen again.